STARFIGHTER RISING

THE STARFIGHTER RISING SERIES
ONE

DANIEL SEEGMILLER

STARFIGHTER RISING

For information contact: www.danielseegmiller.com

Cover Artwork & Design by Jeff Brown Graphics

Edited by Ryan Quinn

ISBN: 978-1-7357375-1-5

First Edition: September 2020

DEDICATION

For Jayrin, Gabe, Lizzie, and Kian, and for everyone else who dreams of rising.

To all my readers, thank you. Check out
www.danielseegmiller.com/free
for access to two free short stories.

Finally, a special thanks to my family, especially my mom, for tremendous dedication in helping me bring this book to life.

PROLOGUE

Konran Andacellos approaches the Nolvaric defenses, yet undetected in his LTOM-58 Sparrowhawk starfighter. With the scythe-like shape of a wide, concave spear tip, the Sparrowhawk's black hull reflects no starlight as it slices through the vacuum of space—straight into the enemy's backyard. Konran's fingers drop to his flight stick, settling onto the leathery grip as he prepares to drop out of autopilot.

The Nolvarics had no reason to suspect his approach. They thought him dead, blown to pieces with the rest of Attack Group Bravo Twelve in a decimating deep-space ambush three hours ago. But four parts skill, two parts luck, and ten parts instinct had saved him for all the same reasons the United Space Federation Navy, desperate for bodies to push back the Nolvaric Invasion, had elected to put a twelve-year-old boy behind the stick of a Sparrowhawk. There was something about pure ability that simply mattered when things started blowing up.

And things were about to start blowing up.

Konran's passive sensors indicate a distance of ten thousand kilometers to target, and he punches the throttle. He comes in hard, swerving and spiraling and pulling the trigger. At his touch, orange plasma belches from his Sparrowhawk's four plasma cannons: one on each wingtip, and two on the nose. Explosions pop in the distance as his guns cut a path through a double perimeter of proximity mines blockading his way. Nolvaric starfighters surge toward him through the gaps, but he evades them, wishing for more missiles. His bay of twelve antimatter missiles rides empty below him, however, depleted hours ago along with the lives of his wingmen.

His shoulders press into his seat as the solar system's sleekest, deadliest starfighter rockets through the gap it just blasted in the enemy's defenses. The Sparrowhawk's quantum-controlled, gravito-nuclear engine rumbles like a racehorse below him, splitting gravitons into raw energy like Earth's ancient atomic

1

weapons split plutonium, and spewing that energy out the aft exhaust nozzle.

In Konran's hands, the Sparrowhawk's flight stick responds like the wand of a symphony conductor. Maneuvering thrusters along its fuselage discharge microbursts of gravito-nuclear energy in rhythmic harmony to his commands, allowing him to change direction in the blink of an eye. Inertial compensators within the craft combat the horrendous g-forces exerted against his body, as does his flight suit's barometric regulator—which, among other things, prevents his blood from cavitating and exploding his heart.

Finally, his target comes into view. Barely visible despite the sparkling backdrop of one hundred million Milky Way stars, an icy, gravitationally bonded cluster of space rocks emerges through the inky darkness of deep space: one of a hundred Nolvaric operating bases lurking out here in the Kuiper Belt.

Some of the ice rocks loom large with the diameter of Neptune's Nereid. Others glisten like meteors, swirling dangerously throughout the chaotic cluster on rapid, angular orbits. Ambient light is scarce at 4.9 billion kilometers from the sun, but Konran has no trouble seeing. Holographic overlays enhance his vision, displaying the objects teeming about by rendering their infrared emissions and quantum gravity distortions. Augmented so, the scene almost looks like a video game from the '80s—the 2180s, to be precise.

Nolvaric starfighters converge on Konran like bloodthirsty mosquitos at sunset. With four wings like crab legs, pointed fuselages like herons' beaks, and shark-fin masts protruding from the top and bottom, the enemy starfighters glint like demon spiders against the galactic backdrop. Known as Askeras, these are the nimblest, nastiest, most infamous of all Nolvaric starfighters. No longer able to ignore the escalating starfighter threat, Konran's plasma cannons unleash upon his foe. Mounted in rotating turrets at his Sparrowhawk's wingtips and nose, the cannons gyrate in every direction, tracking Nolvaric targets and spraying plasmic death in all directions. Enemies surround him, and Konran jolts and jags through their ranks. Askeras explode like firecrackers as he evades their return fire.

Passing through their midst, he stabilizes his trajectory and slows down just enough, letting them get close. The Askeras flock behind him, closing in as if for the kill.

Works every time, he thinks with a grin.

Konran inverts his Sparrowhawk, and his cockpit and craft reorient in an instant, flipping his point of view toward his aft thruster. In the same instant, his wingtip and nose-tip plasma cannons transmute from guns to gravito-nuclear rocket engines, providing him maneuvering capability as his formerly aft thruster assumes the role of megacannon.

Konran's fingers find the targeting solution before his computer signals a lock.

He pulls the trigger, unleashing a concentrated kiloton blast of plasmic devastation from what moments before had been his backside. Fifteen Askeras disintegrate as forty more scatter. Konran reverts his Sparrowhawk, his weapons and propulsion systems resume their standard roles, and he rockets once more toward the gravitationally bonded cluster of chaos that was the Nolvaric operating base.

His Sparrowhawk careens around the diameter of an ice-encrusted, Texas-size rock, skirting no more than a dozen meters above its surface. More crablike Askeras descend upon him, and he releases his orbit, quickly dodging through a cloud of man-size space debris before losing the Askeras between a scattering of larger space rocks.

Gravity switches constantly within the agitated anarchy of asteroids, but Konran adjusts effortlessly, surfing the gravitational gradients like he was born for this kind of action. His guns tear through another pack of Askeras as he winds around an oblong icicle half the size of Portugal. And then there it is: a glowing, pulsating ice rock at the center of the swirling chaos—the heart of the Nolvaric operating base.

It rotates there, seemingly slower than the surrounding bedlam. It beckons to Konran, washing his cockpit in an ethereal, incandescent green. More Askeras focus on him, and he diverts all power to his aft thruster, jetting forward on the power of a thousand sequential gravito-nuclear explosions.

This will be the only attack run, the one chance to win or die.

Konran inverts his Sparrowhawk. His cockpit flips and his craft reorients in preparation for the killing stroke. A green light appears at the edge of the energy source, then another and another, revealing the deadliest of the Nolvaric defenses: concentrated plasmic energy bundles propelled like cannonballs from the heart itself. Green plasma balls fill the vacuous space before him. They destabilize as they get close, exploding with vicious stored energy and rocking his Sparrowhawk with relentless plasmic shockwaves. Konran dodges one, then ten, then fifty of the blasts, intent on his target.

His megacannon comes within range, and he depresses the trigger.

A column of orange plasma leaps from his Sparrowhawk: a kiloton of destruction inbound on the target as if someone had just hooked a firehose up to a hurricane and funneled in all the lightning at once. The green Nolvaric heart shudders, wracking and cracking beneath the blast. Konran's sensors indicate massive fissures forming within the glowing green asteroid—but it isn't dead yet. His trigger finger itches as his megacannon cycles and he dances between waves of green plasma balls.

One more well-placed shot will complete the job.

Konran knows the spot, feeling it more than seeing it within the monstrosity of a space rock. He takes aim, angling slightly with a careful boost from his dual nose-tip cannons—which, inverted so, are presently providing propulsion to his Sparrowhawk.

He squeezes the trigger.

And with an enormous green flash, a Nolvaric plasma ball smashes straight into his cockpit. And everything goes black.

Konran sits there, shirt covered in sweat down to his belly button. Two dozen kids stand around him, every eye fixated on the fading holographic simulation.

"Do it again!" one of them shouts.

"That's all my money," Konran states, glumly staring into the still-darkening hologram. Cold from adrenaline, covered in sweat, and shaking too hard to get up, he realizes he just spent his hover-bus fare. Again.

Looks like I'll be walking home again, he thinks. *At least it's warm out tonight.*

"This one's on me," a cheerful voice rings behind the crowd. It's the arcade owner, who passes through the crowd and keys in a code, restarting the simulation. "Anyone want pizza?" he asks excitedly. "I've just grown six pies!"

Konran doesn't hear the replies. He just melts back into his starfighter.

CHAPTER 1

Five Years Later

Konran Andacellos tears across the sky above Sacramento, California, in his F-620 Cutlass starfighter. Older, but still lithe and trim, the Cutlass slices through the California air with two fin-like wings. In tight formation with five other F-620s, Konran pulls back on his flight stick, pushing his starfighter into a tight upward spiral. Together, the team of six Cutlasses rockets skyward before suddenly arcing down toward the city, their graceful paths like the six ribs of an umbrella stretching its canopy over the cityscape.

The crowd below cheers. Konran can't hear them, but he smiles. As part of the Madera Starfighter Exhibition Team, Konran and his teammates had been selected for seven such shows across North America, each part of Earth's global celebrations commemorating the Scattering. That the exhibition team from the lowly College of Spaceflight in Madera, California, had been selected as the flight demonstration squadron for seven of the Northern Hemisphere's biggest shows was an incredible achievement. And once the dust settled from their tour, Konran's admission into a top-five starfighter school next fall was all but assured.

He had worked his entire life for this—not just because he wanted it so badly, but because it had always been inevitable.

He was meant to be here now.

He was born to be a starfighter.

The compulsion for Konran had always been instinctual, like the child who, first handed an instrument, simply knows how to make it sing.

But instincts born for improvisation tire beneath the redundancy of rote performance, and today is destined as such a day.

Had he been a pianist, Konran may have recognized the moment as one where his fingers remember the music but his brain forgets what to do. Having played baseball throughout his youth, however, he feels almost like a batter failing to hit a fastball despite doing everything right. The stance is there, the hip rotation and elbow drive and weight shift all synchronized, the bat angled perfectly by the wrists, but the umpire calls strike three anyway.

Konran's Cutlass curves back toward the flight-staging area, converging above the crowd with his five companions. He prepares for their final maneuver, a spectacular six-way starfighter weave in a mesmerizing geometric pattern over the crowd. They begin. His Cutlass weaves this way and that. And then, for a split second, his flight stick doesn't remember where to go. The team recovers quickly from the momentary loss of cohesion. But after they land, they learn the Scattering Celebration Committee from Omaha, Nebraska, has dropped them from their show.

When the same thing happens to Konran at the next show, above Alberta, Canada, the Madera Starfighter Exhibition Team is dropped from their remaining five performances that spring.

Two tiny failures in an otherwise pristine career, and in a galaxy so filled with talent that single chances are all anyone gets, Konran's only chance slips away.

Five Years Later

Konran stares out the viewport of the *Viona Grande*, maintaining an orbit eleven hundred kilometers (give or take one hundred meters) above Earth's moon without even glancing at his ten-thousand-ton astrofreighter's controls, awaiting cargo transfer from the lunar base below. The gibbous Earth hangs out his portside viewport, its crescent of deep oceans and chalky clouds lustrous against the blackness of space. Out his forward viewport, ten thousand tiny specks of light glint everywhere: not stars, but starcraft, the myriad specks bustling to and fro, scurrying between the vibrant planet, its plentiful array of space colonies, and every imaginable deep-space destination.

Konran's fingers drum rhythmically along the *Viona Grande*'s glossy, gray, titanio-composite control panel. His eyes gaze past everything to the distant stars.

I wonder if the Tiyaka Reservists have re-secured the geothermal power plants from the Nolvarics yet, he thinks, his mind definitely on his work and not the starfighter battles presently taking place around Barnard's Star, not more than six light-years away.

Two days ago, a band of Nolvarics had launched a daring attack against the frigid super-earth Raschon-2 orbiting Barnard's Star. The conflict had escalated quickly into what was easily the largest Nolvaric offensive of the past decade. Even now, as Konran floated here around the moon, Barnardian militia was busy routing the aggressive Nolvaric cyborgs with help from the Tiyaka Reservists.

Konran's fingers drum their way subconsciously to a small, golden disc on his control panel. The disc hums to life at his touch, and a holographic message appears in the space above it.

Captain Konran Andacellos
In commemoration of five years of commendable service
ISSA Astrofreighter Fleet
10 August 2212

Konran looks at the holo-medallion as the words convert into a holographic depiction of an ISSA astrofreighter docking effortlessly with a rapidly gyrating asteroid. The rendering was incredibly realistic, and if he looked closely, he could even make out constellations in the pocket-size starry background.

ISSA, or Intra-Solar Supply and Acquisition, only hired the best pilots (mantra: *Precision is Perfection*, or *"PIP,"* for those too busy for the six extra syllables). In return for the honor, Konran and two hundred other ace pilots flew astrofreighters between the moon and predetermined locations throughout the solar system, picking up freshly mined minerals and transporting them on strategically determined routes and schedules back to the moon for processing. There was a lot to master: constant Keplerian motion, solar winds, solar flares, and coronal mass ejections; punctilious monitoring of space lanes; tracking and navigating space debris; not to mention adjusting on the fly to constantly changing geospatial politics. The ISSA pilot had more than a few daily challenges to surmount.

Or so they told you. Aside from the occasional political entanglement, astrofreighting was not the most rigorous business in the solar system. Everything was already calculated, and most of the job boiled down to pressing go, opening doors, and chatting with other pilots as the machines did all the work. If not for the mandate that all spacefaring craft with cargo or equipment valued above \$250 million retain human pilots (which pretty much included every single spacecraft), Konran's job wouldn't even exist. He could thank the Nolvarics for that law.

That's not to say the position of ISSA captain came without perks. According to inter-pilot ISSA gossip, an astrofreighter captain like Konran had one of the best paths up ISSA's sprawling corporate ladder. In fact, after seven to ten years running freighters across the solar system, a captain was essentially a shoo-in for a command post on one of ISSA's Mobile Supply Stations (MSS) orbiting the gas giants. Or, with the right network of connections, even a manager of one of the corporation's Venus Gas Mine Quality Monitoring Facilities (VGMQMF).

And it didn't get any better than that.

Konran's gaze turns from his ISSA holo-medallion back to the stars, but his daydreams no longer wander to the starfights of Barnard's Star or even to yesterday's rumors of possible Nolvaric activity near Pluto. The ISSA ladder required climbing, and the rungs were more than crowded.

"Hey, sir," a Sri Lankan accent speaks behind him. "A transmission from the *Relrick* for you." Alandie, Konran's pilot in training, lightly taps Konran's shoulder.

Konran's attention shifts from the stars to starboard, where the astrofreighter *Relrick*, twin sister to the *Viona Grande* and flagship to their upcoming dual mission, awaits its portion of the cargo transfer from the lunar base below.

"This is Captain Andacellos," Konran speaks into the comm.

"Konran!" Captain Natauli Joluna's voice comes in loud and clear. "Watch the orbital precession! If you drift another twenty arcmins axially you'll be in violation of ODFP C-45 in less than six minutes."

Konran shares a glance with Alandie, and the uncharacteristically tall Sri Lankan nineteen-year-old rolls his eyes. The ODFPs, or Orbital Docking and Flight Procedures, were the set of rules and policies governing all ISSA activities. Every

ISSA captain knew them forward and backward, and ODFP C-45 had been considered obsolete since before Konran flew his first ISSA mission. But ISSA policy makers had better things to do than dust out cobwebs from their manuals (still printed in paper and stored in orange-painted cabinets in every ISSA cockpit and control station), and the outdated procedure technically remained an active requirement.

"Did you say C-45—" Konran begins.

"Not to mention C-34, B-77, and B-11," Natauli breaks in. "You've got to look sharp for this mission, Konran, remember? We went over this in precheck. Are you leaving this to Alandie? I don't think he is ready yet."

"We are currently on autopilot, Captain Joluna, ma'am," Alandie replies cheerfully. "Per ODFP A-26, which you encouraged us to review during precheck yesterday, we are laser-syncing our position with our flagship every five hundred microseconds."

Silence for a moment, then Captain Joluna responds, "Fine. Just follow the flight plan, and don't forget to turn on the receiver lamps again."

Alandie winces at the last words, having omitted that step a week ago during a routine tugboating maneuver. The captain of the tug had furnished more than a few choice words when his locking boom snapped off as a result. News like that spread fast, and while every ISSA pilot knew about it, most had chosen not to rub it in.

"Yes, ma'am," Konran replies, offering Alandie a rueful, *you kind of asked for it* look as the younger pilot throws his hands up and spins away from the comm in his copilot seat.

That was unusual of Natauli, Konran thinks. *Something's got her stressed today.* Of the two hundred ISSA pilots out there, Natauli was among the more friendly—not to mention among the most skilled.

Less than a minute later, and without either Konran or Alandie touching the control panel, the *Viona Grande*'s orbital precession resolves itself as the *Relrick* corrects its orbital pattern.

"Everyone has a hard time with the tugs at first, PIT," Konran reassures Alandie, using ISSA jargon for "pilot in training."

"Yeah, but nobody breaks the boom off," Alandie moans, still smarting. "I mean, that's a get-thrown-back-into-simulators stupid mistake."

"Speaking of docking with the tug," Konran tries changing the subject, "did you hear that members of the Kazakhstani National Cricket Team are coming on the *Viona Grande* today?"

"What?" Alandie blurts out. "You're kidding—the back-to-back interplanetary champions are coming on the *Viona Grande*? Natauli didn't say anything about them during precheck."

"I just got an updated passenger list," Konran replies with a chuckle. There were a few last-minute changes. They'll be on the *Viona Grande* in less than a half hour."

Sometimes, rather than hauling expensive space rocks across the solar system, ISSA pilots were asked to ferry dignitaries, celebrities, politicians, and other high-profile, high-paying individuals on tours of the deep-space war sites from the Nolvaric Invasion of 2158. Today's mission is one of those, and Konran laughs as Alandie launches into an enthusiastic, chronological recap of Kazakhstan's cricket accomplishments from the past decade.

When the Nolvarics first invaded the solar system more than fifty years ago, they bypassed the United Space Federation's deep-space navy easily, slipping warships, machines, and materials into the Kuiper Belt with nothing more than patience, trickery, and advanced biotechnology (it turns out space is quite immense and highly difficult to fully observe and defend).

Once there, the Nolvarics meticulously set up hidden operating bases, building them by usurping Kuiper Belt objects from their orbits and gravitationally binding them together in clusters across deep space. Of course, alarms triggered as automated satellite observatories detected the mass change in Kuiper Belt orbits, but by then it was too late: space was too big, the United Space Federation's deep-space patrols too thin, and the Nolvaric warships wiped out the first wave of defenders quickly.

As the bulk of the United Space Federation Navy scrambled to mobilize and react, the Nolvarics began hurling massive space rocks at colossal velocities toward Earth, Mars, and Venus. And then, as soon as the USFN fleet passed Neptune's orbit, the

Nolvarics unleashed a second attack from the asteroid belt, the multidirectional assault focused directly on Earth itself. If the Nolvaric infiltration of the Kuiper Belt was a shocking surprise, this second attack from the asteroid belt was absolutely devastating. To this day, no one had figured out how they did it.

As every schoolchild in the twenty-third century knew, the Nolvarics started out as humans on Earth. But that all changed in the mid-2090s when, through experimental (and highly illegal) anthroelectric biomutation, a small, savvy group of multinational rejects transformed themselves into walking, breathing, semi-robotic super-beings. While the plodding political systems of the day debated the Nolvarics' right to self-effect the transformation, in 2109, the self-made cyborgs usurped control of many of Earth's autonomous warfare systems. By 2110, the world was at war. By 2111, Venus and Mars became embroiled in the conflict as Nolvaric aggression spread to the thriving space colonies.

After seven years of brutal warfare, human ingenuity—or perhaps desperation—began to prevail. The Nolvarics were driven back and cities retaken as humanity developed robust autonomous systems capable of resisting Nolvaric hacking and control. Man and machine fought side by side against the man-machine onslaught (and woman, too, but less alliteratively so), and slowly the Nolvaric advantage disappeared. With the inevitability of defeat growing more certain each day, in 2120, the Nolvarics fled the solar system on the wings of infantile interstellar warp technology, their trajectory toward Canis Minor.

Decades earlier, life-supporting planets had been detected amidst the stars embedded within Canis Minor. With an exuberance hastened by ever-straining natural resources, Earth's nations collaborated to build seven Generation Ships to travel to and colonize the systems. Volunteers came readily from across the globe, and within a few short years the Generation Ships departed: sailing gloriously away from the solar system to distribute human life amidst the stars. Although generations would pass before any of the subluminal ships would arrive at their destinations, the calculated probability that at least one of the ships would achieve colonization was higher than 99.9 percent. Humanity had cheered, their smiles broad whenever they looked to the stars (that is, when they could see them through the haze).

As it was, in 2120, Nolvaric warp technology crossed the distance to the Generation Ships in a matter of days. Then the Nolvarics captured the passengers, biomutated them all into Nolvarics against their will, and ferried everyone to the intended target colonies at speeds much faster than light, their numbers greatly increased.

When they snuck back into the solar system in 2158, the Nolvarics encountered a humanity much advanced from the chaos of 2120. The same autonomous artificial intelligence that spurred the Nolvarics' original defeat had likewise spurred an economic revolution. Farming, mining, manufacturing, healthcare, transportation, and education boomed under the boost of true, artificial autonomy, and humans found themselves free to do with their time as they pleased. The contributors contributed, the freeloaders were fed, and humanity cheered again. When the Nolvarics returned, they found a humanity prospering, a humanity proliferating not only into the solar system but into the stars beyond: a humanity armed with the greatest weapons of all time, prepared to defend itself.

The Nolvarics didn't care.

While the intervening decades had seen scores of fresher, softer targets emerge across the near galaxy in the form of interstellar colonies, the Nolvarics had eyes only for the blue planet, Earth. Their warships came cloaked and undetected into the bustling asteroid belt. Their hulls came protected by gravity-enhanced energy shields. Their forces made it within the orbit of the moon before Earth's defense and detection systems raised an alarm. And they defeated the defenders with awful strokes, tearing apart warships like piranha on the bone.

Without waiting for the rest of the solar system to come to its progenitor's aid, the Nolvarics descended upon Earth. Autonomous defense systems turned against their human creators as Nolvarics bent robotic systems to their will. Suddenly no city was safe, no spaceport secure, no defense incapable of bending. With Earth on the verge of capitulation, the Nolvarics spread their attack toward Venus and Mars. And when Venus fell mere weeks

13

later, the small, red planet remained the lone detractor at the wedding supper between Humanity and Enslavement.

Luckily, the Martians had a trick up their sleeve.

In a turn of fate that fifty years later didn't favor Konran's chances of becoming a starfighter pilot himself, Martian Deep Space Exploration Incorporated was the only source successful at producing warships capable of competing with the Nolvarics. Some scholars, mostly from Earth, believed MDSE had been withholding starfighter technology in order to incrementally "develop" space warfare "innovations," thereby ensuring a constant stream of weapons-related income for decades to come. Regardless of the motives, by 2160, Martian-built starfighters began pouring from the red planet and into the fray.

By mid-2161, Martian starfighters had wrought enough havoc that Earth got to her feet and started punching back. By 2162, the Nolvarics retreated, abandoning what hadn't been demolished of their asteroidal bulwarks and retreating to their bases in the Kuiper Belt and, after defeat there, to Canis Minor.

Humanity hit back even harder in the spring of 2164, when a USFN armada of MDSE-built warp cruisers attacked the Nolvaric home planets orbiting Luyten's Star and Procyon. Defeated, outmatched, and outgunned, the Nolvarics scattered: their last known direction kind of everywhere and anywhere. Humanity had done it again.

Today, nearly fifty years since their final defeat, Nolvaric clans and tribes still attacked regularly across the inhabited galaxy. Although none of the attacks were as coordinated or as large-scale as the original invasion, space battles and skirmishes were not a thing of the past, and stories of starfighter heroics were popular news across the vast network of inhabited space.

Eventually the *Viona Grande*'s cargo arrives, and Konran almost grins in spite of himself—this was going to be entertaining. Today's passenger list included seventy-nine VIPs and one poodle to be ferried to see Kuiper Belt war sites X19AA57 and Y25LM90. In the twenty-third century, it was a mark of prestige for rich and famous Earthlings, Venusians, and Martians to visit Nolvaric war sites that nobody else had visited. And, although all the war sites in the asteroid belt and Kuiper Belt had already been visited by someone famous, it was still a thing to visit a war site that hadn't been visited recently. As far as Konran was concerned, ferrying dignitaries around was light-years better than a multi-month expedition to gather exotic ice minerals from the Oort cloud.

Although Nolvaric war sites X19AA57 and Y25LM90 were originally part of distinct, widely separated Nolvaric operating bases, they had drifted quite close in recent weeks, offering a rare opportunity to step on separate Nolvaric war sites within the same Earth day. As Konran's cargo disembarks from their transport shuttles, the *Viona Grande* fills with higher-than-average tiers of the rich and famous.

Konran dons his pilot cap and coat, preparing to greet the honored guests, and the comm buzzes. Alandie puts it through.

"Konran," Natauli's voice crackles in, "you've got two senators, a district space justice, and half the cast of *Andromeda Uncharted* on board now. Remember what we talked about ODFP A-99 in precheck," she says, referring to the Official Procedure for Greeting and Accommodating VIPs. "Distribute the personalized ISSA space medallions before we leave orbit, and use what we practiced in our training session on engaging in-flight commentary. Let's all impress Director Zieshal today!"

"Thanks, Natauli," Konran replies, sharing a glance with Alandie. Natauli was already pushing this mission hard, and they hadn't left orbit yet.

"She didn't mention the cricket team," Alandie complains.

"Put on your cap and coat," Konran says. "You can meet them yourself."

Alandie springs at the thought, and in moments the two pilots walk through the bulkhead, out of the cabin, and into the *Viona Grande*'s elegant VIP hall.

The trip to the Kuiper Belt will be of moderate length, with travel time to the destination calculated at 153 hours. After several voyages of this kind, Konran has learned to take things slowly, and he mingles easily—if not forcedly—with the crowd: greeting the various VIPs, committing their names to memory, and passing out commemorative ISSA medallions for the journey. Alandie, on the other hand, can barely contain his excitement, and by the time he reaches the Kazakhstani cricket team he is bursting with smiles and compliments.

The time for departure arrives, and flight stewards escort the VIPs to private, custom-arranged quarters in which they can buckle in for the acceleration phase of the excursion. Konran settles into his captain's chair and engages the *Viona Grande*'s engines. Side by side with the *Relrick*, the two astrofreighters rocket away from the moon toward deep space.

"So, I saw the way Shira was looking at you out there," Alandie remarks nonchalantly as the *Viona Grande* accelerates toward its steady-state velocity (as prescribed by intrasolar statute) of thirty-eight million kilometers per hour. He grins, tipping the pointy goatee on his chin in Konran's direction. "It would solve your problems—just saying."

Konran looks over at Alandie. "Just because LiMei dumped me doesn't mean I'm automatically looking for a new girlfriend," he replies.

"If one door of love closes upon your face," Alandie says, his voice taking on a scholarly air, "shake it off and open your eyes to those opening around you."

Konran groans, pulling up a three-dimensional holographic radar display and turning away.

"No comment."

"You can't ignore fate," Alandie insists, edging over to Konran, "or beautiful stewardesses with eyes for you."

"Fail," Konran grunts.

"Come on," Alandie prods. "You refuse to see it because you're still grieving LiMei. Shira's gorgeous, she's available, she's totally into you, and she's definitely more understanding of your occupation—I mean, she comes on these voyages with you."

"I'm not grieving LiMei," Konran retorts. "And trust me, PIT, nothing good comes from interoffice romance. Just wait until you've been around a year. You'll see."

Still, Alandie has a point, Konran thinks. The Scandinavian stewardess was quite striking.

"I still can't believe LiMei broke it off with you just because you're gone half the year," Alandie says. "I mean, she just up and left you."

"Thanks, PIT, for the reminder," Konran replies. "She wasn't wrong, you know. It wasn't going to work out."

"Clearly," Alandie says, his smile dropping a degree and his eyes growing distant.

"All right," Konran says, "who is she?"

"She what?"

"The girl," Konran presses. "The one you're head over heels for."

"What, er, ha, no," Alandie replies. "It was that obvious?"

"It's not like it was hard," Konran says, "the way you stared off into the instrument panel all of a sudden."

Alandie shakes his head. "You got me. Her name is Mareta Kona—she just moved into my orbital condominium complex. We have pretty much everything in common. It's been so fast and perfect, it made me think of you and LiMei."

"Well, thanks for driving that dagger deeper," Konran replies. For all of Alandie's virtues, tact was not among them.

"Sorry man," the PIT replies. "But now I'm gone for half a month, and I can't help worrying about it."

"Why don't you take your first break now?" Konran suggests. "I'm good down here—there won't be much to do until we reach Mars's orbit at least. Go give Mareta a call if you want. That's something I could have done better with LiMei."

Alandie jumps at the offer, fist-bumping Konran and climbing up a ladder into his personal quarters.

Less than ten minutes later, Alandie descends. He resumes his place in the copilot chair.

"So ... how did it go?" Konran asks tentatively, not unaware of Alandie's glum expression.

"She said it was weird for me to call so soon," Alandie says. "Thanks for the quarking advice."

Standing, Konran slaps the PIT on the shoulder. "There's always Shira," he says cheerfully, dodging Alandie's punch, donning his cap and coat, and heading through the bulkhead to visit with the VIPs.

The usual pace of spaceflight assumes its rhythm: long shifts followed by short breaks, with time allotted for sleeping every fifteen hours. After a particularly challenging shift involving three

17

VIP gambling disputes, intense negotiations with Saturnese flight control, a bite from a spacefaring poodle, and a higher-than-average number of reprimands from Natauli, Konran makes his way into his quarters for some much-needed rest.

He spends a few minutes gazing out his window at Saturn. The yellow, ringed gas giant is still near enough to be appreciated with the naked eye. The presence of anything but stars is unusual on these voyages—space is simply so big—and Konran appreciates the beauty of the sight, hanging for a moment with the planet as it hangs delicately in its infinite cocoon of blackness and starlight. He sets his computer to record the scene, not wanting to miss the moment, and settles into his evening routine.

After a half hour on the bike, and another half hour of rigorous exercise, Konran nestles into the couch, which doubles as a bed in his small quarters. With a wave of his hand he pulls up his most recent library acquisition, and a holographic book flickers into existence before him: *Tars Urume: A Starfighter's Autobiography*. Before he can settle two pages in, however, his comm buzzes. With an ocular gesture he dismisses the book.

"This is Captain Andacellos," he answers the comm.

"Hey," Natauli's voice speaks, "you still up?"

Of course, she knows he's awake. Every pilot's status is broadcast at all times to all other pilots during these missions.

"Yeah," he replies. "What's up?"

"You mind if I holo over?" she asks.

"Er, sure," is all he says. Natauli hadn't uttered a non-business-related sentence the entire voyage, and now she wanted to holo over?

In moments, Natauli's holographic form appears in his quarters. Her short, black hair is wet against her tan skin as if she just finished bathing. She is dressed in a relaxed-fitting T-shirt and sweatpants. Natauli, senior flagship captain of the voyage, was visiting in her pajamas. She sits on her own couch, holographically transmitted, which fills the opposite corner of Konran's room.

"I just needed to talk," she says.

"Ah," Konran replies.

"It's been a long day," Natauli adds.

"Yeah," Konran says.

"Thanks for your help today."

"For Saturn?" Konran asks.

"I didn't think we were going to receive admission through Saturnese space this time," she says.

"I worried for a minute there," Konran replies. "But we managed it. I thought you did good."

"I'm sorry if I've been uptight on this mission," Natauli apologizes abruptly. "There's just so much riding on this one, you know?"

"Don't worry about it," Konran says, surprised by her sincerity. "VIP-hauling always adds extra stress." Every ISSA mission was big, and although Konran had grown accustomed to the ubiquity of pressure in his daily life, it could get to anyone.

Natauli sits there, looking distant.

"How are you, Natauli?" Konran ventures, unsure what else to say.

"I'm fine," she says with a dismissive shake of her hair. But she looks up at him with what seems the closest thing to vulnerability Konran has seen in the woman's ever-intense gaze. "I just needed someone to talk to tonight."

"I'm all ears," Konran says, cupping his hands around his ears to make them appear larger. Natauli looks at him like he's an alien before rolling her eyes.

"I know I've been hard on you guys," she continues. "It's not about you—you should know that. I just really need to get this mission right."

Konran considers her words, piecing things together. She wasn't going to say why she came here; he was going to have to guess.

"So," he guesses, "did you apply for the MSS or the VGMQMF?"

Natauli visibly relaxes. "Neither, actually. Min Hosun recommended me to Director Zieshal as a candidate for warp fleet commander."

"Wait, what?" Konran blurts out. "ISSA is getting into the warp business already? I thought that was three years out at least. Natauli, that's huge!"

"Don't tell anybody—it hasn't been announced yet. Onus Shipping already pulled it off, so ISSA's scrambling to catch up."

Onus Shipping Corporation, colloquially known to ISSA pilots as O-Ship, was ISSA's biggest competitor.

Konran whistles low, an impressed sound. "So they must leave the planetary ecliptic before warping?" he asks, referring to the disc-shaped slice of solar system the planets all orbited the sun upon.

"Yeah," Natauli confirms. "They have to travel far enough out of the ecliptic to avoid solar warp prohibitions, and then they warp to the Kuiper Belt or the Oort cloud for materials. They say it's dropping cycle times by 97 percent. ISSA's even talking about opening routes to some of the nearby brown dwarves."

Konran exhales, also an impressed sound. "Wow. There must have been a technological breakthrough to make warping such short distances economical." With the tremendous energy required to initiate warp compression fields, warp travel over short distances was generally reserved for the military or the ultrarich.

"Yeah, seriously," Natauli agrees. "As far as I know, O-Ship has that completely under wraps, and ISSA isn't saying anything about our own capabilities."

"I can imagine," Konran nods. "Remember me when you're warping out of the solar system next month."

"I wish," Natauli replies. "Zieshal gave me this mission as a test—he holoed over and everything to explain it. There are twelve candidates and only two positions, and this is only the first test." She rubs her hands against her eyebrows and forehead, massaging out the tension of her words.

"I was wondering how we got the double Nolvaric sites *and* the Saturn flyby in one go," Konran says. "I can see why you've been feeling stressed."

"I don't know if I'm up to it," Natauli interjects quickly, her voice rising. "I want this so badly—I know I'm good enough for it. But warp travel is so much more complicated than this, and if I'm struggling with a little Saturn flyby, how am I going to manage that? If you hadn't convinced that Saturnese controller to let us through ..." She trails off, forehead pressed against her fingers, peering at the floor.

Konran doesn't reply, risking silence rather than speech in the face of such sensitive emotions. Sometimes women just needed you to listen—he hoped this was one of those moments.

Their silence persists for a moment, and finally Natauli looks up, but not at him.

"Anyway," she says abruptly, and without another word her hologram disappears.

Konran blinks, surprised at the swiftness of her departure. A sense of confusion washes over him, followed by awkwardness and then frustration before repeating all three.

"What...?" he asks the empty room.

No one answers.

I must have embarrassed her, he berates himself, finally realizing she had been looking for support when he gave her silence.

He almost calls Natauli back, and then stops himself, arguing internally for two minutes whether it's a good or terrible idea. When he finally tries, she doesn't reply.

At a loss, Konran calls his book back. Its contents hover beside his couch, and he stares at them, mind racing. He stands up and dismisses the book, leaving the room empty again. He paces, shakes his head, and finally just sits back down.

He calls up a news feed, setting it to play the latest news broadcasts. Its hologram fills the opposite end of his room with a depiction of a woman in a bulky environmental suit. Her face is visible through a globe-shaped helmet, and she stands beneath a layer of churning, brown-yellow clouds. Konran immediately recognizes the surface of Venus.

"We're on location at the Yablochkina crater, where, as you can see behind me, a massive protest has broken out against the Venusian Terraforming Act." The anchor gestures behind her where a large, black, metallic structure stands on Venus's surface. Its shape is that of a large cone with the tip cut off—almost like someone dropped a squat, synthetic volcano onto the planet.

"As you recall," the newswoman states, "the landmark piece of legislation passed Venusian Parliament two days ago and was signed into law by Prime Minister Fasnikov yesterday. In response, EarthMaker Incorporated dropped twenty-five atmospheric vortex engines like this to the planet's surface this morning. These engines are designed to perform the crucial first step in terraforming Venus: cooling its atmosphere so water can be reintroduced to the planet. As you are aware, Venus's water all boiled off billions of years ago due to the planet's runaway greenhouse effect. Although the reacquisition of water has long been considered to be economically infeasible, anonymous sources at Onus Shipping confided in me that the freighter company has developed a viable way to mine and transport water from the trillions of icy comets within the Oort cloud—easily providing enough capacity to sustain multiple biodomes upon the planet's surface."

"Quarks," Konran mutters to himself. "That's why ISSA wants into the warp business."

The news hologram zooms in toward the vortex engine, showing a throng of people dressed in bulky environmental suits not unlike the newswoman's. Their snowman-shaped forms surround and struggle to climb the massive vortex engine. The anchor continues her narration.

"It is unclear how EarthMaker was able to provide such an immediate response to the Venusian Terraforming Act, but rumors suggest they had been preparing for this moment for more than five years. As you see behind me, not everyone is happy about the changes, and these cloud-colony locals are risking Venus's tremendous atmospheric pressure to protest such fundamental changes to their planet."

Konran waves his hand in front of him to move on to the next story, and the news hologram changes to show a ring of metallic, noodle-shaped structures tethered together somewhere in space. The area inside the ring shimmers, distorting the starlight on the other side. Tiny space shuttles flit to and fro about the superstructure, which Konran judges to be enormous. A deep male voice narrates the visage.

"After months of negotiations, the SecondSun Initiative received a massive boost in the form of a United Space Federation research grant, demonstrating the federation's commitment to improving life within the solar system through fundamental research and development."

Konran perks up at the mention of the SecondSun Initiative, having captained several missions that provided raw materials to SecondSun manufacturing facilities. The hologram transitions to show two women in business attire standing next to each other aboard a spaceship. The same massive, ring-shaped superstructure is visible through a window behind them. The newswoman speaks, addressing the camera.

"I'm here with Vo Kinto, SecondSun vice president of technology. Vo, this is a big day for the people at SecondSun."

"Indeed, it is," Vo Kinto replies. "In the 250 years since humankind first set foot on Earth's moon, we have established ourselves into the depths of the solar system and beyond. But the real effort has only just begun. Even as we speak, more than two billion individuals live daily without access to adequate natural sunlight. We at SecondSun do not accept this, nor do the fine members of the United Space Federation Research and Development Subcommittee. With this grant, we intend to put an end to the solar disparity."

"So tell us how it works," the news anchor prompts.

"The sun emits 386 quadrillion watts of electromagnetic power every second," Vo Kinto explains, "most of which radiates uselessly into space. SecondSun harnesses this wasted energy through strategically placed gravity lenses, which bend and redirect the sunlight toward more purposeful locations. With variable focal lengths beyond the aphelion of Makemake, SecondSun gravity lenses will provide Earth-quality sunlight to 95 percent of solar system inhabitants."

"Can you explain the advantages gravity lenses provide over traditional reflecting mirrors?" the anchor asks.

Konran gestures again, and the news feed moves on. A man in a tidy, pinstriped suit speaks from a podium. His accent is a mixture between the long round vowels of Eastern Europe and the short syllables of Chinese. Konran has to squint to understand.

"... that the damage is superficial in nature, and we expect the Triton Insect Harvesting facility to make a full recovery within two weeks," the man says. "Efforts to recover the insects affected by the breach are underway, and there is no reason to believe these will not retain their nutritional value. Reports that the Neptune

23

Commonwealth is in a food crisis are both hysterical and irresponsible."

The hologram shifts to flyby footage of Triton, where warships mill protectively around the Neptunian moon. The footage zooms down, toward Triton's surface without cutting, until a sprawling web of interconnected structures becomes visible, stretching across the moon's icy horizon. One particularly large building stands out, its side completely blown away. The explosion had been huge, throwing debris outward more than two kilometers from the epicenter. Workers in space suits sort through the rubble, and a number of spacecraft land or take off from the site. A somber reporter's voice-over accompanies the footage:

"You're watching a live stream of what remains of the Triton Insect Harvesting Plant. This morning at 8:14 a.m. Solar Standard Time an explosion rocked the facility that processes thirteen trillion edible insects every day. While most of the organic matter is expected to be recovered, the full impact of the accident remains to be seen, with experts suggesting a 38 percent drop in regional food availability to be expected over the upcoming weeks."

Konran moves the news feed on. A regal, dark-skinned woman fills the opposite side of his cabin, whom he recognizes as the Prime Minister of Ceres. She looks angry. As Konran watches, her hologram transitions to a three-dimensional depiction of the inner solar system.

"For the past 175 years," the prime minister narrates with a huff in her voice, "Earth has been deflecting near-Earth asteroids and comets away from their original Earth-crossing trajectories."

On the hologram, thousands of tiny specks appear, marking the location of all the space debris inhabiting the "empty space" between the sun and Mars. An accelerated montage shows hundreds of these asteroids and comets angling away from Earth as Earth-launched satellites systematically blast them from their original orbits.

The prime minister's voice-over continues.

"This work of deflection was accomplished without any regard for the future inhabitants of Venus, Mars, Ceres, Vesta, Pallas, or any of the other inhabitable celestial bodies near Earth. Now we are forced to bear the cost of Earth's carelessness. In fact, today, in

2212, Ceres must contend with 250 times more Ceres-crossing objects than would have been encountered in 2040. Many of these are large enough to completely demolish our populace, and continued defense against them places an unfair strain upon our people."

Her voice grows louder, angrier.

"We do not have the riches and rivers and mountains and plains of Earth upon which to build our wealth. But instead of owning up to and correcting this deadly debacle, Earth hides behind United Space Federation statutes—unwilling to address the condition that she herself caused."

Konran gestures again and again, and news stories cycle past: a debate on the merit of warp restrictions within the solar system ("The antiquated reliance on obsolete legislation is costing the solar system uncounted trillions every day"), a story on the resurgence of artificial intelligence systems in the military ("Within the next seven years, autonomous systems will surpass their pre-Nolvaric Invasion levels for the first time in fifty-four years"), an exclusive report on the shocking state of intrasolar pollution ("The concentration of thorium-230 within the solar vacuum has grown by a factor of ten million within the past three years"), and a Uranian diamond-smuggling scandal connected to the Duke of Callisto's secret mistress ("I assure you, I know nothing about it").

Konran dismisses the news feed altogether. He walks over to his window, exhaling deeply. Saturn still hangs there: a distant yellow marble alone against the unending backdrop of galactic grandeur. He can see his face floating next to it, reflected softly by the dim light of the room.

CHAPTER 2

Ten hours later, but only a couple into his next shift, Konran is already tired. After Natauli's visit the night before, his designated sleep hours had dwindled below half their usual allotment before he availed himself of their purpose. He enters a command into a holographic computer interface floating within his left palm, signaling for his dosage of "sleep in a pill" to increase. His mind becomes foggy for an instant, and then refreshment courses through his body.

This is going to be a long shift, he thinks, sighing. *And I only get a two-hour break before the next one.*

It would have to do.

Shortly, the *Relrick* and *Viona Grande* arrive within the orbit of Uranus. Although the frigid ice giant is on the other side of the sun at the moment, its L3 Lagrange point is directly in the convoy's path. Here, in the gravitationally favorable point in Uranus's orbit, the *Habragon-3* space station lurks in the darkness of space.

The *Relrick* and *Viona Grande* don't stop at *Habragon-3*, but they do acquire a new companion. Per standard protocol when faring beyond the orbit of Neptune and into the Kuiper Belt, they rendezvous with a protective escort from the space station. Today's escort is a Brazilian-made Trovão-class heavy fighter, a truly cutting-edge war machine—at least it was before the days of the Nolvaric Invasion.

"You'd think the electron pushers back on the moon could get us something built within the last fifty years," Alandie complains after double-checking the comm is off. "I know *Habragon-3* has newer ships than this."

"It meets minimum requirements, and that's all they care about," Konran remarks as the *Viona Grande* overtakes and matches speed with the accelerating Trovão-class fighter. At least this escort had been built within the last fifty years.

26

Out the forward viewport, Konran watches the bulky starfighter assume its protective position in front of the two astrofreighters. Its name appears within the *Viona Grande*'s registry as the *Borboleta*.

"Did they seriously get us an escort called the *Butterfly*?" Alandie groans after translating the name.

"Appears so," Konran replies, entering a command on the *Viona Grande*'s console to hail the newcomer.

Static. Konran tries again. More static.

"I can't believe this," he mutters to himself.

"What's that?" Alandie asks.

"Natauli blocked us from transmitting with the escort."

"She can do that?"

"Technically the convoy flagship controls communications with all third-party craft, but usually..." Konran trails off as the comm buzzes.

"It's the *Relrick*," Alandie says, putting it through.

"Captain Andacellos," a courteous male voice speaks from the other side, "we have noticed your attempts to hail the *Borboleta*. Do not worry. We will handle all communications with the escort, freeing your time for your internal duties." The voice pertains to Racho Miccero, Natauli's PIT.

"Thanks, Racho," Konran answers as Alandie's face strains to restrain his reply to the news. "I'm sure the VIPs will appreciate the extra attention."

Four and a half days later, Konran still hasn't spoken directly to Natauli or the *Borboleta*. But Racho's relentless professionalism is pleasant enough to deal with, and the convoy presses without incident beyond Neptune's orbit and into the Kuiper Belt.

Finally, and within the designated arrival threshold of 153 hours (plus or minus five), the *Relrick*, *Viona Grande*, and *Borboleta* arrive at Historical War Site X19AA57. It's a medium-small Kuiper Belt object, no more than twenty kilometers in diameter. Nolvaric garrison ruins scatter across its cratered girth, marred by long gouge marks where USFN energy weapons had impacted the space rock. Cheers ring out within the *Viona Grande* as VIPs and stewards celebrate the arrival.

Konran lets Alandie perform the landing (per ODFP A-55, Revised Procedure for Non-Atmospheric Mooring of Class-A Freighter Craft with Unimproved, Gravitationally Minimal Landing Sites). The *Viona Grande* sets down at its predetermined landing coordinates beside the *Relrick* as the *Borboleta* flutters protectively overhead. Stewards help the VIPs don space suits—a process so streamlined it takes less than a minute per VIP—and one, then five, then eighty lights blink green on Konran's status display, signaling all space suits are RFS, or "ready for spacewalk".

Konran enters the code to allow disembarking through the airlock, and three by three, the dignitaries debark for X19AA57. The *Viona Grande*'s eighty VIPs mingle with eighty more from the *Relrick*, and shortly the frozen asteroid mills with more excitement than one hundred sixty snowmen arriving upon the beaches of Fiji for the first time.

VIPs wander the space rock's dusty, gray landscape in their puffy suits. They pick up mineral specimens. They point at abandoned structures. They photograph the tiny sun, themselves, and the raw galactic cosmos—posting holographic, high-definition, virtual reality photos on the trendiest of social media outlets across the inner planets. Intelligent ion thrusters in the VIPs' suits keep their centers of gravity from displacing too far from the surface of the war site, and Konran tracks their status on a series of displays within his cockpit.

The *Viona Grande*'s comm buzzes, and for the first time in nearly five days Natauli's urgent voice comes in.

"Konran, is your transmission antennae up and calibrated yet? We can't allow half of the VIPs' first posts to show up later than the others!"

Alandie looks up from his copilot chair. "I *just finished* the procedure, ma'am," he replies, a smile on his words but not his lips.

Five hours later the convoy leaves Historical War Site X19AA57, and after seven hours of continual wining, dining, and celebration, they reach Historical War Site Y25LM90. The medium-large Kuiper Belt rock looms out *Viona Grande*'s viewport, large, gray, and shadowed, with a horizon approaching two hundred kilometers. Alandie lands the astrofreighter, sets up the transmission antennae in record speed, and the dignitaries debark for the surface of Y25LM90 in their snowman suits.

"Great job, guys," she says, her voice relaxing as if the weight of the solar system had finally fallen from her shoulders. "I just need to say thank you. You did an astro job this week. I really mean it. We nailed our arrival schedules and asteroidal moorings. Our VIPs are having the time of their lives. Their transmissions are hitting the nets without problems. I couldn't have asked for a better sister crew. Thank you both."

Konran almost laughs at Alandie, who is frozen, dumbfounded, his sleeves halfway rolled up, ready to fight about transmission antennae.

"You're welcome, Natauli," Konran replies. "Same to you. I think Zieshal will approve of this flight report."

The comm clicks off without another word, but Konran can almost hear Natauli breathe the phrase, *I hope so.*

Konran and Alandie settle back into their command chairs. They observe the cavorting VIPs through the *Viona Grande*'s optically enhanced viewport and sensor displays.

After a few minutes, Konran calls up a holographic news feed. One article appears promising, and he reads:

After days of heavy fighting, Tiyaka Reservists liberated twelve of the seventeen Raschonian geothermal power plants held by Nolvaric raiders, capturing eight live Nolvarics in the process.

I wonder when they will open applications again, Konran broods, having been too young the last time the famous militia group posted contracts.

In other news, three Indo-Austran supply vessels had gone missing yesterday en route to Estera-5, the massive deep space colony which shared Neptune's orbit. Abnormal traces of antimatter neutrinos had been detected in their last known vicinity, but no accompanying release of radiation had been observed. Analysts suspected an attack may have been connected to the Triton Insect Harvesting accident earlier that week.

Speaking from Saturn's moon Titan, Yanhua Hsuilan, governor of the Independent Republic of Saturno-China, called the event "another unfortunate failure of security typical to the perpetual oversight prevalent amongst the Indo-Austran Interspace

29

Alliance." She denounced deployment of the United Space Federation Navy's supercarrier *Estrellas Vigilantes* into the region to supervise recovery operations as "an excuse for belligerent infringement of territorial rights."

The politics and logistics aside, Konran can't help but think of the 150 Martian-built starfighters stowed in the belly of the five-hundred-thousand-ton supercarrier. He finds another article from a journalist aboard the *Estrellas Vigilantes*, which includes an interview with the ship's starfighter commander.

Maybe I could become a freelance space journalist—or even a protective escort pilot, he muses, glancing out the viewport where the Borboleta circles lazily overhead. *I could take the pay cut*, he reasons for the thousandth time, unable to resolve the ever-recurring question: *But what next?*

His mind drifts along the subject, traversing well-worn paths in no real pattern. *What if I get stuck making no money and having no fun? Why don't I just go for it? I'm good enough to make it as a starfighter pilot. I just need to find the right chance. And I can always pick up another job as a pilot if worse comes to worst—ISSA would probably have me back. Or I might just end up on Callisto, monitoring Jupiter's Van Allen belts like Starkos Galdini from spaceflight school.*

Konran's mind wanders back to his days at the Madera Spaceflight School. He closes his eyes at the sting of memory. He had his chance to become a starfighter pilot—had worked for the moment, training in the school's F-620 Cutlass starfighter for hours upon hours on top of his normal coursework. After two years of persistence, he earned a spot on the school's flight demonstration team. After a year of resounding local success, the team had been invited to perform for Scattering celebrations across the globe. And then Konran had failed in the stupidest way imaginable, messing up maneuvers he had mastered a hundred times over.

Alandie speaks, breaking Konran's toilet bowl of a reverie from plunging further. "Uh, sir, several of the stewards have disembarked the *Viona Grande* and are traversing the asteroid."

"You know we're allowed to go out there, right?" Konran replies.

Alandie's eyes widen at the thought. "But I thought we were not to disturb the VIPs during their spacewalk, per ODFP A-99."

"That's correct," Konran agrees. "We are not to disturb them. But ICP-94A expressly allows all personnel involved in recreational missions to participate in the event as long as their fundamental duties are not compromised."

Konran closes the news feed, minimizing a live stream showing the *Estrellas Vigilantes* rocketing through space, and accesses the ICPs, or ISSA Corporate Policies.

One minute after reading ICP-94A himself, Alandie is suited up, excitement brimming like radiation from a gamma-ray burst. Konran activates the comm, calling the *Relrick*.

"This is Natauli," the comm crackles.

"Hey, Natauli," Konran says. "I'm going to take Alandie out. He's never been on a deep-space asteroid walk before. Just per ICP-94A."

Heavy silence lingers before Natauli sighs, clearly unhappy with the proposition. "Fine," she says. "Just don't do anything careless. And be back early."

"Roger that," Konran agrees. It had been some time since he had availed himself of ICP-94A. This would be fun.

"Hurry, man," Alandie urges. "We're burning starlight, let's get out there."

By now the VIPs have diffused quite thoroughly across the war site. Their puffy figures wander like 160 space snowmen across the stark, asteroidal landscape, exploring wreckage from a USFN Havoc-class destroyer as well as the sprawling remnants of a burned-out Nolvaric flight-staging area. Konran and Alandie keep their distance, jogging instead for a deserted hill. The ion thrusters in their space suits synchronize with their gait as they run, keeping their feet close to the ground.

The mild exertion, alien environment, and Alandie's utter glee dispel Konran's earlier gloom, and he enjoys himself easily. There really isn't anything like standing atop a frozen rock, billions of kilometers into deep space, separated from the raw, unrelenting vacuum by mere centimeters of space suit.

I really should do this more, Konran realizes with a sudden sense of purpose. He would never stop trying to figure his way into the starfighter ranks, but ISSA had its perks in the meantime.

"Quarks!" Alandie exclaims. "I just posted a photo of us and got a hundred thousand views—in two seconds!" The PIT's glee broadens into a cackle of joy.

Now thoroughly separated from the VIPs, the two pilots take their time. They climb to the crests of asteroidal craters. They photograph everything from the war debris to the Milky Way to the *Relrick* and *Viona Grande*. They laugh, jumping from the ridges and forcing their space suits' ion thrusters to jet furiously to keep them firmly on the ground. Time runs out more quickly than Konran would have liked, and he and Alandie begin the migration back to the *Viona Grande* ahead of the VIPs' return schedule. While traversing the lip of a jagged meteoric crater, Konran pauses, staring for a moment at Y25LM90's not-so-distant horizon.

Was something there, on the far side of the asteroid?

He adjusts his visor's filter, viewing the scene through different electromagnetic frequency bands. He detects nothing unusual, but a sinking knot in his gut argues that something is amiss.

Was I imagining things?

Did I actually see something?

He looks up, spotting the *Borboleta* a couple kilometers off, hovering dutifully above the landing site. Nothing changes in its flight pattern.

I should speak to them, he thinks. He opens a channel to Natauli.

"Natauli, I think something's out there."

She laughs.

"No, I'm serious. Can I talk to the *Borboleta*?"

"Give me a minute," she replies. "Racho's practicing the re-embarking sequence and doing his best to jam up the airlock."

Konran starts running back to the *Viona Grande*. Then he slows down. He was being stupid. This was the Kuiper Belt: there was literally nothing else out here for fifty million kilometers in any direction. But the knot in his gut nags even harder. He checks the time. Several minutes remained before the VIPs would re-board the *Viona Grande*.

There's time to take one more quick look, he reasons, making his way up the side of the nearest hill. The exertion is minimal in the pitiful gravity of Y25LM90, and he ascends rapidly. He searches the horizon, unsatisfied. He needs a better view.

Konran finds another crater with a taller crest. It's out of his way but he runs to it anyway. He still has time. He climbs the crater's side at full speed as Alandie scurries behind him. Now with a better view of the asteroid, Konran scans across Y25LM90 again, filtering through electromagnetic frequencies at finer resolutions. This time, in the mid-ultraviolet range, a slight glare appears upon the horizon.

Sparks ... could that be ...?

He looks up, finding the *Borboleta* still on its circuitous pattern.

"Natauli." He activates his comm. "I really need to talk with the *Borboleta*. Something's wrong out there."

"Konran!" Natauli barks, nearly hysterical. "You're still out there? We're already re-embarking! What are you doing? Get back to the *Viona Grande*!"

"I've been trying to tell you, sir," Alandie says, pointing toward the *Viona Grande*.

Konran notices for the first time that his VIPs and stewards are already waiting at the *Viona Grande*'s access hatch, unable to enter because their captain hasn't opened the door. And ODFP A-12 prohibits re-embarking before the captain is on board.

Quarking crap nuggets, how long did I spend up here?

Konran runs down the ridge, ion thrusters pulsing like beluga blowholes to keep him from springing off Y25LM90. He arrives at the astrofreighter and unlocks the hatch, out of breath. Three by three, the VIPs board the *Viona Grande*; their general sense of incense is thick as Konran pushes past them and into the pilot cabin.

"I can't believe you did that, Konran." Natauli is back on the comm, furious. "I *told* you to get back early, and you ... Oh sparks, VIP posts are hitting the nets about it. You're screwed. We're all screwed now."

"Natauli, don't take off yet." Konran barely processes her words.

"Seriously? ODFP A-14. They board, we take off. No wasting the VIPs' time. There isn't more basic protocol."

While Konran frantically configures the *Viona Grande*'s more powerful sensors to bear on the horizon, the *Relrick* follows standard protocol, rising above the Y25LM90 and hovering five meters above the asteroid's surface, preparing to launch into space. The *Relrick's* repulsor exhaust washes across the *Viona Grande*, rumbling rhythmically through its hull.

"Natauli, stop, don't go yet," Konran reiterates, breathing so heavily it's hard to focus on the control panel. "I need to figure this out. Let me talk with the *Borboleta*!"

He engages the *Viona Grande*'s engines but doesn't ascend like the *Relrick*, Instead he maneuvers so the forward viewports provide a direct line of sight to the suspicious spot on the horizon. He sets his sensors to perform a continual spectral sweep, outputting the results to a holographic display.

"Konran!" Natauli's voice crackles back into his ear. "Are you even checking the nets? We're trending, and they're slaying us."

"At least have the *Borboleta* run a scan," Konran begs. "I'll send you the coordinates."

"Seriously?" Natauli demands. "We're going now!"

"Hold on," Konran pleads. "Just have them do a quick scan." He glances at the spectral scan data, and sudden terror surges in his gut. The sensor display shows the frequency increasing over the past minute from the mid-ultraviolet to the upper X-ray range.

"Natauli! I've got X-rays on my scanner! Right on the other side of the asteroid," Konran bellows. "Don't go!"

But the *Relrick* has had enough, and the astrofreighter takes off Y25LM90 with its cargo of eighty VIPs, two pilots, and five stewards.

"ODFP A-117! ODFP A-117!" Alandie shouts into the comm. "We're invoking ODFP A-117. Emergency override of standard protocol."

"Alandie's right!" Konran says, struggling to control his breathing. "You have to descend! Now, Natauli!"

"Are you serious?" Natauli's voice is sarcastic, nearly shouting back. "We're in space, and you're freaking about some cosmic radiation?"

"Uh, it's, um..." Alandie stammers as Konran works the scanners more. "Just let us talk to the *Borboleta*."

"This is going on your records," Natauli mutters. The *Relrick*'s ascent stops, and it begins a slow descent back toward the asteroid.

"I sent the *Borboleta's* transmission code," Natauli grunts. "Make this fast."

"*Borboleta*, this is Captain Andacellos!" Konran shouts into his comm. "I need you to run a scan for me. There's electromagnetic activity on the far side of the asteroid. Transmitting coordinates."

"Please repeat the request, sir," replies the *Borboleta*'s pilot, whom Konran doesn't even know by name yet.

Suddenly Konran's spectral scan jumps into the gamma-ray range, and his brain finally catches up with what his subconscious mind already figured out. A green light appears on the horizon, growing larger very quickly.

"*BORBOLETA*, EVADE, EVADE!" Konran screams. He doesn't know if his words will make any sense. They don't make any difference. The *Borboleta's* final reply is lost as green energy slams into it, ripping it apart with momentum before blasting it to pieces with vicious stored energy.

An instant later, two more green plasma balls track the *Relrick*. They miss high, but explode as they pass overhead. Their shockwaves feel like an earthquake through the *Viona Grande*'s hull. Natauli's scream comes shrill over the comm, and the *Relrick* swerves wildly before crashing against the asteroid. A cloud of dust kicks up and into space.

Konran's heart thunders and his own scream runs dry. He stares blankly at the *Viona Grande*'s now-obscured viewport, unable to see anything, unable to cry, unable to breathe. Debris clatters against the *Viona Grande*'s hull like rain on a tin roof— whether from the *Borboleta* or the *Relrick*, he cannot say.

There are Nolvarics here, Konran realizes, his consciousness finally registering what his intuition already knew. He starts to hyperventilate.

They just killed the Borboleta.

The Relrick *is down.*

We're trapped.

They'll blow us away just as easily as they did the Borboleta.

We can't outrun them.

We can't hide.

We can't abandon ship.

Konran stares out the viewport, his mind sending a thousand neural commands, his body receiving none of them. His breaths come shorter and shorter. Then he remembers: *the gun-craft.*

Since the days of the Nolvaric Invasion, every spaceworthy craft had been equipped with some form of self-defense. The *Viona Grande* had one GR-29 Defender gun-craft stowed in its upper compartments between the communication and life-support equipment. It had one plasma cannon, a small gravito-nuclear engine for propulsion, and cockpit space for one pilot. Konran had trained with the GR-29: it was mandatory for all pilots to renew their certification every three years, but no ISSA pilot had ever used one in actual combat.

"Natauli, do you read?" he asks, pressing his mouth way too close to the comm.

"Konran..." Natauli's weak voice crackles back in, coughing. "What happened?"

"Nolvarics," Konran repeats, almost whispering.

Natauli panics, not speaking, but her hyperventilation over the comm matches Konran's own.

"Natauli, I need you to see if your GR-29 is still operational. It's our only chance."

"OK, the gun-craft," Natauli breathes back. "It's reading operational."

"I need you to go to it. We have to take out those guns."

"Take them out? How?" Natauli's breathing becomes harder.

"Trust me," Konran replies. "There's no time to waste. Go now."

Another shockwave rumbles through the *Viona Grande* as more Nolvaric plasma balls detonate overhead. Natauli screams again and Konran crashes into Alandie, knocking them both to the ground.

"OK," Natauli's shaky voice crackles in. "I'm going."

Trembling from adrenaline and fear, Konran pulls his space suit back on. "You've got command now, Alandie," he speaks through quivering lips. "Transmit SOS on every USFN emergency signal. Tell them there are Nolvarics."

His space suit on, Konran runs from the pilot cabin and into the VIP hall. He pushes between their terrified faces, moans, sobs, and screams.

"Everyone put on your space suits!" he shouts. He scampers up a ladder, which had just descended from the ceiling, allowing him access to the *Viona Grande*'s upper maintenance bay. He wiggles upward, through the confined space of pipes and cables, finally reaching the GR-29 Defender. Cramped into the space like an afterthought, the gun-craft sits there, nothing more than a small, round cockpit with an engine slapped to its backside and a long, pointed plasma gun protruding from its nose. Konran shoves his way inside the cockpit and straps himself in. He feels the familiar buzz as the craft's inertial compensators come online, and the telltale tingle as the barometric regulator interfaces with his space suit. And in seconds, the humble, narwhal-nosed GR-29 gun-craft is powered up.

"Alandie," he calls with heartbeats racing ever faster, "release the gun, release the gun."

Alandie doesn't know how to do it, so Konran has to calm down enough to think clearly and walk him through it. Finally the bay doors open above him, exposing Konran's little gun to the darkness of space. The gun rises above the freighter, repulsed and balanced on magnetic fields. Konran holds his breath.

Alandie disengages the lock, and magnetic fields throw the gun-craft like a javelin into raw space and away from the *Viona Grande*—a mechanism designed to protect sensitive equipment atop the freighter from the gun-craft's exhaust. At a distance of two hundred meters, Konran's gravito-nuclear engine engages, and the gun-craft shoots forward like a matchstick rocket, careening above the asteroid on its lone flame.

Konran scrambles to gain control. And then, like unexpectedly running into an old friend on a really bad day, he finds the balance: the momentum of the ship, the haptic harmony of yaw, pitch, and roll vibrating through the joysticks and rudder pedals, the slight tug of gravity as he jets at a flash across the heartless, space-hewn landscape, the release of forty-four thousand hours of disillusioned discouragement at his failure to rise from his situation. Konran, at least for the next few moments, is alive.

In an instant he sees his target: the familiar shape of three Nolvaric plasma cannons, sleek and sinister, risen from holes cut into the asteroid. Beside them lies a large, oblong rock—no, a camouflaged Nolvaric transport craft, just like the ones from the Invasion vids, distinguishable only by its silvery landing gear reflecting the distant-yet-still-there sunlight.

Konran aims the gun-craft manually—no sophisticated auto-tracking starfighter cannons here. He releases his grip slightly, allowing the gun-craft to wobble and increase his firing spread, and depresses the trigger. The craft's narwhal nose fires, releasing lasers that act as photonic pathways for destructive flashes of fiery-orange, gravito-nuclear-induced plasmic energy to conduct along through space. To Konran it sounds like an oscillating staccato whine. Silent, sequential explosions of superheated space rocks pop along the alien landscape, and two of the three Nolvaric cannons explode.

Konran zooms past, circling the narwhal-nosed craft for his next approach as the third Nolvaric cannon takes aim. Green plasma glows from its barrel and leaps toward Konran's predicted path. Konran yanks on and releases his controls, sending the GR-29 matchsticking randomly into open space. The plasma ball soars past. Its shockwave hits Konran, and he lets it push him rather than fighting its force. Out of the corner of his eye, he sees Natauli's GR-29 flash by, firing at and missing the plasma cannon.

Konran's rudimentary life-support system struggles to keep up with the stress of battle, and his stomach lurches. He fights to sight back in on the target, but he is disoriented. His hands and arms are momentarily too heavy, too light, and too heavy again, and his vision dims. But years of study melds with tens of thousands of hours of simulator practice, and Konran counts the seconds until the cannon can fire again, even as he considers the inadequacy of his space suit's inertial compensation.

One—I am going to be so sick if I survive this. He rejuvenates, the GR-29's life-support system catching up and compensating for what his body can't. He retakes control of his flailing gun-craft, pulling another, though less drastic, high-g turn and orienting toward the target.

Two. Nausea and dizziness wash over him again, replaced by another life-sustaining infusion from the life-support system.

Three. Konran stares down the Nolvaric plasma cannon, which is now glowing green, but it's not aiming at him.

"Konran, it's tracking me!" Natauli yells. "I don't know how you did that—I can't shake it!"

Konran pulls his trigger, maintaining a solid grip on the controls this time. Orange pulses end in superheated flashes as his narwhal-nosed gun scores direct hits. The Nolvaric cannon explodes, as does the plasma ball within it, erupting into a vicious fireball and destroying the oblong, camouflaged transport craft in the process.

"Ahg," Natauli breathes over the comm. "Oh. Thank you. I tried to get it, but I missed."

"You did great, Natauli," Konran reassures her. "You gave me a window to hit it."

"Yeah," she says, sounding uncertain. "What now?"

"Is the *Relrick* still spaceworthy?" Konran asks, circling his kills from a bird's-eye vantage.

"I don't know," Natauli says. "Racho?"

"Yes!" Racho's cheerful, if not terrified, voice chimes in. "We ran all the checks, and she's spaceworthy!"

"OK, take off. We need to get out of here ASAP," Konran instructs. "Natauli and I will stay in defense mode for the next two million kilometers or so."

"Quarks, that's far," Natauli says.

"We can magnet-lock the gun-crafts back to the astrofreighters' hulls," Konran says. "But we'll need to be ready if anything else is out there."

Then, like realizing he had forgotten about a class on the last day of the semester, except a thousand times worse, despair hits Konran like a comet to the gut. Low and dark and scarcely visible in the dim sunlight, three craft emerge from an opening in the asteroid. Two slender shark-fin masts extend above and below each craft's beaklike fuselage as crab-leg wings protrude from all sides.

"Nolvaric Askeras!" Konran yells as his eyes widen in terror and awe. The trio of crablike starfighters jets away, ignoring his small fish in hunt of bigger prey: the *Viona Grande* and *Relrick*.

They know if they can get them fast enough, Natauli and I have no chance of survival, Konran realizes grimly. Alandie and Racho have already distanced the astrofreighters from Y25LM90, but they aren't nearly far enough away yet. No SOS transmission will save them.

"Alandie and Racho, go full thrust!" Konran orders. "Three Askeras are closing on you fast! Get out of here, but stay close to each other—I can only protect you if you're close. We'll delay them as much as we can." The PITs' responses are lost to Konran as intensity narrows his focus to one singular task.

"And make sure everyone has their space suits on," Natauli adds.

Missiles—they're going to use missiles, Konran thinks, gritting his teeth. *The astrofreighters only have a few defense drones left. They won't hold out long. We have to get ahead of the Askeras.*

"Alandie! Racho!" Konran calls on the comm. "Release your defense drones now! "Natauli, stay close to me," Konran adds. "We have to get our GR-29s' defense drones between the Askeras and the astrofreighters ASAP."

Without waiting for her reply, Konran sets his own thruster to full power and rockets forward. His little craft is faster than the Nolvarics'—it's not hard to accelerate nothing but a guy and a gun with a quantum-controlled gravito-nuclear engine—and Konran rounds on an angle ahead of the Askeras to cover the *Viona Grande* and *Relrick*. The gun-craft's sensors are simple yet effective. As expected, multiple Nolvaric missile launches register.

Konran skids the gun-craft, using maneuvering thrusters to careen sideways along the astrofreighters' path. His thumb tunes a knob on his joystick, decreasing his gun's photonic focal range and widening its firing spread. He pulls the trigger, and orange plasma conducts outward on unfocused photonic pathways, spraying like a cloud behind the *Viona Grande* and *Relrick* rather than outward in a cohesive bolt. Although the GR-29's diluted plasma wouldn't be enough to damage an Askera, silent explosions pop as Nolvaric missiles detonate against Konran's crude plasmic shield. Several missiles get past him, but the astrofreighter's defense drones intercept them, initiating miniature black holes, which, collapsing in colossal yet tiny bursts of energy, destroy the incoming missiles.

Seven, Konran counts. *They only used seven missiles.*

Unwilling to make an easy target of himself, Konran accelerates. He darts toward the *Viona Grande* before yanking the controls and maneuvering into a broad, helical, figure-eight pattern behind it and the *Relrick*. The maneuver allows his gun to face toward the Nolvarics while his momentum carries him along the astrofreighters' vector. Deft usage of maneuvering thrusters lets him present the Nolvarics a continually moving target. His hand finds a switch on his control panel, and a set of eight small drones deploys from the back of his GR-29 gun-craft. The drones whiz toward the astrofreighters as Konran's system registers another missile launch.

Konran sprays the space again, detonating two more missiles with his plasma cloud, but three more make it past. His defense drones surge behind the *Viona Grande* and *Relrick*, racing to intercept. Brilliant flashes crackle and disappear around the astrofreighters as the drones' tiny black holes do their work.

"Natauli, where are your drones?" he asks. "I estimate they've still got twelve missiles left—we need your drones now."

Unable to wait for her reply, Konran darts off again, changing his trajectory and matchsticking up, around, and in front of the *Viona Grande* as a third wave of missiles launches. He sprays the space behind the astrofreighter with diffuse plasma, his mind barely registering that much of the wave is meant for him and not the *Viona Grande* or the *Relrick*. Suddenly aware that he is the intended target, Konran gyrates the gun-craft wildly, showering plasma everywhere. Missiles detonate around him, sending his gun-craft careening like a pinwheel firecracker. But he is still alive.

"Konran! They're coming!" Alandie's voice crackles in as Konran fights for control of the gun-craft. Scarcely reorienting himself, his tracking system registers all three Askeras in hot pursuit of the astrofreighters.

"I've got you!" Natauli says. "Drones deployed!"

A fourth wave of missiles detonates harmlessly in empty space as Natauli's drones do their work, neither impacting the *Relrick* nor the *Viona Grande*.

But the Askeras were still coming for them.

No, you don't, Konran thinks, gritting his teeth and punching his throttle.

From a steep angle below the direction of the chase, Konran jets upward to meet the enemy. Sighting on the lead starfighter, his thumb retunes his gun's focal range to project beams instead of diffuse energy. Angry fireballs erupt on the aft section of the *Viona Grande* as the Nolvaric marks its prey.

No people in the cargo hold, cyborg, Konran growls, whether to himself or out loud, he couldn't say. He pulls the trigger and tight bursts of plasmic energy stream into the Askera's underside. The Nolvarics' shields give way to Konran's concentrated plasma, and the craft converts into a fireball.

Two to go, Konran thinks, disbelieving he is actually giving himself a chance in the fight.

"You guys alive?" he asks, punching his throttle again.

Konran hurtles his matchstick on a deep, arcing loop, searching for the remaining Askeras. In his focus on the leader he lost the other two. He searches the tracking system overlaid on his viewport's heads-up display.

But he can't find them anywhere.

Where are they? Where are they? He panics, holding his breath as his eyes search back and forth, seeking for some sign of the starfighters.

"We're alive! But they got our engines! We're drifting!" Alandie replies, startling Konran, whose last question to Alandie may as well have been an hour ago.

Konran angles back toward the *Viona Grande* to survey the damage, keeping an eye out for the remaining two Askeras. Sure enough, the astrofreighter is no longer accelerating, drifting at constant velocity into open space.

Ferrospit. We'll have to get them to the Relrick. *Wait ... where is the* Relrick?

"Do you have sensors?" Konran asks Alandie. "I can't find the Askeras or the *Relrick* anywhere." His neck hairs prickle as a sudden kinship with a bull's-eye sinks into Konran's gut.

"Scanners show nothing," Alandie replies, fear in his voice. "What do we do?"

Konran rockets away from the *Viona Grande* before performing a shallow, inverted loop and rocketing back toward the astrofreighter. Ending up upside down and backward from his previous orientation, he releases his controls, matchsticking aimlessly in hopes of throwing off any Nolvaric plasma directed his way. His mind goes over what he remembers of the infamous Askera starfighters. *Multi-angle pulse cannons, intelligent target tracking, organic movements, weakest from behind and on the vectors directly above and below the shark fins.*

Telltale blue flashes of Nolvaric plasma burst suddenly across his view. The enemy has him in their sights. Konran sends his guncraft flailing this way and that in stomach-churning fishtails. Nausea gnaws him like a pit bull on the bone, but he maintains focus on his tracking display.

Where are they? he wonders, frantic. With so much space to scan, his rudimentary tracking system wasn't locking on anything. He matchsticks again, and vomit froths in his throat. More blue flashes streak past him, and he dives, twisting and swerving, furiously trying to maintain a semblance of closeness to the *Viona Grande* while staying alive.

One of them will go for it again, he thinks, gagging on stomach acid and feeling faint. *I just have to outlast them.*

Finally, three blips show up on the tracking system: a large object moving toward open space, a small object hovering protectively nearby it, and one medium-size object bearing down on them both.

Konran had found the *Relrick,* and so had the Nolvarics.

"Konran!" Natauli screams. "I can't hold it off!"

"I'm coming!" he yells back. Steeling against the nausea still wracking his body, his lip snarls.

He grips the controls and zooms in pursuit of the Askera. A second enemy blip appears behind Konran as the other Nolvaric takes its place in the deadly race. Just as Konran's life-support system finally catches up with his body and his nausea wanes, he releases his controls again, trusting in the resulting, unstable flight to throw off his pursuer's targeting system. Blue flashes of Nolvaric plasma sparkle past his viewport.

It isn't going to miss forever...

Konran closes quickly on the lead Askera. His knuckles go white around the controls as he aims his narwhal gun and fires. The GR-29's cannon whines with a succession of staccato plasmic pulses, and its orange plasma blasts off two of the lead Askera's crab-leg wings. The Nolvaric diverts its attack run on the *Relrick*, peeling off sharply to avoid Konran's guns—but not before an explosion rocks the astrofreighter. The Askera had gotten off shots of its own.

With no time to consider the fate of the *Relrick*, Konran senses the trailing Nolvaric peering straight into his kidneys. Desperate, he performs an emergency stop, flipping the matchstick on end and firing wildly into the Askera behind him. Orange plasma blasts holes through its fuselage. An instant later, nothing but fiery space dust remains of the Nolvaric.

Konran barely notices the kill, his own craft impacted in the exchange. Atmosphere vents from his cockpit, and he feels the negative force of evacuation pull his hands off the controls. His vision blackens as his intestines wrap around his lungs. More from instinct than volition, his hands fight their way back down. Gripping the flight stick and throttle and swallowing his swirling bowels, he flips the gun-craft back toward the *Relrick* and rockets like a radioactive toothpick for the astrofreighter.

OK ... I'm alive, he understands more than cogitates. His space suit maintains pressurization, allowing him to continue breathing for the moment. His oxygen supply won't last long at present levels of exertion—not that oxygen will matter if he and Natauli can't beat this last Askera. He orients himself to the *Relrick*, scanning for the Nolvaric.

But he can't find the *Relrick*.

"Racho?" Konran asks.

No reply.

"Natauli?"

Nothing.

"Natauli? Racho?" Konran repeats. "Come in!"

He can't find them anywhere. All he sees is one medium-size blip, angling toward him from where the *Relrick* should have been.

The Askera was coming for him.

"Alandie!" Konran calls out, and sweat and snot pour into his mouth. He coughs the remaining words, "You there?" He pulls on his controls, performing a set of evasive hijinks as blue plasma flashes about him.

"I'm here ... we had a secondary explosion." Alandie's voice falters. "It's bad."

"Roger. Do you have sensors? I can't find the *Relrick*."

"Negative," Alandie crackles in. "We barely have comms."

Konran cuts off his conversation with Alandie as the final Askera occupies his full attention. This Nolvaric wasn't making the mistakes of its ill-fated companions. Continually creating an unpredictable target, it weaves back and forth as it comes at Konran. He tries to evade wide, but it cuts him off. He dives low, quickly altering his trajectory and taking advantage of three-dimensional space to create more distance between the Askera. Konran searches and searches, but he can't find Natauli or the *Relrick* anywhere. The Nolvaric closes on him, and he lets go of his controls, letting the matchstick wobble as bluish Nolvaric energy flashes past his viewport. But the Askera stays on his tail.

"I can't find them, Alandie," Konran croaks, gagging on the bile rising in his throat. "I can't find them. I don't think I can beat this one."

"What do we do?" Alandie whimpers more than asks.

Konran glances back at the *Viona Grande*'s distant speck, and one final idea strikes him.

"Jettison everyone and get as far from the *Viona Grande* as you can," Konran orders. "It's going to get hit again."

With the Nolvaric fully focused on him, Konran's life-support system lags further and further behind. His stomach froths and his eyes dim and his throat gags and his head throbs, but he continues to evade death. There isn't a way to beat this Askera in a straight dogfight. He had only killed its sisters through combinations of distraction and surprise: two commodities deep space holds in short supply.

Konran races toward the *Viona Grande*'s hapless form, now more than three thousand kilometers from Historical War Site Y25LM90. He lets go of his flight stick, allowing his GR-29 to matchstick again and again. He throws up, swallows it, and continues breathing as blue Nolvaric plasma flashes past his cockpit. He closes the gap on the listless astrofreighter quickly, maintaining his trajectory while dodging the Nolvaric's continued attacks.

"Almost there. Almost there," he grunts through clenched teeth, expecting any moment to be vaporized into dust.

Instants before collision with the *Viona Grande* he juts downward, diving below and looping around the astrofreighter in a hellacious arc. His gun-craft shakes and his stomach twists and his vision blackens and his blood goes cold, but Konran holds the arc.

Straining with every ounce of remaining stamina, he screams. The *Viona Grande* explodes beneath him, decimated point-blank by the Askera's plasma cannons. Konran finishes his loop, firing his gun-craft as its narwhal nose angles on vector with the beaklike, crablike Askera's top shark fin. Orange plasma cuts straight into the weakest part of the Nolvaric's hull, and the enemy starfighter detonates into a ball of fire and energy. So near to its shockwave, Konran's gun-craft goes flailing like a toddler on a trampoline with a teenager.

But he doesn't notice. His life-support system finally overcome, Konran vomits again and blacks out, drifting with ten thousand pieces of Nolvaric starfighter debris.

CHAPTER 3

Konran wakes up in bed, disoriented.

Where am I? he wonders. His brain feels as if it hasn't booted up in four days.

Mental function returns slowly, and suddenly he notices how much it hurts between his ears, behind his eyes, below his hair, and above his ... feet? His eyes close again and he braces himself, breathing sharply with the throbbing pain. It subsides, easing into a background sense of exhaustion.

"What happened to me?" he asks, hoping the universe will venture a reply. He can sense the answer slipping from his mind like water through a sieve. He opens his eyes again.

Am I in a hospital? he wonders, turning his head and looking around. Tubes run from blinking equipment into his arm.

Yep, I'm in a hospital.

The room is austere, with metal floors, cream-colored polymer walls, and no decorations or windows. The gentle hum of medical monitoring equipment reaches his ears. Suddenly, he hears hurried steps running by his door. Agitated voices echo down a hallway on the other side. People are shouting, urgency in their tone. Konran tries to sit up, but he's strapped to the bed. He's not tied down, rather secured with gentle straps—like the ones used to keep you from rolling off the bed and pulling your IV out. He works them off and sits up.

Artificial gravity, he realizes, the subtle, rhythmic gravitational pull unmistakable. *I'm on a ship somewhere in space!*

The light in his room brightens from dim to medium dim at his motion, and the door opens. A short robotic creature rolls inside: shiny, polished, white; informational screens in place of head and neck; several manipulator arms folded above and to the side of its compact cuboidal structure. A blue light shines from one of the robot's appendages, scanning across Konran's body. His vitals post on its screen.

"My name is Fritz, Patient Andacellos," the robot says, mispronouncing Konran's name, emphasizing the second syllable as *and-Ah-selos*. "Do you request any assistance?"

"Where am I?" Konran asks. "What's going on?"

"I may only provide medical assistance, Patient Andacellos," Fritz says. "Do you require any assistance?"

"My head hurts," Konran says, blinking. The sounds in the hallway have faded.

"I can step on your toes to take your mind off the pain in your head," Fritz offers, laughing with human awkwardness.

Konran takes the bad joke as a good sign—Fritz's programming would not have prescribed humor if there was anything terribly wrong with Konran.

I'm OK, he realizes with relief. *I'm just experiencing the last of the symptoms from my dogfighting maneuvers.*

My dogfighting.

Sudden awful memories hit him with the intensity of a solar flare. Konran's headache explodes, and he raises his hands to his head, groaning. He is vaguely aware of Fritz's scanner traversing him again.

"Kindly do not move, Patient Andacellos."

Fritz touches Konran on the forehead, and a device contours to Konran's skull. Fritz moves it back and forth slowly. Momentarily, Konran's headache disappears.

"Your vitals have stabilized, and your condition is now simply neural shock, Patient Andacellos. I have calmed the affected neural pathways. I recommend thirty-seven minutes of light massage twice per day, and 1.33 liters of water every two hours at a minimum. If you wish, you may ingest a portion of the liquid in the form of chamomile tea. I also recommend you continue to rest, as activation of your motor pathways has served to worsen your state somewhat. Is there anything else you require, Patient Andacellos?"

"Yeah," Konran says as he lays gingerly back down on the hospital bed, "can I have one of those massages now?"

Five hours and thirty-seven minutes later Konran wakes up. He gets up slowly, making sure his head doesn't spin before sitting up all the way. A glass of water sits on a tray next to him, filled to the

1.33-liter mark. Konran takes a slow drink of the cool water. His parched throat rejoices at the liquid's touch, and he takes another longer drink.

He sits on the bed, allowing confidence to build that his head won't explode again. Finally, he rests his feet on the floor. He sees himself in a mirror on the other side of the small, square, cream-colored room. He doesn't look that great.

Then he remembers: *Alandie, the* Viona Grande, *the VIPs ... the* Relrick.

Natauli.

Racho.

How am I still alive?

He stares at the mirror, staring at nothing as an overwhelming sense of loss overcomes him. He takes his water in hand but doesn't drink. Closing his eyes, he exhales slowly. Visions of his dogfight with the Askeras fill the darkness behind his eyes, so he opens them, looking again at himself in the mirror.

His hazel eyes are bloodshot and baggy, his sandy-brown hair disheveled, his skin pale and gaunt. With his eyes open, the battle at Y25LM90 seems like a memory from another life: like the way the nine-dimensional movies made you feel—you were there, but you weren't actually in it. Except he was in it. He did it.

He stops trying to make it make sense.

Instead, he stands and walks across the room. His legs feel like tree trunks protruding from his hips, but he manages the short distance. His bare feet are cold on the metal floor, but he doesn't really care; the temperature gradient is refreshing. He opens his door and enters an empty, dimly lit hallway with closed doors lining either side. Apparently, wherever he is, it's "nighttime" right now. Low voices emanate from down and around the corner.

"Patient Andacellos," Fritz's familiar robot voice speaks behind him, mispronouncing his name again. Konran turns to find the squat, polished, multi-armed medical bot. "Kindly return to your room," Fritz continues. "Would you like another massage?"

"He's up," a new voice speaks from the other end of the hallway. A short, ruddy-faced nurse stands there.

"Patient Andacellos should return to his room," Fritz says. "Please assist me in escorting his return."

The nurse waves the bot away while waving Konran forward. "Bug off, Fritz. Come on over, Konran."

Konran steps delicately down the hallway. The short nurse watches him approach.

"How are you feeling?" he asks.

"Patient Andacellos is biologically stable, although his brain-wave patterns suggest a combination of confusion, grief, and denial."

Konran turns to see two of Fritz's arms nearly touching his face.

"Fritz, shut it off," the nurse orders. "Come sit, Konran."

Around the corner, Konran finds a nurses' bay lit by several low lights. Two more nurses sit there on late-night duty, considering him.

"Fritz pretty much summed it up," Konran says, sitting down next to them. "How long have I been here?"

"Four days," a female nurse replies. Her deep black hair is striking against olive, Middle Eastern features.

"Your vitals were very low when we found you," a third nurse says. He is a tall man with dark skin and gray streaks in his short, black hair. Konran places his accent as Western African.

"Your core temperature measured 35.2 centigrade when we found you, but your life-support and rescue beacon were still holding on—as were you," the African nurse continues. "You're a very lucky man, Mr. Andacellos." He pronounces Konran's name correctly but with an overemphasis on the consonants.

Konran wraps his arms around himself, considering the words. The female nurse hands him a light blanket with a "Here you go."

"Natauli and the *Relrick* died, didn't they?"

The African nurse places his hand on Konran's shoulder. "I'm afraid so, my friend. You did everything you could for them."

Konran sits there, hugging the blanket and closing his eyes. He nods, trying not to think of that awful space battle, trying to convince himself he had done enough. It doesn't work.

"How many from the *Viona Grande* survived?" he asks at last.

"Fifty-six," the ruddy-faced nurse says, "and one poodle." He shakes his head. "I've never seen a poodle in a space suit before."

"Alandie?" Konran ventures after a long moment, his voice almost a whisper.

50

"Alandie is well," the tall African answers. "He had the VIPs tethered together, floating outside what was left of the *Viona Grande* when we found them. I was among the rescue crew sent to retrieve them via spacewalk. I can tell you, Mr. Andacellos, I have never in my life witnessed such a sight. To see a man's eyes in the moment he realizes he is saved from certain death. It is incredible."

"You're a hero, Konran," the woman says, emphasizing the "o" as *kOHn-ran*.

"I, I..." Konran replies, looking down.

"They can't stop talking about you," she adds, considering him from under long eyelashes. "You should hear them rave about how you single-handedly destroyed those Askeras with nothing but that GR-29 Defender. You're *the* topic on the web—well, that and the war."

Konran looks up and his gaze locks with hers. For a moment he forgets what they are talking about. She can't be far from his same age. Her eyes are a deep, unfathomable brown—almost black.

"Four days," he finally repeats, simultaneously realizing how long he has been unconscious and how long he has been staring.

I am really out of it. Wait, did she say "war"?

"You are a true hero, Konran," she repeats, touching his elbow.

Konran looks up, looks down, smiles pathetically, and says, "Could I get some chamomile tea, and maybe something to eat?"

"Certainly," the ruddy-complexioned nurse says, tapping commands into a control device on his forearm. A few seconds later Fritz rolls up with a tray of steaming tea and toast. One of his robot arms stirs the chamomile with a small spoon.

"Is there anything else, Patient Andacellos?" Fritz queries.

"Do you have any pudding?" Konran asks. "I hear these space hospitals are famous for it."

Another Fritz arm extends forward with two pouches. "Will chocolate and vanilla suffice?"

"Perfect, thanks," Konran answers, grabbing the pouches.

Fritz retreats and Konran is left with the night watch watching him.

"I guess I should say thank you," he ventures, looking up from the food, "for saving my life."

51

"It was nothing but our pleasure, young man," the tall African replies. "Indeed, it is we who should be thanking you for what you have done."

Konran smiles a little better than last time, managing a tight line with his lips and a nod of his head. "You're welcome, I guess."

"You missed a lot in your four days unconscious," the woman says, brushing bangs from her forehead to her ear. "You have no idea how much you've done."

"I don't know how I did what I did out there," Konran says. "I had to try. There were Nolvarics on that asteroid. When the *Borboleta*..." He pauses, choking back the awful vision of destruction burned forever into his mind.

"When the *Borboleta* was hit, I couldn't believe it. I remembered every freighter has that gun-craft. It's all I've ever wanted to be, a starfighter, you know. I thought it would be so exhilarating out there in the stars, life and death on the line, power and speed at my fingertips. And it was, but it all happened so fast. There was so much panic and fear—terror that we were all going to die. When the Askeras came out, I knew I was dead, but something inside me refused to let them have my passengers and my PIT and that stupid poodle. I had to stop them."

Konran pauses, realizing he is rambling. "Sorry, this is the first I've thought about it, let alone talk about it. Apparently, you're the first people I've spoken with in four days."

"You have no need to apologize, Mr. Andacellos," the African replies. "What Cazmira said is true: you have done much more than you realize. Your SOS transmission saved the inner planets from a second invasion."

Konran blinks, reeling at the statement. Before he can form an intelligent response, the squat, ruddy-faced nurse chimes in.

"We were patrolling in trans-Neptunian orbit when we received your SOS transmission from the *Viona Grande* and were the first to respond. The Nolvarics were a close second. We've been in battle with them on and off for the past four days. More than a hundred USFN craft are actively engaged, scouring the Kuiper Belt. The Saturnese sent over forty craft, and the IGF even added another fifteen, not to mention their extensive network of surveillance satellites in the region—not that those did anyone any good."

"Whoa," Konran says. "Even the IGF joined—that's big."

"Yeah, not that the Ice Giant Federation wanted to help," the ruddy nurse says. "But those quarking cyborgs set up bases in the IGF's backyard and nobody knew a thing, so they had no choice. Fighting's been pretty hot in some sectors. We tangled with a few of the Schrödingers ourselves not six hours ago—smoked 'em."

Konran closes his eyes and runs his hands through his hair, taking and holding a deep breath as he digests the news. "Oh," is all that comes out with a long exhalation.

He looks at the three nurses, suddenly realizing something that should have been obvious the entire time. "You're all military, aren't you?"

All three laugh at that. "Of course, young man," the African replies with a wide smile. "What else would you expect aboard a Riot-class battle cruiser?"

"A Riot-class?" Konran repeats as he pulls up his mental USFN database. "I still have a model Riot-class I built as a kid. Which ship is this?"

"You're on the *Nova Scotia*," the ruddy-faced man says proudly, "of the Twenty-First Interplanetary Task Force."

Riot-class space cruisers were third largest in the United Space Federation Navy's not-inconsiderable armada, coming in at half the size of supercarriers such as the *Estrellas Vigilantes* and two-thirds that of the Crusher-class heavy battleships. The *Nova Scotia* was one of the newer vessels off the Martian docks—not one of the relics left over from the Nolvaric Invasion. It could even partition itself into three separate sub-ships for increased warfare logistics and survival.

Konran takes a bite of toast and squeezes a mouthful of vanilla pudding, considering the awesomeness enshrouding him. Speaking with his mouth full, he asks, "How long have you served aboard her?"

"Four years now, as part of the original crew," the ruddy-faced man replies. "Been across the solar system two dozen times, and she's as good as the day she first sailed."

"I have been aboard eleven months now," the African nurse adds, "as has Cazmira." He gestures to the Middle Eastern woman. "We transferred from the *Mindanerite* when she was retired from service. I agree with Declan, though." He gestures to the shorter, ruddy-faced man. "This ship is one of a kind."

Konran realizes he knows two of the nurses' names without ever formally asking for any of them. "So it's Declan and Cazmira, but," he nods to the tall African man, "I haven't gotten your name yet."

The nurse chuckles, extending his hand to shake Konran's. "My father always told me, 'No man is a stranger if he knows your name and shares your path.' I am Geoffroy Massone III, Mr. Andacellos, but my friends may call me Geoff."

"Nobody calls him Geoff," Cazmira smirks, her dark eyes twinkling. Declan laughs.

"Then Mr. Andacellos may be the first, as it has been my pleasure to serve beside him against the Nolvarics." Geoff smiles broadly.

"Geoff it is. You can call me Konran," Konran replies, feeling better than he had all night. Did the nurses realize how good this simple conversation was for him?

They exchange conversation for a few minutes before Konran's mind wanders to the survivors of the *Viona Grande*. At a lull in the conversation he asks if he can visit them.

"You realize everyone else is sleeping right now, right?" Declan says. "It's what normal people do at 0345."

"Oh three what ...?" Konran repeats, puzzled.

"It's three forty-five in the morning, *civilian*." Cazmira rolls her eyes at him.

"Oh yeah," Konran says, taking the last bite of his toast, "military time."

He chases the bite with the last of the chamomile tea.

"The problem is, I just slept for four days," he says. "I'm wide-awake now. I can't believe I'm in the middle of a war on a Riot-class cruiser."

Then, an idea striking him, Konran asks, "Do you think the hangar bays are open? Maybe I can check them out?" Riot-class

54

space cruisers had four hangar bays stocked with five Martian-made LTOM-92 Sparrowhawk starfighters each.

"Funny you should ask," Cazmira says. "The captain already authorized you for a tour. No time like the present." She stands as if to leave.

"Not so fast," Declan interjects, entering commands into a forearm computer. "Last I checked your shift doesn't end until 0600."

Cazmira gives Declan a look that says, *Since when does accompanying a recovering patient to his destination—who also happens to be an emerging celebrity, hero, and possibly attractive when he doesn't look like he just awoke from a coma—not fall within my medical duties?* and actually says, "Since when does accompanying a recovering patient to his destination not fall within my medical duties?"

"Since they gave us CK-84-A7," Declan replies matter-of-factly.

A small aerial drone flies up. Its slender, glossy white body is supported by small circular engines on either side, held aloft not by mechanical rotors but by the transfer of ionized air molecules across its engines. It barely makes a whisper as it approaches. Two gentle, blue stripes glow along its polished, polymeric fuselage.

"Nice. Old school," Konran says.

"Good morning, Patient Andacellos," the drone speaks, its deep, cordial voice touched by a Spanish accent. "Please follow me."

"Thanks, guys!" And with that, Konran follows the drone around a corner and out of sight.

The drone guides him down a short, clean hallway full of more closed doors. Comfortable amber lights glow from the sides of the floor, illuminating the otherwise empty corridor. The drone makes a left turn, then a right, and they come to a sealed bulkhead. It opens with a metallic hiss and thunk.

Two guards stand on the other side, dressed in crisp, gray combat suits: helmets, visors, guns and all. Konran pauses, his confidence wavering until one of them states with a Lebanese accent, "Welcome, Mr. Andacellos, right this way."

She gestures down the hallway where a second drone awaits, bulky and tough-looking and gray like the soldiers' uniforms.

The new drone makes no sound except to say, "Follow me." Konran finds its husky German accent fitting.

A long, spartan corridor runs on this side of the bulkhead, lined with pipes and ducts along its length. Crisp overhead lighting shines in contrast to the muted glows of the hospital wing's cozy floor lamps. The drone leads Konran straight down the militaristic hallway, which curves gently as if matching a contour of the ship. Sub-hallways sprout at right angles, but the drone ignores them. Finally, they reach another bulkhead.

How big is this ship? Konran thinks, knowing the answer (250,000 metric tons) but still amazed.

The bulkhead doors slide open with a hiss and thunk, revealing a pair of guards on the other side. Konran follows the drone, entering a wide mechanical room. Four freight elevators line the room's left side like four caverns, their freight doors gaping open and empty.

The drone enters the second of the four caverns, stating, "We descend now." Konran steps aboard, the freight doors close with a hydraulic whoosh and click, the elevator descends, the doors open, and...

"Whoa..."

Konran steps onto Hangar Bay 3. Not more than ten meters away rests an LTOM-92 Sparrowhawk—sleek, beautiful, black, amazing. Its shiny, black-domed cockpit gleams beneath the hangar bay's white lights. Plasmic energy cannons extend elegantly from the Sparrowhawk's wingtip and nose-tip turrets: two cannons at the nose, and one at each wingtip, all capable of independent, multi-directional fire. Konran sees himself as a kid, flying ten thousand simulated combat hours. He sees himself in spaceflight school, his failed emphasis on starfighting. He stares at the Sparrowhawk, awestruck; the object of every minute of the last two decades of life stares back at him with cold glory. He can almost see his reflection in its sweeping, concave wings.

Konran reaches out to touch it, having covered the distance from the elevator without noticing one step. His lungs refuse to exhale as his fingertips grace its molecularly perfect, nano-composite skin. Did a tear just spill across his cheek?

"Konran!" an unfamiliar voice calls from somewhere nearby. Konran's hand yanks away like it had been caught scratching its name into the Taj Mahal. He whirls toward the sound, his heart in his uvula, still failing to exhale.

A man in his late forties or early fifties stands there. His short hair is peppered gray, his immaculate navy-blue uniform adorned by medals and ribbons above the left breast. Konran stares blankly at the man, suddenly acutely aware of his hospital garb, bare feet, and I-just-slept-for-four-days hairstyle.

"Sorry to startle you," the man says. "The medical bay informed me you were on your way."

He extends his hand, which Konran grabs and shakes by rote.

"Captain Darius Granicks. Would you like a tour?"

Konran's shock intensifies as he realizes he is shaking the hand of the captain of the *Nova Scotia*, and his lungs scarcely replenish their supply before the words spill out.

"Captain Granicks! Sir!" he blurts, shaking the hand more vigorously as embarrassment melts before budding enthusiasm. "Sir—uh—yes, sir, that would be awesome—yes, er, thank you!"

Konran follows Captain Granicks around the hangar bay. Granicks points out the various maintenance equipment, safety equipment, and tractor tugs for moving equipment before advancing to the equipment Konran cares about: spacecraft. There are three V10-37 landing craft designed to haul, protect, and deploy marines for atmospheric and vacuous combat operations. There are two S-220F Longbow missile frigates, each capable of firing 450 guided artillery shells beyond the distance between the earth and the moon in a matter of seconds. There is an AURA-3100X reconnaissance craft, which Konran is uncertain whether he is allowed to look at this closely. There is a Ramrod Long-Range Ultrafast shuttle, and even a few wheeled and tracked vehicles for land-based exploits. Konran gapes at the size of the hangar bay, recalling the three other bays like it on the *Nova Scotia*.

What would the Estrellas Vigilantes *look like?* he wonders, considering the hundreds of craft stowed aboard the massive supercarrier.

The tour does not go unnoticed by the personnel and pilots bustling about the hangar at the early hour, and soldiers and sailors salute their captain as he guides Konran through the deck. More than a few glances follow Konran as his hospital garb and bare feet also fail to go unnoticed, but one part embarrassment dilutes quickly in nine parts euphoria, and Konran barely notices.

Finally the captain brings him full circle, and Konran finds himself peering—salivating—once again at the LTOM-92 Sparrowhawks. His heartbeat quickens.

"I take it you are already familiar with these craft," Captain Granicks observes.

"Um, yes, sir, I am, sir," Konran replies, still staring at the craft. "In a way, I guess, at least. Hours on the simulator as a kid. I could pass all 455 missions of *NolvaRetaliation 2164* with my eyes closed. Hours training in spaceflight school, double-majoring in starfighting. I've dreamt of flying one. Never touched one until today."

Konran looks from the starfighter to Captain Granicks, feeling like a part of his soul had just come home. "Thank you for the tour, sir."

Captain Granicks raises his left arm, revealing a forearm computer not unlike that worn by Declan in the nurses' bay— apparently everyone had them on the *Nova Scotia*. He enters a command, and the black-domed cockpit on the nearest Sparrowhawk slides open. A ramp extends from the polished metal hangar bay floor, forming a ladder to the now-exposed pilot seat.

"I've always wondered how these compare to the arcade simulators. Why don't you take a seat and let me know," Captain Granicks says, his words reminiscent of an official naval order.

Konran's uvula swallows his heart again (and possibly everything south), but he knows when not to ask for confirmation. His bare feet touch half the rungs as he climbs the ladder and, for the first time in his life, sinks his weight into the auto-adjusting pilot seat of the LTOM-92 Sparrowhawk, bane of all Nolvarim.

His hands fall to the joysticks like an experienced golfer palming a cherished putter. His fingers tap along the various buttons, dials, and switches like a drummer subconsciously tapping out a riff on the dashboard. The cockpit conforms to his anthropometry, shifting subtly to accommodate his weight, height, limb lengths, and even hand preference. He closes his eyes, breathing deeply and smelling the richness of the cockpit, absorbing the moment like a desert lizard soaking up water through its skin. Finally, he exhales—deep, satisfied, peaceful— another lost piece of his soul falling perfectly into place.

"Yep," he calls from the cockpit. "It's way better than the simulators. It's so perfect I could sleep here."

"Man, we found you in the middle-of-nowhere space sleeping in your sorry GR-29 excuse for a fighter. You could sleep anywhere, if you could sleep a minute," a much-younger-than-Granicks voice calls back with a thick Martian accent.

Konran raises from the cockpit to see a whole group of men and women assembling around Captain Granicks: pilots.

Starfighter pilots.

Konran clambers out of the cockpit and down the ladder, not sure what to expect but unsure of what else to do. He stands there, bare feet cold on the polished hangar deck. *What do I say?* he wonders.

Before he can formulate a reply, he is surrounded, an arm around his shoulder, pilots on all sides of him. They're asking questions: Something about the rescue, being a hero, where is he going to paint his kill stripes, what was going through his mind, can they *have an autograph?*

Captain Granicks steps in and the group recedes apace, though the arm around Konran's shoulder doesn't let up. It's a young man, near Konran's age, dark eyes twinkling against brown skin. His military haircut tapers up into a set of short dreadlocks atop his head. The soft patch on his flight suit reads *A. C. MARTIN.*

"You can call me Ace," he says, a twinkle in his eyes.

"All right, give him some room," Granicks commands, but with a grin on his face. "Konran's just woken up; let's not kill him off yet."

Just then another pilot runs up to the group, carrying something in his arms, which he hands to Ace. It's a flight suit.

"We almost had to wash it again, you kept us waiting so long," Ace says. He hands the gray suit to Konran. "Welcome to the Tharsis Wildlynx, man."

"Wait, what?" Konran stammers.

"You're one of us now, man—honorary member and everything," Ace says. "Put it on."

Konran takes the suit, trembling as he holds it up to his shoulders and lets it fall to his ankles. It looks perfect. A pair of boots are passed to him through the group, and he is encouraged to put the suit on. Without severe discomfort, he pulls it on over his hospital garb, which is light enough to play the temporary role of underwear, tucking the loose-fitting clothing into the tighter-fitting flight suit as necessary, ignoring the awkward bulges it creates. He zips the suit up and takes a seat on the Sparrowhawk's ladder, slipping the boots over his bare feet.

A cheer goes up as Konran stands, his smile as wide as Hangar Bay 3.

Another pilot, of Asian descent by appearance, makes his way through the group and places a patch on Konran's left shoulder, depicting a fierce cat set against a red Martian landscape and black backdrop. The cat peers at a series of eight diagonally arranged stars on the right side of the patch, and Konran instantly recognizes the Lynx constellation.

Tharsis Wildlynx were a famous breed of cat, bred eighty years ago to survive on Mars through highly controversial REMEDI (Rapid Evolutionary Manipulation and Embryonic Design Iteration) genetic engineering. The cats had taken especially well to the Tharsis Highlands in Mars's western hemisphere, subsisting on the generosity of colonists and the handouts of scientists until suitable prey had been designed and deployed on the cold, red planet. The ecological system wasn't nearly self-sustaining yet, but it had gained a foothold.

Suddenly overwhelmed, Konran takes a few steps backward and sits down on the ladder. He feels weak, like his body just remembered what it had been through. Pilots mill around him, concerned looks across their faces.

"Could I get some water?" Konran asks with a rueful grin. "One point three three liters, to be precise. I think I'm overdue."

He raises his left hand in a fist. "Go Wildlynx," he cheers weakly, dropping the hand to support his head as the group cheers in approval.

"Why don't we get you back to medical," Captain Granicks says, stepping protectively toward Konran.

"I'll be fine," Konran replies, waving Granicks back as a pilot returns with 1.33 liters of water. Konran takes a long gulp, hoping for another excuse to delay his return to medical.

"Maybe we can find another place to sit?" he asks.

"The briefing room has some nice chairs," Ace chimes in. "We'll catch you up on news. It'll be good for you."

Two pilots give Konran a hand up, and the group escorts him across the hangar bay.

"Pilots," Captain Granicks mutters to Konran. "You're going to fit in just fine, Andacellos." Then, more authoritatively the captain continues, "Commander Martin, I'll be returning to my quarters for the night. Mr. Andacellos will be under your care and supervision. Don't do anything stupid."

"Yes, sir!" Ace replies. The two exchange salutes, and Captain Granicks departs the hangar bay.

Konran walks on cloud nine into the briefing room and takes a seat, Captain Granicks's comment about fitting in giving him a boost of vitality. Ace enters a command into his forearm computer and a holographic projection initiates in the center of the room. The pilots show Konran recent footage from the Kuiper Belt, some of it shot by journalists, some of it actual combat footage from USFN frigates taking on the Nolvarics. Konran is shocked to learn that two USFN destroyers went down by Haumea—the Nolvarics somehow amassing a heavy presence in the region despite the population of humans permanently inhabiting the dwarf planet. Many Haumeans had been evacuated to settlements on nearby space rocks in the Kuiper Belt.

Journalists reporting on the story appear baffled at the magnitude of the fighting, questioning how this was possible and otherwise reveling in the shocking news story. Journalists reporting on the story also frequently mention ships called the *Relrick* and the *Viona Grande*, a Kuiper Belt war site called Y25LM90, and a heroic pilot named Andacellos. Konran suddenly feels faint, taking another drink of his water and opening the chocolate pudding packet given him by Fritz.

I'm going to need some more chamomile, he thinks as a solemn journalist displays a hologram of Konran from his ISSA personnel file and says the words "modern-day hero."

"Check this vid!" a pilot calls excitedly from the far side of the room. "It posted ten minutes ago and has 985 million views."

He keys his forearm computer, and Konran sees a man—himself—in a space suit, standing on the meteoric ridge from Y25LM90 and staring over the horizon. Alandie stands next to him as disgruntled commentary plays over the holographic video.

"And there is our delinquent captain, doing nothing while we wait here, stuck on this rock."

The video feed changes to another perspective, showing Konran and Alandie from a slightly different angle.

"Typical," a haughty female voice plays over the video, "that we would be the ones to receive incompetent service amidst our most singular voyage." Konran recognizes the voice as pertaining to the district space justice aboard the *Viona Grande* that day.

"Hold on, I don't think this is a good idea," a female pilot with green eyes and a dark brown ponytail calls out, standing up. She enters a forearm command and the montage pauses. Her soft patch reads *V. MELENDEZ, USFN.* "He's been through a lot. Will you be OK watching this?" She directs the last question to Konran.

Konran considers the question, realizing he is watching a video montage of footage taken by VIPs aboard the *Viona Grande*. These first videos had likely posted to social media before Konran ever re-boarded the *Viona Grande*, as evidence against the "delinquent captain."

Konran steels his mind, suppressing thoughts of what inevitably comes next. He was here, in his flight suit, in the briefing room, with the pilots.

I can handle it.

Man, her eyes are green.

"Yeah, I think I'll be fine," he says, adding, "as long as you'll sit close for moral support." He scoots over, opening up a sliver of space and spreading one arm across the seat back.

V. Melendez gives him an *oh, I didn't realize you are an idiot* look and sits back down. The room laughs.

What was that about? Konran pummels himself mentally. *Where had that even come from?*

Before he can settle his internal debate, the montage resumes and he sees his distant form staring at the horizon from yet another perspective. The video pans and shows the *Relrick* sitting nearby, already powered up and ready for departure. Natauli's voice breaks in, making Konran jump.

"Please pardon the delay; Captain Andacellos has been engaged in a routine procedure."

The video changes again, showing Konran running to the ship and Alandie scrambling to keep up behind him, and the voice of the first VIP mockingly asks if this is also "routine procedure."

The montage then jumps to inside the *Viona Grande*, with several clips of passengers showing off souvenirs and commiserating about the service. Next is a feed from the *Relrick*, peering down at the *Viona Grande* still moored on Y25LM90. Konran's throat constricts and muscles tense down his body, but he forces himself to watch.

Suddenly screams ensue as passengers aboard the *Relrick* become aware of the Nolvaric attack. An explosion sounds, cameras jerk and spin, and the *Relrick* crashes back to Y25LM90. The view switches again and a camera catches some pieces of the *Borboleta* crashing into the asteroid through a viewport on the *Viona Grande*. An audible crash is heard as the plasma ball's shockwaves vibrate through the astrofreighters.

"Oh. Oh, oh," Konran moans, the words escaping as his head drops. His hands come to his face as his elbows hit his knees. Then, against his will, a giant sob wracks his body. He gasps against it, coughing, gagging, and sobbing all at once. And then bile rises up his esophagus, and his mouth fills with vomit. He spits and hacks against the acrid viscosity. Semi-cognizant of the struggle to compose himself, Konran's mind only thinks of that day, when Natauli and the *Relrick* disappeared forever.

Natauli.
Racho.
All those VIPs.
Oh.

A hand rests on Konran's shoulder, squeezing it gently but firmly. Another hand wraps around his own, helping him sit up. Konran recognizes the touch of those who understand. He looks up, finding the eyes of the pilots. None are laughing, none judgmental—except V. Melendez, who stands and, with an *I told you so* shake of her head, exits the room with a quick click of heels.

"Hey, man, it's all right," a pilot speaks to him. He's stocky and bald-headed, with Asian eyes and Latino features. "We've all been there, man. We've been there." He slaps Konran on the back. "It's all right."

"Tibo's right," Ace says from Konran's side, his arm around Konran's shoulder. "You're one of us now."

Konran breathes for a moment, collecting himself. Finally he speaks, swallowing a sob and wiping his nose with his sleeve.

"Thanks, guys. I want to watch the rest of it."

"You sure, man?" Ace asks.

"Yeah," Konran says. "I can't hide forever. I need to face it now. It's only going to come out later if I don't."

"It always will, man," Tibo replies. "But that's not the half of us pilots. What you did next—that's the real half."

"I think what Tibo's attempting to say," Ace says, "is that what you did next—what comes next in this holo-feed—despite the losses and death, will define you more than your grief. Sometimes you just can't save someone."

"Yeah, man, Ace gets it."

Konran breathes again, nodding. "I'm ready. I have to do this."

The holographic montage resumes from the perspective of the *Viona Grande*. VIPs are screaming and crying. Konran rushes through the group in his space suit and disappears up the ladder. A sound like a massive hammer resounds from above the *Viona Grande* as the magnetic launch system throws Konran's gun-craft, causing several VIPs to cower and huddle in fear. Although the *Relrick*'s crash had kicked up a dust cloud, cutting-edge cameras still manage to track Konran's flight from multiple angles. He watches himself gain control of the GR-29 Defender and rocket across the barren landscape. The sequence appears much more graceful than it felt when he was actually doing it. Moments later, Natauli launches in her GR-29 and rockets after him.

The Nolvaric plasma cannons are not visible from the camera angles, but their explosions above the horizon are. Konran comes around for another pass, and a green energy blast flies past him. It looks a lot closer than it felt in real life, and his erratic dodge looks a lot more skillful. Konran watches himself right the ship, reorient himself with quick precision, and blast the third cannon to flaming debris. VIPs erupt in shouts of joy.

Alandie's voice sounds over the montage, relieved, "Everyone, Captain Andacellos has neutralized the threat, and we are cleared to take off. Please take your seats and..." Alandie gasps, then says quietly, "*Nolvaric Askeras. Murugan save us all.*"

The announcement cuts off and VIP cameras search throughout the dark, vacuous space for sign of the Askeras, utilizing the many, multidirectional viewports set up on the *Viona Grande* for their viewing enjoyment during the voyage. Soft cries and whimpers join the montage as the scene shifts from one camera to another. Some of the *Relrick*'s VIPs had recovered enough to begin filming as well. Alandie's voice breaks in, reminding everyone to put on their space suits, and the *Viona Grande* takes off, making its break into space. A VIP's camera tracks energy blasts as Konran fires diffuse plasma blasts from the GR-29 Defender's narwhal gun, and missile detonations erupt in the cloud, filling the camera view for a moment.

He watches as he deploys the drones, watches himself defeat the second missile attack, and watches himself go careening under the third. Suddenly the *Viona Grande* shakes violently, and people stumble and fall, screaming in terror. One camera shows Natauli's GR-29 deploying its drones and defeating the final wave of missiles. Another camera catches a small explosion in space: Konran destroying the first Nolvaric fighter. His tiny GR-29 gun-craft rockets upward toward the enemy, as the other two Askeras split up.

Alandie's voice sounds, announcing the engine power is gone, and he recommends praying. VIPs wail, and then a secondary explosion rocks the *Viona Grande*. Cameras from both the *Viona Grande* and *Relrick* catch Konran dodging the two remaining Nolvarics—the prestige of capturing the best footage, posthumous or not, apparently providing them powerful cinematic motivation.

Again, Konran's maneuvers look more skillful than they felt. He can actually see his erratic movements confusing the Nolvaric pilots, throwing off their attacks. Bluish blasts from the enemy ships fire ineffectually into space.

One of the fighters heads for the *Relrick*, and Konran jets in pursuit, his matchstick flame extending like a streak behind him. He fires, scoring a few hits and then, suddenly, the Nolvaric craft *behind* him explodes. Konran's maneuver happens so fast the camera doesn't pick up his abrupt reverse flip, but the pilots all know what he did. Whoops of triumph ring out as they celebrate the kill, and they rewind the footage and watch it several times. Konran laughs with them about how sick it made him feel, especially after doing the second reverse flip. One of the pilots remarks that Konran is "going to love the Sparrowhawk," and that he will "barely even feel it," and Konran decides he knows what cloud eleven feels like.

They resume the montage, and Konran cringes, knowing what comes next. Screams and shouts break out on the *Relrick* as its VIPs film Natauli trying to fend off the final Askera. She charges valiantly, but her GR-29 Defender is blown to pieces in a brutal instant. Next comes the *Relrick*, and its VIPs' camera feeds go black.

Konran breathes slowly, deeply, clenching his teeth against the anguish inside him and looking down at his feet. He realizes the montage has stopped again.

"You couldn't get both Askeras," Ace says. "And you wouldn't have saved anyone if you hadn't pulled that crazy flip to nail the one on your tail. It's the Nolvarics' fault Natauli and the *Relrick*'s passengers died. But you're the reason some people lived."

Konran looks up, tears streaming down his cheeks in solid streaks of water. He blinks, nods, breathes, and wipes his face. "OK, go ahead," is all he says, and the montage resumes.

A camera catches his GR-29 rocketing toward the *Viona Grande*. Alandie orders everyone to tether together and jump through a gaping hole in the side of the craft. He yells at the stragglers to "Move if you want to live!"

Now floating in raw space, VIPs' cameras show the *Viona Grande* exploding under a savage, bluish barrage from the Askera.

Their trailing line of tethered passengers looks tiny and pathetic against the backdrop of raging fireballs and the intergalactic cosmos—so dramatic it could have been an advertisement for a sci-fi movie.

Some cameras pick up Konran as he zooms around the *Viona Grande*. Others catch orange plasma raining down from his gun-craft narwhal nose as he completes his circle around the decimated astrofreighter. A massive explosion erupts as Konran destroys the third Askera.

The holographic montage slows down, and dramatic music accompanies the scene. It's barely discernible in the chaos, but in the corner of one frame Konran can see a plasmic energy blast impacting on vector with the Askera's top shark fin. The pilots go crazy, standing and cheering and slapping Konran on the back and talking about the "textbook kill."

The next shot shows Konran's gun-craft rotating lifelessly as it drifts into space. The VIP, who sounds a lot like the VIP who had mocked Konran earlier in the montage, thanks Captain Andacellos for saving their lives.

Next comes footage of the VIPs cheering and crying at the *Nova Scotia*'s arrival. Konran thinks he can identify Geoffroy and Cazmira as spacewalking rescuers herd beleaguered VIPs aboard the Riot-class cruiser. One VIP refuses rescue until her poodle is taken safely aboard first.

The final shots show Konran's GR-29 Defender coming aboard the *Nova Scotia*. Many of the VIPs are there, recording themselves talking about their hero. Utter silence prevails as Konran's limp form is pulled from the gun-craft. The announcement is made that he is alive, and a tremendous cheer breaks out. VIPs' cameras switch from him to them and back to him again. Then a platoon of marines pushes everyone out of the way, and the montage ends.

Konran finishes his last squeeze of chocolate pudding, drains his remaining water, and, wet tears still on his cheeks, loses himself in conversation with the Tharsis Wildlynx—his squadron.

CHAPTER 4

Konran can't shake the Nolvaric Askera behind him. He yanks the flight stick this way and that, careening wildly in an attempt to escape, but the Askera doesn't miss a beat. Konran can feel its targeting system lock onto him, can sense its plasmic pathways energizing. He closes his eyes, bracing himself.

Bam, bam, bam.

"Konran?"

Konran bolts upright. He's in his hospital room, flight suit still on.

It was a dream, he realizes, heart pounding.

Bam, bam, bam.

"Konran?" a female voice asks. She sounds familiar.

USFN security protocol did not allow personnel to use modern holographic computers aboard USFN vessels, and Konran consults the forearm computer Ace Martin had given him after the welcoming party last night. The computer displays the time as 11:16—he's barely slept for four hours.

"Just a minute," he calls to the door.

"OK," the voice replies.

He gives his left arm a quick flick and the forearm computer slides down his wrist and into his palm.

So old school, he thinks, wiggling his fingers and signaling the computer to sync with his biosignature.

The system brings up his recent messages, suggested news, and ISSA notifications. He has 265 unread messages in his ISSA corporate inbox, and 82,807,346 new notifications across his social media platforms.

That's a lot of notifications, he observes with wide eyes. It jumps to 82,830,102 before he dismisses the computer, which glides in standby mode to the back of his hand.

"I can come back," the voice at the door says.

"No, it's OK." Konran stretches, stands, and realizes he doesn't feel like death walking anymore.

Thanks, Fritz, he mentally acknowledges, looking in the mirror.

His hair is a mess, but his face doesn't look as bad as it had. He walks to a hygienic station across the room and, hoping for the best, requests the *Basic Hair Styling and Facial Cleansing* option via his now hand computer.

The subsequent tingle on his scalp and evaporation of water on his face are refreshing, and he steps back to evaluate the result. His hair doesn't look normal—just a standard part down the left side, but at least it doesn't look like four days of coma-head anymore.

After the Wildlynx welcoming party last night, Konran hadn't removed his hospital garb from beneath his flight suit before crashing to sleep. It's a little bulky in places, but not that bad, and he elects to ignore it for the sake of time. Taking a breath, he opens the door. Shira, the Scandinavian stewardess from the *Viona Grande*, stands on the other side.

"Hi," she says with a shy smile.

"Hey," Konran replies. With long, golden hair falling behind her back in dual braids, and a crisp, white jump suit highlighting the frosty blue of her eyes, Shira may as well have been an angel.

"We learned you had awoken, so Alandie sent me to check on you."

"Alandie sent you?" Konran asks, suppressing a grin. *Of course Alandie did.*

"Everyone wanted to come, but Alandie didn't want to overwhelm you," she explains. "And..." she pauses, looking down at a pastry box in her hands, "I thought you might like this."

"Oh yeah?" Konran says, taking the small box and opening it. A slice of golden pie sits within.

"Wait, is this banana cream pie without banana chunks?" he asks.

"You like it that way, yes?"

That settles it—she is 100 percent angel.

Konran takes a bite, wolfing it down with the provided spoon.

"Oh ... this is perfect."

"Patient Andacellos!" Fritz rolls up in a huff, mispronouncing Konran's name as he appears in the doorway. Shira has to jump back a step.

"I do not recommend ingesting such quantities of sucrose at this stage of your recovery," Fritz chides as one of his arms reaches out and, with incredible dexterity, snatches the open box before Konran can take another bite.

"Come on," Konran complains, lunging, but the bot rolls backward before Konran can grab the pie. Pie smears across Fritz's chest as the bot hastily stows the pie within an internal compartment.

"I will preserve the confection for your later consumption, Patient Andacellos," Fritz says, still backing away, "as I see you are rather attached to it. Please let me know if there is anything else you require." A Fritz-size door panel slides open in the hallway, and the medbot disappears inside.

"That bot," Konran says, dumbfounded, "just stole my pie."

"And wiped it all over himself," Shira adds, laughing.

In spite of the chagrin of losing his pie, Konran laughs with her. The effort feels good.

"There's more back in the mess hall," Shira says. "I only brought the one slice."

"Tempting, but I should listen to Fritz—he really has done a great job with me."

"Well, I am sure it will keep," Shira responds brightly. "The culinary facilities are extraordinary on this ship. So, would you like to go see everyone?"

"That would be so awesome," Konran agrees, stepping into the corridor and matching pace with Shira. The two talk pleasantly as she leads him from the medical bay, across a wide, transverse hallway, and to a set of double doors labeled, *MESS HALL*.

"They'll all be in here," she says. "It's the gathering place."

Konran takes a deep breath as she opens the door. The mess hall is packed with people, and as he steps inside, the room erupts into a roar. In moments he and Shira are surrounded, and then, like a piece of driftwood eddying near the bank of a quickly moving river, he is sucked into the throng.

Konran recognizes the VIPs, their memorized names coming as they each vie for his attention. Some intelligent corner of his brain realizes he should smile, and his lips effect the shape easily and generously.

Konran shakes hands. Konran gives hugs. Konran is kissed randomly on the cheek, forehead, and hand. Konran's flight suit gets teardrops on its shoulders and collar. Konran feels something he's never felt before—something indescribable, and he thinks he understands what Geoffroy was talking about last night when the nurse spoke of the VIPs' eyes when the *Nova Scotia* rescued them via spacewalk.

Shortly Alandie presses through, and another cheer erupts as the two embrace. Seeing the younger pilot is like a bucket of ice water to the face, and words come out in elated chunks rather than grammatical sentences.

"We're alive!" "We did it!" "We made it!" "You saved us!" "You saved them!" "Can't believe your flying!" "Can't believe yours!" "Three Nolvarics?" "I thought you were dead!" "I thought we all were!"

VIP cameras are everywhere, hovering above the crowd, raised on palms and fingers, implanted as gems between eyes for perfect point-of-view presentation, recording Konran and Alandie from dozens of angles. One of the hover-cameras perches on Konran's shoulder for a better view of the reunion, and Alandie flicks it away with an index finger.

"You'll get used to it," he says, laughing with the crowd.

Together, Konran and Alandie receive their adoring fans. VIPs gush to Konran about Alandie, describing how brave he was and how he saved them. More VIPs gush to Konran about Konran, describing how amazing he was and how he saved them. One senator almost brings Konran to tears with her heartfelt, eloquent expression of gratitude. Another VIP promises to buy Konran his own island on Earth. Yet another commends Konran for the tremendous gift he gave the solar system by saving his life so he could keep making holo-movies. The district space justice wedges herself before him and, thrusting her now-famous space poodle into Konran's arms, sobs that he "saved her Fufu."

71

Fufu goes crazy, growling and snapping at Konran's face and neck. The district space justice laughs it off as adorable, telling Konran he has a way with dogs just like he has a way with starfighters. Straining to keep the increasing saliva spraying from Fufu's teeth away from his face, he wishes he could show the dog his way with a starfighter.

Suddenly a young woman is standing next to Konran, her hand on his arm displacing the poodle just as quickly. Her long, brown hair is pulled back and colored with twisting streaks of glowing light, and several artfully placed rings of skin diamonds sparkle around her violet eyes. She smells like a midsummer's night bathed in the light of a thousand comets (an actual scent), and Konran's stomach auto-fills with helium. She says something to him.

"Wha ... huhm, what?" he stammers, uncertain whether his brain-mouth connection has been severed.

"Are you hungry?" she asks again, laughing through a smile that could have launched the United Space Federation Navy to the Oort cloud in a minute.

"Uh ... yeah ... yeah, I am," Konran replies, his stumbling brain finally placing the young lady as Kyalia Rennasent, co-star of the wildly popular holo-series *Andromeda Uncharted*.

He smiles back, suddenly appreciative of the odd, spontaneous awesomeness afforded by his newfound celebrity. Fufu makes an oh-so-precious lunge at him, and he has to dodge to avoid the canine's canines. Kyalia steps with Konran, gracefully maintaining her grip as if long practiced at this dance. She raises her hand to the crowd, signaling their attention with another Oort cloud of a smile.

"Our hero is hungry!" she proclaims, linking her arm through his. "Set the tables!"

The milling throng erupts in another cheer and the mess hall converts from a reception hall back into itself.

"Franco, we require your assistance!" Kyalia says, and with motion so assertive that the room itself follows suit, Kyalia leads Konran to a table and sits him down. Alandie gives Konran a subtle elbow nudge as they part, stepping away with a *good luck, you're gonna need it* look, and joins a table filling with

Kazakhstani cricket champions. Konran doesn't see Shira anywhere.

Though technology had long displaced humans as the preferred means of food preparation in many sectors of society, the *Nova Scotia* boasted several galleys full of living, breathing, culinary masters (the increase in morale more than compensating for the loss of efficiency and precision). In moments from Kyalia's call, a diminutive man with penetrating eyes and an unmistakable chef's uniform appears at the tableside.

"Ms. Rennasent, will you have the usual today?" His accent places him of Russo-Venusian heritage, undoubtedly from one of Venus's many cloud colonies.

"Of course, Franco!" she beams, giving the chef her best smile yet.

"And for you, Mr. Andacellos?" Franco inquires, not requiring Konran's name.

Konran has absolutely no idea what to order. "Well, I haven't eaten much of anything for five days now, and the medbot said I shouldn't have any sucrose yet, so can I just have something that won't make me sick?" he asks.

Franco smiles. (Chefs smile even if a customer insinuates their cuisine could displease anyone, let alone make them sick.) "We have your medical reports, Mr. Andacellos," he says succinctly. "I will see you are brought something that agrees with you and your medbot."

The chef returns to the galley, leaving Konran feeling alone in the room full of people, brunching with Kyalia Rennasent—holo-star, icon, bachelorette.

She called me her "hero," he realizes, the thought quickly fading to, *Her eyes are deep blue now, like Earth's oceans from orbit.*

Konran searches for something to say, trying not to fidget with a bulge of loose hospital garb, which had found its way under his armpit. Suddenly he senses the ocular pressure of someone watching him, and his eyes flick to a nearby table filled with good-looking, overly perfect individuals staring at him.

Other cast members from Andromeda Uncharted, he recognizes, looking back at Kyalia, whose ocean-blue eyes smile

73

back at him, dimpling dazzlingly at the corners. His mind races as his tongue binds.

What do I say? he demands his mental faculties to answer. Quickly considering the factors and calculating to minimize risk, Konran's brain doesn't disappoint, settling on safe, simple small talk as a first attempt at conversation.

"So, I guess I saved your life," he says, his tone casual, ignoring the bulges of clothing making their way up his right leg.

Kyalia's brow furrows, and her chin droops slightly. Her nostrils flare and her eyes squeeze shut and she inhales slowly, her beautiful face stiffening. Finally, she opens her eyes, and Konran feels he is staring through two stained glass windows into the raw depths of a child who just realized she can't find her mother. Kyalia blinks as her lip begins to tremble, and two tears pool and spill, running in delicate lines down each side of her face.

She reaches across the table as tears fall more freely, grabbing Konran's hand and squeezing it with both of hers. She lowers her head, pulling his hand and resting her forehead atop it, his hand between hers. Tears drip through her fingers and onto Konran's as her glowing hair pulsates with her sobs. Konran reaches and rests his free hand beside Kyalia's. He is acutely aware of the room of VIPs staring at him again, holo-cameras rolling.

"I ... I'm sorry," he attempts, "I didn't mean..."

"No," Kyalia sobs, "no, don't apologize." She squeezes his hand more firmly, desperately, breathing deeply as if trying to control herself.

"Thank you. Thank you, Konran," she finally manages. "Thank you for saving my life." Sobs continue in waves as Konran sits there, holding her hands: conspicuous, awkward, immobilized, and cognizant of it all.

Suddenly, Franco is there. "A napkin, Ms. Rennasent?" he inquires, offering a hand towel to the weeping holo-star.

Kyalia sits up, tears sparkling with skin diamonds as she takes the towel and dabs her now-turquoise eyes. Red sclera accentuates the striking color, and Konran's helium returns as she looks back at him, still clinging to him with one hand.

"Thank you, Franco," she says, tears abated. "I don't know what came over me."

"I have found the *agua de flor de Jamaica* to provide the most calming of effects, especially when cultivated in zero gravity," Franco replies, placing two glasses of deep-purple liquid on the table. The chef hadn't appeared to be carrying anything except the hand towel. He adds a few flower petals of *Malva sylvestris* to each of the drinks with a practiced flourish and disappears back into the galley.

Kyalia raises her glass, her expression lighter but stained-glass somber as ever.

"To life," she says.

He raises his glass, and the rich, purple juice sloshes gently against its efficient, hydrophobic surfaces. "To life," he replies, touching his glass to hers.

"To life!" the entire mess hall cheers in unison, breaking into applause and tipping back glasses of their own. Awkward tension flees as Konran smiles back at the room. Toasts to "Konran!" and "Life!" and "Konran!" break out before attention ebbs back to its customary, table-by-table stasis.

Conversation comes easily for Konran now that much of the tentative vulnerability inherent in every human encounter has been obliterated, and he chats with Kyalia about that day, less than a week ago, when the Nolvarics failed to kill the *Viona Grande*.

Their food comes (oysters and sauerkraut atop slices of morel mushrooms for her, a creamy, grainy soup for him that tastes good but he has no idea what it is). She talks about how excited the cast had been to go on an actual space adventure, how terrible it had been to see the *Borboleta* go down, how she had cried upon learning of Natauli and the *Relrick*'s fate, and how her heart paled with fear and leapt with hope as Konran had fought for her: like a lone knight standing between hope and oblivion (she actually said that).

Konran talks about his respectable but uninspiring tenure at ISSA, about spaceflight school, and about failing to become a starfighter pilot. Kyalia stops him when he mentions his parents.

"Wait, you never knew them?" she asks, her hand touching his again.

"Nope," he confirms. "With all the possibilities afforded by genetic engineering these days, a couple can simply drop off a baby and never be traced. It happens more than you think. I've read a lot about the subject."

"So who raised you?" she presses.

"Just a boys' home in Merced, California. They actually do a really good job with kids—I got lucky."

The ocular pressure of eyes gazing upon him returns, and Konran pauses, glancing over at the table of fabulous-looking *Andromeda Uncharted* cast members staring his way. One in particular, Philipe Cziklof, looks particularly antagonistic.

"What's up with Philipe?" Konran asks, turning back to Kyalia with his voice low.

"Oh, is Philipe staring?" Kyalia remarks with a dismissive shake of her head. "He thinks he's in love with me. Don't take it personally."

"And the others?" Konran asks, noting the other five people at the table.

"They're his clique," Kyalia explains matter-of-factly. "He's the most popular cast member, so they follow him. When they deserve it, he pulls strings and gets them more lines, more screen time, better scenes, guest appearances, famous-people stuff. Since he's 'in love' with me, they all glare at anyone I do anything with."

Konran nods, her words a mystery to him. "Sounds super fun."

"Get used to it, Hero," she says, playfully squeezing his hand. "You're one of us now."

Chef Franco returns and the table is cleared. "I trust everything was agreeable," he states, facing mostly Kyalia but speaking mostly to Konran.

"Oh yes, Franco," Kyalia responds enthusiastically, "as always." She reaches and touches his arm. "And thank you."

"Of course, Ms. Rennasent," Franco says simply. "Do you require anything further?"

"As a matter of fact, could we have some—" Kyalia begins but is cut off as an alarm sounds. Not blaring, but clear, the sound is accompanied by small red lights flashing from the corners of the room. The mess hall becomes still, and then a woman—Fufu's owner—begins to wail hysterically.

"Another attack," a calmer VIP observes. "Fourth one."

76

Alandie stands from his seat across the mess hall. "OK, everyone, don't panic. Please return to your rooms and buckle in. I will pass along updates as I receive them."

As the crowd rises to follow Alandie's instructions, a pair of marines enters the double doors. One speaks loudly over the din.

"Konran Andacellos!"

The room quiets, parting out of the way so the marines have a direct line of sight to Konran.

"The captain requests your presence, Mr. Andacellos," the marine continues. "Please come with us." It sounds more like an order than an invitation, and Konran jumps to his feet as the crowd roars its approval. VIPs shout his name.

"Konran! Konran! Konran! Konran!"

Kyalia tugs his arm as he steps past, and Konran catches her eyes—now a vivid, Amazon green.

"Find me when you're done, Hero," she says with a smile. "Franco makes the best malasadas—you have to try them."

"Sorry for... " Konran begins.

"Don't you dare apologize. Now, go be a hero!" Kyalia's words feel as much of an order as the marines' request, and without another word Konran passes through the mess hall corridor of cheering VIPs and joins his escort.

"Let them have it, Andacellos!" a VIP shouts emphatically. "Blast 'em to bosons!"

"Don't you mean, 'blast them to fermions'?" someone else asks.

"Sounds better the other way," is the last thing Konran hears as the marines whisk him from the mess hall.

They walk briskly across the wide hallway, straight into the wall. Konran's brain is puzzled at the pace until the wall simply gives way, opening up with a quick hiss just long enough for the three to pass inside.

They step onto a narrow, militaristic platform within a long, glossy, cylindrical tunnel. Thin lines run along its circumference like a miniature, much-less-dirty version of a grav-lev subway line. A shuttle zips silently up to them, a door opening without a sound. Konran and his escort step on, and it carries them away.

Konran feels as if he is falling face-first toward the end of the tunnel, recognizing that gravity has reoriented within the tunnel to

77

propel the shuttle forward. A marine says, "Lean to the left," and Konran mimics them as they lean. Suddenly he feels like he is falling to the left, and the shuttle abruptly changes direction, shooting left down a side tunnel. An instant later the shuttle stops without a hiss and Konran feels gravity right itself. The three of them step out, pass through another invisible door in the wall, ascend an elevator, and enter a spartan antechamber adorned with neatly arranged, high-powered weaponry on the walls.

Six marines occupy the room; one steps up to Konran, raising a device to his face—like the kind used in courtrooms to make sure someone is telling the truth.

"Konran Andacellos," she states. "Under direction of Captain Elwin Darius Granicks and according to the needs and codes of wartime, you are hereby inducted as captain's aide, to serve aboard the USFS *Nova Scotia*, this the fourth day of March, 2204. Do you accept this position and swear, under pain of treason, to abide an oath of complete fidelity to the rights and permissions given you as a fully endowed member of staff?" Konran stares at the device, glowing green less than a meter in front of his face.

"Um, yes, of course," he replies, uncertain what he has just agreed to; better to not argue with a marine.

She removes the device from his face and another invisible door slides open behind her with a hiss. On the other side Konran recognizes Captain Granicks standing in his service uniform with two other officers. The marines escort Konran inside, salute, and depart through the door, which is clearly visible from this side. The entire process hasn't taken more than two minutes.

"Konran, welcome," Captain Granicks states, looking up from a large dais at the center of the room. A woman with ebony skin and intensely intelligent eyes stands next to the captain, joined by a man maybe ten years younger than Granicks. Her angular face is a picture of serenity; his square jaw is fixed, gray eyes flashing for the conflict.

"Allow me to introduce Commander Exeunt and Commander Revenshal," Granicks says. "Commanders, Konran Andacellos."

"No need for introductions on my part," Commander Revenshal says, extending his hand and shaking Konran's. "Glad to have you aboard, kid."

"Your actions to save your crew and passengers were highly commendable, Captain Andacellos," Commander Exeunt says, inclining her head slightly his way. Her accent is unlike any Konran has ever heard, not exotic nor unclear, but certainly not derived from any earthbound language: individual syllables were too sharp, but entire words still their usual length. Something about the dignity of her words makes Konran feel as if his entire life's existence has just been validated.

"I've exercised my wartime authority to appoint you as captain's aide, Konran," Granicks explains before Konran could reply to the commanders' praise. "This grants you a level of security clearance and will allow you to join me on the bridge."

"Er, sir, thanks..." Konran replies, still uncertain what is happening.

"That means come and join us, son," Captain Granicks says, gesturing him over. "We're in the middle of preparations for a pending engagement with the Nolvarics. And I want you here for this."

Konran steps up to the dais, standing between Granicks and Revenshal. The dais contains a two-dimensional map of the inner solar system. The location of USFN and allied forces, Nolvaric positions, and other astronomical points of interest are marked by various colors and symbols, and Konran is amazed to see traces of Nolvaric activity as deep as the asteroid belt. The *Nova Scotia* is marked on the map with a star inside a diamond floating out in the Kuiper Belt, and Konran instantly recognizes the location as less than ten million kilometers from Y25LM90.

They've barely moved at all since rescuing me five days ago.

"This is what you got us into," Granicks says, indicating the plethora of red markers designating Nolvaric activity across the outer solar system. "And if not for that, you can imagine what kind of a mess we would be in if the Nolvarics had done it their way. No one knows how they managed to amass such a force so close."

Konran considers the map, noting the highest concentrations of Nolvarics to be *nearest* the more heavily populated Kuiper Belt settlements.

"It's like they were ready to pounce," Konran says, his view of the politically-tumultuous-yet-otherwise-placid solar system flipping on its head. "And I stepped right into it."

"You weren't the first," Granicks replies, "but you do appear to be the first to have survived the encounter. Several disappearances over the previous weeks have been traced to similar confrontations. We estimate they were less than two months from rolling the Kuiper Belt into New Nolvariz."

"So we don't know where they came from?" Konran asks.

"Our best guess is that they're from the clans inhabiting the Oort cloud," Granicks explains. "Evidence suggests they may have leveraged an abandoned manufacturing facility around the Luhman 16 binaries to build their fleet, which they snuck into the solar system over time."

"Luhman 16?" Konran asks. "The co-orbiting brown dwarfs? But wouldn't any Nolvaric activity have been easily detectable by Alpha Centauri? There are almost two hundred million people in that system now, and they're so close to Luhman 16."

At a modest 6.5 light-years away from Earth, the binary dwarf stars did not seem like the most logical resource to supply an attack—but then again, the logical resources had all been taken by humans already.

"Do you recall how the Luhman 16 colonies failed?" Commander Exeunt questions him.

"Oh yeah, the influenza virus mutated like crazy out there," Konran says. "Nobody went back after the rescue parties succumbed, too."

"And the carizans have a knack for sneaking into places unnoticed—like a bunch of cockroaches," Commander Revenshal adds with disgust. Konran recognizes the statement as a derogatory reference to the *carinalin-feroxilanodite-tozanase* super enzyme critical to the Nolvarics' ability to bio-assimilate circuitry into their nervous systems, as well as a reference to the ubiquitous insect of order Blattodea, which had thoroughly carved its own niche within the inhabited galaxy.

"No matter how they did it," Granicks continues, "the Nolvarics are here and there are a lot of them. And it's our job to stop them." He turns back to the map.

"Our position," he indicates the *Nova Scotia*'s diamond-shaped marker, "has seen intense enough Nolvaric activity that Task Force Command has not deemed it safe for us to transport your VIPs back to the inner solar system."

"And Nolvarics are masters of the ambush, as evidenced by the current mess, so it's not safe to simply cruise out of the Kuiper Belt to the warp margin and warp out of here," Konran observes.

"Sharp kid," Revenshal remarks, cocking his head. "Can I take him on the *Gamma*?"

"Nice try," Granicks replies. "And yes, Konran, exactly right. Our progress has been slow of necessity, involving scanning possible hiding locations via drone and cleaning up whatever we can."

"Kind of like poking around the beehive until you get the bee," Revenshal cracks.

"Kind of like that," Granicks grunts. "Now, less than an hour ago our probes sparked an extensive series of Nolvaric detections throughout the sector. Although specific targets have yet to be identified, we have strong reason to believe a coordinated attack is being mounted against the *Nova Scotia*."

The dais-map zooms in until Konran can make out a series of USFN warships, eight in total, comprising the task force of which the *Nova Scotia* was a part. Although separated from one another by more than twenty million kilometers, the vastness of space causes the ships to appear close together on the dais-map. Red probability clouds swirl between the USFN formation, marking the estimated location and strength of Nolvaric forces in the region. The red clouds cut a swath between the *Nova Scotia* and the rest of the task force, effectively cutting them off from their nearest allies. "This all happened within the past hour," Granicks says. "As you can see, this rapidly emerging Nolvaric force has separated us from our task force."

"Masters of the ambush, all right," Konran reprises his previous comment as a knot forms in his throat. "Sparks, that looks like a lot of Nolvarics. So what are we going to do?"

As a Riot-class warship, the *Nova Scotia* was more than capable of self-defense. Armed to the teeth with plasma cannons, rail guns, warp-capable cruise missiles, and an array of starfighter craft, each Riot-class warship could self-partition into three separate, autonomous warships, transforming into a mini armada of its own. This consisted of two larger, heavy-hitting sub-ships known as the *Alpha* and *Beta* (each with a complement of ten starfighters and support craft) and a smaller, faster, quick-strike sub-ship known as the *Gamma*. Staring at the ever-growing Nolvaric probability clouds on the dais-map, Konran is grateful to be aboard a Riot-class warship today.

"You'll be assisting me on the bridge of the *Alpha*, Konran, while Commander Exeunt will take the *Beta* and Revenshal the *Gamma*."

"I still think he would like the *Gamma* best," Revenshal insists. "Small, fast, and deadly is his style."

"Nevertheless," Granicks replies, keying something into his forearm computer, "he's with me today. You'll still have him via holo-link."

"It's just not the same," Revenshal mutters wistfully as a door opens. A small man enters. His skin is brown, his forehead Andean, his cropped hair dark, and his age right around Konran's—if not a bit younger.

"Captain!" the man says enthusiastically.

"Konran, this is Chief Science Officer Salazar. He is going to get you plugged in while we finish up in here."

"Salazar Salazar at your service," Salazar states amiably, shaking Konran's hand. He couldn't be taller than Konran's shoulder.

"Salazar Salazar?" Konran asks.

"You can thank my parents later," he replies flatly, leading Konran from the room via the door he just entered. "Have you ever used a space-time emulator?"

"Sure," Konran says, "space-time fundamentals is core curriculum in pilot school." Besides gaining a better understanding of the weirdness that was space-time, Konran had never used anything more than the basics from the notoriously confusing class during his pilot career at ISSA.

"Good," Salazar says, "because here you go."

He leads Konran into a well-lit, semicircular room with data consoles along its edge and an arcing row of command chairs at its center. Naval officers turn to look at him as he takes it all in. Konran is on the bridge.

Salazar stops at the curved row of command chairs and motions for Konran to take a seat. He steps forward, swallowing the same emotion he felt last night when touching the Sparrowhawk.

"You want me to sit there?"

"Yeah, how else are you going to aid the captain?"

"Er... " Konran says, feeling as if he were being requested to take up residence in the Taj Mahal.

"Dude, it's just a space-time emulator," Salazar says, "and this seat is yours."

Konran obliges. His heart flipping like a pancake, he sits down in the *Nova Scotia*'s command deck, two seats to the left of the captain's chair. He gazes around the bridge, taking in the pods of data consoles flanking the perimeter of the room, set lower than the command deck. A hybridized, modern command center, the *Nova Scotia*'s bridge was a streamlined combination of the combat information centers and command bridges of the ancient, seafaring warships.

"So you're familiar with the way space-time can warp in unintuitive ways, depending on the gravity and velocity between points in space?" Salazar asks, sitting beside Konran.

"Right," Konran replies, "we run space-time corrections to adjust for time dilation every time we're in orbit around anything bigger than Enceladus, so our clocks run at the same rate as those in the control stations below. It helps synchronize our docking processes."

"Precisely." Salazar continues his explanation. "Under conventional propulsion, the *Nova Scotia* is fast enough to dilate time between ourselves and a stationary point in space at the rate of 1.9 percent. This means if we are two hours away from an allied base when the Nolvarics attack it, and we aren't in position to use our warp drive, from the base's perspective they will need to hold out for two hours, two minutes, and sixteen seconds before we arrive to support them."

Konran nods. "Makes sense. The solar standard speed limit for us civilians is 2.2 seconds of time dilation per hour."

"Yeah, I haven't obeyed that speed limit for twelve years," Salazar says. "The next thing you need to understand is that the *Nova Scotia* is equipped with powerful gravitational generators capable of warping the geometry of space-time around us. This is different than simply inducing synthetic gravity fields within the ship.

"Right," Konran says. "That's how you generate gravitational shielding for the ship."

"Precisely," Salazar agrees. "But, the external grav fields can be used for offensive capabilities beyond mere shields. And when we partition the *Nova Scotia* into the *Alpha*, *Beta*, and *Gamma* sub-ships, each section is equipped with its own gravitational generators. Just yesterday, Granicks and Exeunt used the grav fields to disable a Nolvaric destroyer without even touching it."

"Ah, they must have flanked it first, like in a Cianiza Cicatrice maneuver," Konran replies. "Did the *Gamma* finish them off from below?"

"Quarks, did you read the report?" Salazar asks, surprised at Konran's response.

"No," Konran laughs. "I just recognized it from a level on *NolvaRetaliation 2164*. Most of the later levels couldn't be beaten without compensating for Nolvaric gravity traps. I may have played the simulator too much as a kid." *And through college, and sometimes still in my spare time,* he adds mentally.

"No way!" Salazar replies. "I love that game! Still play it to stay sharp. You know it's used with modifications for training purposes at the academy? There are some intense competitions around it."

"Really?" Konran says excitedly. "It was by far and away the most realistic starfighter simulation, but I didn't know the military used it. The way the arcades linked it to real starfighter simulators made it incredible. I'd save up credits for two weeks as a kid and then go beat the whole game."

"That settles it," Salazar declares. "We're playing when this is done. I have to see if I can beat you."

Someone clears their throat emphatically, and Konran and Salazar look up to see the entire bridge of officers staring at them.

"Right, it's wartime," Salazar says, and the *Nova Scotia*'s chief science officer resumes explaining the space-time emulator.

"So, in its most basic formulation, space-time is composed of three spatial dimensions and one time dimension for a total of four dimensions. Although there are twelve classical dimensions, the four primary dimensions are the only ones we really care about during macro-scale space combat."

"Up/down is left/right is forward/backward," Konran repeats an adage ingrained into him by his first starfighting instructor—meaning that in gravity-less space all three spatial dimensions are equivalent.

"And time is always on your side," Konran finishes the quote, repeating the line in unison with Salazar.

"OK, what's your connection to Andu Crajvic?" Salazar asks. "Nobody quotes that unless they're connected to him somehow."

Konran is impressed. "My flight demonstration coach flew with Andu before getting injured and taking up teaching. She repeated that all the time."

"Name?" Salazar asks.

"Zulim Daio."

"No way, ha!" Salazar exclaims. "She graduated the academy a year before me. She was one of the best pilots in her class."

Konran pauses, considering Salazar. Zulim would have graduated over a decade ago, before Konran had even entered high school. Either Salazar was older than he looked, or the small Andean man had graduated the academy at age thirteen.

Salazar pauses, too, considering the eyeballs staring at him from around the bridge. "Sorry, guys," he says unapologetically. "He just knows my old friend."

Business as usual returns to the bridge, and Salazar resumes the lesson.

"All right, it looks like you've got the basics. Space and time interrelate with each other and stretch and bend as influenced by changes in gravity and velocity, blah, blah, blah. Let's fire her up."

Salazar enters a command via forearm computer, and Konran is engulfed in a holographic sphere of light. It's space: the space around the *Nova Scotia*, to be precise. Salazar zooms and rotates the space-time emulator about Konran, explaining how to orient oneself within the emulated space. Konran watches with wide eyes, soaking in Salazar's instructions. The space-time emulators at spaceflight school were like toys compared to this one, and Konran feels like he just stepped foot in Disneyland (which also had better emulators than his flight school).

The scientist shows him how to manage the various layers of the system, peeling back and displaying pertinent information for the objects around him, such as mass, heading, composition, kinetic and potential energy, centroids and moments of inertia, shield strength, distance to target, time to target intercept, optimal route to target, time to weapons range, optimal firing solution, suggested attack patterns, suggested defense patterns, levels of hostility, survivability, and otherwise pretty much anything he wants or needs to know.

Next, Salazar demonstrates how the system can display geodesics, or the space-time version of lines on a topography map. Konran zooms in to see the small warping effect that nearby Kuiper Belt objects (including Y25LM90) have on space-time. The space rocks bend the geodesic lines like the depressions made by marbles spread across a soft mattress.

Suddenly curious, Konran tracks the space-time emulator to the nearest known Nolvaric position. It takes him a moment, but he finally locates seven narrow, chevron-shaped objects, each with the same heading and velocity. The space-time emulator immediately marks them with red blips, indicating their status as hostile vessels. Less than eight million kilometers from the *Nova Scotia*, seven Nolvaric Rezakars dimple Konran's space-time emulator.

The geodesic lines pop and sway around the Nolvarics, distorted by the midsize warships' energy and gravitational shields. Konran thinks he recognizes the wide, M-shaped formation of Rezakars, but before he can place it, Salazar interrupts him.

"No, do it this way," Salazar explains, zooming Konran's space-time emulator away from the Nolvarics and showing how to make it auto-track the enemy.

As the seven Rezakars zoom into view, Konran finally discerns their formation.

"They're using wolf formation," he says, feeling adrenaline displace the blood in his veins. "Which means they expect to engage on only one front."

He zooms out farther, exploring the space-time vicinity of the *Nova Scotia*'s task force. "Yep, they've got the *Jakarta*, the *Okhotsk*, the *Gaza*, and the *Lagos* cut off here," he says, referring to the three Riot-class battle cruisers and one Crusher-class battleship in the task force. "And here they have us cut off from the *Havana*, the *St. John*, and the *Wichita*," he adds, locating the three Havoc-class destroyers rounding out the task force.

"I bet this area is salted with mines." He indicates a patch of space-time in between the *Nova Scotia* and the Crusher-class *Lagos*. "And they've probably set up an ambush here." He points behind the *Nova Scotia*. Konran zooms in to examine the space dividing the *Nova Scotia* from its three Riot-class sisters.

"Sparks," he exhales. "Those are Nolvaric Nicransins. How did they sneak three heavy warships into the Kuiper Belt—let alone into the middle of the task force? No wonder the seven Rezakars went with wolf formation."

Konran gyrates the contents of his space-time emulator, the geodesic lines flipping and tumbling holographically about him as he considers the impending battle from every angle.

"Captain on the deck," a voice calls out, and Konran startles as a hand rests on his shoulder. He looks up to see Captain Granicks there.

"Good observations," Granicks says. "And completely correct. Do you recognize the overall pattern?"

Konran turns back to the formation, considering its nuances and cross-checking them against memorized lists of Nolvaric tactics.

"Oh... " He finally breathes, the air catching in his trachea as blood drains from his face. "It's the Vaanderbak Scythe—from when the Nolvarics took out Admiral Vaanderbak during the Battle of Procyon in 2165. And we're Vaanderbak this time."

Granicks's hand squeezes around Konran's shoulder, and the captain takes his place in the command deck, two seats to Konran's right.

"You could just do this," Salazar says, leaning over and entering a command into Konran's emulator. The words, *Vaanderbak Scythe, 87 percent match,* display near the Nolvaric formation.

"Lieutenant Vilkoj," Captain Granicks states, addressing the officer of the deck. "I have the conn."

"You have the conn, sir," Vilkoj replies, nodding sharply from a command pod near the front of the room.

"Thank you, Lieutenant," Granicks answers. "All right, people: status report."

"Twelve point four eight meglicks to target," an officer calls out, using the naval contraction "meglick" for "mega-click," or one million kilometers. The Nolvarics were 12.48 million kilometers from the *Nova Scotia.* At warship speed, the enormous distance wasn't really that big.

The reports continue.

"Time to target is 1.7 hours at present relative velocity. Flank speed time to target is fifteen minutes, including acceleration and deceleration phases."

"Tesseracts within range in minus one meglick. Point defense systems initiated. Countermeasures initiated. Gravity shield wells nominal. Partico-energy shields nominal. Weapons nominal."

Konran doesn't geek out at the reference to the tesseract—the USFN's ultra-sophisticated, extra-dimensional, relativistic cruise missile. He doesn't break into a boyish grin as Commander Ace Martin's voice reports "status ready" for the four starfighter bays. He doesn't do mental cartwheels when Commander Exeunt and Commander Revenshal holographically appear next to him within the command deck, their holograms projected to the *Alpha* from command decks within the *Beta* and *Gamma* subsections of the *Nova Scotia.* He doesn't revel as Captain Granicks interacts with the bridge officers, confirming details of their situational readiness.

He just stares into his space-time emulator.

"Excellent," Captain Granicks says at the conclusion of the bridge reports. "Commanders Exeunt and Revenshal, please report."

"*Beta* status green, Captain. Flight Deck 2 ready for combat, Flight Deck 1 reporting standby," Commander Exeunt reports in her sharp, alien accent.

"*Gamma* status green, Captain, and trigger fingers itching," Revenshal says with a jaguar's grin. "Let's rock 'em."

"Excellent," Granicks repeats, "and agreed."

"All right, folks," he says, addressing the bridge, "as you know, we've got a situation here. Less than two hours ago, probes sparked a series of widespread Nolvaric detections within our sector, resulting in positive identification of seven Rezakars on an intercept course with the *Nova Scotia*. Konran here correctly identified this situation as a coordinated Vaanderbak Scythe with us as the focal point."

The bridge is silent, all eyes on the captain.

"This amounts to three facts," Captain Granicks states, raising a finger. "First, we can expect no aid for the duration of our conflict with the Rezakars. We do not need it."

Granicks raises a second finger. "Second, this level of Nolvaric coordination is beyond anything they have mounted so far. When Konran spooked their hive five days ago, Nolvaric forces across the Kuiper Belt broke rank in frenzied, individual, uncoordinated attacks. The forces we face today are operating in crisp military harmony with their peers. We can expect them to be superior to those we have faced so far in nearly every way. This does not matter. We will out-execute them, we will outperform them, and we will defeat them."

Captain Granicks raises a third finger. "Third, upon review of this coordinated campaign of isolation against the *Nova Scotia*, Task Force Command agrees that the offensive only makes sense in one light: these cyborgs know who Konran Andacellos is, what he's done, and where he is, and they are coming for him themselves.

"Let me be clear: they cannot have him."

CHAPTER 5

Coldness; ice trickles down Konran's spine, percolating throughout his body at branches in his nervous system.

Me?

The weight of fear begins to crush upon him.

The Nolvarics are coming for me?

The seven red Nolvaric blips in his space-time emulator seem so close, their approach an implacable countdown. The need to flee grips like an icy hand around his neck, but he cannot move, let alone breathe, the ice preventing him. All he can think about is that day, five days ago, when the *Relrick* was obliterated forever along with its captain, crew, and cargo of eighty VIPs.

They want me?

The bile in his throat. The terror in his spine. The soft pressure of the GR-29's trigger beneath his right index finger. They all seem so long ago, yet so fresh. Konran pulls the trigger in his mind's eye, blasting each of the three Askeras from space once again.

They want revenge.

There hadn't been time to think five days ago at war site Y25LM90, only time to react. Somehow he'd won. Somehow, through raw desperation, he'd lived to see another day. But his lot had been drawn on that forsaken space rock, and his audacity to defy the call could only delay the grim inevitability.

They won't stop.

He struggles to breathe. His body tingles with the need to run. And then he feels foolish. Run? Where could he even go? It's not like the Nolvarics would forgive or forget his part in their growing disaster of an invasion.

Ridiculous. Pathetic. Foolish—

Ridiculous for his tiny, insignificant efforts to save the *Relrick* and *Viona Grande*; pathetic for his desires to be a starfighter; foolish for even trying, for swimming so long, so hard, so pointlessly against the ever-churning current. There wasn't anywhere to run. There never had been.

Did I ever do anything that really matters?

The enemy craft are mere minutes from missile range now. Konran stares at their red, chevron-shaped blips in his emulator, feeling the dread of ending too soon, too young, before ever becoming anything truly important, his one spark extinguishing just as it finally managed to burst into heat—a futile flame against the frigid, heartless wind. It feels strangely calm, the iceberg within his heart.

"You won round one, son," Captain Granicks states, "against ten-thousand-to-one odds."

Konran looks up, blinking. He'd only been in thought for a few seconds, but it felt like six hours had just passed.

"They can't take you," Granicks says, the lines around his face hardening. "Not those seven ships; not a hundred more lurking out in the blackness. No one can without your permission."

The eyes of the command bridge are focused on Konran. Men and women of all races stand around the oval room, backlit in their smart, gray uniforms by the comfortable glow of weapons, sensors, navigation, operations, and propulsion control displays. Konran looks back at them, his eyes flitting from one officer to the next, taking them each in. The holograms of Commanders Exeunt and Revenshal sit next to him in the command deck, she piercing and confident, he resolute and eager.

Ten-thousand-to-one odds.

Captain Granicks's words echo between Konran's ears, and he realizes the ice within has halted, obstructed by something fresh yet familiar. Instinctually he knows it.

No one can take me.

He knows the feeling from the mess hall, from Kyalia and Cazmira and every conversation since he awoke from unconsciousness. He knows it from the moment the *Viona Grande*'s magnetic lock released, from the moment he first pulled the wobbly gun-craft's trigger. He knows it from more than a decade of bulldogged, shove-the-odds-you-know-where-because-I'm-doing-this determination that someday, somehow, somewhere he would become a starfighter. Hope—the nagging kind that

91

doesn't ever quite go out: the brick wall existing for the sheer sake of existing.

Fear fills with courage as ice turns to steel, changing nothing and everything at the same time. And suddenly the red Nolvaric blips look a lot like ants.

"They've got us cornered, sir," Konran says, looking up at the captain. "As I see it, those Rezakars just cut off their only chance for escape."

"Indeed, they did," Captain Granicks agrees with satisfaction.

"Let's hit 'em where it hurts, boys!" Commander Revenshal's hologram yells, and the *Alpha*'s command bridge bellows in reply.

Commander Exeunt's hologram doesn't yell, but she briefly catches Konran's eye. Something about it sends a visceral thrill surging inside him—the certainty of the seasoned huntress behind her gaze foretelling the Nolvarics' impending demise more clearly than all the shouting on the *Nova Scotia* ever could.

Konran settles into his emulator like a second baseman preparing for the first pitch of the championship baseball game. His breath is smooth and controlled, his muscles relaxed yet ready, his mind focused, his eyes keen and watching.

"Initiate *Gamma* partition!" Captain Granicks orders, and the bridge jumps to action, preparing to launch the sub-ship from the rest of the *Nova Scotia*.

"*Gamma* atmospheric isolation confirmed," Lieutenant Vilkoj calls out.

"You'll want to watch this," Salazar says, and a new holo-screen pops to life in Konran's space-time emulator. The holo-screen fills with a video feed from the *Nova Scotia*'s hull, where the warship's armored surface glistens like soft fire beneath rays of distant sunlight. Pre-partition diagnostics display on the screen, indicating how close the *Gamma* is to separating from the *Nova Scotia*. Little status bars press their way from yellow into green.

"*Gamma* gravitational isolation confirmed," Lieutenant Vilkoj suddenly calls out, to which Commander Revenshal's hologram barks back, "*Gamma* green for partition!"

"Partition!" Captain Granicks orders.

"*Gamma* partition a go!" Vilkoj declares, and Salazar leans toward Konran.

"Check this!" he enthuses.

An audible roar rumbles through the bridge, and Konran's holo-feed shows the tip of the *Nova Scotia*, the *Gamma*, break away and blast off into space. At ninety meters in length and sixty meters in diameter, the *Gamma* is shaped like a sleek, stretched ellipsoid. The *Gamma's* shape cuts off at its backside, where it melds into three powerful rocket engines. Bulges run along the *Gamma's* length from tip to tail, housing sensitive sensor, jamming, communication, and countermeasures equipment—not to mention a substantial array of plasma and rail gun cannons. Known as a cutter rather than a cruiser, the *Gamma* packed a hefty punch while optimizing speed over size.

Accelerating faster than its size should allow, in less than a moment the *Gamma* disappears from Konran's holo-feed, trackable only as a small blue blip blinking within his emulator: space-time's version of the cavalry charge.

"Starfighter bays, report cold-launch status," Granicks requests.

"Packed tight and green to go," Wildlynx Commander Ace Martin's voice buzzes into Konran's emulator.

Salazar tosses a new holo-feed into Konran's emulator. The feed is split into four quadrants, each showing one of the *Nova Scotia's* four hangar bays. Sparrowhawk starfighters line the launch zone in front of the bay doors, sitting on the cusp of outer space.

"Excellent," Captain Granicks says. "Bay 1: cold-launch three Sparrowhawks on *Gamma*-support trajectory. Bays 3 and 4, cold-launch forward attack groups: four Sparrowhawks and one Longbow each on target ACOM. Bay 3: plus sixty. Bay 4: minus sixty. Bay 2: follow Bays 1, 3, and 4 with full rear guard cold-launch. Launch when ready."

"What?" Konran whisper-asks Salazar.

"We're cold-launching the Sparrowhawks with the Longbow missile frigates," Salazar explains. "It means we're using magnetic launch systems to throw them out there on designated trajectories, without them using active thrusters—it makes them almost impossible to detect. They already have stealth skins activated. Both the Sparrowhawks and Longbows can ooze the stealth skins out of pores within their nano-composite outer skin when they need to become undetectable. They'll be virtually invisible, but when things get hot, they'll have to pull them back in. Stealth skins tend to fall apart during combat."

"I know what cold-launches and stealth skins are," Konran says, keeping an eye on his holo-displays. "What about that other stuff?"

"Ah, that," Salazar says hurriedly. "Granicks ordered Hangar Bay 1 to cold-launch three Sparrowhawks to directly support the *Gamma*. That bay will have two Sparrowhawks left in reserve, in case we need them. Hangar Bay 2 is cold-launching a rear guard, which means sending all five of its Sparrowhawks, its two Longbow missile frigates, and its AURA-3100X reconnaissance craft. They'll be floating in space behind us in case any Nolvarics sneak up that way. Bays 3 and 4 are cold-launching forward attack groups with four Sparrowhawks and one Longbow each. We're launching them on the Nolvarics' ACOM, with Bay 3 launching sixty degrees above ACOM and Bay 4 launching sixty degrees below ACOM. It will put them in a flanking position."

"Bay 1, launch!" Lieutenant Vilkoj calls, and Konran's holo-feed shows three stealth-shrouded Sparrowhawks hurling out into the blackness. Konran tries to track them on his holo-feed from the *Nova Scotia*'s hull, but they're already gone from view.

"Yeah, but what's ACOM?" Konran asks. "I've never used that term."

"Anticipated center of mass," Salazar hisses impatiently.

Konran's holo-feed shows the *Nova Scotia* rotating in space—which he discerns by the motion of the stars behind the ship's hull. He can't feel a thing from the bridge.

"Bays 3 and 4, launch forward attack groups!" Vilkoj calls, and four stealth-shrouded Sparrowhawks and one stealth-shrouded Longbow immediately evacuate Hangar Bay 3. Hangar Bay 4 hangs on for a moment as the *Nova Scotia* rotates farther, and then its complement to Bay 3's forward attack group launches into space. Like Bay 1, as soon as they launch, they're gone.

"Bay 2, cold-launch rear guard," Vilkoj calls, and Bay 2 evacuates everything: all five Sparrowhawks, two Longbow missile frigates, as well as its ever-mysterious AURA-3100x intelligence craft.

"I'm still not sure what ACOM means," Konran whispers, trying to keep up with the progression of the battle.

"Here," Salazar says, and a blip pops into existence in Konran's space-time emulator. It floats in between the seven Rezakars at the center of their formation.

"That's the Nolvarics' center of mass, or 'COM.' It's the geometric center of their formation."

"OK," Konran says as things start to make sense.

"This," Salazar continues, adding another blip to Konran's space-time emulator, "is the Nolvarics' anticipated center of mass, or ACOM." The blip floats in space in front of the Nolvaric formation. Konran can see it moving as the Nolvarics move, tracking the point in space where the Nolvarics are heading.

"The Nolvarics' ACOM is where we predict their formation to be in the future," Salazar explains. "Watch this." He activates a "friendly trajectories" layer within Konran's emulator, and lines appear tracking the progress of the cold-launched fighter groups.

Konran follows the lines tracking the two forward attack groups with his eyes. They diverge in triangular fashion: one line on an angle above the Nolvarics' ACOM, the other below ACOM. Together, they create a neat dual-flanking maneuver.

"OK, got it," he says. "It's like what the simulators referred to as predicted trajectories—except they always showed probabilities instead of one targeted ACOM."

"Yeah," Salazar whispers, "they've gotten better at this since the days of the Invasion."

"*Alpha-Beta* dead ACOM," Captain Granicks orders. "Give me a convergence rate of 0.33 hours."

"Dead ACOM means," Salazar adds hurriedly, "that we're charting a dead-intercept course with the Nolvarics' anticipated trajectory."

"Got it. Thanks, man," Konran repeats, returning his attention to the battle.

The forward attack groups progress across his emulator toward the enemy, diverging along their triangular lines and spreading out toward the Nolvaric position.

The Wildlynx are out there now, Konran thinks, suddenly wishing the patch on his shoulder allowed him to be out there with them. But, he couldn't complain; being here as captain's aide was still incredible.

"Hostile weapons launch detected," an officer calls out. "Three fishbones from each of the seven Rezakars. All on *Nova Scotia* intercept trajectory. Point eight minutes to impact."

Konran's heart jumps and his muscles coil at the announcement. Nothing said "Nolvaric attack" better than "fishbones incoming." The infamous missile was the bread and butter of Nolvaric space warfare—and for good reason.

War footage replays through Konran's mind: dozens of fishbone missiles fragmenting into a thousand shards and tearing the hulls from USFN ships, installations, and anything in their way. Once fragmented, fishbone shards became individual mini missiles of their own. From gamma-ray pulses to concussive blasts to chemical or electrical attacks to swarms of nanobots to thermonuclear capabilities, there was a bit of everything packed into each fishbone.

The tiny, red fishbone blips swim across Konran's emulator like a school of piranha. Not a single fishbone targets the *Gamma*, however. The Nolvarics want the biggest fish first.

Just like on Y25LM90—except this time I'm the biggest fish.

"Seven sets of three," Salazar mutters bemusedly into his space-time emulator. "Nolvarics and their precious prime numbers."

"Fishbones locked," Commander Revenshal's hologram says calmly, and a status alert appears in Konran's emulator.

Konran maximizes it with a gesture, revealing a holo-feed from the *Gamma*'s hull. Revenshal gives Konran a smug look, and the holo-feed overlays with targeting information. Twenty-one small, red, circular indicators move across the screen, marking the incoming missiles.

"Take them out," Revenshal commands.

Crisp, orange flashes burst from photo-plasmic cannons along the *Gamma*'s hull. One, then two, then fifteen tiny fireworks explode against the backdrop of outer space as the guns strike true.

"I give you six evasives," Revenshal states, glancing at Granicks and Exeunt and extending his hand. Six fishbones dodge chaotically in Konran's emulator, plunging ever closer to the *Nova Scotia*.

"Gunners, finish the job," Captain Granicks orders.

Reengaging the holo-feed from which he witnessed the *Gamma* rocket away into space, Konran watches now as the Riot-class cruiser's guns burst to life with flashes of orange, sizzling plasma. Two more tiny fireworks burst against the backdrop of space as two more fishbones go down.

"Remaining fishbones have auto-detonated," an officer calls out. "The resulting splinter cloud has a radius of 8.4 millicks, traveling our way at 180 kilometers per second. Sparrowhawk attack groups will not be affected."

Similar to the term "meglick," which indicated one million kilometers, the term "millick," or one thousand clicks, was USFN jargon for one thousand kilometers. Konran considers the implications. While the initial Nolvaric attack had been easily defeated, the Rezakars still managed to seed a sizeable region of space with deadly fishbone splinters. Depending on what came next, the intelligent fragments and their myriad of randomly configured detonation methods could quickly become more than a nuisance. But that isn't what bothers him.

Why didn't the missiles warp-jump? They hadn't reached warp-to-target range, but they could have at least dodged Revenshal's attack better.

"Salazar," Konran says with some anxiety. "Why didn't any of the fishbones warp-jump? It doesn't make any sense."

"The *Gamma* didn't let them," Salazar says hastily, some sort of calculation absorbing his focus.

Before the scientist can explain further, a schematic appears in Konran's emulator depicting a pair of warp inhibitors installed in the nose of the *Gamma*. The schematic is labeled *SECRET*, causing Konran's eyes to bulge.

Just how much security clearance did Granicks's wartime authority give me? Konran wonders as Revenshal's hologram turns and winks at him.

Then something changes at the edge of his emulator. He looks, and three of the Rezakar blips break off from the main formation. While four of the seven Rezakars continue their original course toward the *Nova Scotia*, the other three angle toward the *Gamma* at flank speed.

"Here they come!" Revenshal states eagerly. "Let's reel 'em in."

The *Gamma* changes course as if fleeing from the Rezakars. Konran recognizes the maneuver as a variation of the classic Yang-Tian Noose, which had risen in tactical popularity toward the end of the Nolvaric Invasion. If played out per script, the *Gamma*, which was faster than its three pursuers, could double back through three-dimensional space and catch the other four Rezakars in a crossfire with the *Nova Scotia* before the pursuers caught up. When Konran had first learned of the maneuver at age thirteen, it had taken him a week of puzzled concentration before his mind had wrapped around the three-dimensional nuances involved.

But won't the Nolvarics just recognize the ploy? he wonders.

Sure enough, the three Rezakars spread out, cutting off the *Gamma*'s optimal route of retreat and reengagement. Konran studies the battle, his mind racing. The four other Rezakars were still over five meglicks away from the *Nova Scotia*, heading on a cautious yet direct intercept course. The *Gamma*, three meglicks from the *Nova Scotia* now, holds fast to its Yang-Tian Noose trajectory, ignoring the counter maneuvers of its three pursuers. If Revenshal didn't act soon, Konran feared the *Gamma*, which was severely overextending itself, would be in for the fight of its life.

"Hook, line, and sinker!" Revenshal's voice is ecstatic, sounding more like bait than prey.

"Excellent," Captain Granicks says. "Commander Exeunt, please send our welcoming gift."

"With pleasure," the tall woman's ebony-skinned hologram replies in her sharp, alien accent. "Tesseract cold-launch on *Gamma*-intercept trajectory, two per each Rezakar, warp on *Gamma* signal."

Konran watches intently, an understanding forming in his mind.

"Fire!" Commander Exeunt orders, and six tesseracts launch silently from cruise-missile tubes within the *Nova Scotia*. Visible briefly as blurs on Konran's holo-display, their blue blips converge rapidly on the *Gamma*. At just over a meglick, their engines

98

engage, and the missiles rocket even faster, arcing still toward the *Gamma* rather than the Nolvarics.

"Here come the fishbones," Revenshal reports, "and even some cattails with enough juice to get us." Konran recognizes the term "cattail" as the USFN designation for Nolvaric gravitational bombs. Typical cattail range was shorter than that of the long-range fishbones, and the weapons shouldn't have been in range of the *Gamma* yet.

An upgrade from usual Nolvaric specs, he observes.

Nolvaric fishbones and cattails zip like tiny, gnat-size blips within his space-time emulator. Konran receives a new holo-feed from the *Gamma*'s hull, and he watches as the cutter's guns pick off the incoming threats. Starbursts pop in response against the starry space.

Geodesic space-time topography lines twist and bend in Konran's emulator as gravitational bombs detonate, warping the fabric of space-time around the *Gamma*. Colloquially known as gravitational soup, the unfurling space-time distortions spread quickly across the *Gamma*'s anticipated trajectory, cutting off its Yang-Tian attack vector. Fishbone splinter clouds flow erratically throughout the gravitationally warped region, a favorite Nolvaric death trap.

Sudden patches of blue and green splash across Konran's *Gamma*-transmitted holo-feed. He peers at the ephemeral blotches, puzzled before realizing that the Rezakars had drawn within energy weapons range of the cutter. Their attack dissipates against the *Gamma*'s shields like an aurora borealis across Norwegian sky, to which the *Gamma*'s silent blasts of orange return fire provide an oddly harmonious juxtaposition of color.

Commander Exeunt's tesseracts are mere millicks from the *Gamma*, still arcing toward the USFN cutter. The three Rezakars are relentless, their barrage of fishbones and cattails turning space into a bowl of writhing spaghetti.

"Fire tesseracts!" Commander Revenshal's bellow startles Konran, and he looks up as the commander continues: "One per Rezakar, dead trajectories."

An instant later, $120 billion of science and technology launches from the *Gamma* and into space, streaking toward the three Nolvarics. Konran mentally counts down the approach:

Three, two, one ... warp!

Then $120 billion detonates in harmless fury, defeated by Nolvaric shields. Konran's zoomed-in emulator performs a remarkable simulation of the detonation unfurling in expensive, fiery ripples across space.

And then, without warning, one, then two of the Rezakars are annihilated, transitioning from solid machines of war into expanding clouds of dust as Commander Exeunt's tesseracts punch straight through their shields. Twin fireworks blossom blindingly on Konran's holo-display, the Rezakars' deaths like supernovas against the Milky Way.

The third Rezakar fairs better than its sisters, shuddering but not disintegrating beneath Exeunt's surprise attack. A fresh holo-display appears in Konran's emulator from the *Gamma*, this one with advanced, close-up imaging of the surviving Rezakar. Plumes of gas vent like geysers as fissures burst across its silvery hull. Diagnostic messages buzz across the holo-feed, assessing damage and indicating optimal locations for follow-up attacks.

Salazar leans toward Konran. "The Rezakars were blinded to Exeunt's tesseracts by the *Gamma*'s electronic warfare systems," he explains. "They never saw them coming. Revenshal's attack collapsed their shields to a definite quantum state, allowing Exeunt's tesseracts precise knowledge of that state and free passage through."

"Close and kill, boys!" Revenshal orders, more interested in the application than the theory of the physics at play. "Finish them before they stop the bleeding. Rail guns and plasma cannons!"

Given any respite, Nolvarics could return a damaged ship to fighting shape in shocking time, and the *Gamma*'s guns crackle with the fury of Zeus in response. Plasma hammers Nolvaric shields. Magnetically accelerated rail gun rounds slice through destabilized sectors, impacting in violent concussions upon the surface. The Rezakar rotates, exposing fresh hull to the *Gamma*'s punishment.

"Revenshal, get it done!" Salazar urges. "They've diverted on you!"

Konran activates his emulator's auto-zoom function and instantly sees the scientist's cause for alarm. Diverted from their attack run on the *Nova Scotia*, the remaining four Rezakars hurtle toward the *Gamma*. Konran studies their approach, searching for any advantage the cutter could exploit.

They're using a variation of claw formation, he understands, recognizing the Nolvaric ships' orientation in relation to the *Gamma*. Like vertices of a trapezoid angled in space, two forward Rezakars are trailed below and behind by two rearward ships. The lead craft fly closer to each other than their lagging companions.

"Starfighters incoming!" Konran states moments before the enemy fighter craft launch.

"Nolvaric starfighter launch confirmed!" a bridge officer replies, a tinge of surprise in her voice. "Thirteen per Rezakar: mixed Askeras and Miratans."

They usually only have seven starfighters, Konran recalls, mentally logging yet another upgrade to the Nolvaric forces.

The red starfighter specks swarm like angry bees in his emulator, racing from the four main-pack Rezakars to aid their wounded companion.

Come on, Gamma, *come on,* Konran urges, but the damaged Rezakar continues to do an impressive job of not dying. If the Nolvarics could save the ship, it could swing the tide of the rapidly unfolding battle.

"Fifteen more seconds, Commander," Captain Granicks says, "and then you get out of there."

The *Gamma*'s guns unleash with new urgency. Rounds punch through the Rezakar's shields. Meteoric fireballs explode on its surface. The knot in Konran's gut tightens as something feels amiss. Nolvaric armor gives way slowly—too slowly.

Why isn't it dead yet? he worries. And then his eyes widen in disbelief. *There was no other explanation.*

"Their armor!" Konran blurts. "I think it's adapting to the attack!"

"Schrödinger's cat, he's right," Salazar sputters. "Commander, cycle your firepower levels and frequency—see if you can throw them off."

"No, Revenshal, get out of there, now," Granicks orders. "Forward attack Longbows, dispose of that Rezakar. Sparrowhawks, provide escort and cover. *Beta* partition authorized: Commander Exeunt, give them some space."

"Aye, Captain," rings across the bridge as officers execute the orders.

The forward attack Sparrowhawks and Longbows retract their stealth skins, and fresh, friendly blue blips appear on either side of the Rezakar. Three more Sparrowhawks appear near the *Gamma*, close, but not entangled within the mess of grav soup.

The Longbows don't hesitate to contribute. Tiny blue blips burst like welding sparks from their positions: scores of artillery shells approaching the bleeding Rezakar on two angles. Space-time geodesics bulge like a balloon between fingers as the Nolvarics' shields compress beneath the onslaught. And then, beneath so much brimstone on judgment day, the Rezakar shreds into pieces of oblivion.

But the Nolvaric cruiser hadn't gone down without a fight.

"Target cattails!" Commander Revenshal shouts as tiny red blips billow like dandelion spores toward the *Gamma*.

"Set shields for dynamic shock attenuation!" he orders. "Full thruster reversal!"

That's so many cattails, Konran worries. *They should have already been depleted.*

As quickly as the cattails emerge, they detonate, and space-time twists like an eel against the fisherman's grasp. The *Gamma*'s guns attempt to stop the cattails, but their orange blasts careen at weird angles as their energy reflects against powerful, rapidly shifting gravitational gradients. Revenshal's hologram fuzzes.

"*Beta* partition a go!" Lieutenant Vilkoj calls out, and Konran pulls up his holo-feed from the *Nova Scotia*'s hull. A terrific rumble shakes the bridge, and the *Beta* partitions from the *Alpha* and blasts away into space. Commander Exeunt's hologram sits lithely in her command chair, her dark eyes flashing like a lioness after her prey.

"Kill main engines!" Commander Revenshal's voice is staticky, as is his hologram. "Maneuvering thrusters only. Optimize for rolling two-second, least-turbulence trajectory."

Constellations tumble within Konran's holo-displays as the soup tosses the *Gamma*. Then the backdrop of space flips, spins, and goes black as the holo-displays cut off altogether. Revenshal's hologram pops in and out of fuzzy existence. Rather than fear, however, Konran sees the cowboy holding to the bull in the commander's eyes.

"Permission to engage enemy starfighters directly," Commander Ace Martin's voice crackles in.

Less than a meglick away from the *Gamma*, two groups of four blue Sparrowhawk starfighters advance toward the oncoming Nolvaric threat. The Nolvaric starfighters are close, and Konran can feel the Wildlynx itching to engage.

"Not yet," Captain Granicks replies. "I need you with those Longbows."

"Copy that, Cap," Ace replies, and the Sparrowhawks fall back. In Konran's emulator a volley of Longbow welding sparks takes their place, dropping the Nolvaric starfighters from a population of fifty-two to forty-one.

Now distant from the *Alpha* but not yet arrived at the *Gamma*, Commander Exeunt's *Beta* dives toward the four main-pack Rezakars. Her guns blaze with ruthless precision, but the enemy craft absorb the punishment, intent on the *Gamma*.

Konran's heart pounds in his throat. His eyes flick this way and that. His mind studies his emulator, absorbing his holo-feeds and calculating at the pace of battle.

Longbow artillery shells defeat one wave of fishbones, and then a second, and then a third. But the fourth wave makes it past. In reply, the *Gamma*'s three defensive Sparrowhawks rapidly deplete their internal stores of twelve small yet potent missiles, destroying the fourth wave of fishbones. Konran exhales, eyes riveted to the struggling *Gamma*.

The *Beta* fires tesseracts of her own, three for each Rezakar. One punches through a Rezakar's shields. Wounded, the Nolvaric cruiser does not slow down.

They want the Gamma—bad, Konran thinks, holding his breath. Something about the way this is unfolding feels wrong to him.

"Longbows, get out of there," Captain Granicks orders. "Forward attack Sparrowhawks, provide cover. Revenshal, can you extract from the grav cloud yet?"

That's it! Konran realizes.

"The grav cloud!" he yells, nearly stammering the words for excitement. "It ... it's not diluting! It's lasting too long!"

"Kepler's beard, he's right!" Salazar exclaims. "The magnitude hasn't attenuated since the initial barrage, but the frequency is no longer cascading randomly."

"Revenshal," Granicks says, "get out of there now."

"On it."

The *Gamma*'s engines ignite, but like a Greyhound bus into sand dunes, the cutter stops with a brutal crash, not five waves into a sea of fifty. Revenshal's hologram disappears and reappears, fuzzy and scattered like the four-letter words the commander is hurling.

More fishbones and cattails spew from the Rezakars. The Longbows and Sparrowhawks reply, but their depleted ammunition stores aren't enough. The *Beta* fires, as does the *Alpha*, but the sheer magnitude of the Nolvaric attack makes the math easy to compute: *No matter what, the Gamma is going to get hit.*

Konran looks around the bridge, helpless. Everyone is busy: officers scramble at their consoles, Captain Granicks gives orders, Salazar works so fast it looks like he's dancing, Commander Exeunt presses the *Beta* ever closer.

Konran closes his eyes, visualizing the *Gamma*. He feels the gravitational waves tumbling over the cutter, perceives them punishing its every move. He becomes the wave, undulating, crashing, crest after trough after crest, pulsating like a heartbeat within deep space. And then Konran understands.

The grav waves are no longer self-generating. They're only self-perpetuating.

Konran clenches his jaw and fists, thinking hard. The solution dances across the tip of his brain.

The warp engines! he suddenly realizes. *They compress space-time! Could they drive the grav cloud?*

"Warp!" he yells, opening his eyes. "Revenshal! Warp! Use your warp engine to drive the grav waves—and then warp out of there!"

"Yes! Yes! Yes! Yes! Yes!" Salazar blurts with mad enthusiasm. "Perform a near-field warp through the nodal plane when you hit the first harmonic—the gravitational field will be zero there! Don't go far, just go far enough!"

"Do it, do it, do it, do it, do it!" Revenshal's urgent, staticky voice bellows to his unseen crew.

Konran watches, standing, staring, gripping the side of his space-time emulator. With synchronous, Euclidean harmony, the waves surrounding the *Gamma* dance together, driven by the cutter's warp engine.

And then the fishbones and cattails hit.

Dozens detonate within the gravitationally warped region ensconcing the *Gamma*. Space-time twists, buckles, and shears before exploding into unmitigated chaos. The *Gamma* is gone—any sign of the USFN cutter completely eviscerated.

And then Commander Revenshal lets out his biggest shout yet, shrieking with a tremendous, "Yee-ha, boys, that's how it's done!"

Konran's space-time emulator auto-adjusts to show the *Gamma* floating in free space beyond the Rezakars. Still in weapons range, the cutter fires a fusillade of its own.

The *Beta* has already reacted, adding more firepower to the barrage. Tesseracts streak toward the wounded of the pack, raining upon it like thunderclouds. In the time necessary for fifteen cruise missiles to converge, warp-jump, and penetrate the wounded Rezakar's shields, she, too, joins her fallen sisters in the dust of oblivion.

Three to go.

"Yeeaahh!" Konran yells, pumping his fist and jumping with relieved elation. The entire bridge is staring at him, but he doesn't care. Neither does Revenshal.

Sweaty and fierce-eyed, the commander's hologram steps to Konran. They lock eyes, and Revenshal's lips part into the snarl-smile of the still-standing gladiator.

"That's how we do it, son. Now let's finish these carizans."

Captain Granicks's orders come fast and hard, and the *Alpha*, *Beta*, and *Gamma* take to the work of ending the battle like a farmer to the shovel. Konran's heart still pounds, but his breathing slows and his body relaxes. He wipes his forehead, and his sleeve comes away soaked. He sits down, allowing his mind to reengage with the battle. There is still work to do, but the worst is past.

And then Salazar says, "Oh crap." And space-time explodes anew.

So many cattails, Konran realizes.

Mushrooming with raw energy, the space around the Rezakars looks like the Mariana Trench swallowed the Grand Canyon and threw up an earthquake. The monstrous gravitational distortion licks outward, driven by Rezakar warp engines. Grav waves reach like fingers toward the Wildlynx. Other waves swell around the Rezakars themselves, a protective barrier about their position.

"I think Konran just developed a new form of space warfare," Salazar adds.

CHAPTER 6

"Longbows taking fire!" an officer shouts. "Longbow 1 down! Longbow 2 down!"

"Ace, sitrep," Granicks orders with some urgency. Konran recognizes the abbreviation "sitrep" to mean "situation report."

"Actively engaging enemy starfighters," Commander Ace Martin's voice crackles in. "Longbows both went down, but we confirmed escape pod release on both ships. Grav soup is getting nasty out here. It's like they can manipulate it so only we get hit."

"They can," Granicks confirms. "Transition to close-range engagement with the Nolvaric fighters. The Rezakars are keeping the soup away from them—should give you some breathing room."

"Got it, Cap."

"Exeunt and Revenshal, status," Granicks orders.

"*Beta* systems nominal," Commander Exeunt's hologram replies in her alien accent.

"*Gamma* energy cannons at 60 percent due to surface damage," Revenshal says. "Countermeasures systems substantially damaged. Warp inhibitors down, but engineering thinks we can get them back up. Shields at 53 percent."

"All right," Granicks continues, "*Alpha*: give me staggered double-tesseract salvos every fifteen seconds. Set for space-time disturbance along the Rezakar-Wildlynx vector. We need to break up their soup. *Beta*: punish the Rezakars. *Gamma*: stand off until warp inhibitors come online. Save your ammo."

Gravitational soup reaches in all directions in Konran's emulator, pulsating with the irregular, tempestuous rhythms only Nolvarics can understand.

Wildlynx blips zip across his emulator, dodging gravitational tendrils and engaging waves of mixed Askera and Miratan starfighters. Konran can almost see the blitzkrieg-quick Askeras and their crablike, beaklike forms glinting in and out of distant sunlight. He can almost feel the sheer strength of the larger, sharklike Miratans and their array of plasma cannons—cannons of the variety that destroyed the *Borboleta*.

He can sense Sparrowhawks carving elegant, evasive arcs through space: can perceive targeting systems locking onto targets, can feel the pressure of the trigger, can discern the weight of inertia as maneuvering thrusters ignite in orchestral bursts of synchronicity with powerful aft engines. He detects the advantage afforded by the galaxy's supreme starfighter—the edge which kept the outnumbered Sparrowhawks one step ahead, always ready to pounce.

So why did it all feel so wrong?

Sparrowhawks strike and Nolvaric numbers dwindle from forty-one to thirty-eight. Sparrowhawks evade, and aspirant Nolvaric hunters find themselves as prey.

So what is it? Konran demands, but his faculties refuse to relinquish the subconscious solution.

He changes position, shifting from a sit to a crouch within the emulator. He turns himself about, ducking, raising up, craning, squinting, examining the battle like a chimpanzee examining a melon-size ruby. His breaths quicken, but while he notices everything else, he doesn't notice that.

The Rezakar grav cloud has become an entity unto itself. The *Beta* drives forward regardless, entering the fringes and fighting back with warp engines of her own. The Rezakars respond with an outpouring of turbulent grav waves. Shaking and rocking in the onslaught, Commander Exeunt holds fast to the attack, trusting in Revenshal's engineers to bring the *Gamma*'s warp inhibitors back online. Tesseract blips emanate from her location. The missiles circulate through the grav soup, seeking routes to the Nolvarics.

Alpha-launched tesseracts invade the grav cloud around the Wildlynx. The multidimensional cruise missiles detonate with furious gravitational distortions of their own, which open bubbling voids in the Rezakar's soup. While the *Alpha*'s attack waxes, its effectiveness wanes, and Rezakar-driven grav waves slosh into the voids, filling them as fast as they form. Shortly, the Sparrowhawks find themselves cut off from the rest of the force, fighting for their lives within the roiling, anarchic soup.

"How's it coming, Revenshal?" Granicks asks the commander, whose hologram has disappeared from his command chair. "We need that warp inhibitor up now!"

"We almost had it," Revenshal's strained voice crackles in, "but the leptonic modulator crapped out, and we had to jettison it before it bathed us in radiation." He grunts as if lifting something heavy and then says to someone unseen, "Go for it, Sanikan, I've got this. No, Mogric said to do the other one ... yes, I'm sure." Another moment of grunting, and Revenshal adds: "We're patching a workaround through the particle accelerator—almost got it ... I think."

"Make it happen, Revenshal" Granicks replies, looking at Commander Exeunt, who nods. "We'll buy you some time."

"We'll get it, Cap," Revenshal grunts again.

And then Konran sees it.

The Nolvaric starfighters—they're too fast, too nimble.

"Ace," he shouts. "Ace, can you hear me?"

"A little busy, man," the flight commander's voice crackles in. "What you got?"

"The Askeras and Miratans," Konran says, "some of them are too fast. They were hiding it before, but they're definitely upgraded from normal specs."

"So that's it!" Ace replies, his voice choppy. "I noticed something but couldn't pin it down."

"Stay sharp," Konran says. "It might not be the only upgrade."

"On it," Ace crackles back. "Can you ... comms ... other groups." His transmission breaks up.

"What was that?"

"Can you spread the word? Comms are shot. Can't reach the other groups."

"Will do," Konran affirms. And then he realizes he has no idea how to do that.

"Salazar," he asks, "I need to talk to the rest of..."

"Gotcha covered," the scientist replies, and a holo-display appears in Konran's emulator with a list of Wildlynx attack groups. The list reads:

FORWARD ATTACK GROUP I
FORWARD ATTACK GROUP II

GAMMA SUPPORT GROUP
REARGUARD

The four groups inhabit various places in Konran's emulator. Due to their original launch trajectories, Forward Attack Group I is on top of the battle with respect to the *Alpha*. Forward Attack Group II is below, but otherwise in line with Group I. The Gamma Support Group is farther away than Groups I and II, struggling against the same grav soup the *Gamma* itself had escaped. Finally, the Rearguard is drifting several meglicks behind the *Alpha*, still shrouded in stealth skins and patiently awaiting any attack from that direction.

With Ace's Forward Attack Group I already accounted for, Konran selects Forward Attack Group II from his display. Then he selects the name of its leader, a pilot with call sign Valkyrie.

"Valkyrie, this is Konran Andacellos," he says. "Do you read me?"

Static.

"Valkyrie, do you read me?"

"What, did you throw up again?" Valkyrie's voice crackles in, and Konran realizes he is speaking to V. Melendez—the same V. Melendez he had offended during his Wildlynx reception last night.

"Er, no, er ... It's the Nolvarics—they're upgraded from usual specs: some of them are faster than they should be. Just wanted to let you know."

"How much faster?" Valkyrie's voice is nearly all static.

"I'd say 10 to 20 percent," Konran answers. "Hard to say—they were hiding it until you guys closed on them."

"I can work with that."

"Do you need me to contact your group?" Konran asks.

"Repeat?" her voice crackles back.

"Do you need me to contact the rest of your group?"

"Negative, I'll spread the word."

"Great. And watch for more surprises."

"Roger."

Konran selects the Gamma Support Group and opens communication with their leader, call sign: Hot Sauce.

"Hot Sauce, do you read me?"

Static.

"Hot Sauce, do you read?"

More static.

Konran tries the other two pilots in the group but gets the same results. He tries Hot Sauce again, but he already sees the problem: the group is entirely embroiled in grav soup. There is no getting through to them.

"Salazar, I can't reach these guys," he says. "I have to reach them now or ... or else ..." Konran trails off, panic rising.

"They're too deep," Salazar states the obvious. "We'd have to dive in ourselves, or the *Beta* or *Gamma*."

"Helmsman, make maximum advisable speed for the Gamma Support Group," Captain Granicks orders. "Authorized to enter the grav cloud. Communications: get us in contact."

The *Alpha* dives toward the grav cloud. Gravitational tendrils wick toward the *Alpha* in response, uncurling like burgeoning thunderheads as the Rezakars react.

"Prepare warp engines for space-time manipulation," Granicks orders. "Configure for convex space-time compression at 5 percent capacity. Drive that grav cloud away from us. Commander Exeunt: bring the *Beta* and coordinate efforts."

The *Beta* changes course, skirting the outer layers of grav soup and making toward the *Alpha*. Space-time geodesics take shape in Konran's emulator as the two ships dive into the grav cloud together, their warp engines carving a pocket of smooth sailing around them. The effect is short lived.

Rezakar warp engines bend space-time in reply, and space-time geodesics convulse like pythons on the barbeque as grav waves hurtle back and forth between the USFN and Nolvaric ships. Then, overcome in a deluge at once, the *Alpha* shakes like a central-Californian earthquake.

"We can't out-math the Nolvarics!" Salazar shouts, his voice vibrating, hands working feverishly in his emulator.

"I know," Granicks replies, as if oblivious to the earthquake. "Do it anyway."

"Agh, er, yes, sir," Salazar gripes, bouncing in his chair next to Konran.

Abruptly, a staticky female voice crackles into Konran's emulator.

"Sauce ... urgent ... "

"It's Hot Sauce!" Konran exclaims, struggling to work his emulator while shaking within it. "I've got her!"

"Communications, strengthen that signal!" Granicks orders.

"Hot Sauce! Do you read me?" Konran asks again.

More static, and then, "Situation urgent! Stickman's down. Can't find Fideo. Nolvarics everywhere."

Konran has no idea what she's talking about until he notices the pilots' call signs on his holo-display. Hot Sauce, Fideo, and Stickman are the three pilots making up the Gamma Support Group.

One down, one missing? Konran's heart sickens at the thought. He searches his emulator for Fideo's Sparrowhawk. He finds it, separated from Hot Sauce by more than a millick, surrounded by fishbone splinters. Konran searches for something to do, some way to get the pilot out of there, and then the fishbones detonate.

"No," Konran breathes. "NO! No, no, no, no, no!" he shouts, ignoring the bridge officers looking at him over their shoulders, ignoring the still-shaking *Alpha*.

"Konran!" Granicks commands. "Do what you can with what you have."

Konran steels himself, Granicks's words reining in his failing composure. He sets his jaw, and his grief replaces with a simmering heat.

You cannot have her, he mentally vows to the red blips in his emulator.

"Hot Sauce, I need a holo-link to your cockpit."

Static. And then, "Here!" A holo-display appears with point-of-view footage from Hot Sauce's helmet. For a moment, Konran can see everything she sees, and then the link breaks and the holo fades.

"Get me closer, Granicks!" Konran demands. "I need that holo-link!"

"Do it!" Granicks orders. "Make it happen, people!"

The *Alpha* and *Beta* fight against the relentless Nolvaric gravitational assault. The *Alpha* shakes and officers shout and

Salazar scrambles in his emulator next to Konran, but the holo-link reestablishes, and for Konran everything else fades.

He buckles into his command chair, tugging the straps tight like a starfighter pilot. He maximizes Hot Sauce's holo-link and fills his emulator with her cockpit. He reads her targeting display, checks her shield capacity, and notes her weapons status in an instant. The view out her cockpit is overlaid with rippling space-time geodesic lines: Konran can feel her Sparrowhawk riding the gravitational topography.

She—now he—swerves wildly, dodging blasts from the five Askeras and three Miratans on her tail. A school of fishbone splinters swims nearby. Geodesic lines fluctuate unnaturally, and smaller, easier-to-move fishbone splinters swirl directly into Hot Sauce's path. She jukes upward, catching a fresh, un-splintered grav wave. The move loses ground on her pursuers, however, and enemy starfighters close in.

The situation is as hopeless as any before it.

Except Y25LM90.

"Too fast ... Can't shake them ... Hold on!" Hot Sauce's voice crackles in ragged bursts as her Sparrowhawk flees for all it is worth. Her guns fire deliriously, spraying out suppression fire at every angle.

"Hot Sauce!" Konran yells. "Cut through the grav field, don't surf it. Trust your Sparrowhawk!"

"I can't!" she replies, breathless. "Shrapnel density too high ... AAAGGH!"

A green plasma ball detonates nearby—fired from one of the Miratans, no doubt. The detonation crumples Hot Sauce's left wing, destroying its wingtip photo-plasmic cannon in the process.

Konran's blood runs cold at the impact, but even as Hot Sauce's point-of-view holo-feed spins, she groans and the Sparrowhawk rights itself.

She's alive!

In space with no aerodynamics to worry about, the robust Sparrowhawk could lose both wings and still fly, but the suddenly imbalanced mass and loss of thrusters makes the fight thirtyfold more difficult.

"Break now!" Konran shouts, leaning subconsciously to the right. "Into the gradient. Cut through the splinter cloud with your guns. Go, go, go!"

Hot Sauce breaks hard down and right, away from her pursuers and into the swirling, accelerating shrapnel cloud. She grunts like a tennis champion volleying for match point as her Sparrowhawk plunges deeper into the gravitational gradient. Her holo-feed jostles brutally beneath the ever-changing forces, and her guns, set to fire diffuse rather than focused plasmic bursts, blast a pseudo-path through the swirling shrapnel. The move causes the five Askeras to give up direct pursuit, their crablike, beaklike structures preferring to surf the gradient. The Miratans and their more powerful, sharklike hulls, however, plunge in after her.

"Watch the Miratans!" Konran yells.

Hot Sauce banks, emerging from the gradient and catching a new wave. The maneuver grants her speed, and she angles for a shot on the Miratans. Then her Sparrowhawk lurches like a sailboat encountering an oceanic geyser. The impact sends her hurtling against the gradient, and her Sparrowhawk tumbles through another wave.

The Miratans have gravitational bombs! Konran grasps, noting yet another heretofore unknown upgrade to the Nolvaric forces.

"Hot Sauce! The Miratans have grav bombs! Can you hear me? Cut the gradient again—get out of there!"

Hot Sauce responds admirably, cutting across the churning gravitational gradients and firing photo-plasmic blasts from her remaining cannons. Nolvaric fire splays angrily at her, but she evades, maneuvering her tattered Sparrowhawk like the starfighters from the Invasion vids. Her quick breathing comes audibly across the comm, but to Konran it may as well have been his own.

"Go head-on against the seven o'clock Miratan," Konran instructs. "Get in so close it can't use its grav bombs!"

Hot Sauce dives through a grav wave, catches the next, and uses its push to round on the Miratan. Her Sparrowhawk dodges like only a Sparrowhawk can, jumping left and right, up and down, slowing and speeding up as she closes for a head-on attack run.

Her guns fire, blasting from her nose and right wingtip. Orange plasma slices into the Miratan even as its own attack sails wide. Hot Sauce's guns rotate and track the sleek Nolvaric fighter as it flashes past, pounding it further.

"Stay close! Not too far!" Konran yells, and Hot Sauce corrects her arc, maintaining close to the Miratan. A gravitational bomb detonates where she would have been, further warping space-time in the vicinity. The awkward turn kills her momentum, and the discerning Miratan pilot angles immediately for the kill.

Before Konran can say anything, Hot Sauce inverts her weapons and thrusters—exactly like he wanted. She maneuvers deftly with her wingtip thruster and fires her megacannon. An orange column of photo-plasma erupts from what moments before had been her aft thruster, erasing the Miratan from space.

"*Incoming!*" Konran warns as two Miratans and five Askeras converge on her.

Flashes of blue photo-plasmic energy and green plasma balls fill Konran's emulator. Hot Sauce reverts her Sparrowhawk to its primary propulsion mode and jets away. Miratan grav bombs burst in her wake. The two sharklike pursuers come in fast on her flank. The five Askeras come in hard on her tail. Konran senses the distant Rezakars twisting the gravitational gradient to Nolvaric favor, glazing their passage and congealing Hot Sauce's to molasses. Facing such partisan odds, Konran sees a thousand ways to get her killed but no way to get her out.

Except ...

"Stealth skin now!" he yells, reaching for the controls himself.

Hot Sauce's hand almost touches his as she activates the stealth system.

"Go evasive," Konran directs, "and then straight into their middle. The stealth skin won't last long."

But Hot Sauce doesn't need it to. Like the champion trap shooter given seven targets at once, she dives her now-invisible Sparrowhawk up, around, and into the midst of the enemy. Her guns flash as her stealth skin disintegrates. A Miratan explodes. She inverts the Sparrowhawk and the ensuing mega blast of plasma destroys two Askeras at once. She doesn't wait, and a quick Sparrowhawk reversion and flick of the trigger takes out the last

Miratan and two more Askeras. She catches a grav wave even as the final two Askeras react to her attack, and, surfing it down and around, releases the final two missiles from her internal missile bay. Konran lets out a whoop of triumph, and the final two Askeras culminate in puffs of space smoke.

"Wooo! Yeaaahhh! Now that's what I call starfighting!"

The *Alpha* rocks, and Konran bounces in his command chair. He minimizes Hot Sauce's cockpit and his emulator returns to its normal mode. He can't make sense of what he sees, until the *Alpha* rocks again. And then he understands: the *Alpha* was embedded so deeply within the mass of churning gravitational soup that geodesic lines look more like children's scribbles than space-time topography. The ship's warp engines and gravitational shield generators strain mightily against the impending grav waves. Even as he watches, more waves strike, and the *Alpha* rocks again.

Nearby, the *Beta* experiences the same abuse. In a brief moment of triumph, the two ships' efforts synergize and the grav soup pushes backward, like an invisible force repelling the ocean at high tide. But the Nolvarics on the other side react just as quickly, and gravitationally warped space-time crashes with a vengeance upon the *Nova Scotian* sub-ships. And the *Alpha* trembles again.

Then Konran notices the enemy starfighters—twenty at least, swarming about the USFN position like flies to a hippopotamus. They waft within the grav soup, circulating easily upon its undulations: moving in for a strike, drawing back to safety, an uncanny coordination with the chaotic soup keeping them out of harm's way. And methodically they chip away at the *Alpha* and *Beta*.

Konran's attention broadens, taking in the bridge. Officers remain professional, but there is a tension that wasn't there before—like everyone knew they all were in real danger and everyone was making sure every action counted.

The *Gamma* doesn't even show on sensors anymore, nor do the Rezakars at the center of it all. Captain Granicks gives orders, coordinating efforts to counter the soup and curtail the starfighter attack. Commander Exeunt's *Beta* harmonizes with the *Alpha*, and the two ships hit back again and again, the dogged pugilist keeping the opponent at bay—if only barely.

"You can't out-math a Nolvaric. You can't out-math a Nolvaric," Salazar mutters over and over again in the command chair next to Konran, struggling to keep up with the scientific side of the cybernetically advanced cyborgs' attack.

The *Alpha* shakes again, and Konran nearly panics—

This is my fault; I got us into this; I demanded we dive into the grav soup; it's my fault we're all stuck here. How are we going to get out of this? What now, what next?

And then, as fear swells back up inside Konran's heart, Captain Granicks catches his eye. There is a grin hidden within the hard lines of his face, a twinkle next to the determination in his eyes, a certainty about his stance that says he, the captain, was right where he wanted to be. And then it dawns on Konran:

Granicks chose this so I could save Hot Sauce. He isn't just surviving this grav soup, he still thinks we can win.

"Commander Martin," Granicks orders, "combine the forward attack groups and go take out a Rezakar. Proceed gently, with stealth skins up. The *Alpha* and *Beta* will broadcast fishbone positions to you on a one-way channel."

"I knew you loved me," Ace crackles back. "Forward Attack Groups I and II, disengage starfighters," he orders. "Stealth skins up, we're going in—easy style; make those skins last."

In Konran's emulator the blue blips marking the forward attack group wink out as the two groups of Sparrowhawks (Group I above the *Alpha* and *Beta*, and Group II below) enrobe in stealth skins, leaving Nolvaric starfighters to play by themselves.

"Aide Andacellos." Granicks looks at him. "I have a pilot to collect. You are to coordinate elimination of all enemy starfighters within the vicinity."

"Yes, sir," Konran says, liking what he was hearing but unsure how to do it. A holo-display appears in his emulator with a list of the *Nova Scotia*'s hangar bays. Hangar Bay 1 aboard the *Beta* still houses two Sparrowhawks, and Bays 3 and 4 aboard the *Alpha* both have one each. Granicks's cool, gray eyes nod at him.

"Hangar Bays 1, 3, and 4, Sparrowhawks, report status," the captain says.

"*Alpha* Sparrowhawks revved and ready to go," a pilot reports back. His call sign, Tibo, lights up in Konran's holo-display.

"*Beta* team golden as a goose," a female voice, call sign Antic, crackles in.

"You are to perform an offensive action, eliminating all enemy starfighters within two millicks of the *Alpha* and *Beta* under the direction of Aide Andacellos."

"Right on, boss, that's what we're talking about," Tibo replies.

"Hangar Bays 1, 3, and 4, launch Sparrowhawks," Granicks orders, and the bays evacuate. Two Sparrowhawk blips appear in Konran's emulator near the *Alpha* and two more near the *Beta*.

Suddenly, the *Alpha* dives through the grav soup with a strategically placed space-time nudge from the *Beta*'s warp engines. The *Alpha* almost closes the gap to Hot Sauce's Sparrowhawk before the three Rezakars deep within the soup react. A grav wave crashes in, impeding the *Alpha*. A second wave propels enemy starfighters toward the *Nova Scotian* flagship, determined to halt the rescue effort.

And Konran goes to work.

"OK, guys, send me cockpit holo-links," he instructs, and four holo-links appear in his emulator. He considers the enemy position, and then pulls up Tibo's link.

"Tibo, two Askeras are separated from the pack. Do you see them?"

"Yeah, man, I see them. We take them out first?"

"Yeah, they're not taking the gradients as aggressively as the others. You and Forest cut through the next wave and you'll be right on top of them."

"You got it, man," Tibo replies, and he and his wingman, call sign Forest, make a break for the next grav wave. The two Askera blips wink out.

"Tibo, you've got incoming now," Konran advises. "Three Miratans. Take a partial dive into the next wave, and then let it spit you back out. Angle so you come in behind them, but watch the grav bombs. The Miratans are upgraded with them."

"I like it," Tibo replies, and he and Forest dive into the next grav wave.

118

Konran turns to the two Sparrowhawks near the *Beta*, call signs Antic and Slydog. He splits them up, using Antic as bait while Slydog catches a grav wave and comes in behind a trio of Askeras. The pair make short work of the enemy fighters.

Konran shifts attention between the two groups, coordinating attacks, staying away from grav bombs and evading counterattacks. Nolvaric numbers dwindle to half their initial total, and, as Tibo and Forest are about to eliminate their portion of the enemy force, Slydog's urgent voice crackles into Konran's emulator.

"Konran!" his voice comes, breathless. "It's like the wave grabbed me and spit me out! I can't get an overshoot, and my breaking angles are all gone! I make one move and they've got me in a double-high-side gun pass anywhere I go!"

Slydog's blue dot spirals and twists in Konran's emulator, narrowly avoiding four Miratans and two Askeras hot on his tail.

He can't outrun them, Konran understands, pulling Slydog's cockpit into his emulator.

The pilot's multidirectional wingtip cannons fire wildly above and behind him. His Sparrowhawk scarcely dodges Askera and Miratan return fire, bouncing like a pebble atop a landslide in the gradient. Y25LM90 tickles the back of Konran's spinal cord as he strains with Slydog to stay ahead of the enemy guns.

"Execute hard break right into their trap," he orders, "followed by immediate engine inversion hard stop. Kill your speed and pick your target."

"I don't think—" Slydog begins.

"Don't wait! Do it now!" Konran yells into his emulator. Slydog obliges, stopping dead on his trajectory, inverting his Sparrowhawk, and firing wildly with his megacannon. The six Nolvaric fighters whiz past, but neither they nor Slydog are damaged in the exchange of weapons' fire. Then the *Beta*'s rail guns pulverize the Nolvarics into dust. Accelerated to 65 percent the speed of light, the magnetically propelled projectiles leave afterimages in Konran's retinas at such close range.

Commander Exeunt's hologram smiles at the shocked look on Konran's face. "Do not forget to utilize all your assets, Mr. Andacellos."

Konran nods, minimizing Slydog's cockpit and returning to his emulator. The area around the *Alpha* and *Beta* is clear of enemy starfighters, and Hot Sauce's Sparrowhawk shows docked in Hangar Bay 3. They had done it—for now. More Nolvaric starfighters stream toward the *Alpha* and *Beta*, left behind by the forward attack groups.

Here comes round two, Konran prepares himself.

"Warp inhibitors online!" Commander Revenshal proclaims as his hologram reappears in the command ring.

"Excellent," Granicks replies. "Tibo and company, hold tight. Revenshal, let them have it. Ace, sitrep."

"Perfect timing, Cap!" Ace's voice crackles in. "Just about there."

Garbled grav soup melts into organized waveforms as the *Gamma* inhibits Nolvaric warp engines. This was more like the soup the *Gamma* had been trapped in earlier—still dangerous and difficult to navigate, but no longer actively trying to kill everyone.

"Ah, I can finally see again," Salazar says with relief. "The soup was making me claustrophobic."

Indeed, even the three Rezakars themselves come into view, residing in their pocket of calm within the sea of gravitational waves. Eight blue blips pop into existence there, joining the Rezakars within the eye of the storm.

"You've earned this, bro," Ace says, and Konran receives a new holo-link. He opens it and finds himself riding in Commander Martin's Sparrowhawk. Three Rezakars loom like giant, chevron-shaped beasts before him. Ace dives, plunging with the rest of the Sparrowhawks for the attack.

"You heard of the Zanbatō?" Ace asks.

"Oh, have I," Konran replies. Named after the feudal Japanese sword famed for stopping cavalry with one strike, the Zanbatō required precise coordination between multiple Sparrowhawks to be effective.

"Valkyrie," Ace barks, "designate target. Wildlynx, prepare to engage on my mark. Make this look like a standard strafing run."

A targeting designator appears on Ace's cockpit, hovering over a point in space above the lead-most Rezakar.

"Target designated," Valkyrie crackles in.

"Let's do this," Ace orders, and the Wildlynx Sparrowhawks break for the cruiser.

The fighters close rapidly, skillfully skirting Nolvaric suppression fire, which fills the black sky with blue bolts and green plasma balls. Konran can almost feel the g-forces jerking the pilots side to side, up and down as the Sparrowhawks stay true to their target while staying alive. Their guns spit return fire as if invading the beaches of Normandy.

"That's why I like you, Ace," Commander Revenshal states. "You always pick on someone bigger than you."

"Rezakars and your momma," Ace crackles back.

"Here's one for my momma, then," Revenshal replies and coil gun rounds burst into the eye of the grav soup. Bright lines streak toward the lead Rezakar, popping in brilliant explosions across Nolvaric energy shields. Some projectiles punch through, slamming into the Rezakar's tough hide in mushrooming balls of fire.

"And here's one for your daddy," Ace crackles.

Abruptly, the Wildlynx's winding, evasive strafing pattern ceases. For the briefest instant they stop in unison, every Sparrowhawk inverted, every megacannon sighting in on Valkyrie's target designator. Konran can almost feel life-support systems preventing pilots' insides from exploding under the rapid deceleration. The Rezakar's multi-layered surface glares up at him like the skin of a great dragon. Despite a thousand simulated encounters with the Rezakar, Konran feels the sensation viscerally—as if poised over the great beast, mere inches from its teeth.

Then Konran's body stills and his finger twitches, and Ace pulls the trigger.

Eight columns of sizzling, photo-plasmic destruction flash into the Rezakar. Its shields erupt more than yield as septillions of subatomic particles convert into volcanic, flaming chaos. Catastrophic energy writhes about the point of impact. And then, in a ceremonial display of starship hari-kari, everything collapses inward, sucking flaming chaos like a vortex into the ship's heart. And the Rezakar becomes a miniature star. Backlit by the blast, the eight Sparrowhawks have already moved on to the next target.

"Excellent, Wildlynx, now fall back," Granicks says, bringing Konran back to the bridge. "Salazar," he continues, "coordinate warp inhibition activity. We're going in."

With strategic timing, the ships of the *Nova Scotia* push into the gravitational soup. *Gamma* warp inhibitors turn off, and *Alpha*, *Beta*, and *Gamma* warp engines engage, driving the soup backward. The warp inhibitors turn on, silencing the Rezakar counterpunch. Cycle after cycle, the USFN forces converge, and within minutes they break from the grav waves and into the eye of the soup: three spider wasps into the tarantula lair.

The Rezakar counterattack comes with withering ferocity, but it doesn't matter. Konran watches on holo-displays from all three sub-ships as the *Nova Scotia* engages in close-quarters combat. Exeunt's *Beta* spirals like a martial artist, her strategic bursts slicing meticulously, viciously into enemy hulls. Granicks's *Alpha* comes in like a boxer, plastering the Rezakars with space-time's version of the jab-cross-hook combo. Revenshal's *Gamma* is the gunslinger, unleashing everything as it comes in fast and hard. Rezakar shields succumb, and the remaining two chevron-shaped ships break in half, and those pieces crack in half again. And Revenshal pulverizes the remainder out of existence for good measure.

Weapons fire ceases.

Debris chunks hang in space.

Nova Scotian warp engines dispel the soup, and space-time resumes its accustomed stillness.

The Rezakars are no more.

Konran's fingers move to the Tharsis Wildlynx patch on his shoulder, feeling its significance now more than ever.

Then he notices his hospital garb under his flight suit, hot and sweaty and shoved worse than ever up his armpits and legs.

CHAPTER 7

"All right, people, let's get cleaned up," Granicks says. "Commander Martin, designate a pair of Sparrowhawks for escape pod retrieval—the rest of your pilots are to come in for refit and repair. Rearguard Sparrowhawks and Longbows to remain active, but bring your radius in to two meglicks out. Commander Exeunt: supervise escape pod recovery action. Commander Revenshal: let's get the *Gamma* back together."

A series of affirmations ring across the bridge, and Captain Granicks pauses, allowing a moment for execution of his orders.

"Ladies and gentlemen," he addresses the bridge, "that was some fine fighting today. Now stay sharp while we clean up. A warship can be most vulnerable when she thinks she's just won victory, but not us. Palm your bio-readers and eat whatever the galley brings you, whether you think you need it or not. Trust me, you do. Sensors: continue to monitor and apprise me immediately of all threats. Communications: verify the status of the task force— we very well may be needed elsewhere. We will remain at General Quarters until escape pod retrieval completion, at which point we will reassess."

Salazar leans over to Konran and sticks his hand into Konran's emulator. A bio-reader materializes around Salazar's hand, shimmering as he scans his palm on it.

"It'll be kale-quinoa-lima-bean chips and lemon water for me," the scientist remarks. "Same thing every time."

Konran scans his palm next, and even the small motion exacerbates the sweaty stickiness that is his hospital garb beneath his flight suit.

"I've gotta get out of this," he says, raising his arms in disgust. "Is there anywhere I could find a change of clothes?"

"Let's see what we can do for you," Captain Granicks states. "Come with me."

"Er, yes, sir, thanks," Konran says, surprised at the captain's personal attention so soon after battle. "See you, Salazar," he adds.

"Lieutenant Vilkoj, you have the conn," Granicks addresses the deck officer.

"I have the conn, sir," Lieutenant Vilkoj replies, stepping sharply into the command console ring. The man, who has a sharp, eagle-shaped nose, thin face, and thick black hair, only has one hand. Its partially formed fingers protrude beneath Vilkoj's left sleeve.

Weren't birth defects like that done away a century ago? Konran wonders. Then he notices Vilkoj noticing him noticing his hand, and he turns to follow the captain.

He steps through a door at the rear of the bridge and finds himself once again sitting in a grav-lev shuttle, encompassed within its long, glossy subway tunnel. The shuttle whisks away, goes left, goes down, and stops at a militaristic platform. The doors open, and Konran steps out. A woman and a man, both decked in camo-gray combat gear, stand in the center of the platform.

"Major Hentagkol," Captain Granicks addresses the woman, "thank you for meeting me. Allow me to introduce you to Konran Andacellos."

The woman steps forward lithely, grasping Konran's hand in hers similar to the way he would escort a woman down from a step. The barrel of a large, repeating plasmic shotgun protrudes above her left shoulder, but if she felt its weight, Konran could not tell.

"A pleasure, Mr. Andacellos," she says, bowing slightly in the still-traditional Southeast Asian manner.

"Likewise, sir, er, ma'am," Konran replies, unsure how to respond to such a graceful, apparently destructive creature.

"Corporal Andresej Cassio here," Major Hentagkol says, releasing Konran's hand and gesturing to the brawny marine standing next to her, "will act as your assistant for the foreseeable future."

"Thank you, ma'am," Konran says, wondering what this had to do with getting a shower and a change of clothes. He turns to the corporal, who, standing at least a head above Konran and two above the major, doesn't smile. His MMP (medium-range, multi-phase plasma rifle) doesn't, either.

"Mr. Andacellos," Cassio acknowledges with a curt nod. His Venusian accent sounds like it's from Venus's Baltic colonies, but Konran can't be sure. The corporal's winter-blue eyes don't blink as the two exchange a brief handshake.

"With your permission, sir," Hentagkol says, "I will return to my forces. We are executing a series of Nolvaric suppression drills."

"Of course, thank you, Major," Granicks replies.

Hentagkol bows slightly before hopping in a shuttle and zipping out of sight. Cassio stiffens as she departs, and Konran realizes he probably interrupted something the marine had been looking forward to.

"Corporal," Captain Granicks addresses the tall marine, "thank you for taking this assignment. Please follow me."

Granicks leads them from the tunnel into a corridor. Lined with doors on the right and windows on the left, it reminds Konran of his old college dormitory. About halfway down and on the door side of the hallway, a man crouches. He moves as the trio approaches, and Konran realizes the man hasn't been crouching, but hovering: he has no legs. Nearly as wide as he is tall, the plump half man scowls up at Captain Granicks from beady eyes. Konran hadn't seen a more bizarre human being in space since the Kashmiri trillionaire brought his half-robot daughters to "behold the wondrous asteroids" more than two years ago. Although Konran consciously knew there was nothing to fear from such people, the resemblance to Nolvarics inevitably made his skin crawl. He shivers, and sticky hospital garb moves with him, clinging obnoxiously to his back and armpits.

"Sir," the hover-man states with a lax drawl, "are you sure about this?"

"Excuse me?" Granicks replies.

"Are you sure you want to do this?" the half man repeats, floating upward so his eyes reach eye level. His shoulder bears the rank insignia of warrant officer.

"Mr. Laske," Granicks says, "why do you think I am here?"

Laske sighs, a gruff sound. "It won't be trivial to set the wardroom back how they like it once the commissions start complaining. Just warning you—they're a special breed of particular."

"It won't be trivial to regain your current pay grade once I demote you back to petty officer, either. Which do you prefer?"

"Agh. Rmph. Fine, bring 'em in. The initialization protocol finished already; all I need are preferences."

"Very good," Granicks says. "Gentlemen, after you."

Konran follows Laske through a door and into a spacious room filled with an arrangement of couches and cushions. Glowing stripes of dim but comfortable lighting illuminate the space, demarcating the couches and cushions into distinct booths and mingling areas. Four sub-rooms split from the main space at arcing partitions in the walls, two to either side. Similar accommodations are visible within their shadowy bowels, and Konran gets the feeling he has stepped into an upscale discotheque.

"OK, it's this one," Officer Laske says, passing the booths and crossing to the first sub-room on the right. "Corporal, would you like to import your current preferences?"

"That will do," Cassio replies, appearing less than pleased with whatever is going on—either that, or he always looks that way; Konran isn't sure.

"Can I ask what we're doing here?" Konran ventures, shifting uncomfortably within his flight suit.

"Did you really just ask me that?" Laske drawls. "What's it look like?"

"Er," Konran says.

"Mr. Laske," Granicks interrupts, "please afford my new aide the respect he deserves. Or do you not recognize the hero of Y25LM90?"

Laske peers at Konran with extra interest, floating upward to get a better look at him. "That was you?"

"Not only that," Granicks adds, "but he played a pivotal role in our victory this morning, so if you would prefer I don't send you to bunk with the junior rates, then please show some respect."

126

Laske swallows, sinking back to floor level as his Adam's apple drops in his thick throat. He swallows again once descended, and then speaks.

"To answer your question, Mr. Andacellos," he drawls with the courtesy of a Louisianan butler, "I am preparing to turn this space into your personal cabin, to be shared with the corporal here. I will need your preferences in order to complete the setup process."

"Er," Konran says again.

"What do you want your bunk to look like?" Laske presses, his newfound formality barely clinging to his vocal folds. "I need something, or you get the standard gray-drab that nobody wants, and I..." he trails off, looking at Granicks. "If so, I would be happy to return, were you to change your mind."

"Uh, could you just make it like my apartment? It's in the Apogees complex, orbiting Earth," Konran ventures, still unsure what was about to happen.

Laske works his forearm computer interface for a moment, and then projects a hologram of Konran's apartment room into the space. Konran blinks before realizing the man had pulled it from an old image Konran had uploaded to his StellarConnections social media account.

"Yeah, that will work," Konran says.

Laske nods, enters another command into his computer, and the elegantly crafted discotheque sub-room wall behind him ripples, sending a hundred mechanical clicks echoing into the wardroom. The wall caves inward before spreading with a thousand more clicks into a new arrangement. Discotheque furniture likewise ripples, dissolving in a flurry of clicks and transmogrifying into a pair of beds, a common desk, and a bathroom. An image of Venus appears next to one of the beds, the golden sun rising over a golden, swirling horizon, backlighting a series of cloud colonies, which stretches into the distance. The wall beside the other bed becomes a muralized version of a photo Konran took during his first orbital spaceflight of Earth. Despite having orbited the blue planet hundreds of times since that moment, he'd never succeeded in surpassing the beauty of that first shot. Apparently, he and Cassio had similar tastes for home, if not different planets.

Finally, a new wall encloses the room, and a door clicks into existence in its center. One last click sounds as a nameplate appears next to the door, reading:

K. Andacellos, Capt. Aide.

Cpl. A. Cassio, Asst. Capt. Aide.

"Excellent," Captain Granicks says. "Konran, meet me in my office tomorrow at 0800. Until then you are free to relax and rest up." Shifting his attention, Granicks nods to the other men. "Mr. Laske, Corporal Cassio." And with that he departs the wardroom.

"Right, then," Laske says. "Hope you like it. The door will activate at your touch. Your personal items should arrive within the next quarter hour, Corporal, and you should have a set of clothing in your locker already, Mr. Andacellos." He hovers back down to ground level and whisks toward the exit.

Konran looks at Corporal Cassio, who is giving him a *you going to stand there forever?* look.

Konran reaches out and touches the door. A slight tingle pulsates into his fingertips, and he pushes against the sensation, sliding the door open and stepping inside.

"I will begin your training tomorrow after your meeting with the captain," Cassio says. "Until then, you may rest."

"Training?" Konran asks, turning back. "I thought you were my assistant."

"Yes, to assist you with not dying."

"Ah. Right," Konran says, understanding Cassio is his new bodyguard—duh. "You coming in?" he asks.

"Not now," Cassio says, assuming a guard-like posture next to the door.

Konran steps in, letting the door slide shut behind him. And the past five days hit him like a sack of bricks.

How did my life get so crazy?

He sighs, sinking onto his new bed and closing his eyes, feeling the bricks settle heavily across his chest, neck, and shoulders. His mind replays his conversation with the nurses, the tour with Granicks, sitting in the Sparrowhawk, meeting the Wildlynx, Fritz stealing Shira's pie, the gawking celebrities, Kyalia's tears on his hands, the bridge, the emulator, the battle. He stops when his mind jumps to the *Relrick*. He couldn't go there again—not yet, at least.

Y25LM90.

He opens his eyes, finding them staring at his muralized, low-orbit photo of Earth. He feels sticky and smelly, but he just lays there, staring. Slowly, his breathing relaxes, and the weight pressing down on him diminishes. He always loved how the sun glinted off the snowcapped Sierra Nevadas in the image, how the mountain lakes gleamed blue, how the pines dotted verdant green across the lower elevations and the white clouds softly gave way to the blackness of space—all at the perfect angle. The complete, idyllic serenity of it all always made him feel whole: something about the way it captured the only two places he'd ever considered home.

"Play Juggernaut, by Calipsolar," he states, trying a hunch. Sure enough, the familiar sounds of Calipsolar's masterpiece of down-tempo, ambient-space-age jazz begin playing, filling the room without emanating from anywhere. His new bunk room wasn't much, but it still had the essentials.

Konran lays there, letting one song lead to another, listening, drifting, dozing—anything but thinking.

He wakes up as the album finishes and cuts off the music with a casual flick of his wrist computer.

All right, where's that change of clothes and the shower?

* * * * *

One long shower and a change of clothes later, Konran is back on his bed, bare feet kicked up, hands propped comfortably on a pillow behind his head. Although simple and nondescript, the clothes he had found waiting for him in the room fit well; they could have been silk compared to his hospital garb.

A holo-display hovers easily in front of his face, which he peruses via ocular and verbal commands. While ocular commands were less sophisticated than direct neural commands, neural interfaces had fallen out of style around the time evil, bionic super-beings invaded the solar system and usurped control of the interfaces themselves. But Konran doesn't care, having lived his entire life in a society terrified of neural interfaces. If only he hadn't chosen the moment to check his social notifications and ISSA corporate messages, the setup might have been relaxing.

In Konran's defense, the 83,265,345 notifications clogging his social inbox had been pretty hard to ignore. But, after suffering through several thousand variations of "YOUR GD AT FLIYNG, BRO" and "MERY ME, PLZ," he'd left his notifications (now diminished to 83,261,633) and turned his attention to his ISSA corporate message system: mistake number two. Mentally berating himself for not checking in on the *Estrellas Vigilantes* instead, Konran reads the fifteen most recent subject lines:

RETURN TO WORK—NOTIFICATION 18

CEASE AND DESIST EXTERNAL EMPLOYMENT—WARNING 2

FINE: RECKLESS ENDANGERMENT OF STAFF—PENALTY WAIVED

FINE: RECKLESS ENDANGERMENT OF PASSENGERS—PENALTY WAIVED

FINE: RECKLESS ENDANGERMENT OF ISSA PROPERTY—PENALTY OWED

FINE: RECKLESS DESTRUCTION OF ISSA PROPERTY—PENALTY OWED

FINE: RECKLESS DISREGARD FOR DIRECT ORDERS—PENALTY WAIVED

RETURN TO WORK—NOTIFICATION 17

CORPORATE AWARD: SELFLESS HEROISM AND BRAVERY

CORPORATE AWARD: OUTSTANDING ACTION UNDER EXTREME DURESS

NOTICE: GR-29 GUN-CRAFT PRIVILEGE SUSPENDED, PENDING REVIEW

NOTICE: FREIGHTER CRAFT PRIVILEGE SUSPENDED, PENDING REVIEW

YOU ARE INVITED: FORMAL DINNER WITH SENIOR LEADERSHIP

CONGRATULATIONS! PROMOTION PACKAGE ATTACHED, LEVEL-V CAPTAIN

RETURN TO WORK—NOTIFICATION 16

Without reading any of the message details, Konran closes the holographic interface with an ocular gesture, diminishing it with a blink. He stares up at the ceiling and sighs. He looks down, bringing one hand to his forehead and staring at the door. Then he covers his face with both hands and lets out a long groan.

ISSA.

He had completely forgotten about ISSA. Memories of the *Viona Grande* and *Relrick* flood back without invitation, combining nauseously with thoughts of steely ISSA bureaucrats slavering to cross-examine every pebble of the mountainous paperwork invariably awaiting his return. Konran rolls weakly onto his side, bracing himself against the sudden urge to throw up.

He doesn't, and the brunt of the emotion passes. Laying there, he extends his left hand away from the sofa, holding it out in open space. A small tray responds to the gesture, levitating from its position on the floor and raising a cup into his open palm. Sitting up slowly, he drains the contents in one gulp and replaces the cup, which gently returns to the floor on its tray.

The concoction—whatever it was, had arrived during his shower as part of his post-battle meal. A pleasant-but-not-sweet taste lingers on his tongue, and in a few moments his body reacts to the bio-metabolically balanced influx of nutrients. He closes his eyes, melting back into his pillow as a soft surge of vitality fills his chest.

He extends his hand again, the tray levitates, and he takes a handful of colorful nuts from the tray. It pleased him that levitating tray technology had been incorporated into the *Nova Scotia*'s officers' quarters, he himself having splurged after his last ISSA promotion and purchased a set of levitating dishware.

Whatever those nuts are, they're good, he thinks, wondering if they were among the many non-Earth-originated varieties popular around the solar system these days. *Probably.*

He grabs another handful before dismissing the tray, chewing the nuts slowly, and savoring the color on his tongue.

I could get used to this biometri-whatever food service.

Confidence bolstered, Konran blinks at his wrist computer, and his ISSA messaging system jumps back into existence.

It's now or never, he coaxes, trying not to think too much about what he is going to do. *I can't go back—there is no way I can go back to that now.*

"Message Director Zieshal," he states firmly.

A blank input box appears before him.

"In light of recent events, I hereby submit my resignation, effective immediately. Thank you."

Konran stares at the message. It stares back, daring him to cut ties with everything he's known for the past five years. He had never actually wanted to be a freighter pilot; it had just happened when reality forced him to find a job after he failed at his starfighting goal. He hesitates, and old arguments pry their way to the forefront of his consciousness.

Could he really walk away from ISSA? It was his job, his lifeblood, and the only means by which he contributed to society. It was the reason he had that nice apartment in the Apogees instead of his stale old bed in a central-California boys' home.

Sighing, he disengages his holographic ISSA inbox from its point-of-view link and sends it to hover beside his levitating meal on the floor.

Despite never developing a passion for the job, Konran had developed quite the comfortable ISSA groove over the years: show up on time, receive a flight plan, traverse a few billion kilometers of open vacuum, follow procedure like a boss, bring some fresh space rocks wherever ISSA wanted, rinse and repeat. It was consistent work, and the need for astrofreighters was only growing. It was something he could count on, and it paid better than almost every attainable, non-extreme job within the inner solar system (not that there was anything wrong with being a solar flare dive guide or one of those spelunkers who rescued those robots that always got stuck exploring the inner crust of minor planets).

I'm doing OK for myself. I'm making a good living. My life is stable.

Konran glances at his resignation message hovering faithfully above the floor.

"What am I thinking?" he asks out loud, raising his palms to his face and staring back at the ceiling. "I don't want to be an astrofreighter. I'm on a quarking Riot-class space cruiser. They made me an honorary member of the sparking starfighter wing."

He looks back at his message. It doesn't reply.

"What am I thinking?" he asks again. "I don't even know how much—or if—they're paying me here. This could simply end tomorrow. And then what?"

He looks back at his message, moving it with an ocular command from the floor back to head height.

Resignation.

He had been so eager as a child, so determined as a teenager. Now, after a major punch of failure to the gut and a fistful of life to the face, things had changed. He still wanted it just as much, but something had eroded between his desire and his belief.

Was it even still really there?

He thinks about today's battle with the Nolvarics. The experience had been a blur—terrifying, yes, just like Y25LM90, but so natural, invigorating, and refreshing. The mixture of emotion feels strange, but its message is clear.

I'm in the right spot now, no matter what happens next.

He returns to his resignation message, prepared to send it. An icon at the top of the screen indicates two new messages have appeared since he last looked. Curious, he switches to his inbox:

RETURN TO WORK—NOTIFICATION 19

DECISION: ASTROFREIGHTER AND GR-29 PRIVILEGES

He opens the second one.

Captain Andacellos,
In regard to a thorough analysis of your activity during Mission Record Number ISSA46-9952P-00FR, we regret to inform you

133

the Official Review Board has found your performance deficient per ODFP A-121 and has hereby enacted full suspension of your flying privileges (including, but not limited to, all ISSA-bonded freighter and support craft), to be released pending your successful recompletion of Flight Training Core Courses 110, 110B, 242, 302, 330A-C, 350, 370, and 425, as well as a minimum of 250 hours of simulator training and 130 hours of supervised flight training. Although your courageous actions in the face of trying circumstances are to be commended, please understand this suspension is based upon the following well-documented behaviors:

- Willingness to disregard multiple direct orders from a superior officer
- Failure to maintain VIP comfort and schedule
- Failure to fully protect wing ship from known danger
- Excessive maneuvering of astrofreighter craft on thrusters with VIP personnel aboard
- Repetitive usage of unapproved flight patterns with GR-29 gun-craft
- Negligent, willful damaging of astrofreighter craft
- Willful and unprofessional self-aggrandizement during official ISSA business
- Irregular orders given to pilot in training while acting as...

Konran stops, blinks, switches back to his resignation letter, and sends it without another thought. Then he authorizes his ISSA message system for full deletion.

"Sorry, sir," a polite voice speaks from his computer. "Fifty-seven messages are delete-protected within this inbox."

Konran closes the application, accesses his computer's system controls, and deletes the ISSA app from existence.

"I've got to get out of here," he vocalizes, standing abruptly and kicking his levitating food tray. Nuts go flying, but the tray manages to catch most of them while keeping the beverage from spilling. Already out the door, Konran doesn't stop to watch the culinary acrobatics.

"You have an odd idea of rest," a Venusian-Baltic voice calls from across the wardroom. Konran spots Corporal Cassio lounging on a sofa on the other side of the room.

"It wasn't happening," Konran says. "Where is everyone?"

"The ship is at General Quarters," Cassio answers. "Those not required to sleep are prepared to fight. The captain does not feel we are out of the conflict yet."

"Ah, right."

"You are going somewhere?" Cassio asks.

"Yeah, the mess hall."

"You understand they will deliver your food to you?"

"Yeah, but being alone wasn't working out so well," Konran replies, feeling exasperated. "I've only been back from the dead for a day, and company would be nice."

"I will accompany you," Cassio says, moving to get up. "It is next to the wardroom, but on this side of the ship they call it the dining hall."

"I'm actually heading to the one by the medical bay, if that's OK."

"The *Nova Scotia* has three medical bays, one per sub-ship."

"I'm going to the mess hall by Hangar Bay 3."

"Why? The dining hall is right here."

"I just like it better."

"How do you know that if you have only been back from the dead for one day?"

"I'm just hungry and know the chef there already," Konran retorts.

"You do not sound hungry," Cassio responds, eyes narrowing.

"That's just where my friends hang out, and I want to see them."

"So why didn't you just say that?" Cassio asks.

"Agh," Konran grunts. Crossing the wardroom in frustration, he exits through the sliding door. He makes it twenty steps down the corridor before stopping. Turning around, he sees Cassio already standing there, leaning against the wall by the wardroom door.

"Would you like me to show you the way?" Cassio asks.

"Yeah," Konran sighs, "that would be good."

Konran feels nervous as he and Cassio step from the grav-lev shuttle, exit the tunnel, and pass through the doors of the mess hall. As expected, the hall bursts into cheers upon his appearance, and he is immediately swarmed by effusive VIPs. He smiles, shakes hands, and accepts congratulations, but although his eyes look for someone, he doesn't find her in the crowd. And then, to his chagrin, Alandie is nowhere to be seen, either.

Instead, he finds himself seated at the head of a set of pulled-together tables, answering questions and dishing out details on the recent battle. VIPs hang on his every word, gasping in amazement and shouting with elation in all the right places during the narration. The process and the praise feel mechanical, but with nothing else to do and the captive audience holding him prisoner, Konran presses on. After the third time redescribing Hot Sauce's escape from the Nolvaric starfighter-grav-soup death trap, a voice rings out from the front of the room.

"Hero!"

Konran jumps to his feet, bumping a VIP senator who was close enough to be bumped by the jump. A path clears path between Konran and the young woman at the head of the room. Twisting rivers of glowing highlights pulsate softly along her long, brown hair.

Cassio jumps, too, but, after seeing Kyalia, he gives Konran a knowing, *so that's why you wanted to come to the mess hall* look and resumes his bored posture against the wall.

Kyalia had that effect on people.

The actress runs across the room (which isn't really that big), catching Konran in an embrace and nearly spinning him off his feet. Konran hugs her, feeling embarrassed but giddy at the same time. Her deep, navy-blue eyes swallow him, and he finds himself swimming in their depths. Then she punches him in the shoulder.

"Why didn't you tell me you were coming, Hero? I've been waiting to hear from you all day."

"I'm sorry. It's been a long day. And ..." Konran stops to think for the first time since leaving his cabin. "I don't actually know how to contact you. So, I just came here."

"You could just accept my StellarConnections request," she says, pushing him with a playful nudge. "Or use the onboard directory, or ask your marine."

Konran glances at Cassio, who shrugs.

"I think I could use some of those masdalas you promised me—it's been a long day," Konran says.

"You mean the malasadas?" Kyalia laughs. "Franco!" she calls. "We'll take you up on that dessert now."

"Your dish, Ms. Rennesant," Franco speaks from behind her, and Kyalia starts with a gasp and a laugh.

"Franco! You startled me! Thank you!" She beams at the chef who delivers a platter of egg-size balls of savory, sugar-glazed fried dough.

"They're donuts," Konran says, happily taking a bite of one. "Oh, wow, they're good!" he adds through the mouthful.

"I told you, Hero," Kyalia says.

A sudden Sri Lankan accent rings across the mess hall.

"Konran!"

Delighted, Konran looks up to see Alandie.

"We came as soon as we heard you were here." An entire group of VIPs stumbles into the mess hall behind Alandie, and Konran is swarmed again.

Cassio acts quickly, and grunts and growls of pretention pop as the marine pulls his way through the crowd to Konran.

"I apologize," he says unapologetically, keeping the VIPs at bay. "Konran has to go now—official naval business."

As if on cue, another voice rings out, this one robotic.

"Patient Andacellos," it calls loudly, mispronouncing his name as *and-Ah-selos*. "You have failed to report to medical for seven hours. This behavior is simply unacceptable."

Fritz the medbot rolls through the crowd, pushing past Cassio and scanning Konran with an assortment of medical appendages.

"Your neural stress levels are unacceptably high," Fritz chides, "and your sleep levels are unacceptably low. I detect you have not taken your chamomile supplement as prescribed, and you missed your morning and afternoon massage sessions. Please come with me, and we will correct this delinquency."

Cassio pulls Konran to his feet. "Exactly," he affirms. "Sorry, everyone." He pulls Konran through the crowd, following Fritz, who rolls into the lead, happy to have secured his patient.

Instead of taking Konran into the medical bay, however, once through the mess hall doors Cassio pulls Konran down a new corridor. They walk quickly, almost furtively, and Konran ducks below low pipes and around bulky equipment as Cassio directs him through a web of interconnecting maintenance corridors.

"Where are we going?" Konran asks, the question a whisper due to the marine's urgency.

"Evasive action," is all Cassio replies.

They emerge a minute later, exiting the maintenance maze and setting foot on a wider, more normal corridor. It stretches out for a dozen meters in either direction before arcing out of sight around gentle bends in the structure. Windows run along the left-hand side, affording periodic views of outer space.

"This way," Cassio says.

After another minute Cassio opens a new door and leads Konran down a ladder. When they stop, Konran is standing in a comfortable, semicircular room with a large, U-shaped couch along its rear wall. The front wall isn't a wall at all, but a large window with a spectacular, unhindered view of space. Spacecraft scurry about, effecting Captain Granicks's post-battle orders. The *Gamma* floats less than three kilometers away with a repair scaffold wrapped around its girth.

"This is better," Cassio says. "I will have your friends and food delivered here."

"Thanks," Konran says, sitting down. Maybe the marine wasn't so bad after all.

Ascending the ladder, Cassio parts with, "It is my job."

* * * * *

Konran, Kyalia, Alandie, Cassio, and an assortment of *Andromeda Uncharted* cast members sit around the U-shaped couch, chatting, eating, and watching out the viewport as *Gamma* repair operations continue. Konran could have done without the bulk of the holo-stars in the room—most were annoying prats—but Cassio

138

could have done worse when collecting Konran's "friends" for the private luncheon. And with Kyalia at his side, it was hard not to feel on top of the world. Or was it on top of the Kuiper Belt? Or the solar system? However that phrase worked out here. What was there to be "on top of" in space, anyway?

"When I get off this ship, I'm going moon jumping," Philipe, Kyalia's oft-brooding co-star says smugly. "I'll rent out the spacepark on Deimos—even if it costs $100 million—and I'll spend the entire day moon jumping."

"I've heard of that park," Alandie says. "So you can really jump around Deimos?"

"Oh yes, it's the best," Philipe brags with know-it-all self-assurance. "Deimos has so little gravity, you run and jump, and you go right into orbit. You'll never get better views of Mars or the stars—I guarantee you. You're coming, of course."

"No way, ha, are you kidding? I could never afford that." Alandie balks.

"Alandie," Philipe croons, "the cost is on us. We couldn't go without you. You, too, Konran."

"Astro, count me in," Alandie replies. He was adapting better than Konran to his newfound stature with the VIPs, although he did have four extra days of practice under his belt.

"All right, make that two of us," Konran says, going with the flow. Kyalia cheers and Philipe raises a glass of chamomile tea (the chic thing to drink among the *Nova Scotia*'s elite these days), nodding with self-satisfaction.

"Not me," Chaisna Tiscionne, a popular recurring cast member, interjects. She brushes black bangs out of her deeply shadowed eyes. "Makes my stomach turn. I don't know how you do it."

"How will you spoil yourself, then," Philipe prods, "when our adventure comes to an end?"

"Encelada," Chaisna replies. "All I want is a nice, big encelada."

"*Ensalada*?" Cassio asks, the words his first in an hour. "All you want is a salad?"

"Not *ensalada*," Chaisna glares at him, "*Encelada*. Like from Enceladus, Saturn's moon."

"You just said the same word twice," the marine replies, "and pretended it was special if it came from Enceladus."

"Encelada comes from the subterranean oceans of Enceladus, and it's the most incredible cuisine you've never heard of, not a salad."

"So what is the difference?"

"The difference?" Chaisna flushes. "How can you compare precision-extracted geothermal steam-vent barnacles to a pile of foliage? I'm not surprised you're ignorant, though. You're just a marine—how would you know anything?"

"Do you know where I intend to go once this is over?" Cassio replies. The marine pauses, allowing a moment for everyone to wonder, and Konran is impressed by the calm restraint with which he brushed off Chaisna's insult.

"I intend to watch the auroras flash from a front-row seat above Jupiter. Have you ever seen anything more beautiful than a Jovian aurora? They are utterly glorious—one hundred times as powerful as any on Earth."

He pauses again, looking directly at Chaisna before adding, "I apologize. You need military clearance to get close enough to Jupiter to revel in their beauty. But can you imagine it? Ah, wait," he shakes his head in mock regret, "you are an empty-headed actress. A pity, really."

Chaisna stands in a huff and struts to the ladder. "I didn't pay to listen to this monkey," she snarls before clambering up and out.

Philipe follows her, and the room vacates of *Andromeda Uncharted* cast members save one, who remains at Konran's side. Shortly, it's just he, Kyalia, Alandie, and Cassio watching the stars out the viewport.

"Dude, you can clear a room," Alandie says.

"Speaking of such," Cassio says, "I require your assistance, Mr. Cabrameda." The marine stands and indicates for Alandie to follow him, and Konran finds himself alone with Kyalia.

He tells her of growing up in California, a poor but lucky orphan in his boys' home. She tells him of her own upbringing in Abu Dhabi as the daughter of an American actress and European businessman. He talks of scrimping and saving every penny to play starfighter simulators; she talks of lavish birthday presents and elegant parties. He reminisces of anticipating bus trips to Modesto Bay—California's vast inland seashore. She describes helicopter diving with dolphins off the Australian coast. They sit together, watching through the viewport until the scaffolding falls from the *Gamma* and the three sub-ships of the *Nova Scotia* form back into one.

Hours later, Cassio returns and Kyalia bids them goodnight. Konran's feet tread upon air as he follows the marine back to their bunk cabin, the weighty heaviness of the day evaporated.

CHAPTER 8

Chanziu Guan didn't like what he was hearing. It didn't help that he had been holed in the maintenance shaft for seventeen days now. Not to mention the thirteen days it had taken to prepare and get into the hiding place, the sixty-five days prior to that floating in space, cloaked in his ship, logging every traceable transaction and conversation arising from the massive, mobile, supra-Jovian USFN space fortress, nor the four hundred and fifty-nine days before that just figuring out where to start looking. No one ever said being a spy would be easy.

Not even Chanziu could have predicted the fruit hanging before him today. But fortune favors the prepared, and, as a result of recent action at Y25LM90, Chanziu's infiltration efforts placed him at the center of one of the most pivotal conversations in the history of inhabited space. Chanziu had only sent four nanobots down the shaft. Four insignificantly tiny bots, practically impossible to detect: the minimum required to form a transmission line long enough to eavesdrop.

Chanziu knew he may never get this close again. And so, today, right now, 13,300 hours of patience, persistence, and luck boiled down to the next few moments. Gratefully, the nanobots had been made in China—Saturno-China's finest war-research laboratories, to be exact. Chanziu could only hope they would hold out long enough.

Voices crackle back into the spy's ear, and Chanziu releases his breath. Despite periodic gaps in transmission, so far the nanobots were working.

"I say we move to Phase 4 now. Send in the Krona; let them have at the inner planets. You want chaos? That will give you chaos."

Chanziu's eye fills with data on the speaker, a woman identified through previous effort as Ambassador Hasina Ikavanoric of Alpha Centauri.

"Chaos, bah," a second voice speaks. "You realize our timetable has already been pushed forward seventeen months, or don't you recall the endgame?"

Chanziu's system identifies the speaker as Vadic Heesor, the United Space Federation's oily minister of defense.

"I agree with the ambassador. Your blunders have already thrust our cause to the precipice of failure, Minister."

That was Admiral Carlo Lewiam—commander of the USFN's Twelfth Oort Fleet.

"Do you wish to be more specific, Admiral?" Minister Heesor speaks.

"You cannot be so ignorant."

"Enlighten me."

"Your algorithm, Minister. Your *perfect* algorithm. As spectacular a failure as the man that created it."

"Are you referring to the algorithm that made our plan possible in the first place? The reason you stand here, on the cusp of more glory and power than your puny mind can comprehend? That algorithm?"

"I'm referring to Andacellos. You missed him. Your algorithm never so much as hinted at Y25LM90. And now this."

Silence. The nanobots can't have gone down yet. Chanziu weighs his options, preparing to launch three more. It's worth the risk. Heesor continues just before Chanziu executes the command.

"My algorithm has accurately identified over twelve million militarily serviceable prodigies—a million of which serve under your personal command. Not to mention the 6.7 million we've sent undetected to—"

"We know the numbers, Minister," a fourth voice breaks in, soft yet imposing. "Now choose your next words carefully: Can you explain Andacellos?"

Chanziu closes his eyes, breathing slowly, causing his parasympathetic nervous system to trigger and curb his spiking adrenaline response. This was it. He was finally listening in on the man known only to him as the Leader.

"Yes, my Lord. And no." The words emerge precariously from the minister, reluctant, as if their conversion from mental process to physical vibration cost the man dearly.

"Continue."

"I computed his scores since his emergence. He is at least a Level 19 tactically and, given his contributions to today's battle, potentially a Level 20 in spatial combat."

Silence. Chanziu can almost feel the Leader's grave expectancy demanding further information. Finally the minister continues.

"But given his prior history—none of which escaped my algorithm—he averages no better than a twelve in any category, peaking at moments at a fourteen, dropping at times as low as an eight. The algorithmic results align perfectly with his current astrofreighter position. Better than average, yes, but practically normal. His deceased superior scored two orders of magnitude nearer selection than he."

More silence. Then the ambassador speaks up.

"What kind of Level 19 or 20 are we talking about here?" the Alpha Centauri woman asks. "We regularly see Level 19 performance from even our Level 16s or 17s. They're all smart; they're all geniuses at that level. But what makes it truly unique is when it doesn't go out—when the spark of utter brilliance persists."

"I was getting to that," Minister Heesor says. Even through the infinitesimally tiny nanobot uplink, Chanziu detects hesitance in the words.

You weren't getting to that, Chanziu understands. *You couldn't wish for this interrogation to end sooner.*

"It's impossible to speak certainly with so little data," the minister goes on, "but Andacellos's performance indicates Class-A Level 20 capability. A tactical performance like his yesterday doesn't just spark into existence—simply put, Andacellos made too many correct decisions in too short a time span. Current predictions indicate he is capable of consistently performing at such a level."

More silence: this thicker, heavier than before.

Finally the Leader's voice enters Chanziu's ear: "Tell me, Admiral, of your one million *prodigies,* how many Class-A Level 20s do you have under your command?"

"Two, my Lord, possibly three."

"And how many have we delivered to the Krona?"

"None, my Lord. We have reserved them all for our strategic advantage."

"As we discussed," Ambassador Ikavanoric adds, "there is no sense in giving up an Alexander the Great or Genghis Khan to such an unpredictable, unstable force."

"So what do you propose we do about this Andacellos?"

"Try again. Use more force. Kill him now." Admiral Lewiam's voice is steel.

"You can't simply defeat a Level 20 with greater force, or haven't you studied your Hernàn Cortès, Admiral?" the ambassador challenges. "The entire solar system saw what Konran Andacellos did when your impetuous Nolvarics burned his boat."

"We don't have to defeat a Level 20 yet," Admiral Lewiam retorts. "His ship dies, he dies. Darius Granicks is barely a Level 18 strategist. Three Level 18s fell to the Nolvarics this week. They're a dime a dozen in the navy."

"And what of the ten other Level 17s or higher serving aboard his ship—eleven, counting Andacellos. That's well more than any ship outside your hand-selected battle fleet. The man crushed your Rezakars like a rhino stomping dung beetles," Ambassador Ikavanoric observes.

"Thank you, Ambassador, for the illuminating analogy."

"Why destroy Level 20 talent when you can just take it?" That was the minister.

"Why? Because he is an anomaly. Because he is not within our—"

"Proceed, Minister," the Leader's cool timbre interrupts the admiral.

"Among the eighty-seven known prodigies at Level 19 or higher, his combination of skills is nearest the skill set that turned the tide of the Nolvaric Invasion. Why not take him? Isolate him from his preferred environment, stage an attack, and snatch him in the conflict. Pin the attack on the Saturnos and Phase 3 initiates itself. Then you take all the time you want to groom the Krona."

Cold adrenaline rushes through Chanziu's chest cavity. Despite his months of effort, even he hadn't known the danger to his people. This would thrust Saturno-China into outright war with the United Space Federation.

We will lose, he understands, reflexively letting the thought go, calming his mind, and refocusing on the conversation.

"My contacts among the Chinese extremists on Earth are eager to act," Ikavanoric adds. "My spies confirmed they recently secured two Huoxing star cruisers from Saturnese defectors. They just need the right target and motivation. Their commandos are most effective."

"It won't be enough against Granicks," the admiral warns, "which is why I urged for more force. Overwhelming force this time."

"Agreed," the ambassador confirms. "So can you coax your pawns into another attack?"

"Can I coax them? Get me those Huoxings, and I'll get you all the Nolvaric backup you can wish for."

"I believe we have come to an agreement," the minister states almost smugly. After following the United Space Federation's minister of defense for over ten months, Chanziu understands the undertone. The man was a master of manipulation, and the admiral and ambassador had just agreed to execute his desires for him.

"I shall stoke the public opinion of Andacellos in the meantime," Minister Heesor continues, "in order to hypersensitize the emotional effect when he is abducted. If you are in further need of my services, you know where to find me."

"No," the Leader's iciness echoes against squeamish silence. "Your *services*, Minister, will ensure this Andacellos does not escape our trap—that is, if you wish to witness Phase 3 initiate itself."

More silence. Chanziu studies the readings on his optical overlay, paying particular attention to the countdown timer. He has fourteen minutes to vacate his current position before this shift's maintenance crew sweeps the area. He stays motionless yet relaxed, continuing to prevent sympathetic nervous responses from spiking his vitals. Even within his infiltration suit—which rendered him invisible and inaudible on most observable frequencies—a surge in biologic indicators could reveal his presence to the detectors aboard the space fortress. This was no time to fail because his heart thumped a little too hard.

"We are agreed?" the Leader's hard voice queries.

"Yes, my Lord," three voices respond, their vibrations a mixture of fear and anticipation.

"Do not fail, and your places will be assured when I bring the inner planets to their knees at the hand of the Krona."

We will lose, Chanziu realizes, wriggling easily yet urgently backward out of the maintenance shaft.

We will all lose.

* * * * *

Three hours ahead of his optimal, secure-withdrawal schedule, Chanziu Guan works his way along the ceiling of a long, moderately populated hallway deep within the USFN space fortress. Unseen by the soldiers and staff passing below, Chanziu's infiltration suit allows him to adhere to the ceiling without exerting his weight upon it—his mass made nearly transparent to the gravitational waves pulsating throughout the fortress.

As far as Chanziu knew, the Saturnese were still the only power in the galaxy to possess such technology, but that didn't make using it in broad daylight any less dangerous. Some moments were simply worth the risk, and it didn't take Chanziu's years of meticulous training to know that this was one of those moments.

Chanziu knew he couldn't disclose his recording of the conversation. Not yet, at least. There were too many dominos in this game, thousands of them, stacked meticulously across every odd corner of the galaxy. Chanziu had found enough of them over the past 554 days to lead him here, to the heart of the plot. But now what? How to win? He didn't know the Leader's identity or his whereabouts. All he had was the plan. It was like standing in a room full of mousetraps—one wrong movement and nobody in the galaxy would outrun the ensuing catastrophe, least of all his people.

Chanziu shudders, pausing in his rhythmic descent of the corridor to collect himself. If even a whisper of the recording's existence were to get out … it would mean disaster. War. Invasion. Destruction. Desolation. The Leader would not hesitate to unleash the Krona—the clan, Chanziu had gathered, of ultra-advanced

Nolvarics populated over the past decades (thanks to the Leader's ambition and the minister's algorithm) with six million abducted, brainwashed, and meticulously groomed geniuses, their particular aptitudes suited for war. Armed and prepared for combat against the inner planets, the Krona waited out there, somewhere in the vast, vacuous void, eager for the call to action. Five hundred and fifty-four days ago Chanziu hadn't even known of their existence. War with the United Space Federation would be terrible; war with the Krona would be nothing short of doom.

As Chanziu saw it, he only had one play remaining, one final unobstructed step on the floor of mousetraps. He needed a Sun Tzu, or at least the closest thing to a game-changing war tactician he could find. He had to get to Andacellos first and convince him to win this fight. He could only hope the minister's algorithm had it right this time, and that the man didn't get to Andacellos first.

So Chanziu crawls, upside down, along the ceiling of the USFN space fortress, as fast as his fingertips and toes can take him.

CHAPTER 9

Konran wakes, rested and rejuvenated and feeling better than he had for ... apparently forever. And then he realizes someone is shaking him.

"Konran, get up," Cassio says.

"I'm up, I'm up," Konran groans, pushing the marine's hands away. "Did I sleep in or something?"

"No, you have company."

Again?

"Who is it?"

"Commander Martin, of the Wildlynx," Cassio says. "Fritz sent him away an hour ago so you could complete another sleep cycle."

"Fritz is here?" Konran asks, getting up. Cassio hands him a fresh set of pressed clothing, and Konran adds, "What's this?"

"Fritz left a half hour ago. This arrived this morning—your new uniform."

Konran puts the clothes on, and the gray slacks and collared shirt fit well, toeing the line between functional and official. A pair of similarly styled boots round out the uniform, and Konran opens the door.

"Konran!" Ace shouts. "I love what you've done with the place. I felt like I was waiting to pick up a date, your medbot kept me waiting so long."

"Hey, Ace," Konran says, exchanging a man hug with the pilot. "This is Corporal Cassio," he adds, stepping away from the door.

"We met when your robot kicked me out," Ace replies, shaking Cassio's hand. "You from Venus?"

"I am. Was it the accent?" Cassio replies.

"Name, actually. I knew a Cassio back in flight school. Named Raf, from the cloud colonies. He was a beast with a Sparrowhawk."

"I do not know him, but I have distant cousins who moved to the other side of Venus. You are from Mars?"

"Yep, just like most of the Wildlynx," Ace confirms. "You guys ready?"

"For what?" Konran asks.

"Breakfast, what else?" Ace says. "Come on. Everyone's hungry."

A few officers on break offer "good morning" as Konran departs the wardroom with Ace and Cassio. After a quick shuttle ride to the *Beta* section of the *Nova Scotia*, Ace leads them to the Wildlynx's pilots' lounge, just outside of Hangar Bay 1.

"How did you obtain this space?" Cassio asks before they enter.

"Swapped space with the ordnancemen and the mechies," Ace says. "Exit appreciated the efficiency and let us keep it."

"Wait, who's Exit?" Konran asks.

"Ha, you haven't heard that one yet?" Ace replies as the door to the lounge opens. "That's what we call Commander Exeunt."

Konran enters the room, and, as was becoming customary on the *Nova Scotia*, a cheer breaks out at his appearance. Instead of red-carpet shouts and raucous applause, however, this one takes the form of a quick chant, accelerating from a vigorous "Rah, rah, rah, rah" into a crescendoing roar, which abruptly cuts off with a piercing "Woo-rah!" And instead of adoring, slabbering VIPs, Konran finds himself slapping backs with instant friends.

"Man, Andacellos." A pilot with tan skin, a shaved head, and lean features approaches him. "You're a sick Chupacabra, if I've seen one. You've got some moves, man, even from the command chair."

"Tibo thinks he's going to give you a call sign already," another pilot says. "He tries to start everyone's signs."

"Yeah, and where'd yours come from, Digger?" Tibo asks the squat but trim pilot.

"Not that he's unsuccessful," Digger concedes. With brown skin, thick black hair, and keen, round eyes, Digger's features marked him as likely coming from Noachis Terra—the Martian highland region populated significantly by Nepalese descendants.

Konran laughs. Recalling Tibo and Digger's part in yesterday's battle, he says, "You guys were astro out there—really, it was awesome to watch you in action."

150

"It was all you, man," Tibo replies. "Come on and meet the posse." He indicates the man and two women standing beside Digger. "Slydog over here, Antic there, and this is Forest."

Tall, lanky, and apparently very strong for his wiry frame, Slydog lifts Konran off his feet in an embrace. "Chilla, you saved my life out there. I couldn't believe that worked—every instinct said I was dead if I pulled up like that, but you convinced me."

Slydog sets Konran down, grasping his hand instead and moving it through a sequence of advanced handshakes, which Konran does his best to imitate. "That was astro, chilla; solid astro." With a high, dark brow line and sharp features, the pilot could have been from the Turkish settlements within the Martian volcanic caldera of Apollinaris Patera.

Konran doesn't recognize the appellation "chilla," but he goes with it, telling Slydog, Antic, and Forest how great they all did. Speaking with them makes him think about the other pilot he helped, and at a lull in the backslapping he asks, "So, how's Hot Sauce doing?"

"She's great, man," Tibo says, "resting it out in medbay. She used to be my wingman, you know? But I wasn't there for her, and now Fideo and Stickman ... Man, you know, they're gone; Nolvarics turned them into dust. But you saved her, man—you made them pay for what they did. Watching you do it, I knew you were the Chupacabra. No one can touch you, man."

"We ain't calling him Chupacabra, Tibo," Ace interjects, cutting through the thicket of pilots to Konran's side. "It's way too long. Besides, we've got to get him into a Sparrowhawk first. Right?" Ace addresses that question to Konran.

"I like the sound of that," Konran agrees enthusiastically.

"Maybe just Cabra," Tibo spouts. "Yeah, we call him Cabra. Or Cobra, like the way he flew that gun-craft; like a snake out there."

"Maybe we call you Mouth," Ace counters, and everyone laughs.

"Speaking of mouths, anyone else hungry?" Ace calls to the group, and the group yells back.

Unlike the semi-enclosed booths of the more compartmentalized wardroom, the pilots' lounge had a long table running down its center, with seating for the entire squadron. Ace's arm on Konran's shoulder nudges him to take a seat. And, allowing himself to move in that direction, Konran runs straight into a pair of green eyes, a short brown ponytail, and a soft patch that reads, *V. Melendez.*

Valkyrie.

"Or Barf," she says, her face ten centimeters from his, eyes unblinking. "We don't have anyone called Barf yet. Is that why you kept us all waiting so long?"

"Er," Konran stammers before catching his balance. "Well, if you'd sit with me, I'd be happy to demonstrate again."

Valkyrie's stone face breaks into a grin, and to Konran's surprise, after saying, "You're all right, Andacellos," she actually sits down next to him.

"So, Tibo," Konran asks across the table as Ace sits on Konran's other side, "if you're so into call signs, what does yours mean?" Cassio doesn't join them, remaining at the side of the room, not sitting, but not standing, leaning against the wall and watching.

"It's short for Tiburón, man. That's Spanish for shark," Tibo explains with pride.

"So, that must come from your ferocity in battle?"

"Nah," Antic replies with a shake of her head, "he's just a shark. He'll take your money and bust your knees." One of her eyes squeezes and her nose wrinkles as she makes a sideways face. "Like a shark," she finishes, and Konran laughs.

"Only if you're a Nolvaric lover," Tibo grins with a wink. "Only if you're one of them fools."

"Here it comes!" a new voice calls out from behind Konran. "What you've all been waiting for!"

Two pilots, one male with dark, almost black skin and the other female with some of the whitest skin Konran has ever seen, carry in platters of steaming food. They serve Konran first, and he stares at his plate with widening eyes. Two perfectly round pancakes stare up at him, eggs Benedict baked into their centers. An assortment of chopped pistachios adorns the fluffy crust, which oozes cheesy sauce onto an arrangement of simmering scallions and sizzling bacon peeking from beneath.

"What?" he states in delighted disbelief. "This! I haven't had this in forever. How ...?"

"We have our ways," the man states smugly. His soft patch reads, *H. Shellegal.*

"You could say," the woman adds, "that Ms. Fruryakova told us."

"Wait, you talked to Shuya Fruryakova?" Konran asks. "How did you even find her?"

"We didn't," she replies, "but you posted holos every birthday from six to sixteen, and the nets never forget."

Konran stares with wonder at the woman, whose thick white hair pulls back in neat cornrows into a tight bun. Then he notices her soft patch, which reads, *K. Shellegal.*

"The Twins are magicians, man," Ace says. "They can cook anything."

"Twins?" Konran asks through a mouthful, unable to avoid shoveling in the first bite. "Oh. Oh, wow, you nailed it. So, wait, you guys are twins?"

"Can't you see the family resemblance, man?" Tibo asks. "Pearl here is albino, man, which is why we tried to call her Bleach at first, but her brother kept threatening to shove my spleen up my throat so we just settled on Pearl, you know, man."

Pearl rolls her eyes and serves Tibo, letting some of the cheese sauce drip off the plate and onto his flight suit.

"Oh, I'm sorry, shark bait," she cracks with mock penitence. "Maybe you can bleach it out."

"Yeah, man, I deserved that," Tibo says, wiping the cheese sauce onto his fingers and licking it. "But seriously, girl, this sauce is palladium. For real, palladium."

"For real, palladium, indeed," Konran speaks through his fourth mouthful, relishing the dish. "So what's your call sign?" he asks Pearl's brother.

"Spleen," the pilot replies, raising his chin in a quick reverse nod with a *you know that's right* sort of grin.

The Twins finish serving everyone, and Konran eats with the Wildlynx, laughing, joking, and chatting. In between the exchange of words, the pilots wolf down platters of oozy-pistachio-egg pancakes, savoring Konran's old favorite dish with him. It feels easy. It feels right—like sitting in the middle of a group he was always destined to be part of. Finally, 0800 approaches, and Ace stands.

"Welcome to the team, man," he says, slapping his hand on Konran's shoulder. "Everyone's glad you're here, especially after the fight yesterday."

Slydog raises a forkful of pancake and shouts, "To Konran!"

"To Konran!" the Wildlynx cheer, raising forks of their own.

"Thanks, guys. This was amazing," Konran says, pausing from his third helping to smile. "I quit my ISSA job yesterday, so I've thrown all my cards in with you now."

"First time I saw you fly," Ace continues as the cheering subsides, "I knew you were a real pilot, man. You belonged with us. You belong in a Sparrowhawk. Anything else is putting falcons in a cage."

"That's exactly how it feels," Konran says through a final bite. "But really, thanks for this," he says, raising his fork to Pearl and Spleen on the other side of the table. "This is incredible. You two are the best."

Taking one final bite, an idea strikes Konran. He makes a face as if gagging. His stomach dry heaves and his neck muscles strain. He bends over as if choking, turning toward Valkyrie. She reacts quickly, but Tibo, wise to the ploy, reacts faster, leaning over and poking Konran with his fork as Valkyrie pulls him to his feet. A mouthful of partially chewed eggs-Benedict-pistachio-pancake-bacon spews out of Konran's mouth and splatters across Valkyrie's neatly pressed flight suit.

Wide-eyed, Konran swallows whatever is left in his mouth. "Oh no," is all he says, looking up to meet Valkyrie's intense green gaze. Then, with all eyes on her, the Wildlynx's lieutenant commander wipes Konran's sputum off her clothes and grabs it in her fist.

"You are such idiots," she sputters, flinging the fistful of vomit at him.

Konran flinches, and Valkyrie is gone, storming past Cassio, who had nearly made it to Konran's side before stopping to watch. And the room bursts into laughter.

"Maybe we call you Ohno," Tibo wisecracks as Ace, laughing nearly to tears, helps clean Konran. "Or Shangel, you know, man, short for Shoulder Angel. 'Cause you're always saving us and you wear that puke on your shoulder like a shoulder angel."

Ace finishes wiping Konran down and, curtailing his laughter, commands the attention of the entire room with a sudden air of authority.

"All right, people, Konran has to go. I expect the *Nova Scotia* will remain on alert throughout the day, so stay focused. We're doing head-to-head round-robin rotations in the simulators today, so study up and be ready. The battle yesterday revealed our enemy has advanced weapons and starcraft, and we will be ready next time they come to play. And, Tibo," Ace looks over at the lean, bald-headed pilot, "you're on muck duty, so get cleaning."

"Yeah, man, I deserved that," Tibo replies.

Ace leads Konran from the pilots' lounge and into the grav-lev shuttle tunnel.

"I'll let you take him from here, Corporal," he says, slapping Konran on the back and shaking hands with Cassio. "And next time, please sit at the table—you're one of us now."

Ace gives Konran and Cassio a sharp nod and an easy grin, and the shuttle whisks them away.

* * * * *

Cassio stops and Konran steps up to the door labeled, D. Granicks, Captain. He moves to knock, and the door slides open.

"Konran, good morning," Captain Granicks speaks from behind a mahogany desk in an efficiently decorated office. "Please, have a seat."

Konran sits in a comfortable armchair across from Granicks.

"How are you feeling today?" Granicks asks.

"Better," Konran replies. "Definitely better."

"I understand you quit your job at ISSA?"

"Yeah, you should have seen my inbox last night. They couldn't figure out whether to promote or reprimand me."

"And you wish to stay aboard the *Nova Scotia*?"

After throwing his entire basket of eggs into the *Nova Scotia*, the thought of pursuing an alternative hits Konran like a punch to the spleen. "Uh, yes, sir ... if I can. That's why you made me your assistant, right?"

"It is," Granicks confirms, and Konran's heart slows by twenty beats per minute. "So, how are you coping with recent events?" Granicks adds. "A lot has happened to you this week."

"Seriously, sir. But I'm doing all right. Every time I open my eyes something else crazy happens to me, but I'm getting used to it."

"I wouldn't expect that to stop anytime soon. I understand you had breakfast with the Wildlynx?"

"Yeah, it was great," Konran says. "They made me this dish the old cook at my boys' home used to make for me. Ms. Fruryakova just made it up for me one day, and the Twins figured it out from holos I posted years ago."

The talk of breakfast reminds Konran of a question he wanted to ask Granicks, and he adds, "By the way, could I ask you something?"

"Of course."

"Well, uh, I hope this is OK to ask."

"It's fine, son, you're my aide. Ask away."

"OK, um, well, I've noticed a lot of people on the ship with ... genetic quirks, you know? Like Laske with no legs, and Vilkoj with no hand, and Pearl who's albino. I'm just curious. I mean, you don't really see genetic defects like that much anymore."

"It's a good question," Granicks replies. "You could say I am particular about the people I bring aboard my ship. Rather than genetic defects, I see unique perspective and opportunity in those people."

"So you picked them on purpose? I mean, that's not a bad thing, I'm just curious."

"As much as I can, I do," Granicks says. "Experience has taught me that diversity of people, when cultivated correctly, engenders a synergy that you cannot find elsewhere. You simply cannot duplicate the resourcefulness of a man without a hand, the determination of a man without legs, nor the resilience of an albino woman of African descent. As a result, the *Nova Scotia* can do things other ships can't: like perform an intrasolar warp to pick you up."

156

Konran's eyes widen at that. "Wait, you *warp-jumped* to get to me? Really?"

Granicks smiles. "Correct. When the footage of your action at Y25LM90 posted, I recognized a pilot I wanted on my ship. The Nolvarics were going to close in fast, so I warp-jumped to get there first. Luckily, Commander Exeunt is particularly skilled in such matters, and we beat them to you."

"But intrasolar warping is illegal," Konran says, realizing the comment bordered on arguing about the reason he was alive.

Granicks smiles again and shrugs. "When you're really good at it and use it to fight Nolvarics, the details tend to go overlooked."

Konran considers that, feeling extra grateful to still be breathing. "I'm certainly not complaining—it's just impressive. Thanks again for saving me, and wanting me on your ship, and making me your aide and everything." He grins.

"You're certainly welcome, son," Granicks says. "That, in fact, brings me to our conversation this morning."

Konran sits up, edging forward on his seat. "Yeah, go ahead."

"To be blunt, there are forces in motion in this galaxy, and I'm afraid you have fixed yourself right at the focal point."

Konran absorbs that, mentally bracing himself.

Here we go.

"You said the Nolvarics yesterday were coming for me, but this sounds like something more."

"It is," Granicks affirms. "In fact, your position as captain's aide is not just so you can participate in military action on my bridge. It is also so I can share secure information with you."

"So, like a security clearance?" Konran asks.

"Yes. In times of war I have limited authority to grant such access. Our conversation this morning falls squarely within this realm."

"So I can't say anything outside this room?"

"For the present, make that your rule. You will receive further training as time permits."

"I can do that."

"Very good," Granicks acknowledges. "Now, some of this conversation may be difficult to swallow. Are you prepared for this?"

"Yes, sir, I am."

"Excellent," Granicks states, satisfied. "To begin, the USFN maintains a massive database of Nolvaric technology levels, activities, and locations, which updates instantly upon every reported encounter. Our best algorithms comb this data, parsing it with intel from millions of additional sources. The process is so precise, in fact, that we can calculate with high accuracy when and where any given Nolvaric clan will strike, as well as what technological advancements we will see next."

"Let me guess," Konran explores a hypothesis. "The advancements we saw yesterday were beyond the predictions."

"If only we were so lucky," Granicks says grimly. Standing and taking a step backward, the captain swings both arms upward as if lifting an object from the ground with his mind. A three-dimensional holographic projection of the solar system arises in response, filling the office. Now within the outer edges of the hologram, Konran stands and takes a step back of his own. The captain gestures again and the map scales logarithmically, altering the distances between planetary orbits so everything, both near (like Earth) and far (like the Kuiper Belt), fits compactly within the office.

Konran instantly knows the date from the planetary configuration, a date every child in the solar system knew by heart: April 3, 2164—the Scattering, or the day the Nolvaric Invasion ended. Granicks gestures again, and the 3D hologram flattens into the usual, easier-to-understand two-dimensional depiction of the solar system that everyone knew and loved.

"Do you recognize the date?" Granicks asks.

"Definitely. It's the Scattering. The day the Nolvaric Invasion ended. They had already been kicked out of the solar system, but on this day their bases around Luyten's Star and Procyon were overrun, and the Nolvarics scattered into the galaxy."

"Correct. Contrary to popular opinion, however, this is not the day the Nolvaric Invasion ended."

"It's not?"

"Observe." The holo-map cycles forward in time, and the planets move dutifully around the sun on their compressed Keplerian orbits.

"For three years after the Scattering, we see no activity, then in 2167 we have ..."

"The Battle of Neptune," Konran says as a red indicator blip appears near the ice giant's position in the holo-map.

"Very good. What do you know of it?"

"Just the basics," Konran says. "Some Nolvarics snuck back into the solar system and were detected just as they left the Kuiper Belt. The USFN supercarrier *Convictions End* engaged them before they attacked the Neptune colonies. The task force commander—Admiral Vincer Cummersen, I think—employed a Hajikini gravity generator to transform a linear flanking maneuver into a spherical siege around the Nolvaric position. After that it was like fish in a barrel. Since then, gravity generators have been a mainstay on all warships. At one point—"

"Yes," Granicks cuts him off, "you have the basics. Now, the only new technology used in this battle was the Nolvarics' ability to heal their ships, which averaged 1.25 times faster than during the Invasion. The Battle of Neptune occurred long enough after the Scattering that historians don't consider it part of the Invasion; however, this was essentially a delayed counteroffensive, with near-homogeneity to Invasion-era strategy and tactics."

Granicks pauses, and, as if throwing a Frisbee, tosses the solar system onto his wall. It minimizes automatically, resizing to fit the space. A new 3D holo-map appears in its place, filling the office with a depiction of the Orion Spur of the Milky Way galaxy. A faint star hovers in the center of the room, and Konran knows its name without thinking: *the sun*. Granicks flattens the map to a near-2D projection (maintaining some, but not all, of the spatial three-dimensionality between stars) and scales the map so its outer edge terminates at a radius of thirty light-years from the sun. The majority of inhabited space floats effortlessly there, encompassed easily within Granicks's office.

"After the Battle of Neptune," Granicks goes on, "we have the Battle of Sirius, the EZ Aquarii Trinary Offensive, the Battle of Lacaille 9352, and the Battle of Tau Ceti, all of which fit the previous mold, and none of which introduced any significantly new technology."

Red blips flicker into the galactic map after the mention of each battle, hovering dutifully next to the stars they were named for. Granicks stops after the Battle of Tau Ceti in 2170.

"This is the true point the Nolvaric Invasion ended," he instructs. "Hereafter, Nolvaric attacks devolve from coordinated militaristic assaults into tribal raids. By 2172, we had identified at least eighteen distinct Nolvaric clans, each with unique tactics, staging areas, subtribes, and rates of technological development. This is where our analysis begins in earnest."

The two holo-maps jump forward in time, and red blips begin popping like fireflies, methodically marking the time and location of every Nolvaric attack. After a few seconds, red lines begin sprouting between indicators blips, connecting and reconnecting them like the nodes of a rapidly reshaping cobweb. Numbers fill in the remaining free space, obscuring the stars and planets as an algorithm takes over. The lines, blips, and numbers change too rapidly for Konran to derive meaning from, but he watches raptly, drawn in by the mesmeric, holographic dance.

Suddenly, turquoise and yellow regions flash within the maps, adding their splotchy shapes to the blips, lines, and numbers, and Granicks pauses the algorithm.

"These are predictions," he explains, indicating the regions of turquoise and yellow across the two maps. "Only a few years have passed by so far, but the algorithm already has sufficient data to reliably predict future Nolvaric states."

He zooms in on the galactic map, focusing on a particularly big turquoise region near the K-type star Epsilon Eridani, 10.5 light-years from Earth.

"This turquoise region indicates a Nolvaric attack was predicted in the Epsilon Eridani system in February 2175. Had this region been highlighted with yellow as well, an advancement in Nolvaric technology would be expected during the attack. Details can be accessed like so."

He reaches into the holo-map, taps the turquoise region, and a holo-display appears next to it.

"At this point we've only processed a few years," Granicks continues. "Tell me: How good is the prediction?"

"Well," Konran says, squinting at the region, "it missed the actual attack by about two months and seventy-eight million kilometers, but it all falls within the uncertainty bounds. So I guess it did pretty well. And it got the orbital radius from Epsilon Eridani almost spot on."

"Very good. Pay attention to this accuracy as we progress."

Granicks zooms the galaxy back to its thirty-light-year radius, and the simulation resumes. On Granicks's wall, the four planets of the inner solar system dart about the sun like moths to the flame. The five larger, outer-solar-system planets crawl more gracefully around the solar epicenter, but what truly amazes Konran is the map in the center of the room. Even with more than a quarter quadrillion kilometers compressed into two square meters, he watches as the stars of the Orion Spur creep ever so slightly across the galactic firmament. Despite living in a day when humankind traveled to and from the sun's nearest neighbors, it never ceased to amaze him how dynamic everything was out there: while the nine planets and their myriad millions of smaller solar companions orbited the sun, trillions of similar planetary systems soared ceaselessly through space, spiraling around stars who glided upon galactic orbits of their own. If only the ancient mariners had known the utter fluidity of those points they fixed so certainly by sextant each night.

Decades of information flies by in seconds, and the simulation stops, having covered thirty-seven years in less than a minute. Konran peers at the maps, curious to decipher meaning from everything. Then he recognizes the arrangement of the planets, and his hands go cold.

"What is the date?" Granicks asks.

"February 27, 2212," Konran answers, his mouth becoming sticky. "Not quite a week ago. The day I fought the Nolvarics."

"Precisely," Granicks says. "I'm no Salazar, but some things are so clear even an old dog like me can pick them up. Notice that every, and I mean every, Nolvaric attack within the last twenty years falls within the temporal and spatial zones indicated in turquoise by our algorithm. While we can't predict the exact time or place of an attack, we always know when and where to focus our resources. I mean *always*."

Granicks peers at Konran with intensity before continuing.

"Prediction of Nolvaric technological advancement is somewhat less precise, but 99 percent of our yellow predictions still prove true within three months. Until you blew up that Nolvaric outpost on Y25LM90, we effectively had our enemy decomposed into a math equation. Some military scientists had gone so far as to predict the day we would bury our last Nolvaric, with optimistic estimates as soon as the year 2275, plus or minus fifteen years."

Konran whistles long and low, considering Granicks's revelations. "Warfare is some serious science."

And all I ever thought about was getting myself into one of those Sparrowhawks.

"Think of it this way," Granicks adds. "Everything you do leaves a fingerprint on the universe around you. What you choose, what you don't, where you spend your time, who you associate with, how you react to unexpected events, how much oxygen you exhale—everything you do can tell me valuable information about who you are. The more sophisticated my sensors and the more of them in all their various forms I can get around you, the more of that fingerprint I can detect and decipher. That is partially why territorial rights are so hotly disputed. Every pass at a planet or jaunt through a shipping lane provides another upward tick in the war for information."

"And then Y25LM90?" Konran asks, shivering, partially due to the thought of the frigid Kuiper Belt asteroid, partially to the thought of Granicks analyzing him down to his playlists and food decisions.

"Yes. Observe." The algorithm ticks forward and Y25LM90's red blip appears in the Kuiper Belt, marking the second stop on the *Relrick* and *Viona Grande*'s VIP tour. No turquoise or yellow predictions accompany it. It just appears, so insignificant that Konran would have missed it had he not been looking for it.

The simulation progresses forward another four days, and hundreds of red blips burst onto the map, leaping in massive splotches all across the Kuiper Belt. Ominous tendrils of red trickle inward, into the solar system, terminating where the assaulting Nolvarics had themselves been terminated. But neither turquoise nor yellow appears, and, in less than a week, more than four decades of computational brilliance crumbles to bunk.

And I started it, Konran thinks, dryness smacking in his mouth.

"Do you realize what this means?" Granicks asks.

Konran swallows unsuccessfully, trying in vain to get his saliva working again. "Somehow I stepped into the biggest Nolvaric trap in history?" he manages.

"We thought we had them pegged!" Granicks thunders. "We thought we had a strategy! We had minimized the risk and defended ourselves soundly! All evidence pointed in this one direction, convincing us we were right! And in one moment we realize we never knew anything at all!"

Konran cringes beneath Granicks's glare, feeling like the prey beneath the predator's gaze. And the moment passes.

"Sorry, son," Granicks says. "It's not your fault. But this insight—this revelation, this slap in the face that things were never what they appeared—well, let's just say if you hadn't been there in the command bridge yesterday, we might already be forehead deep and looking up."

"What do you mean?" Konran asks.

"Remember when you saved two of my pilots after figuring out the Nolvaric starfighters were more advanced than previous specs indicated?"

"Yeah," Konran says—how could he forget that?

Granicks swipes at the holo-map (like it just peed on his shoe), and the whole thing disappears, fading into a collection of the most recent algorithmic predictions. "What does the yellow say?"

Konran reads the yellow-highlighted predictions. "Nothing," he says. "It missed that. It just has something about an ice sublimation system."

"Like I said," Granicks growls, "we had them at a math equation. That sublimation system surfaced a week before Y25LM90, over on Raschon-2 orbiting Barnard's Star. The Nolvarics used it to steal water from the icy super-earth."

"Oh, right," Konran remembers. "Then they attacked the geothermal plants and the Tiyaka Reservists fought them off. I was following the action from the *Viona Grande*."

He shivers at the memory; thinking of the time before Y25LM90 was like considering the experience of his clone from another dimension.

"Exactly," Granicks confirms. "The algorithm had no problem with that one—just like everything else until now."

"So the Nolvarics that attacked Raschon-2 weren't related to those attacking the Kuiper Belt?" Konran asks.

"Perhaps, but nothing's certain. The Nolvarics who attacked the Kuiper Belt this week didn't display any tech advancements until the battle yesterday. My gut feeling says most of them simply didn't have the tech—which means our friends yesterday were concealing it on purpose. They were waiting for something bigger, and then got called up and sent after you when it all went south. What this tells me is there were multiple clans involved, some of which were more advanced than others, all amassed under the guidance of some higher authority. Your altercation on Y25LM90 spooked the hornet's nest, and the more undisciplined forces broke rank."

Konran tries to swallow, but his larynx has sunk into a pit of quicksand. He circulates his tongue, trying to disperse whatever saliva is left in his mouth.

"Not all of the Nolvarics yesterday had advanced tech," Konran replies at last. "It took me a while to understand what I was seeing. They would use it in spurts, to get an angle or evade an attack, and then they would revert to their normal specs."

"Exactly," Granicks replies. "But, and here is the key: you saw it, Konran—you picked it from that mess of chaos with no real battle training or analytics experience to your name."

"But your people were on to them, too," Konran replies. "Ace and Valkyrie would have figured it out."

Granicks shakes his head.

"Possibly. But when we sent that intel to the rest of the task force it turned the tide. You didn't just save your Wildlynx compatriots, son. That intel jump-started the battle for the *Jakarta*, the *Okhotsk*, and the *Lagos*, which each gained an edge from that point forward. It utterly saved the *Havana*, which was hit so hard the entire crew abandoned ship after defeating their foe. Unfortunately, the *Gaza*, the *St. John*, and the *Wichita* had already fallen."

So many people ...

Konran grips the side of Granicks's mahogany desk, unsure if his legs were still working.

"That feat," Granicks continues, "is more impressive than how you took out those three Askeras with your gun-craft. What you accomplished on Y25LM90 was spectacular and unprecedented, to be certain. But on my bridge, well," Granicks shakes his head slowly, "that was something else. You can't just get lucky with something like that."

Konran stares at the collection of yellow-highlighted predictions still hovering between himself and Granicks. Then he hangs his head and closes his eyes.

"If I had been faster—maybe I could have..." he trails off, sighing against the sudden moisture in his throat. The change in texture from dry to wet was not comforting.

"No," Granicks insists. "The Nolvarics were hiding it. You said it yourself. They obscured it *on purpose*. They were better trained and better equipped than any Nolvarics in the Kuiper Belt. Don't you dare beat yourself up. Your insight regarding the warp drive saved the *Gamma*. Then you saved Hot Sauce and Slydog, and that in turn saved thousands more in the task force."

Konran's tongue sticks back to his pallet, suddenly dry again. He breathes, and his mouth makes a sucking sound, which he licks against before coughing and sitting down.

"Sorry..." he wheezes.

"It's OK, son," Granicks says. "It's normal to feel this way. But you'll never win another battle if you let it stick. You've got to focus on what you did right. Someday soon you're going to have to do it again. And we're going to need you."

Konran nods, taking a deep breath. "It's just hard to give yourself any slack when people's lives are on the line, you know?"

"It is. That's why you need good people around you. One woman or man can never carry the load alone."

Konran takes a few more breaths, internalizing Granicks advice. "So what do we do now?" he asks.

"That's why I called you here," Granicks says. "Let me get you something to drink first."

"That would be great," Konran replies. Despite the burden sagging onto his shoulders, he had good people around him now. Whatever came next, he could face it with them.

Granicks gestures, and a mahogany engraving of the Battle of Celsis splits in half on the wall to Konran's left. A levitating tray emerges from behind the panels. Tendrils of water vapor rise in spiraling wisps from perfectly cooled bottles as the tray touches down on Granicks's desk. Konran chooses the closest drink, pops its lid, and takes a long, gulping swig of the cool liquid. He doesn't recognize the flavor, but it does the trick.

"Ah," he sighs, satisfied. "What is this stuff?"

"Gorosoe tree sap juice," Granicks replies. "Fresh from the Korean settlements on Ganymede. One of the best kept secrets in the solar system."

"I'll say," Konran says. "Can I have another?"

"Help yourself, son. We have more to discuss."

Konran grabs another glass and Granicks goes on.

"Now that you understand the state of the solar system, you will understand how important it is for us to act quickly," Granicks states. "Your contribution to the battle yesterday has attracted high-level attention. In fact, I have orders to bring you in to USFN headquarters at Jupiter. They're sending a supercarrier to escort you in as we speak."

Konran coughs as gorosoe juice squirts behind his nose. "Wait, what?"

"Jovian Command wants you bad, son. I told you, your contribution to the battle yesterday was impressive."

"That's ... oh, that's crazy."

"Don't worry, we're not going."

"We're not?"

Granicks shakes his head. "No. There's no way our Nolvaric predictions suddenly screwed up so completely on their own. Something is at play beneath this, and it's been at play for a long time now. Something like this requires powerful people pulling strings in the shadows. There's no way I'm taking you in to HQ—

166

the one place in the galaxy packed with more power than any other."

"Yeah, don't send me there," Konran agrees. "So what else, then?"

"Have you ever been to Maehn Arziban?"

Konran chokes on his gorosoe juice again. "Maehn Arziban?" he sputters. "I'd have better chances getting to the Horseshoe Nebula. Are you saying we're going to Maehn Arziban?"

"I've been considering it," Granicks replies. "I have a contact there."

"Must be some contact," Konran blurts, "to be able to get you inside their defense perimeter."

Granicks looks at him. "He is."

"You're serious."

"It's a risk, no doubt. But my contact reached out with an invitation immediately following Y25LM90. I wasn't sure what to do about it at the time ... but now ... well, I'm considering it. With his blessing we would be assured entry into Maehn Arziban."

"Who is it?" Konran asks.

"I can't tell you that yet," Granicks replies. "The communication was sent through an old channel we set up years ago—nonmilitary, dark-net tech; not exactly something I'm allowed to keep around. But I do anyway."

Konran stares at the captain. "So, this contact of yours sent you a dark-net message after Y25LM90? It's about me, then."

Granicks nods. "My gut tells me to go. But I needed you to be aware first."

"What did he say? Can I know that at least?"

Granicks considers, then he shrugs. "We're in this together now, son. Here's what I can show you."

The captain scratches at the index finger on his right hand, rubbing it with his thumb in a particular sequence—whatever the pattern was, Konran cannot tell. Then Granicks holds the finger up close to his mouth and breathes a soft phrase: *"Echati changra. Kisanan pon tumali. Echati engara. Ranami gara fainari."*

A small holo-display pops to life, projected from the captain's index finger. The display is empty, except for one line of text hovering within its surface:

Friend. Come in haste. It is imperative I meet the boy.

"All right," Konran nearly whispers, nodding to himself and then to Granicks. "Let's go to Maehn Arziban."

"Excellent," Granicks says, flicking his finger and closing the holo-display. "Time for me to call in an overdue favor with Vice Admiral Chandikarya."

* * * * *

MAEHN ARZIBAN (City)

Founded October 4, 2142, by Sertius Arziban, the reclusive city-moon of Maehn Arziban is the capitol seat of the planet Summanus (see also: Planet Nine; Significant Twenty-First Century Discoveries; List of Massive Trans-Neptunian Bodies), which is the ninth planet from the sun (see also: Sol; Solar System One). The city of Maehn Arziban occupies the entirety of the Summanian moon of the same name (see also: Maehn Arziban (moon)), which has a diameter of 5,103 kilometers, or nearly that of Saturn's Titan. Separated both physically and politically from the rest of the solar system, Maehn Arziban has become a melting pot of culture and a hub of intergalactic trade. Known to proponents as a beacon of economic and political freedom, and infamous for severely restricting access to inhabitants of the other eight Solarian planets (see also: Original Planets, List of Massive Sub-Kuiper Solarian Bodies), Maehn Arziban (as well as its six sister-moon colonies (see also: Arzibanian Collective)) boasts a technologically advanced, multilayered orbital defense system designed to prevent any unwanted starship from entering within eight hundred meglicks of Summanus (see also: NAC (No-Admittance Cannon)). Despite its incredible distance from the sun, Maehn Arziban (moon) generates sufficient internal heat energy through tidal squeezing interactions with Summanus that its inhabitants have consistent access to a reliable source of geothermal energy.

Konran gestures with his eyes, directing the holo-display in front of him to select the hyperlink for Summanus.

168

SUMMANUS (Planet)
First predicted mathematically in the early twenty-first century, it was not until the middle of that century when earthbound scientists first observed the ninth planet using primitive, optico-infrared telescope technology. As with the majority of Solarian bodies, Summanus's name derives from ancient mythology, stemming from the Roman god of nocturnal thunder (see also: Summanus (Roman Deity)). With a mass eight times that of Earth, Summanus orbits the sun with a semimajor axis of 420 AU, or fourteen times more distant than the orbit of Neptune. Summanus originally formed within the protoplanetary disc alongside the other eight planets but was gravitationally ejected to its current orbit by interactions with Jupiter. The planetary composition is similar to the cores of Jupiter and Saturn, consisting of a large, rocky core enveloped within a thick, icy crust.

The door to Konran's bunk room opens, and Cassio pokes his head in. "Enough sulking. Time for training. Come."

Konran stands, and the holo-display evaporates.

"I wasn't sulking," he says, following Cassio through the wardroom and into the corridor.

"What were you doing, then?" the marine asks.

"Thinking."

"Is there a difference? Either way, I have the cure."

Cassio stops, letting Konran enter the grav-lev shuttle first before stepping in behind him.

"Oh yeah, what's that?" Konran says.

"PT."

"PT?"

Cassio looks at him, and the shuttle shoots into the tunnel.

"Yes, PT. Get ready for the workout of your life."

CHAPTER 10

Konran sits in the middle of the large, U-shaped couch at the rear of the semicircular room that had become his viewport on the *Nova Scotia*. Cassio sits on the far side, looking bored again. The unhindered view of the Milky Way is, of course, spectacular as always, and Konran enjoys it, albeit subconsciously. What really draws his attention are his feet, which still feel like boulders dangling from his legs.

The marine hadn't been kidding when he said Konran was in for the workout of his life. Konran had approached the workout with confidence—living in the twenty-third century had provided more than sufficient information and resources to keep himself in shape—but no other training could have prepared him for this. Inside the gravity-manipulation chamber that constituted the marines' gym aboard the ship, Konran had felt his limbs turn to lead. It was one thing to lift weights. It was another thing entirely to become the weight. While he swore he had spent an hour at least in the chamber, Cassio asserted it hadn't been more than fifteen minutes.

"You're sure this will wear off soon?" Konran groans.

"You should feel rejuvenated in less than an hour," Cassio replies flatly, "especially with as much of that drink you are consuming. Gorosoe sap is a fair enough anabolic catalyst."

Konran brings the drink to his mouth again, straining to lift spout to lips. His deltoids, biceps, and forearm muscles burn, and finally the cool liquid pours into his throat. At least Granicks had given him the case of gorosoe tree sap juice. Konran manages to drain the bottle, and the juice case hovers up and over to him, accepts the empty container, and provides a full one, which he takes gratefully—if not painfully. It would be a minute at least before he could attempt raising the new bottle to his lips.

"You know, bodyguards don't usually try to kill the people they're assigned to protect," Konran mutters.

"You said you could take whatever I threw at you," Cassio reminds him.

"I take it back. You're a demon."

"The boost cake will set in soon."

"Not yet. And, about that, I thought all anabolic accelerants were dangerous," Konran says, recalling horror stories of bodybuilders' arms and legs suddenly bulging so large their cardiovascular systems failed, unable to keep up with the increased demand for blood. "If I die from this, I'm going to haunt you. In fact, if I die from anything now, I'm going to haunt you."

"Do any military personnel aboard this vessel appear unwell?" Cassio asks, his Venusian-Baltic accent becoming thicker the more Konran pesters him. "Boost cake is 100 percent stable and completely bio-assimilable. You will be well within the hour, and then we can work out again."

Konran stares at the marine, wishing his arm could lift the bottle either to drink or to throw it.

"You're not serious."

"We do not have the luxury of time. You must be prepared before we reach Maehn Arziban, so we go again. Three more times."

Konran's arm finally actuates, and he drains the bottle of tree sap juice. The hover case exchanges the bottles, and he lets his arm dangle at his side again.

"Fine. Do your worst."

"You understand that you merely accomplished the fundamental warm up? I think I will do less than my worst next time."

"Whatever. Either way, it can't feel any worse than that."

Cassio scoffs. "I suggest you rest. You will know soon enough."

Konran takes the advice, shutting up and sinking back into the couch, watching the stars slip slowly across the galactic void.

Things looked different when sailing through space at the *Nova Scotia*'s cruising speed of 7 percent the speed of light (a paltry seventy-five million kilometers per hour, or twice as fast as the *Viona Grande*).

The speed at which the stars shift behind the viewport isn't the only thing irregular out there in the cosmos.

From his viewport vantage point, Konran can see the sun glaring like a brilliant but tiny sparkler some 5.8 billion kilometers away. Five tiny celestial spheres gleam against its light, and Konran knows them by memory rather than distinguishability from the more distant stars: Mercury, Venus, Earth, Mars, and even Saturn, spreading out like a jagged, pinprick line above and slightly to the right of the sun.

It was strange to see them like that. It wasn't that the planets had all lined up on one side of the sun—Konran enjoyed when they did that. Rather, it was the angle that unsettled him. Due to gravitational efficiencies, spaceflight generally took place within the planetary ecliptic, or on the same slice of solar system where the planets all orbited the sun. Spaceships traveling through the solar system preferred to align their internal gravity with the planetary ecliptic. This meant that, to a typical intrasolar space traveler, the planets always lined up to the "left" or "right" of the sun.

But today the Nova Scotia wasn't being typical. Nor was it traveling within the ecliptic.

When Granicks declared he would not bring Konran to Jupiter, Konran hadn't known what to expect. He certainly hadn't expected to be hurtling on an angle nearly perpendicular to the ecliptic, straight out of the solar system. But the planet Summanus was on the other side of the Kuiper Belt (and had been for centuries due to its long, slow orbit). While the Nova Scotia boasted a flank speed of 19 percent the speed of light, such velocity was reserved for short-range wartime maneuvers, too dangerous for general intrasolar travel. But even if it had been possible to cut a path through the solar system at flank speed, the voyage would have still taken more than two weeks to get to the moon called Maehn Arziban.

Thus, the only expeditious way to get there was to leave the solar system behind—not far, but just enough so the Nova Scotia could safely warp across the seventy billion kilometers separating them from Summanus. Notwithstanding the Nova Scotia's purported penchant for illegal yet effective intrasolar warping, not even Granicks would risk such an immense intrasolar leap. And so, although the warp itself would require no more than a half hour, it would take half the day just to crawl out of and back into the solar plane.

On the bright side, more than an hour had already passed since Konran's meeting with Granicks that morning, meaning the *Nova Scotia* had already covered one-fourth the distance to the warp margin. It was initially counterintuitive to him that the warp margin should be so wide this far from the sun, but Cassio had actually done a fair job explaining how orbital inclinations thickened the solar system at farther distances from the sun. Despite the hundreds of millions of objects larger than one kilometer buzzing about the Kuiper Belt, the probability of impacting one was low. But the odds weren't zero, and despite the *Nova Scotia*'s considerable shields, Granicks didn't like the thought of taking a one-thousand-meter-wide rock to the face at faster-than-light velocities. Even then, with trillions of such objects hurtling through the outer reaches of the solar system, the probability still wasn't zero once you reached the warp margin—but, at least statisticians agreed the odds of randomly exploding into nothingness became a manageable risk.

We're leaving the solar system, Konran thinks for the seventeenth time. As an encore to his first sixteen iterations of the thought, his stomach flops as if spit out by a roller coaster.

I am leaving the solar system—for the first time.

His arm makes it back to his lips, and he drains the next bottle of gorosoe tree sap juice.

Before Konran left Granicks's office that morning, the captain had called to request his favor from Vice Admiral Chandikarya. To Konran's surprise, within minutes the *Nova Scotia* received a fresh set of orders to, "Extend the hand of diplomacy at this time of urgency to assure the Arzibanian defense network obtains sufficient support against the upsurging Nolvaric threat."

When Konran asked how that changed the order from USFN Jovian Command to deliver him to Jupiter, the captain explained that it didn't. But, needing only the premise of an excuse (and affirming that he and Vice Admiral Chandikarya were now even), Granicks had set the *Nova Scotia* churning for the warp margin in less than ten minutes from the communication.

I'm actually going to warp, Konran thinks for the eighteenth time. *I wonder if it really feels as funny as everyone says.*

Under other circumstances, Konran may have been elated for a chance to visit Maehn Arziban. The largest of the six inhabited Summanian moons, Maehn Arziban was said to be prosperous, beautiful, and bustling with interstellar activity; but you had to be connected to receive admittance. For most "Solarians," as the Arzibanians affectionately labeled the folks inhabiting the solar system's lesser radii, Maehn Arziban may as well have been orbiting another star.

And for good reason. Founded before the Second Nolvaric Invasion, Maehn Arziban boasted a layered orbital defense system so impressive that the Nolvarics had ignored the planet in their attempts at conquest. It was said that Arzibanians simply watched and wagered during the Invasion, gambling amongst themselves whether they would have a fresh planet to recolonize when it was all done. Whoever had sent Granicks the mysterious fingertip message from Maehn Arziban, he carried some serious Arzibanian gravity to grant a USFN warship access to the system.

And so, the swirling pit of unease inhabiting Konran's diaphragm persists. Whatever solutions Maehn Arziban could offer him, his gut was convinced they would only make things murkier. Somehow, he, Konran Andacellos, the lowly dreamer, the forever-wannabe starfighter pilot, had become intertwined in the solar system's most nefarious plot. Now he fled to the city-moon of mystery, absconding on the very warship that was supposed to deliver him to United Space Federation Naval Headquarters.

What is going on out there? he wonders, imposing the question upon the stars gliding before him on their unnatural angles.

"Hello? Konran?" a voice calls down the access shaft leading into the viewport, and Konran's stomach careens off the roller coaster again.

"Kyalia?" he blurts, turning at the sound of her voice and regretting the sudden motion. "What are you doing here?"

The glow of Kylia's pulsating hair enters the room first, preceding the holo-star's descent down the ladder. She proffers one of her smiles upon touching down, and Konran feels the distant sun dim by comparison.

"Hey, Hero," she says, taking a seat and sidling up next to him. "I thought I would find you here."

Konran relaxes into her touch, but then suddenly stiffens as he remembers the sweaty workout of not so long ago.

"What is it?" she asks, looking at him with concern.

"Oh, I just did this crazy workout," Konran admits (inadvertently manfully), "and I probably don't smell that great at the moment."

She laughs before nestling back in beside him. "Have you ever spent an entire week on set with the cast? You could do three more workouts and not even come close."

Konran makes eye contact with Cassio at that, and the marine, who still looks bored, gives him a quick double-eyebrow raise as if to say, *Now you have something to look forward to after I'm done torturing you.*

"Franco made these for you," Kyalia continues, pulling out a few nondescript, wafer-size packages from somewhere and handing them to Konran. "He said something about them providing something or other for your recovery."

It was Konran's turn to laugh. "Well, if Franco said that," he replies, taking the wafers, "they've got to be good for me."

"You know he's always right," Kyalia says. "He's the best chef I've met. And you're the reason I got to meet him," she adds, giving him a light elbow nudge.

Konran melts at the touch, choosing to savor the moment and the wafers rather than speak. And, as the glimmering stars suck him in, he feels as if the universe had just crowned him king (albeit one under siege, but still, a king).

"You all right?" Kyalia asks after a moment.

"Yeah," Konran replies. "Yes, of course. I'm great."

"And I'm the Queen of Calisto," she says. Her smell fills his nose as her pulsating hair brushes his arm. Her eyes, now a gentle violet color, wrinkle around the edges as she looks up at him, making her appear mischievous.

"So what's up?" she presses.

"Oh, you know," he replies. "There's just been a lot to swallow lately."

"Talk to me," she offers.

"I don't know if I can, really," he admits. "It's naval stuff."

"It's about Maehn Arziban, isn't it?" she says.

"You know about Maehn Arziban?" Konran asks, unsure what he could say.

"Uh, yeah, Hero, everyone does," she says with an incredulous laugh, somehow edging even closer. Her face feels so close to his that, given the right nudge, gravity just might do the rest. And Konran's mouth goes dry.

"We're doing a crossover shoot with some of their local stars. You should come—I'll get you in it. Everyone would love it!"

Kyalia's excitement is exhilarating, and Konran's brain fumbles to generate words beneath the magnetic interference.

"You ever had gorosoe tree sap?" he finally asks, calling the hover case over and swapping for a fresh bottle. "Best-kept secret in the galaxy."

"Definitely!" she says without missing a beat. "The cast loves the stuff."

Konran opens the bottle, handing it to her before selecting one of his own. Her eyes widen as she lowers it from her lips, and she takes another drink.

"This is amazing. Where did you find it?"

"I'm not sure I'm at liberty to say," he replies, "but I've got this entire case. I may even let you have another one."

"Just one?" She shoves against him. "You have an entire case. And I thought you were my hero."

"I should be your hero for sparing one," he replies, regaining some mental traction in the conversation. "You saw how good they are. Besides, seven of them are already empty." He gestures and the case closes, hovering back down to its spot on the floor.

"Let me guess, you drank them all today?"

"I've had eight so far, counting this one. Two before I got the case. It's been that kind of a day."

"And what kind of a day is that?" she asks, settling back in next to him.

"The kind where you find out the entire universe actually does revolve around you, and that it all wants to kill you—or something like that."

176

"Ha!" Kyalia replies with a laugh. "You're dramatic enough to be a holo-star, Hero. Tell me about it."

"Remember what I did at Y25LM90?"

"Uh, yeah. Why do you think I keep calling you 'Hero'?"

"Well, that kind of set off this huge Nolvaric surprise attack. When they attacked us yesterday, they weren't just attacking the *Nova Scotia*, they were coming after me personally."

"You know, Hero, you really are a hero."

"That's not even all of it," Konran continues, taking a swig of the sap. "After we analyzed the Nolvaric attack—not just the one directed at me, but everything—we came to realize that—"

Cassio clears his throat loudly and Konran stops, realizing he is saying too much.

"Well, I guess it's complicated," he finishes. "That's probably all I can say."

"I get it," she says sympathetically. "I could barely handle being rescued once. For you it hasn't stopped."

It felt good just to hear someone else acknowledge the fact, and the swirling pit of unease in Konran's gut finally stops.

"I'm lucky to have good people around me," he says, parroting Granicks's earlier counsel. "I'd be dead without them." Cassio meets Konran's eye again and winks.

"Well, from what I've heard, Hero, you've done nothing but rescue people since you woke up," Kyalia replies. "I'd say you're even."

Konran smiles at her and takes another sip. "So how about you?" he asks, changing the subject. "How are you?"

"I'm good, Hero," she replies. "Going stir-crazy on this tin can, but I'm feeling myself again. Can you believe we've been in space for almost two weeks now?"

Konran hadn't thought about that. As far as he was concerned, he'd only been on the *Nova Scotia* for around two days, and he'd practically forgotten about the seven days prior to that on the *Viona Grande*.

"Not really, that's crazy, Konran says." Kyalia's eyes are a rich indigo now, and Konran blinks, suddenly swimming in their pools. It was now or never.

"I could take you somewhere special when we get there," he adds. "Just the two of us. Maehn Arziban has to have some fabulous restaurants."

And it will probably cost half of my life savings, but I don't care.

"Hero, are you asking me on a date?" Kyalia asks.

"If that's what you want to call it," he replies.

He leans in, unable to resist the pull any longer. His eyes close as his lips descend toward hers. Her hair tickles his face, and...

Kyalia pushes him away, laughing as if Konran just said something silly. "I can't date you, you're my hero!"

"Whu ... uh ... I, uh ..."

"The publicity would never work out," she adds like it was the most obvious fact in the world. "Besides, Alandie's totally my type. If you set me up with him that would be publicity gold."

As if she needs help from anyone to do that.

"Uh ... yeah. Sure..."

She leans in and gives Konran a light kiss on the cheek. "Thanks, Hero," she says, relaxing back in beside him. "I get so nervous sometimes."

They sit there, side by side, watching the stars together. Kyalia's weight feels perfect snuggled in so close. Juxtaposed so starkly with Kyalia's matter-of-fact rejection, his feelings flip between disbelief, numbness, and the ever-present desire to try the kiss again. Kyalia, as comfortable as ever, just talks to him. Even rebuffed so directly, Konran can't help but take comfort in the holo-star's genuine, if not unorthodox, expression of friendship, and his emotions muddle further.

"I've got a cast meeting in five minutes, so I better run," she says at length. "Let's talk again before Maehn Arziban."

She stands, kisses Konran on the cheek again, and flourishes Cassio with a smile. The glow of her pulsating hair lingers on the walls a moment after she disappears from sight.

Konran turns back to the viewport, staring past the planetary pinpricks on their awkward angle, past the millions of stars, into the cosmic void beyond.

And then Cassio snickers. He tries to hold back, but the next one pops out like a shout. Konran makes eye contact with the marine, and Cassio bursts into side-bending guffaws. He doubles over, leaning with one elbow on the couch for support as the laughter takes control. Finally he stops, but one glance at Konran sends him rolling in a fresh outpouring of verbal mirth.

Konran watches, dumbfounded, as humiliation begins to boil within his heart. Like the bubbles rising to escape from water too hot to contain them, the sensation froths in waves of greater and greater intensity. And then, unable to contain the chagrin any longer, Konran starts laughing: softly and pitifully at first, but growing in strength as he confronts the full, searing stupidness of the situation.

Cassio makes eye contact again, and their chorus of cackles echoes within the viewport for minutes.

Finally, Konran's laughter abates, and an urgent thought fills his mind. He struggles to speak, wiping tears from his face and composing himself while still laughing between breaths.

"Dude," he finally manages. "Show me where the closest bathroom is. I think I'm going to explode."

* * * * *

Chanziu Guan sits in the command chair of his Jinfen stealth craft, watching a small blip move through his holographic astro-display. The blip, near the inner edge of the Kuiper Belt, makes no sense. For the past fifteen minutes its trajectory has angled upward, away from the planetary ecliptic. The last orders Chanziu had intercepted from Jovian Command said the *Nova Scotia* was coming to Jupiter—right into Chanziu's hands. This, however, was completely unexpected.

Chanziu turns away from the astro-display, rotating his chair to a row of consoles on the other side of his cockpit. He inputs a series of commands, querying his databases for the locations of known (and supposed-to-be-unknown) USFN munitions depots, resupply points, mobile operating bases, and any other military assets that could have moved into the region in the last few hours. Nothing. He expands the search. Nothing again: no rendezvous point, no coordinated maneuver, no strategic realignment of USFN forces, not an incoming Nolvaric attack. Nothing. The only thing clear about it was that the ship *was not* coming to Jupiter as ordered.

Almost as if ...

Chanziu turns back to his astro-display. Tracking the blip, he runs a quick calculation. Sure enough, the ship's course charts an optimal angle for the warp margin.

Chanziu curses, restraining his fist from punching through his console—he needed both items functioning at the moment. Instead, he brings his fists to his forehead and rests both against the Jinfen's cold composite wall. He closes his eyes.

Why?

Then a thought strikes him like a hammer to a bell: *Darius Granicks must know something.*

Chanziu rotates back to his row of data consoles and goes crazy. He hacks everything, careful enough to not get caught but sloppy enough to be fast. He pours through data, and in moments the answer flickers before him on the screen.

Vessel: Nova Scotia

Status: Irregular

Cause: Conflicting orders

Description: Reporting to Maehn Arziban in lieu of Jovian Command

Action: Rescind and remit orders

Chanziu rereads the database entry three times before slamming his fist into his console. The console doesn't break (nor the fist), and Chanziu shuts it down. Then he shuts off all light sources in the Jinfen and makes his way to his small cabin. He shuts internal gravity off as he steps through the entryway, and then he sits, not on the floor but between it and the ceiling, floating. Chanziu was in his thinking spot.

With his first thought he curses his marriage to Saturnese stealth technology. Still within Jupiter's gravity well, his Jinfen lurked undetected within the thickest hive of USFN warships known to the solar system. Thanks to Saturnese military bureaucracy, however, the craft had been declared spaceworthy before scientists had worked out the final details, one of which involved preserving the Jinfen's cloaking system while simultaneously igniting her ultrafast subluminal propulsion system.

"An invisible intelligence agent has no need of speed," an all-knowing official had brushed off Chanziu's complaints when he was issued the Jinfen.

Now Chanziu was stuck behind enemy lines with a paltry top speed of 575,000 kilometers per hour, at which rate he couldn't hope to arrive at Maehn Arziban within twelve years. The Jinfen was many things: sophisticated, slippery, subtle, lethal. However, complete, it was not. Hanging there next to the swirling mass of gas that was the solar system's largest planet, Chanziu Guan was going nowhere fast.

Approximately eighty warships and fifteen million kilometers (or just over twenty-six hours) stood between the Jinfen and an unimpeded route to the *Nova Scotia*. And then he still had to make it to the warp margin, warp, sneak back into the solar system near Summanus, and then infiltrate Maehn Arziban and find Andacellos before the *Nova Scotia* picked another destination. Or before Minister Heesor got him.

Simply making a break for it was out of the question. Even if the Jinfen engaged her ultrafast engines and reengaged her cloaking system before being pulverized into space dust, she couldn't outrun a missile, let alone a well-placed rail gun round or plasma bolt. And once detected, it wouldn't take a military-grade computer to run the probability calculations necessary to find her, invisible or not.

A quick mini-warp was out of the question, too. Even without the massive array of warp dampeners protecting Jupiter's moons and their nine hundred million inhabitants, the planet's mass alone prevented warp drive functionality for millions of kilometers in all directions. The warp dampeners were just the cherry on top, designed to prevent terrorists (or really stupid pilots, or cloaked Saturnese spies) from initiating a warp drive within the planet's gravity well and wiping out half of Europa when the warp field destabilized catastrophically.

Chanziu's hand reaches out, and he allows himself to spin slowly, tumbling through the cabin as questions tumble through his mind.

Why Maehn Arziban?
What strategy drives such a desperate move?
Where will I find Andacellos when I get there?
How will I convince him to join me?
How can I get there in time?
How can I get out of here at all?

He stops his body's momentum with a finger against the floor and takes three deep breaths.

"Chanziu, my son," his father always said. "You are more brilliant than the sun at noonday. But you must learn patience, or your brightness will burn before you can make it yours. Light but one thought at a time, and you will have fire to spare."

As a child, Chanziu hadn't paid much attention to his father. Chanziu was too busy being brilliant, too focused on making stuff happen on the small Saturnian moon his family called home. It wasn't until the rival moon decided to attack that he finally saw wisdom behind his father's words. Not until he had huddled, a terrified, whimpering twelve-year-old boy behind the rickety airlock of his family's agricultural shed. Not until that moment, alone in the darkness, trying to force something, anything into his brain to save his family out there, hidden amidst their neighborhood of small, neatly cultivated plots of moonscape. Not until the cries and the screams and explosions had his father's words finally made sense.

Chanziu recalls that moment as he had ten thousand times since. Its urgency feels familiar—much like today's. His mind and body still, and Chanziu breathes again, waiting for that one thought.

* * * * *

Konran steps back into the corridor, relieved by his restroom reprieve. Cassio stands on the other side of the hallway, eyes still red from all the tears he had laughed out. He chuckles again.

"Are you sure you are ready for your next workout?" the marine asks.

"Let's do it. Whatever Kyalia brought me must have kicked in. I feel good enough—plus, I need to punch something with my fifty-kilogram gorilla arms."

"She probably gave you more boost cake," the marine says. "It is the only way to recover so quickly."

"I don't think so," Konran replies, "it actually tasted like food. Definitely not boost cake."

"Bah," Cassio snorts. "Chefs make anything taste like food—it is their job. Let us go."

Konran follows Cassio down the corridor. They make as if to enter the door to the grav-lev tunnel, but a woman steps out as it slides open.

"Konran!" she says, pronouncing his name as *Kōhn-ran.*

"Cazmira?"

"I was looking for you," the nurse says, stepping up close in the already cramped space. "I heard you were down this way. I'm off shift until we warp. I thought you could show me how to play *NolvaRetaliation 2164.*"

"The sim game?" Konran asks. "But—"

"I only have the sim-deck for another hour—you're a hard man to find, you know. Won't you show me how good you are? I would love to watch you in action. Please?"

Stuck there between Cassio, the door, and Cazmira, Konran just stares at the nurse.

"I am afraid Mr. Andacellos is required elsewhere," Cassio says, carefully yet firmly moving Cazmira out of the way and pushing past. "I apologize. Maybe next time."

"Excuse me? What was that about?" Cazmira grumbles as Konran steps onto the grav-lev shuttle in front of Cassio.

"No offense, ma'am," Cassio replies, shrugging as he steps onto the shuttle himself. "It is my job."

"Yeah, and what's that?" Cazmira asks hotly.

"His bodyguard."

CHAPTER 11

Konran eases back into the captain's seat, his hands and fingers comfortable on the controls of the naval landing craft. It was a familiar sensation, one developed over five years at ISSA, like calluses upon palms. Now if he could just remind himself to breathe.

It's just like the simulator. I've practiced this already. I've performed hundreds of atmospheric descents with dozens of starcraft during my career. This is no different than the simulator.

But real life was always different than the simulator—especially billions of kilometers from home, surrounded by the frozen nether reaches of the solar system.

When Cassio had promised boost cake would solve all of Konran's exercise-induced ailments earlier that day, Konran had been more than dubious at first. But each subsequent recovery had progressed faster than the last. Within minutes of the final session, Konran was on his feet, chipper, refreshed, and feeling better than he had since his former flame LiMei had broken up with him. And it didn't take an exaggerated eye to note that his shirt fit more snugly about his biceps and deltoids, his slacks a little tighter about his quadriceps, glutes, and hamstrings.

So when Konran received the message to "report to the Wildlynx simulator deck for immediate training," his smile nearly split his face in half (and if not for boost-cake-enhanced craniofacial musculature, his enthusiasm certainly would have finished the job). Instead of a Sparrowhawk, however, Konran spent the flight's final four hours training on Naval Landing Craft 112-A, simulating the final approach and descent into Maehn Arziban.

It's not like that wasn't totally awesome. Under normal circumstances, preparing to land on Maehn Arziban would have been an experience of unbridled bliss. But after anticipating some

184

serious Sparrowhawk starfighter sparring with the Wildlynx, Konran swore his shirt fit normally again after all the simulator time in 112-A.

This is easy stuff, he coaxes himself. *Not much different than Earth. I've got this.*

"Orbital Twelve, this is Archer-Two-Niner," he speaks into his comm set, "requesting permission to proceed."

"Request acknowledged, Archer-Two-Niner," Orbital Twelve responds. "Please confirm lock-in with chaperone buoy."

Konran glances at his control panel, where an indicator bar changes from yellow to green. Out his forward viewport a small beacon flashes in the distance, marking the location of the chaperone buoy waiting to escort the landing craft through Maehn Arziban's GAZ, or gravitational admittance zone. Beside him in the copilot seat, Commander Exeunt enters a series of authorization codes and nods at Konran.

"Roger that, Orbital Twelve. Locking in chaperone slave," he replies, making a small course adjustment to align with the buoy before relinquishing autopilot control to the chaperone.

"Authorization granted, Archer-Two-Niner. Proceed on chaperone-locked course to your rendezvous point with Sponsor Echo-Bravo-Three-Zero-Juliet-Bravo. Be advised: active targeting systems are locked on your position. Be advised: any course deviations merit immediate punitive action. Be advised: you proceed at your own risk. Please acknowledge."

"Acknowledged, Orbital Twelve. Proceeding as directed."

Konran releases the controls, and the landing craft glides smoothly forward, tugged as if by an invisible chain. The chaperone buoy guide floats less than a kilometer out the forward viewport, its beacon flashing with a distinct pattern: long, long, long, pause, long, short, long, longer pause, repeat.

The Morse code flashes, as Konran learned during simulator training, were an analog backup system confirming connection between his ship and the chaperone buoy. As long as the sequence didn't change, everything was operating properly. Every ISSA pilot knew the code backward and forward, and he easily translates the signal into its phonetic cognate: *O-K.*

"Fighter Wing, report status," he speaks into his comm, glancing at his sensor display. Ace's and Valkyrie's Sparrowhawks fly in close escort formation to Konran's landing craft. The *Gamma* brings up the rear, itself ten kilometers back. No other escort had been permitted for the USFN envoy.

"Fighter Wing holding high and tight," Ace crackles in. "And nice flying, man. I knew you could pilot, but Granicks wasn't messing when he said you could handle this."

"It's not much different than bringing an astrofreighter in to Earth or Venus," Konran replies. "Only Earth threatens you less with instant death if you screw up, and Venus doesn't use the flashing buoys."

"I always like good death threats to start my day," Ace says. "It's like a cold shower: makes me feel alive."

"Because Commander Martin routinely starts every day at 20:15," Valkyrie crackles in. Konran winces at her voice, the pistachio pancake disaster still fresh in his mind.

Play it cool. Just be professional.

"Like every green-blood, baby," Ace crackles back.

"You mean lazy and useless?" Valkyrie's voice is neutral.

"Funny, that would be the exact opposite of what I mean."

"Or were you referring to the hebetudinous effects of consuming too much Martian produce?" she replies innocently.

"The what now?"

"I believe Lieutenant Commander Melendez is suggesting Martian food makes you dull and lethargic," Commander Exeunt replies in her sharp, punctuated accent, not above engaging in the verbal joust.

"Now that stinks, Valk. Kinda like that phlegm you Vestans confuse for food."

"You wish you could stomach kribasa, green-blood."

"I wish you had never brought that mucus-slime recipe off that asteroid."

"Wait," Konran interjects, "Valkyrie, you're from Vesta? You know how to make kribasa?"

"Born there, and yeah. You tried it, Shangel?"

"We ain't calling him Shangel," Ace mutters.

"Only once, on a freighter run to Vesta," Konran says. "The CEO of the Vestan Mining Guild took us to dinner and I couldn't get out of trying it. Turns out that stuff is amazing."

"That wouldn't be old Commandant Krupigan, would it?" Valkyrie asks.

"Yeah, that was him. So, you knew him?"

"You could say that. He's the one who convinced me to be a pilot."

"Small world—or rather, dwarf planet," Konran replies and Valkyrie actually laughs.

"There's hope for you yet, Shangel," she crackles back.

"We ain't calling him Shangel!" Ace complains. "And Konran, man—you can't be serious."

"Totally serious," Konran deadpans. "The guy was over two meters tall—hard to forget someone like that."

"Not that guy," Ace chides, "the kribasa, man. You actually liked that primordial sludge?"

"Definitely!" Konran rejoins. "That stuff is incredible once you get past the mucus-slime consistency. And if you really savor it— let the crystals sit and melt on your tongue—I mean, wow. Nothing like it."

"Man, I just threw up in my mouth."

"I think Ace needs a weekly kribasa intervention," Valkyrie piles it on. "What do you say, Shangel?"

"I think so," Konran takes the next jab. "We'll probably have to slip it into his food at first or drip it into his mouth when he's sleeping—at least until he starts taking it willingly."

"They didn't teach me to sleep with one eye open for nothing, you know," Ace mutters. "Might as well call you Kribasa."

"But seriously, Valkyrie, when are you making some?" Konran asks.

"Find me eight hours and a kilo of mucaescia spores, Andacellos, and I'll whip you up some on Maehn Arziban," Valkyrie replies happily.

"You're on triple watch, forever," Ace retorts. "Effective immediately."

"I'm sorry," Captain Granicks's voice joins in, "but I cannot permit such an egregious violation of naval labor regulations. In fact, Ms. Melendez, I'll grant that request for leave as soon as advisable. It's been awhile since I've had kribasa."

"What? *Et tu, Capitán*?" Ace replies, tone betrayed. "Come on, Rev, Exit—at least one of you has to be on my side."

"Sorry, pal," Revenshal joins the conversation. "You're losing this one."

"In fact," Commander Exeunt adds, "there is a restaurant that serves Vestan cuisine not far from our destination. It will be easy to make the arrangement."

"I'm shutting up now," Ace says, "before we end up drinking from the toilet and calling it fine dining." Everyone except Ace laughs.

"So, Valkyrie, no more Shangel?" Konran asks after a pause, reflecting on her usage of his actual name in her last transmission.

"Ick, no. Worst call sign ever. Ace rode Tibo so much it must have been one of those Freudian slips."

"Nothing Freudian about that," Ace returns.

"All right, kids," Commander Revenshal's voice crackles in. "This is as far as I take the *Gamma*. We'll synchronize our orbital position for optimal response time, should you need us down there. Good luck."

"Excellent, Commander," Captain Granicks replies. "Hopefully we'll be back shortly. I'll send status checks every fifteen minutes."

"Copy that, Cap."

Konran watches his sensor display as the *Gamma*'s blip breaks off behind him. It holds position just outside the dashed line marked as the Arzibanian Defense Perimeter, falling farther and farther behind as the chaperone pulls Konran onward. More than eight million kilometers behind the *Gamma*, the rest of the *Nova Scotia* awaited, patiently docked at the Maehn Arziban's permissible radius for ships of its size.

Suddenly cognizant of his lack of support, an intense sense of naked vulnerability envelopes Konran. Alone and miniscule, he, Ace, and Valkyrie press forward, blanketed within an ocean of unending, unfamiliar blackness billions upon billions of kilometers big.

His gaze returns to the stars. Even so far from the sun, they retain their characteristic patterns, but Konran finds little solace.

And then, what previously had only been an extra-dark patch in the ocean of darkness takes form: the planet Summanus, the ancient god of nocturnal thunder, emerges discernible as an immense black disc.

Konran's sense of foreboding deepens as the unnaturally dark mass slowly grows in size. Planets simply didn't look like that. Even Makemake at its aphelion of nearly eight billion kilometers still had enough light left to look like something when you approached it. But this was nearly eight times that distance, which meant sixty times less light.

I wonder how Alandie's doing? he thinks, willing his mind off the subject.

Alandie had left for Maehn Arziban hours ago, along with Kyalia and many of the VIPs. While Konran and the *Nova Scotian* landing party waited and waited for Arzibanian clearance to proceed toward the restrictive moon, the *Nova Scotia's* non-USFN passengers had booked passage on a merchant vessel in under an hour.

They're probably already having dinner, he thinks, wistful but not jealous. Although Cassio's laughing session had made something right in Konran's heart again, it didn't mean a part of him didn't still wish to be on the other side of the table from the glowing hair, scintillating perfume, dazzling smile, and hypnotic eyes. But once he told Alandie that Kyalia was into him (and after he picked his PIT off the floor and brought him back to consciousness), it wasn't two minutes later that the two of them sat, arm in arm, burbling sweet nothings at each other like the galaxy's perfect couple.

I'm never going to understand how this works, Konran broods. *I mean, it's not like I misinterpreted her signals. Except I did. Completely. How was I supposed to know? What else are you supposed to think when a girl ...*

Ace's voice crackles in, interrupting the thought, and Konran's brain mentally thanks the pilot.

"You'd think they oriented us to pass *underneath* that beast on purpose," he says.

"I would have," is all Valkyrie replies.

189

Above and to the right of the chaperone buoy, Konran sees what the pilots are talking about. The massive orbital defense station known as Orbital Twelve glimmers with bulging arrays of missile batteries, energy cannons, antennae, and receiver dishes. Scarcely illuminated by sunlight so diffuse that its brightest reflection shines less than that of the full moon, the station floats there like a supernatural fortress, its parts fading in and out of perceptibility as it rotates. Konran watches it pass overhead, shivering.

"Konran, look closely," Commander Exeunt speaks, and Konran nearly jumps. "In the distance. You will see what you have been looking for." She points forward, and an indicator pops into existence at the gesture, marking something yet invisible to Konran's eyes.

He peers into the indicated void, attempting to discern shape or form betwixt the starry panorama, but all he sees is the lurking mass of Summanus looming ever larger out the forward viewport. And then he sees it.

"Is that ...? It's a ... That's a NAC!" he begins in a whisper, ending almost in a shout.

The NACs, or no-admittance cannons, were the legendary, ultimate Arzibanian line of defense. Massive, long-range, plasmo-ballistic super-cannons, the NACs had rendered the Arzibanian Collective virtually untouchable to outside military occupation—as the ill-fated Kashnavanori-Humbrick task force found out sixty-five years ago when sent to enforce United Space Federation tax law upon the colonies. Although the cannons hadn't seen large-scale usage since that initial clash, the Arzibanians demonstrated them annually on Arzibanian Independence Day, demolishing mocked-up battleships and old, retired cruisers with one shot apiece. After the Second Nolvaric Invasion, Earth and other inhabited systems had adopted similar defense systems, but none at the same grandeur or audacity as the NACs.

Being part of Solar System One but so far from the collection of debris clinging to its closest radii, the Arzibanian Collective was an attractive, easy-to-reach destination for interstellar traders. With so much trade traffic into the system and such harsh terms of admittance, once or twice a year some ill-fated merchant crew made news by violating Arzibanian protocol and getting blasted to pieces by the NACs. Such actions inevitably drew condemnation across the galaxy (most severely from the Arzibanian's nearest neighbors), but hurt feelings swept quickly under the bridge of minimally regulated trade, and, both because of and in spite of the NACs, the Arzibanian Collective continued to thrive.

"I bet I could fit six of these landing craft in that barrel," Konran says, eyes glued to the NAC. The cannon hovers directly out the viewport, drawing near enough to partially block out Summanus. Undoubtedly, the United Space Federation Naval party had not been brought on this route coincidentally.

"Eight and a half, to be precise," Commander Exeunt replies from the copilot seat next to Konran.

"Eight and a half?" Konran repeats.

"You can fit eight and a half of this craft abreast into that barrel," the commander corrects his estimate. "Do you know the origin of the guns?"

"Uh, didn't Sertius Arziban himself design them?"

"In part. He envisioned them, yes, but they were designed and built by my people."

"Really?" Konran says, realizing he has no idea who Exeunt's "people" are. "I actually don't know where you're from, Commander. I never placed your accent."

The dark-skinned woman looks at him, and something about it makes Konran happy to be friends with the woman instead of enemies. "I am Xolian, Mr. Andacellos."

Since his encounter with Kyalia earlier that day, Konran had been proud that nothing had caused him to need more gorosoe tree sap juice. Not Granicks's offer to pilot the landing craft, nor the orbital defense stations, nor the NACs, not even the ever-growing orb of Summanus had overwhelmed him enough to call upon the exquisite liquid for support. But now he suddenly wished he had at least one bottle with him into the pilot cabin.

"Xolian? You're a Xolian?" is all he can reply.

"I am."

"I'm flying with a Xolian?"

"Indeed," she replies with a smile, this one more amused than terrifying. "You are easily impressed, Mr. Andacellos?"

"Sorry, I've just never met a Xolian before. All the stories, I mean, you're like the most famous space pirates of the twenty-third century. I feel like I should ask for your autograph or something ..." Konran pauses, realizing too late what he had said.

Exeunt just smiles. "That is a common preconception about my people."

"Er, Commander. I didn't mean ..." Konran says, fumbling over the apology.

"But if you want an autograph, you may ask it of my uncle. You will meet him within the hour," she replies with another enigmatic look.

"Your uncle?" Konran asks cautiously, his head slowly realizing its foot wasn't rammed in its mouth to the ankle after all.

"I should probably fill you in, kid," Granicks voice crackles in. Having given Konran authority to captain the landing craft into Maehn Arziban, the captain rode in the back of the landing craft with Salazar, Cassio, and what gear they had been permitted to bring.

"It wasn't appropriate to explain earlier. Yes, Commander Exeunt is Xolian, and technically a royal one at that. Her uncle is my contact on Maehn Arziban. He's the reason we were able to get sponsorship to enter the colony so quickly. He and I go back years, but you may not want to call him a pirate to his face when you meet him."

"Right, yes, sir. Sorry, sir," Konran replies, looking at Exeunt who dismisses the apology with a shake of her head.

"Man, I didn't even know that intel," Ace crackles in.

"I did," Valkyrie replies breezily.

"And how did you acquire more intel than your superior officer?"

"Girl talk, duh."

"Sounds hebetudin-whatever," Ace replies.

"Touché, Commander. Touché," Valkyrie crackles back.

Konran chuckles, feeling better. His life had changed overnight, and as Granicks had warned, the craziness wasn't going to stop anytime soon. Things were simply how they were now. He was flying with Xolians, visiting Maehn Arziban, and fleeing from Nolvarics. Life had been throwing its best curveballs, but as his old coach used to say, "A curveball isn't impossible to hit, you just have to know how to watch for it."

"There are more curveballs coming," he mutters, mentally bracing for the uncertainties undoubtedly out there in the darkness. "You just have to know how to watch for them."

"Curveballs?" Ace asks. "You talking baseball over there, man?"

"Er ... yeah ... more metaphorically..." Konran starts to explain.

A bright light appears at the edge of Summanus's dark disc. The planet itself is near enough now that its surface has changed from an utter black void to a vague, blotchy blackness, but the sudden increase in light casts shadows across the Summanian topography, highlighting a rugged, crater-strewn landscape of ice.

"Solis," Konran says, suddenly awestruck.

The light grows in intensity before separating entirely from the planet, suddenly shooting off into space. But the light doesn't leave, assuming instead an orbit-like path about the planet. Solis, the moon converted into a tiny pseudo-sun by Arzibanian ingenuity (and a fair amount of nuclear fusion reactors built into its surface), had risen.

And then, in its wake, Maehn Arziban appears.

Maehn Arziban rises behind Summanus like a miniature Earth, white clouds and blue lakes so idyllic that Konran can't imagine the solar system existing without them. The white swirls of vapor ride lazy atmospheric convection currents, spiraling in patterns far more perfect than any concocted by the blue planet.

"Archer-Two-Niner, this is Sponsor Echo-Bravo-Three-Zero-Juliet-Bravo, do you read?" a female voice crackles into the comm. Her accent is sharp and punctuated like Commander Exeunt's.

"Acknowledged, Sponsor Echo-Bravo-Three-Zero-Juliet-Bravo," Exeunt answers without missing a beat. "Reading you loud and clear."

"Prepare for chaperone disengagement in two minutes. We will lead you in."

"Acknowledged, Sponsor. *Echati changra*," Exeunt replies.

"*Echati engara*. Welcome home, Yoana."

CHAPTER 12

Chanziu Guan was making good time. The six-hour detour hadn't helped, but once he found his epiphany, it had taken nothing more than patience to evade USFN forces and escape from Jupiter.

It had been simple, really.

After hacking the Jinfen's cloaking generator, rewriting portions of its operating system, and physically reengineering sections of its ultra-advanced, hyper-secret propulsion system, Chanziu had been on his way: over-pressurize the propulsion capacitors, emit a microsecond burst of stealth-killing gamma propulsion, reengage cloaking, maneuver randomly to throw off targeting vectors, and repeat.

The USFN's frenzied efforts to locate, track, and destroy his mysterious reappearing, disappearing ship had gotten close. Impassioned bursts of coil gun, plasma, and missile fire hounded each reemergence like a Fourth of July grand finale. But, like the grandmaster's chess opponent losing their last pawn one space from regaining a queen, they hadn't really gotten that close. The evasive maneuvering had consumed precious time, but once Chanziu had built up sufficient velocity in the direction he wanted to go, he simply let it carry him away.

Now, finally far enough from the hornet's nest that was Jupiter, he ignites the Jinfen's ultrafast engines. With a maximum velocity four times faster than any USFN warship at subluminal speeds, Chanziu had mere minutes before reaching the warp margin.

Still, he worried. The *Nova Scotia* had probably already arrived at Maehn Arziban. She would be through the security scans by now, already making her approach to the city-moon. Chanziu turns to his row of data consoles, working them with a magician's touch, and the Arzibanian orbital docking registry displays before him. Sure enough, he was right. The *Nova Scotia* shows docked eight million kilometers out from Summanus, with a note on the boarding party size and intended destination.

Xolians, Chanziu notes, thoroughly impressed. *Darius Granicks has friends in high places. If anyone can keep Andacellos safe until I get there, the Xolians can.*

He relaxes somewhat, formulating the beginnings of his contact plan. His eyes meander through the rest of the orbital docking registry, his mind more on whether diplomacy or stealth is the optimal tactic for the situation.

And then his gut hits the floor. In plain text before him, Chanziu reads disaster.

The Tartaglia *is set to dock at Summanus in forty-five minutes.*

Frantic, he accesses the *Tartaglia*'s registry entry, praying against hope that some other vessel shared that name. But no. It wasn't just *a Tartaglia* bound for the same destination as Konran Andacellos, it was *the Tartaglia*: Vadic Heesor's personal flagship. Not only that, but its landing party had been preapproved for immediate admission into the system. The USFN minister of defense had outpaced Chanziu.

He probably traded the water from the Caspian Sea for such rapid admission.

Sixty minutes from Summanus at best, Chanziu still had to navigate the Arzibanian's defense network before setting his feet onto Maehn Arziban.

Failure comes to none faster than they who underestimate their enemy, the old adage taunts him, and he pounds his fist into the data console.

"No!" he screams as the tentacles of failure plunge into his chest, wrapping around his heart with icy embrace.

"No," he speaks, pleading. But the math was simple: space was too big, Heesor too fast, and Chanziu too slow.

Despite everything he had done, despite months of tedious effort, despite all the secrets he had uncovered, Chanziu had failed, Heesor had won, and Chanziu's family and his people would be destroyed.

"No!" he snarls.

He hadn't just called upon six PhDs' worth of specialized training to rebuild the Jinfen's cloaking generator and propulsion system for nothing. He hadn't lived in that maintenance shaft for seventeen days to unearth Heesor's treachery for nothing. He hadn't scoured the galaxy for nothing, piecing together in 460 days a plot that amounted to the subterfuge of the millennium. He hadn't fought all those years ago, a child of twelve, singularly defeating more than thirty raiders from that despicable, rival Saturnese moon for nothing.

His family yet lived. His people yet survived. Chanziu stands up, leaving the Jinfen on autopilot and donning his space suit.

It was time to work.

* * * * *

Maehn Arziban grows from a softball to a basketball to a diameter equaling Giza's pyramid as Konran's landing craft draws near. Solis's light reflects brilliantly from the city-moon's surface, its luster dimming the gentle, consistent glow of deep space by comparison. Hundreds of starships sparkle beneath the light, coming and going in all directions.

"Preparing to enter the GAZ," Konran announces, searching for signs of the Xolian escort, which still hadn't shown up on sensors.

The GAZ, or gravitational admittance zone, was a thin, gravitationally modulated bubble surrounding each of the Arzibanian moons. Passage through the GAZ caused distortions in its field, which allowed precise tracking of all craft entering or exiting that system. It also happened to be far enough away that the NACs had time to blast you to smithereens if the Arzibanians decided they no longer liked you.

The landing craft hits the GAZ, rocking and lurching as GAZ-affected space-time shifts about it. Like the passenger of an ancient automobile transitioning from solid asphalt to deep sand at high speed, Konran staggers in his seat. Commander Exeunt, however, could have sipped tea with her pinky raised for all the GAZ affected her. The jostling lasts for another second, and the landing craft sails into undistorted, certified Arzibanian space.

Konran disengages the link with the chaperone buoy, and the beacon flashes brightly three times, signaling the system had deactivated successfully. He makes a series of quick course adjustments, aligns the landing craft with its rendezvous point, and sets scanners for optimal short-range small craft detection.

While over forty craft milled within a hundred kilometers of his position, he could detect no sign of the Xolian escort.

"Archer-Two-Niner, we have visual. Maintain current trajectory," the Xolian sponsor crackles into Konran's comm. Still seeing nothing, he adjusts his viewport's settings, cycling through various combinations of spectral frequencies without luck.

Xolians, Xolians, he thinks, summoning what he knew of the infamous clans. *They come from the moons of Kapteyn b, thirteen light-years away. They're builders and merchants, but some people call them space pirates. They're near-mythological warriors—but that's mostly comic book hype. And they're said to test others, probing for weakness and strength in out-of-the box ways before engaging in the manner most optimal to victory.*

On a hunch he kills his active scanning system, setting it to listen instead to the background signal of space itself. And there they are: a trio of blips zipping up to meet them from Maehn Arziban's southern hemisphere.

"Visual confirmed, Sponsor," Konran replies, figuring that was close enough. "We track you on vector minus fifteen, minus twenty-three, minus seventy. Take us in." He activates the landing craft's Morse lamp, transmitting the standard maritime sequence of hailing flashes.

The three Xolian craft burst into view in response, no longer hidden from either scanning systems or eyeballs. The lead craft blinks with hailing flashes of its own, signaling intent to rendezvous for escort. "Prepare for rendezvous, Archer-Two-Niner. Did Yoana give us away?"

"Negative, Sponsor," Commander Exeunt replies, "that was all Mr. Andacellos."

"I speak with Mr. Andacellos, correct?" the sponsor asks, her punctuated words crackling with a hint of curiosity.

"Yes, ma'am," he replies.

"You should know that no guest to Maehn Arziban has ever passed that test. How did you accomplish it?"

"I figured your fighters were too advanced to track with standard techniques, so I just looked for what wasn't not there, and there you were," Konran replies.

"Impressive," the sponsor replies. "Your reputation precedes you, Captain Andacellos. It is an honor to fly with our most prestigious of guests."

Konran's brain lurches to process the conversation, scarcely able to comprehend that he is flying with, speaking to, and exchanging personal compliments with Xolian pilots—that is until he catches Commander Exeunt rolling her eyes beside him. He gives her a questioning glance, and she mutes their comm system.

"My cousin Zenara pilots that craft. She relishes overstepping bounds for a taste of the dramatic."

"Ah," Konran replies. "How should I respond?"

"Tell her we are excited to meet her father."

Konran unmutes the comm system. "Thank you, Sponsor. We are excited to meet your father."

"You will meet him shortly," Zenara replies. "Initiating rendezvous."

The three Xolian craft split up, looping around and forming into a triangular escort, one ship in front, two to the rear. Ace's and Valkyrie's Sparrowhawks form a similar shape with Konran's landing craft, the USFN triangle encompassed within that of the Xolians. Hands on the controls, Konran matches velocity with Zenara's lead craft. Maehn Arziban looms as big as a mountain, and the duo of trios descends.

Once in stable formation with his escort, Konran engages his optical zoom to study the simple, elegant Xolian craft in front of him. Its shape resembles that of a black, elongated egg—except trimmer, and more dynamic, like a blunted arrowhead. A ring of swooping, triangular winglets protrude from its body just aft of the midline, curving and tapering gently backward until they converge into nothing, like the sleek fletching of a twenty-third-century arrow. The design bears no transition points, edges, or lines; rather, everything melds smoothly from one captivating geometry to the next. A series of seven thrusters glow pale sapphire behind the craft, a hexagon surrounding a central point.

"Beautiful," Konran says under his breath.

"Captain Andacellos, please repeat?" Zenara crackles in.

"Er," Konran looks at Exeunt, shrugging helplessly, "I was just admiring your craft—a beautiful design."

"A worthy compliment from our worthy guest," she replies, spiraling her craft rapidly in a show of enthusiasm. Her starfighter's winglets shift with her motion, growing and shrinking in size, merging into fewer, splitting into many, their motion around the central mass discernible only due to the rotational mismatch between them and the seven sapphire thrusters.

"What's it called?" he asks Exeunt.

"That Xolian starfighter is known as the Xarba," she explains. "The closest translation would be 'health,' but it signifies more than that—a fiery vitality."

"Archer-Two-Niner, prepare for atmospheric entry!" Zenara calls out as the Xarba's dance subsides.

Konran grins in anticipation. He checks his altimeter, which had been pinging radar off Maehn Arziban's surface since they had entered the GAZ: only one thousand kilometers remained before atmospheric entry. Spaceflight—though chic, dangerous, and the crowning symbol of advanced civilization—was generally a remarkably boring undertaking. The same set of basic procedures pretty much got you from point A to point B every time. But no two atmospheric entries were ever quite the same—and it wasn't every day you got to plunge through the protective shell of a new world while piloting a new craft in tight formation with potential space pirates, not to mention the one in your copilot chair, all while descending into the capital city-moon of the most successful yet inaccessible space colonies this side of the Oort cloud.

Konran flicks a toggle switch, and the landing craft's atmospheric entry system engages. Muffled clicks and clangs echo throughout the craft as unshielded equipment retracts from its hull. Muted hisses whistle and gurgle as thermally absorbent coolant pumps throughout its fuselage. Although it would have been feasible to simply dive into the atmosphere with protective shields up, the exotic subatomic particles used in military-grade shielding tended to produce nasty byproducts when intermingled hotly with Earth-like atmosphere such as Maehn Arziban's. And then there were the grav shields, which threw atmospheric molecules into a frenzy of micro-weather systems. Better, consensus had decided, to endure atmospheric entry the way nature had intended: with good old-fashioned materials and geometries suited for heat absorption, resistance, and thermal shock shedding. Konran couldn't help but agree with the consensus, because every time the experience was captivating (and the lack of toxic tornado rain was nice, too).

"Fighter Wing, report entry status," he orders.

"Fighter Wing green for entry," Ace confirms.

"We are green for atmospheric entry, Sponsor," Konran sends back to Zenara. "What place are we in the queue?"

"In the queue?" she asks.

"Yeah, how many ships are ahead of us for reentry?" When descending into Earth, Venus, or Mars, the wait could add another hour depending on the quadrant you were visiting.

"Ahead? No one," Zenara replies, her punctuated accent amused through the comm. "They're all waiting for us."

"Well, all right, then, take us in," Konran says, suddenly feeling at the crest of a roller coaster looking down.

Zenara dives, and Konran presses easily into the controls, reorienting his mind as *forward* transforms into *down*. The Xarba's winglets wrap in around its egg-like arrowhead shape, sucking in like a straitjacket. Konran traces Zenara's decaying orbit toward the city-moon below, brimming with excitement. He mentally tracks the kilometers above Maehn Arziban, intuiting the distance by experience rather than altimeter reading.

Four hundred kilometers to go, three hundred, two hundred, one hundred. Here we go!

Atmospheric molecules convert from invisible vapor into pinkish-white plasma as they ionize under the friction of entry. The landing craft's viewport adjusts to the glow, filtering for continued forward visibility. Telltale heaviness presses upon Konran as the decelerations of reentry pull him into the pilot's seat. Slowly, the blackness of space gives way to the blueness of sky, which appears a fuzzy bluish gray through the viewport filters. Without checking his instruments but at an altitude of twenty kilometers, Konran opens a comm channel to all occupants of the landing craft.

"Here come the bumps, everyone," he announces.

Deceleration thrusters fire, and Konran's weight triples for an instant, fading back to normal as internal gravity adjusts to the dynamics of deceleration. The jets fire seven more times as thermal energy (recently stored within the craft's thermally absorbent coolant) converts into speed-arresting plasma jets. This was Konran's favorite part of reentry, his personal front-row seat to the mighty clash between raw engineering elegance and the ageless forces of physics.

He relishes the moment, grinning at Exeunt. Then the blur of plasma dissipates, automated atmospheric entry systems disengage, and control of the landing craft reverts to Konran. His hands settle back to the controls. His eyes scan sensor displays. The landing craft arcs gracefully behind Zenara's Xarba, whose straitjacket wings have unwrapped into two long, graceful airfoils. Ephemeral vapor vortexes swirl as the craft skim atop puffy clouds.

She dives again and Konran follows. White clouds darken into a thick, stormy fog, billowing tumultuously about the descending craft before dispersing to reveal Maehn Arziban below. Giant biospheres bulge like embedded globes of glass across the landscape, their domes large enough to contain Earth-size cities. In a testament to Maehn Arziban's flair for technological achievement (and one of the galaxy's most successful terraforming projects), the space between the biospheres overflows with meticulous city structure. Towers of commercial districts flow like fields of silver grass in all directions. The monolithic structures give way to rows of solar arrays, bulky industrial centers, urbanized pastures of perfectly arranged dwellings, and, speckled throughout, crystal-blue lakes and neatly manicured forests. A large, snowcapped mountain range runs in the north, bracketing the cityscape in a rolling caress.

Imitating Zenara's arc, Konran guides the landing craft on an easy, downward spiral. Their formation whips around the southern portion of the cityscape before leveling out on the final approach vector, straight toward the mountain.

These guys really get the royal treatment here, Konran observes, noting how the other starcraft and air vehicles around them kept to flight lanes at higher or lower altitudes while the Xolians shot straight through the middle. *They have their own flight lane.*

"Archer-Two-Niner, we will touch down in 1.5 minutes," Zenara's sharp, punctuated accent crackles into the comm.

"Acknowledged, Sponsor," Konran replies. "On your lead."

Now a mere one thousand meters above the ground, they kiss the tops of skyscrapers as Zenara angles them toward one of the more massive city centers. A hundred spires of every elegant variety flash past in sparkling grandeur, melting into urban sprawl at their outskirts. Modest suburban dwellings transition into large homes and then enormous estates, which grow in size with increasing distance into the foothills. At less than fifty meters above the ground, Konran senses curious eyes upon their formation, billionaires about their business, peering up at the military escort coming to consort with one of their esteemed neighbors.

"Here we are," Zenara's accent crackles as her Xarba cruises over a long, curving wall, slipping between two of the many mean-looking gun turrets perched atop its massive girth.

Konran's landing craft crests the wall an instant later, entering a staggering compound of multifaceted structures, probably a sixth as large as the rest of the foothills combined. Zenara cruises forward effortlessly, straight through the outcroppings of towers, warehouses, and offices. They pass rows of structures before Zenara slows, stops in midair, and descends gracefully onto a small landing pad, winglets angling upward as she sets down.

Konran's craft hisses (stabilization thrusters slowing and stopping its velocity), hums (antigravity repulsors balancing it above the ground), and sets next to Zenara's with a crisp crack (metal landing skids tapping down on flexicrete tarmac). He runs a final diagnostic, finds all landing systems reporting green, and, heart thudding within his chest, authorizes the landing craft for debarking.

Konran follows Commander Exeunt from the pilot cabin, squinting as he enters a crisp, Arzibanian spring day. Cassio forms up next to him. Salazar steps up, looking at Konran with a wide, *can you believe this?* look in his eyes. Ace jabs an elbow in Konran's side, and the pilot grins as Valkyrie looks around beside him. Konran takes a step, mentally noting that gravity here was similar to that on Earth. The compound, if not the entire city, employed synthetic gravity generators to compensate for what the moon lacked in mass.

Captain Granicks is several steps beyond, speaking to a tall man with wizened, ebony skin and short white hair salting his temples. The man carries a bearing of authority, which is complemented by a thin robe of green, purple, and black, trimmed at the edges with gold. Three pilots stand smartly next to the man, each wearing a similarly styled flight suit.

Konran identifies the foremost of the three pilots as Zenara, who looks a lot like a younger version of Commander Exeunt. She has the same sharp forehead and piercing eyes—except her straight black hair falls below her shoulders in two tight braids, while the commander's was cut short.

"Konran," Granicks is saying, "let me introduce you to Ruzcier Exeunt, former chief of Xolian Clan Libra."

"It is a great honor, Mr. Andacellos," Ruzcier says, stepping up to Konran with a litheness belying his age. "I am eager to speak with you, for we have much to discuss this day."

"The pleasure is mine, sir," Konran replies as Ruzcier grasps his hand in a healthy, two-handed grip. The man stands there, letting his gaze penetrate into Konran's for a long moment, probing, as it were, beyond the irises and into the secrets contained beneath.

Unsure what to do, Konran adds, "I have heard so much about your people."

"Ah," Ruzcier says, releasing Konran's hand, "but it is that which you have not heard which we shall discuss today."

He places his hand on Konran's back, directing him toward a sprawling latticework of stone archways that extends from the landing pad in both breadth and depth.

"Come, my guest. The city has voted to begin the spring storms early this year, and rain will begin shortly," he says, gesturing to the rapidly advancing storm clouds Konran had passed on his way in. "Let us go to my home, where we may speak in comfort. My servants have prepared well for your arrival."

Konran strides to keep up with Ruzcier's pace, finding himself leading a suddenly ceremonious procession of Xolians and United Space Federation Navy personnel. The flat tarmac quickly changes to smooth cobblestone: not quite white, bright but not glaring under the still-sunny sky. A tall latticework of stone archways looms before him, and Konran follows Ruzcier into their belly. Recherché yet simple, the structure allows light, shade, and open air to swirl around the group as they pass beneath. The hand-carved uniqueness of each pillar whispers that Konran has entered a world of rich, traditional precision—or perhaps it was one of grand, meticulous elegance. Before he can discern exactly what it feels like, they are met by a row of servants standing in front of ...

What is that ...?

Ruzcier leads him to a long, narrow carriage with rows of open seats spaced perfectly along its length. It hovers serenely in place, with only the faintest hum of gravitational repulsors rumbling through the stony archway. Konran barely notices the carriage, his eyes riveted instead on the striped, feathered, and horned animals hitched two by two to the front of the vehicle: zebras, ostriches, and impala in alternating rows, with four of each animal in total. The animals stand with dignified attention at their posts, with only an occasional snort, squawk, or twitch of an ear.

"If you would take your place, Mr. Andacellos," Ruzcier says, gesturing for Konran to sit on the vehicle's front row, "my carriage masters will ferry us to my home."

Konran steps into the carriage, which dips slightly at his weight, bobbing subtly up and down as everyone else takes seats behind him. Last of all, Ruzcier takes his place next to Konran. Carriage masters step onto foot platforms extending from the sides of the carriage, two on either side in the front, two in the middle, and two at the rear, and the animal train breaks into a trot.

The carriage masters chant as they go—a rhythmic almost-song in what Konran assumes to be the Xolian language—and the animals synchronize their pace with the words: two-footed ostrich in time with four-footed zebra in time with lightly jumping impala, the methodical clack of hooves and feet echoing through the vast archway like an ancient drumbeat.

Splashes of light speckle stone pillars, trickling through the intricate archway latticework. Fresh spring air swirls in eddies as the carriage winds forward, gusting with moisture across Konran's face and mussing his uncovered hair. The archway beckons him as he passes through it, each uniquely carved pillar some remnant of a story as vast as the structure itself. Fleeting familiarity pecks at the edge of Konran's consciousness as the carriage veers this way and that, tugging his memory at a turn here, a glint of light there, or at a shape etched into rock. But what exactly it reminds him of, he cannot say.

Finally the carriage slows, and Konran's attention shifts from the world around him to that before him. The caravan exits the archway, and grassy hillocks on either side rise into twenty-meter cliffs as they pass between. Bands of colored stone mottle the grayish-yellow canyon walls, sweeping in patterns of green, purple, black, and gold. Clusters of brush and tufts of trees spring up on either side, and the babble of water gives Konran the impression he is approaching a fertile, hidden valley.

The carriage masters' song echoes rhythmically through the canyon along with the clack, clip, and click of animal feet, and Konran begins noticing other animals amidst the ever-thickening foliage on either side. Monkeys dangle from trees and jump between branches; meerkats raise curious heads from mounded holes; young leopard cubs frolic, wrestling as their mother watches from the shadows of a low tree branch; a group of small, gazelle-like creatures grazes next to a bubbling stream; birds swoop from tree to tree, adding their songs to the Xolians'; a trio of lionesses look up, their keen, yellow eyes considering the carriage, considering Konran.

They round another bend in the canyon, and the fertile valley appears much like Konran had anticipated. Three hundred meters wide, two hundred meters deep, and filled with green, the valley teems with Edenic splendor. Trees tower with trunks five meters thick, topped with lofty platforms of leaves; others sprawl wide, their branches drooping low. Elephants and giraffes amble amidst arboreta, their large frames small by comparison. A herd of wildebeest laze to Konran's left, mingling about the foremost edges of a crystal-blue lake. Fed by waterfalls on both sides, its waters stretch across the valley, filling the half of it from side to side. Behind that, a stately manor sprawls, its geometry scattering the golden rays of Solis across the valley floor.

The carriage proceeds directly forward, neither turning nor slowing as it approaches the lake. At the lake's edge, the Xolian chant suddenly stops. Before either ostrich or impala or zebra touch the water, their restraints release and the animals spread neatly to the left and right.

Did they just bow? Konran wonders as the carriage glides between the handsome beasts, hovering on momentum out over the lake.

Pink flamingoes and gray, long-necked herons turn heads curiously to track the carriage. A hippopotamus sinks into the waters, disappearing with a splash and a ripple. A colorful finch lights upon the carriage next to Konran, peering up at him before casting back to the sky.

Across the lake, architecture melds seamlessly from ancient to ultramodern as arched pillars support a large sweeping balcony below the eaves of a low, geodesic roof. A set of tall, golden doors stand open at the base of the manor's façade, gleaming beneath Solis's light like a pair of outstretched arms, as if beckoning guests to come and enter.

"It has been five generations since my ancestors left humble homes in Africa to seek their fortune in the skies," Ruzcier speaks, startling Konran. The man had yet to utter a word since entering the carriage. "I have lived my life amidst those skies," he continues, gesturing upward, "and logged more than six hundred light-years behind my humble name. This valley is my tribute to those upon whose shoulders I have reached ever upward. What do you think of it, Mr. Andacellos?"

"I, er, this is incredible, sir," Konran replies. "It's one of the most beautiful things I've ever seen. I think your ancestors would be honored."

"As I hope they are, my young friend. A man must never forget his roots, nor the shoulders upon which he stands. Wouldn't you agree, Mr. Andacellos?"

"Uh, yeah. Of course, sir," Konran replies, drawing his eyes back to the lake, his gaze searching its depths.

Unless you never knew them, he adds inwardly.

"We have great technology," Ruzcier continues. "We possess the ability to colonize planets and touch the vastness of the stars. But we will never rise to greater culture or wisdom without the strength of those who came before us. We must know and we must remember, or what are we but shallow impressions, a fraction of our true humanity?"

A pang rises within Konran at the Xolian's words, and he swallows it. Something about the energy with which the man spoke stirred him, making him wish he could share in the man's love of ancestry. He had been bracing for the curveballs that Maehn Arziban would inevitably hurl his way—but he had been completely unprepared for a conversation like this.

"Yeah, I think you're right," is all he says.

"What monuments would you build to your heritage, my friend? Upon whose mighty shoulders does such a warrior as yourself stand?"

Konran pauses, having no idea where to even start.

How is this man doing this to me? he wonders, feeling more sensitive about his lack of family than he had since he was seven. He had never thought of himself as a warrior—just a kid who grew up alone wanting to be one.

"I don't really know," Konran finally replies. "My DNA is mostly American, with some bits of Western European, some Native American, and some Southeast Asian."

"But from whom do you come?" Ruzcier presses.

"I don't know," Konran replies softly. "I grew up in a boys' home in Central California. I never knew my parents; I tried, but I couldn't even trace one generation genetically."

The carriage stops, having crossed the lake. The manor looms six stories upward, its windows, doors, pillars, and balconies rich, ancient, and alien. If the valley was Ruzcier's homage to the past, this estate was his homage to the present. The man steps from the carriage, and Konran reflexively follows, his feet touching down on cobblestone.

"Come, my guest," Ruzcier says, guiding Konran forward, "let us see what we can do about that."

Cassio, Granicks, Commander Exeunt, Salazar, Ace, Valkyrie, Zenara, and the rest of the procession dismount behind him, but Konran is no longer aware of their presence as he ascends the marbled steps, walks between the magnificent pillars, enters the golden doorway, and steps into Ruzcier's home.

CHAPTER 13

Konran sits in a comfortable chair on the far side of a long, elegant receiving room. A knee-height oval table of polished African blackwood stands between Captain Granicks to his left and Ruzcier Exeunt, who sits across from him. Luxurious panels of blackwood line the walls, split into carved, rectangular sections by stripes of warm, marbled stone. A rich rug fills the center of the room, textured with captivating geometric patterns of green, purple, black, and gold. A silver orrery stands in the opposite corner, by the door, depicting the planets of Kapteyn's Star rather than Sol. Sunlight from Solis penetrates large prismatic windows behind Captain Granicks, combining with a sprawling waterfall chandelier on the ceiling to brightly illuminate the room.

Cassio stands comfortably at alert by the door. The rest of the USFN party waits in an adjacent, analogously lavish dining hall, sampling Xolian delicacies to the music of Ruzcier's servants. None of their sound enters Ruzcier's receiving room, however, where the occupants sit in silent attention. Two servants cross the room, depositing two boxes onto the table: one small and wooden, the other large and metallic.

The servants exit, and Ruzcier leans forward, picking up the wooden box and considering it with deep eyes.

"I have had this in my possession for twenty-two years, three months, and eleven days now," he says, turning the box around in his fingers, "though even I do not know the entirety of its secrets."

He looks up at Konran, lines of emotion wrinkling his aged, ebony skin. "And if I am not mistaken, my boy, this is for you," he says, reaching his arm out until Konran reaches forward and takes the box.

Konran examines the box much as Ruzcier had. The wood looks rough but feels smooth—crude, if not carefully built, as if constructed using hand tools. No adornment marks its surface. "What is it?" he asks.

"Open it," is all Ruzcier replies.

Konran searches for a biometric sensor, button, or other mechanism to open the box, but finds nothing. He fiddles with it for a moment, and then realizes the top of the box is simply inserted into grooves cut into the side panels. He gives the lid a slight tug with the pads of his fingers, and it slides off with a squeak of wood scraping wood. He deposits the lid on the table next to the large metallic box.

"There's nothing in it," he says, puzzled, looking in the box. "Just some dust."

"There is only nothing inside if you are not who I think you are," Ruzcier replies. "Touch it."

Konran peers into the dust. His heartbeat accelerates as he reaches his hand downward. What had Ruzcier given him? What secret does he hold right here, in his palm? Konran inserts his fingers into the dust. It feels cold, like dust that hasn't seen sunlight in many years—and that's it.

"What does it do?" he asks.

"You just need to touch it. Put your fingers into the dust," Ruzcier replies.

Konran pushes his fingers deeper into the dust, swirling them around a little for good measure. It feels more viscous than regular dust, like it doesn't want to let go of the box.

"Are you sure this is for me?" he asks, feeling foolish.

"Did you get your fingers in it?" Ruzcier asks, stepping over and leaning beside Konran. "Try the other hand."

Konran tries the other hand with the same results.

"Try both hands."

Konran obliges, feeling more and more like a toddler playing with some magic dust he'd scooped from a street corner.

"This can't be right," Ruzcier says, standing up and pacing. "It has to be him." He looks back at Konran, considering him like he would a key that had inexplicably failed to work.

"Darius," Ruzcier addresses Captain Granicks without removing his eyes from Konran (whose fingers are still in the dust), "we need your scientist."

Captain Granicks signals to Cassio, who obligingly exits. A moment later the marine returns, dragging the *Nova Scotia*'s short, dark-haired, olive-skinned chief science officer with him. Salazar's mouth is still full, and he chews and swallows as they cross the room, eyes darting from Granicks to Ruzcier to Konran.

"Captain?" he asks, wiping the corner of his mouth as Cassio deposits him in front of the table.

"We need you to help us with this box," Granicks explains, pointing to the box in Konran's hands. "Ruzcier suspects it should activate somehow at Konran's touch, but nothing has happened so far."

Salazar's eyes go wide as he brings one hand up, covering his now open mouth. His eyes flit between the box and Konran and then to Ruzcier. "No way," is all he manages.

"Do you recognize the design?" Ruzcier asks.

"Oh yeah," Salazar says. "It's a Churxor. I can't believe it."

"A what?" Granicks asks, looking between Salazar and Ruzcier.

"The scientist is correct," Ruzcier says. "It is a Churxor box— and a very stubborn one at that."

"What's a Churxor box?" Granicks asks.

"Have you ever heard of Damascus steel?" Salazar says.

"Are you saying this box has to do with medieval Near Eastern steel-forging techniques?" Granicks replies.

"OK, yeah, you've heard of Damascus steel. And no, the box has nothing to do with that."

"So what is the point?" Granicks presses.

"True Damascus steel was a technology unto its time," Salazar explains. "Once the art was lost, it took centuries before technology advanced enough to fully reverse-engineer it."

"So, this is..." Konran begins.

"The twenty-second-century version of Damascus steel, only rarer, and more marvelous," Salazar concludes. "The Churxor box."

"A Churxor box?" Konran repeats, looking at the box with renewed interest. "What does it do?"

"It's a locked time capsule," Salazar explains. "It can hold almost anything inside it, but whatever it holds can only be found again by the one who locked it." Salazar stops, looking at Konran with his widest eyes yet. "You ...?" He shifts his gaze to Ruzcier. "Him ...?"

210

"We need it to work now, whatever it is," Granicks says. "Can you fix it?"

Salazar's eyes move back to Konran and then to the box. "I think so," he finally says. "If I didn't have it in front of me, there would be no way I could reproduce it. But, with this sample ... Can I see it?" he asks, reaching out.

Konran hands him the box, and Salazar kneels down at the table, placing the box before him and replacing the lid.

"My servants will bring him another chair," Ruzcier says.

"Too late," Granicks replies, "he's already in the zone."

Salazar doesn't respond. He pulls a multi-tool from his pocket, configures it, and fiddles with one side of the box. He puts the box down, stares at it defiantly, reconfigures his tool, and fiddles more with the side of the box. An electric arc suddenly bursts out, traveling visibly along the scientist's arm before dissipating into his clothing. Salazar doesn't seem to notice. He props the box up on its back panel, delicately clamps his tool across the front, produces another multi-tool from his pocket, and bores into the bottom panel deep enough that the tool sticks in the wood.

"Spit on this," Salazar instructs Konran.

"Spit on it?" Konran asks.

"Yeah, right there where it goes into the wood." Salazar indicates the location with his eyes, his hands still holding the tools in place.

Konran leans over, spits, and white saliva bubbles cover Salazar's hand.

"Oh, my bad," he says, embarrassed.

"Try again. Don't miss."

Konran wipes his tongue around his mouth to gather more saliva, takes careful aim, and spits on the box. This attempt has more spread, but spittle splatters on Salazar's tool instead of his hand.

"Perfect, now hold these," Salazar instructs, indicating his tools. "Carefully."

Konran takes hold of the tools, trying to hold steady as Salazar releases his grip.

"Right there," Salazar says, extracting a thin wire from the tool in Konran's right hand. He strings the wire between the tools, making several loops before stopping.

"Hold it," he says, pulling another multi-tool from his pocket and touching it to the wire.

A tiny but brilliant flash bursts out, and Konran jerks away involuntarily, blinded by the spark. He drops the tools and rubs his eyes, groaning.

"Sorry!" Salazar blurts out, concerned. "I should have told you to close your eyes. Your vision should probably be OK. How many fingers am I holding up?" He holds up three.

"We can fix any ocular damage quite easily," Ruzcier responds. "Shall I call for my medical staff?"

"I think I'm fine," Konran replies, still rubbing his eyes. "I've got a white spot in my vision, but it's fading back to normal."

"I will have them bring you regenerative lenses, just in case," Ruzcier says. He gestures in the air, inputting commands into an interface only he can see.

"Come on, Sal!" Granicks says, angry. "This isn't physics lab. Be careful."

"Sorry," Salazar says, picking up the box. Despite the fall, the tools remain firmly in place. "Should I wait?" he asks.

"I think I'm OK," Konran says. "But I'll take those lenses when they come."

Ruzcier nods. "You will have them in minutes. Do you require any tools or materials for the work, Salazar?" he asks.

"No, I'm actually almost done," Salazar replies, producing another tool from his pocket. "Now that the first one is in, I should be able to do the rest myself."

He glances at Granicks who nods, and the scientist proceeds. Salazar inserts the tool into the side of the box, has Konran spit on it, secures it with wire, warns everyone to look away, welds it in place, and does the same with the remaining surfaces. Shortly, the box looks more like an alien ball. Tools protrude from all angles with wire running between them, holding everything together. Salazar takes a seventh tool from his pocket, removes its power source, and connects it to his wiring job.

"There," he says triumphantly. "That should do it."

"Sir," a servant says, entering the room. "The regenerative lenses."

Konran accepts them happily, opens the package, and inserts them into his eyes. His vision returns to normal and his eyeballs breathe a sigh of relief.

"So, what now?" he asks as the servant exits the room.

"We wait," Salazar replies, not looking up from the box.

Konran stares at the box for what seems like a full minute, but nothing happens. He looks up at Granicks who is sitting back in his chair, a patient yet intrigued look on his face. Ruzcier sits with lips pursed, hands together, fingertips touching his chin. Salazar is motionless, his face no more than ten centimeters from the contraption, willing it to work with a *come on, come on* look on his face. Cassio stands behind him, peering down curiously. His eyes meet Konran's, and he gestures subtly to his plasma rifle, glancing meaningfully at Salazar.

Do you want me to shoot him? Konran interprets. He shakes his head, grinning.

A noise emanates from the box: the sound of a thousand tiny sparks. The sound fades in a moment, and the box goes silent. Salazar laughs and jumps to his feet, beaming like the school nerd taking the homecoming queen to the dance.

"YES!" he exclaims.

"So, it's done?" Konran asks.

"It's done," Salazar says. Still jubilant, he picks up the box and detaches his tools. "Open it," he says to Konran.

Konran slides the lid off again. Charred-out pockmarks mar the inside of the box, corresponding to the locations of Salazar's tools. Rather than burnt dust, however, Konran finds a small device inside.

"What is it?" he asks, removing the device from the box.

"That," Salazar replies, his voice getting giddy again, "is a neural implant—old school, like pre-Nolvaric tech."

"A neural implant." Konran considers the device. Neural implants had gone out of style more than a half century ago due to certain cyborgs' creepy affinity for manipulating their wearers. "Am I supposed to put it on my head?"

"No, my friend," Ruzcier says, a look of elated relief upon his face. "That is meant for me."

"For you?"

"Yes," the older man replies. "A few more minutes, my friend, and we shall fulfill the purpose of our meeting. There is much yet to tell. May I?"

Konran hands Ruzcier the neural implant, which the old man grasps between steady fingers and presses to the crown of his head, above his left ear. He sits back into his chair, gestures with his left hand, and the large metallic box on the table—which heretofore had been silent—buzzes to life, opening up and folding into a small machine. A set of miniature robotic arms surround a central platform nestled into the machine's heart, each bearing different implements, like nozzles, fingers, or grinding wheels.

"Oh," Salazar says. "I haven't played with one of those since I was seven." He kneels back down to look at the device. "A third-generation synthesizer. You can tell by the shape of this shaft here." He points into the machine. "With a, wait ... ah ... This is rigged to receive organically coded input!"

"This second bit of security was my idea," Ruzcier says, reaching forward and tapping his finger lightly against a needlelike instrument within the synthesizer.

A prick of blood on his fingertip wicks quickly into the synthesizer, which whirs into motion when he removes his finger. Mechanical components slide back and forth, up and down as the synthesizer does its work. In less than a minute the machine goes silent: a small cube occupying its formerly vacant central platform.

"Fascinating," Salazar mumbles. "Was that virally encoded?"

"Indeed, my friend," Ruzcier replies, picking up the cube and handing it to Konran. "This one is for you, Konran."

"So," Salazar says, "you kept the program to build the cube encoded in your bloodstream and catalyzed it with a virus from a neural implant, which was reconstituted from dust inside a Churxor box that had been locked by Konran himself?"

"No," Ruzcier answers, "I kept the catalyst for the build program in my bone marrow. The neural implant imparted the program to my bloodstream as virally encoded RNA and also stimulated the release of hormones, which the catalyst then activated. These in turn bonded with the virus and allowed the synthesizer to decode and run the program. The Churxor was indeed locked by Konran, twenty-two years, three months, and eleven days ago, to be exact."

"OK, that makes so much more sense," Salazar replies, nodding.

"This is a holo-projector," Konran observes, recognizing it as an outdated version of a current model. "Wait, did you just say I was here over twenty-two years ago? I would have been less than a year old!"

"Yes and no, my friend," Ruzcier explains. Twenty-two years ago, your hands encoded the Churxor box, but it was far from here, in the HR9038 system."

"HR9038. You mean the star in the Cepheus constellation? That's like," Konran searches his memory, "thirty light-years away. But I've never been on a warp cruiser, let alone outside the solar system. I didn't even leave Earth for the first time until I was thirteen."

"The star is thirty-five light-years away," Ruzcier replies, "and, yes, you were there, or this box would not have opened. I recall the moment vividly, for it was the last time I saw two of my dearest friends."

Ruzcier leans forward, eyes keen.

"Let me tell you a story."

Konran reels at Ruzcier's words, his mind spinning to comprehend what he was hearing. He had steeled himself for whatever curveballs might be slung his way, but then this one had failed to drop like a proper curveball and nailed him squarely in the side of the head. The lone consolation to his throbbing cranial fuzziness was advancing to first base, which in this case involved whatever words Ruzcier had pending on the tip of his tongue. The Xolian's thick, punctuated accent is hypnotic as he begins.

"Many years ago, I was partners with a Martian named Kazrick Anavos. He was a decorated starfighter pilot, which was not uncommon to find in those days. We made a good team, he and I, earning a living as mercenaries of sorts, traversing the charted galaxy and specializing in what we called 'Correction.'"

"Correction?" Salazar interrupts.

"Yes, Correction," Ruzcier continues. "There are over a billion people living more than a light-year from this solar system now, and the farther away you go, the less concentrated the authority of government. As you may imagine, my people have benefited immeasurably from this de facto laissez-faire, as we Xolians have been largely unencumbered in our various enterprises; however, the lack of authority also allows those with baser methods to thrive—especially upon the weak."

"Space pirates," Konran says, glancing at Granicks and cringing inwardly.

"Indeed, and worse yet," Ruzcier replies, unaffected by the comment. "Consider entire populations enslaved, their existence bound to corporations more powerful than Maehn Arziban. Consider warlords vying for territory, ravaging space colonies to make a statement, pressing survivors into their ranks and scattering the remainder to the galactic winds. There is certainly civilization to be had amongst the stars, but the stench of corruption is as thick as policing is thin. My partner, Kazrick, and I specialized in surreptitiously addressing such offenses, or Correction, as we called it."

"So, you were like space cops, then," Salazar says, sitting down on the floor to listen.

"More like space vigilantes, if you must label us as such," Ruzcier replies, "although this is hardly the purpose of the tale."

"Right," Salazar says, "go on."

"It was May of 2174, and the Orion Civil Wars were still ongoing," Ruzcier begins.

"Wait, you fought in the Orion Wars?" Salazar interrupts. "Those were right after the Nolvaric Invasion ended!"

"Sal," Granicks says, "let the man speak."

"Yes, sir," Salazar runs his hand over his lips like a zipper, nodding at Ruzcier to continue.

"I did not fight for any side directly, but yes, I did take part," Ruzcier answers. "While some star systems like Luyten and Procyon grew in stability and wealth after the Nolvarics fell, other systems in the greater Orion Sector fell into considerable chaos as settlers rushed to claim Nolvaric territory."

"Don't you find it ironic that Luyten, Procyon, and the other Canis Minor core systems were the most stable so shortly after the Invasion?" Salazar interjects. "I mean, they were *the* Nolvaric strongholds back in the day—"

"Sal!" Granicks admonishes the scientist. "We're not here for a history lecture." He gestures to the Churxor box and synthesizer on the table and the holo-cube in Konran's hand. "Do I need to have you removed from the room?"

Cassio stirs eagerly at the captain's words.

"No, sir," Salazar replies, abashed. "Sorry, sir," he says to Ruzcier, "your story is just so fascinating."

"No matter, my friend. If you please, I will continue," Ruzcier replies.

Salazar nods in response, like a turtle tucking into its shell.

"Due to the decade-long conflict," Ruzcier explains, "there was no shortage of opportunity in the region. Kaz and I used every means to compile lists of potential clients: news reports, advanced searching algorithms, information brokers, rumors—you name it, we used it. We were quite selective about our clients, you see, and after many days of effort I settled on what I knew to be the perfect job—it was dangerous, but we could do it, I had no doubt. Kaz, however, did not agree.

"For some reason he had fixated upon a small, hopeless missing-persons job back on Procyon. Try as I might, I could not shake the thought from his head. After more than a week of arguing, he relented to take my job, but his heart was never in it. Within two months, we found ourselves on the run, fleeing three sets of warlords with as many prices on our heads. I don't know how many aliases and disguises we burned escaping that mess, but somehow we made it with our lives to the Epsilon Eridani system. There we were hired as astromechanics on the deep-space station *Ridoux-5*—hiding in plain sight, with a fresh set of aliases and readjusted facial contours."

Salazar's eyes bulge, but he keeps his mouth closed. Ruzcier pauses, acknowledging the scientist. "Yes?"

Salazar looks tentatively at Granicks, who glares laser beams at him. "Nothing," he replies with a shake of his head, "I just visited *Ridoux-5* once, for a semester during my postdoc."

"Then you will believe me when I say it was an excellent fallback location," Ruzcier says.

Salazar nods, but says nothing, mimicking the turtle again. Out the windows Konran notices the sunny day has faded to gray, the storm outside arriving overhead.

"One day," the Xolian continues, "after months of lying low, Kaz was abnormally excited. I knew something was up because he took me straight to a bar after work, and that man never touched a centiliter of liquor in his life. There we sat for over an hour, eating and talking about nothing as Kaz forced conversation after conversation. Finally he gave me a hand signal—we had hundreds we used to communicate on jobs—and I understood it instantly. Slowly I turned around, and there, across the bar, I recognized the face of Muirs Daschel, the very client Kaz had wanted to take on all those months ago. Somehow he had convinced the man to travel more than eleven light-years, and had coordinated our meeting without my knowledge. Seeing no alternative, I agreed to meet with the man, and that day our lives changed forever."

Salazar looks like he is going to explode, but Granicks silences him with another laser bolt, and Ruzcier goes on.

"Muirs explained how his daughter, Linaya, went missing more than two years prior. She was attending Genilaerd University on the super-earth Luyten b and had just begun doctoral work in biological astrophysics. One night, Muirs and his wife, Shalti, received news that Linaya had perished in an interstellar warp accident while traveling from Luyten to Procyon for her semester break. The news came as a shock, because Linaya had decided to forego the visit in order to continue her research.

"They tried to explain this to the authorities, but the investigation found extensive evidence indicating Linaya had been among the seventy-three unfortunate souls who disintegrated with the warp cruiser, and the investigation was dropped. Muirs and Shalti explored every avenue to prove otherwise, but the effort only succeeded in bankrupting them. In fact, in order to reach us on *Ridoux-5*—more than eleven light-years away from Procyon— they sold their home, and Shalti went to live with friends while Muirs made the journey."

Ruzcier pauses his narrative, and a crystal glass drifts into his hand from above—the ceiling apparently stocked with refreshment. He takes a long drink, exhales with satisfaction, and four more glasses drift downward, landing within the grasp of each of his guests. Konran takes a sip, feeling invigorated by the mystery liquid as Ruzcier continues.

"The Daschels couldn't pay, which meant no job to me, but Kaz being Kaz couldn't let it go. We argued for a day, me trying to move on, he speaking of a nagging need to take the job. Finally, I relented, and Kaz booked us a warp cruiser to Procyon that same hour."

Ruzcier shakes his head, a nostalgic expression passing across his face before continuing.

"An average Correction job took three months to complete, sometimes six or more, and rarely a year, but only for the really high payouts. After one fruitless year on the Daschel job, I was finished—the case was nothing but dead ends, and I sincerely believed the girl had died in that accident like all the evidence said she did. Being a sensible businessman, Kaz would take other jobs to maintain our cash flow, but try as I might, I could not make him let Linaya go.

"Every time I tried to walk away for good, he pulled me back in, convincing me to try one more lead. I learned more about the workings of the galaxy during that time than any other, for it forced us to challenge our every technique, rethink our every ploy, and reconsider even the soundest of assumptions. Prior to this we managed our work with the utmost discretion, but as our efforts to locate Linaya dragged out, we found ourselves increasingly clandestine. The secrets we unearthed during that time, though they never led to Linaya, served me well when my people called me home to lead them as chief."

Salazar's wide eyes look as if they wish to plug into Ruzcier's brain and download his database, but the scientist remains silent, shifting on the floor between Ruzcier and Konran. Granicks doesn't move, his contemplative posture that of a man deep in thought. Cassio stands comfortably behind Salazar, apparently able to hold the position indefinitely. Konran's mind races to process the story.

This is all leading up to the holo-cube in my hands, he thinks, heartbeats coming faster with every word.

Outside, the spring rain starts falling on Ruzcier's prismatic windows.

"Three years after we first met Muirs, we found ourselves on the super-earth Raiota orbiting the red dwarf LHS 1140 in the Cetus constellation. Our client was a new, legally formed government inhabiting the Raiotan moon Hanrumis. They claimed their water-production systems were being sabotaged by Raiotan-based hackers. Because there were no direct warp routes to Raiota from our home base of Terra Fina, we purchased our own warp cruiser to make the fifty-six-light-year journey."

"Wait, you purchased a warp cruiser?" Konran asks, feeling as if he'd just been told Ruzcier had purchased the sun. "How did you man it? How did you manage the risk of a fifty-six-light-year journey?"

"We were doing well for ourselves," Ruzcier replies modestly. "We manned it with a skeleton crew of Kaz's old war contacts and accepted cargo shipments to finance the journey. Of course, we didn't make the voyage all at once—that would have been suicide. It required four months of extensive planning and six warp jumps before we arrived in the system. Because it was a new warp route, it was not difficult to sell cargo space, despite the risk, and we more than recovered our investment in one trip."

"One trip?" Konran asks, wrestling to refrain from derailing Ruzcier's tale to discuss the challenge of eking out profit in the astrofreighting business. His desire to know the origin of the cube wins out, and he concludes the thought by saying, "That's amazing."

"We arrived in the system five days ahead of schedule," Ruzcier continues. "Raiota is a harsh planet, as you may be aware, experiencing an Earth-year equivalent of weather every Earth month due to its orbital eccentricity and velocity about its star. We planned our arrival for the end of spring, which gave us a window of two weeks to conduct business before the populace retreated underground for the next round of winter hurricanes. While the bulk of our crew conducted trade at the Raiotan warp docks, Kaz,

I, and three crewmembers took a transport down to the planet's surface, posing as Bestiphan gamblers."

"Hold it, you posed as Bestiphans?" Salazar interrupts with nearly a laugh. "How did you pull that off? Those wackos are essentially alien now, what with the evolutionary pressure of heavy Bestiphan gravity, molecular dissimilarities from Earth, the spectral composition of their star, and their fondness for inbreeding. Did you know their DNA differs from Earth-born humans by half a percent on average? That's five times the norm already!"

"Have you ever met a Bestiphan, Mr. Salazar?" Ruzcier asks, his voice controlled.

"No, but everyone knows..."

"I suggest you do so before commenting further. Despite their warlike propensities and cultural eccentricities, they are among the more gracious *people* I have encountered in my travels—which, I assure you, are quite extensive." Ruzcier peers unblinking at the scientist, the lines on his face hard, but his eyes calm. For a moment, the patter of rain on the windows is the only sound.

Salazar's gaze turns to the table, and he mumbles, "Sorry, sir, I understand."

"Very well," Ruzcier says, taking another drink from his cup. "Our lead, in this case, came from a comment Kaz picked up in the Tau Ceti system before warping to Raiota. Apparently, an exclusion region had cropped up on Raiota, suddenly closing down an active mine. Although exclusion regions were not uncommon, this one had emphatically turned away scheduled cargo transports with Longbow missile frigates."

"That happened to me on Mercury once," Konran comments, taking a sip from his glass, "right after the USFN occupied the planet as a testing facility. No one thought to alert the scheduled arrivals that they were no longer permitted into the system."

"I recall that policy change," Ruzcier replies. "I myself withdrew from a lucrative solar-harvesting venture on Mercury, though I did receive fair compensation for the eviction. Now imagine, my friend, if nobody knew why Mercury mysteriously shut off from the solar system—that's what this exclusion region was like on Raiota. Many whispers, but no facts."

"So what did you do?" Konran asks.

"There was no straightforward way into the region," Ruzcier resumes, "but our Bestiphan cover provided excellent means to scout unnoticed. You see, most people cannot differentiate one Bestiphan from another, and by splitting into groups and varying our numbers, no one ever noticed when one of us was missing. We staged our efforts from the neighboring city of Ishak, and within days we had a map of entry points. Further leveraging our Bestiphan personas, we talked our way into the arms-dealing crowd, where we purchased bio-augmentation exoskeletons, a CTT-17 landing craft, two LTOM-75 Sparrowhawks, and one of our favorite toys: drone-swarm EMP bombs."

"Nice!" Konran says. "That's the original Sparrowhawk!"

Ruzcier nods, a hint of nostalgia returning to his face before proceeding. "Using the bio-augmentation exoskeletons, we probed our infiltration points for abandoned mining entrances. Once we found one, Kaz, his friend Amig, and I entered under cover of night, making our way through seventy kilometers of broken, subterranean mining shafts using an old mining map until we reached the fringes of an underground research complex. Amig ran back to the surface to signal our companions, and within two hours of his departure our Sparrowhawks began buzzing the complex, setting off EMP swarms and shutting off their external electric systems.

"Kaz's plan assumed any hostages would be held in convenient, preexisting locations, so while the complex fell into chaos, we made our way to the former mining barracks. What we found shocked us."

"What did you find?" Konran asks.

"Women," Ruzcier replies.

"Women?" Konran says.

"Women?" Salazar repeats.

"Yes, fifty-one women, all held captive in this one facility. We searched amongst them, calling for Linaya Daschel, and there she was. After three and a half years of futility, we had found her—as well as fifty more like her."

"How did you get them out?" Konran asks, drawn to know the end of the tale.

"Wait, did you encounter any resistance?" Salazar asks. "I find it hard to believe you simply waltzed into a complex as heavily defended as you make it out to be without any resistance."

"I am Xolian, Mr. Salazar; the resistance was of no consequence," Ruzcier says.

Salazar smiles, pauses, and then nods stiffly, saying only, "Ah."

"So how did you get them out?" Konran asks again.

"Kaz ran ahead of us, navigating the maze of subterranean corridors using my map. I followed with thirty-seven of the women—fourteen refused to leave—and when we surfaced, Kaz was already airborne. He had hot-wired and stolen an old gunship—which required at least three crew to fly, mind you—and was clearing a path for our exit. Our enemy was on to us by then, and our Sparrowhawks had been pushed back by their Longbow missile frigates.

"You should have seen Kaz there, guns blazing in that bulky, slow gunship, completely untouchable. He fought off at least ten defense-drone swarms while Amig brought in our CTT-17 landing craft, loaded everyone, and took off as Kaz blasted an exit vector. He shot down hundreds of Longbow rounds before destroying the missile frigates themselves, and then, at the last moment, right before his craft was overcome by defense drones, he ejected—and Kazrick timed it so the escape pod vector intersected with the CTT-17."

Ruzcier shakes his head, contemplating a moment etched into his memory. "And then do you know what he did? He burst his airlock, spacewalked to us with minimal protection, climbed through a hatch, and, drenched in frozen sweat and shaking from head to toe, collapsed in the cargo hold. I've never seen such piloting since." Ruzcier points at Konran with a long, steady finger. "Except once now, on a vid that just posted from Y25LM90."

Konran's spine tingles, but before he can respond, Salazar interrupts.

"So what about your other job? The one you went to Raiota for in the first place?" Konran wants to slap the scientist.

"We never completed it," Ruzcier replies. "We got out of that system as fast as our warp cruiser could take us. Fortuitously, before we abandoned our false identities altogether, we received an anonymous payment for twice the sum we had originally contracted for. It turns out the compound we destroyed had been practicing cyber-warfare techniques on the Hanrumi infrastructure systems. When the attacks ceased, our client assumed we had succeeded."

"And what of the compound?" Salazar asks, licking up every detail. Konran's hand twitches.

"It disappeared," Ruzcier explains. "Local authorities mounted an investigation once word leaked what was going on there, but all they found was a burned-out mine."

"Whoa," Salazar breathes out.

"So you found Linaya and escaped," Konran jumps in, encouraging the story to proceed.

"Indeed," the Xolian says, his punctuated accent becoming thick with memory. "We saved thirty-seven women that day, but to Kaz there was only one. Upon returning Linaya to Procyon, Kaz told me he intended to continue helping her. You see, during her time in captivity, Linaya uncovered a plot much greater than the borders of that mining complex. Each hostage was an expert in some field: there were scientists, physicists, biologists, economists, mathematicians, historians, surgeons, you name it. Linaya kept a record of the captives' tasks—not written, of course, but in her memory—and the pattern she found was so disconnected it made no sense at all. Only after hypothesizing that there were more compounds like theirs did the picture begin filling in. So she watched, and she waited, piecing together the puzzle one task, one errant comment, one whisper at a time. She told us of her unequivocal assurance that one day she would be rescued, and of her conviction that when that day came, she would unravel the plot, one string at a time.

"Kaz almost convinced me to stay with them—the man was persuasive—but I saw an opportunity in the warp industry too good to turn down, and we parted ways. Kaz married Lin, and they made a formidable team—twice as formidable as Kaz and I had ever been. I lent what aid I could as my warp-transportation business grew, and we had more than a few adventures over the years. Then my people called, needing a chief, and I answered. By then my fleet had grown to twenty-two warp cruisers and fourteen smaller warp yachts, one of which I gave to Kaz and Lin. As time passed I saw them less frequently, with less contact between our meetings. Their adventures became more harrowing, of which I only know the smallest fraction."

Ruzcier pauses, licking his lips and taking a drink from his glass.

"You wondered why I asked about your heritage, Mr. Andacellos," he says.

Konran nods, the only motion capable of his otherwise frozen frame.

"The last time I saw my friends, Lin had an infant of two months in her arms, and Kaz had the Churxor in his. Kaz put the neural implant inside the box after I encoded its catalyst into my bone marrow. Then they knelt together, son in one arm, box in another, and locked the Churxor with their son's biometric imprint. They gave me the box, leaving instructions to watch for their son if they never returned. They told me they had to hide him and couldn't explain more, but that I would know him when I saw him. They said he would be like his father, and that I should give him the box if that day came. That was the last I ever saw Kazrick Anavos and Linaya Daschel."

A single tear fills the corner of Ruzcier's eye. "Do you know how to operate that cube?" he asks.

Konran swallows and shakes his head, blinking his own burning eyes.

"Speak your parents' names," Ruzcier urges.

"Ka ... Kazrick." Konran swallows again, clearing the lump in his throat. "Kazrick Anavos. Linaya Daschel."

The holo-cube hums in Konran's hands, vibrating cozily before emitting a stream of light that solidifies into a man and woman in the air before him.

Kazrick stands on the left, his arm around Linaya's slender waist. He has Konran's eyes and cheek structure; she has his nose, chin, and hair. Their holos look straight at Konran for a moment, the tenderness in their eyes blurring as Konran's fill with wetness. His parents' gaze is foreign yet familiar, reminiscent of the sensation he experienced while traversing Ruzcier's complex of carved stone archways.

"Konran," Linaya begins, and Kaz smiles. "My precious little boy. If you are watching this message, then terrible things have happened. Our plan has failed, and you have lived your life without us, alone in a world foreign and alien." She pauses, closing her eyes as Kaz squeezes her shoulders. "You are now our last hope for success," she goes on, voice steadying. "You are our greatest hope, our deepest joy, and now, though we are gone, we must ask you to finish the work we have started. Everything depends on this," her voice drops to a whisper, becoming urgent, "for there is more at stake than anyone can possibly imagine, and once you receive this message, it will already be so late. But you have a gift, my son. And that is the one thing that can..."

SLAM! A door crashes open on the far side of the room, causing Konran to drop the holo-cube and everyone to jump to their feet. The message cuts off as the cube bounces under the table.

"Sir!" a Xolian servant shouts, running into the room. Ace, Valkyrie, Commander Exeunt, and Zenara rush in close on her heels. "We have eight USFN ships inbound, already within the atmosphere, heading straight for us; Arziban Permit Control won't release their registry data. It looks like they have a fighter escort, too."

Ruzcier looks at Granicks, the captain's face a mixture of alarm and determination. "What kind of ships?" Granicks asks. "How far out?"

"Heavy landing craft," the servant replies, still breathless, "three minutes out. They've hailed us for permission to land, but I get the impression it won't matter what we reply."

"Sir," Ace says, tone grave, "we've lost contact with the *Nova Scotia*. It's almost like we're being jammed."

"We are," Granicks replies gravely. "Can you get these pilots to their Sparrowhawks before the landing craft get here?" he asks the servant.

"It will be close, sir, but I think so, if we go now."

"Go now," Granicks points at his pilots. "I want you up and in escort formation. Bring our 'guests' in, and try to raise Revenshal while you're up there. Use hard laser links if you can't get through the jamming."

"Yes, sir!" they both reply, sprinting with the Xolian across the room and out the door.

"Who is it?" Ruzcier asks.

"Someone high up," Granicks answers, "with at least a Hector-7 clearance to come in closed hatches like that—and someone with serious Arzibanian connections." He looks at Cassio, and then at Konran.

"This isn't a coincidence. Until we know otherwise, we assume Konran is the focus of the visit. Your priority," he points at Cassio, "is to disappear with Konran. We'll sort out the details if we get that far."

Granicks turns to Commander Exeunt. "Work with Salazar and get me an ID on those ships. I need to know who we're dealing with before they get here."

"Yes, sir," she replies, exiting quickly with the scientist.

Granicks looks at Ruzcier, who nods, turning to Konran.

"Come, my friend," Ruzcier says, "retrieve your cube. We will see to your safety." There is a change in the nostalgic old man, like the crispness in the air before the lightning bolt.

Outside, thunder crashes as rain streams down Ruzcier's large, welcoming windows.

* * * * *

Chanziu Guan's Jinfen pulls out of its warp jump as physically close to Summanus as possible. And then it explodes.

Chanziu rockets forward without it, protected by nothing but his space suit. Its material feels cold but refreshing against his skin-tight stealth suit below.

Salvaged pieces of the Jinfen's propulsion, navigation, targeting, life-support, cloaking, and shield systems drive him toward Maehn Arziban, cobbled together into a mishmashed, one-man rocket booster. He zips into the Summanian system, bypassing the capital ship docks and shooting past the orbital defense stations.

An alarm blares in his ear, signaling that the NACs had picked him up. Chanziu selects his target. The alarm changes tone. Chanziu ejects, and the NACs fire. His rocket booster is obliterated behind him, but he couldn't have gotten past the GAZ with it anyway.

Now he is nothing more than space debris, hurtling down to burn up like so many thousands of particles in Maehn Arziban's atmosphere. One mistake, and fiery atmospheric digestion would become his reality, but Chanziu doesn't need two chances to get this right. He searches his tracking system and reacquires his target.

There. He sees it, identifying a small vessel about to enter Maehn Arziban's GAZ. Chanziu fires his remaining maneuvering thruster, angles toward the craft, locks it into his navigation system, and, as he closes range, engages his magnum opus of hodgepodge space engineering.

A series of detonations flash silently, flipping him around and arresting his momentum. Mechanical restraints huddle his form into a ball as thrusters decelerate him further, and he converges on and matches speed with his target craft.

Now atop his prey, Chanziu fires his tethering system. The anchor clinches, and he feels the tug of the ship's thrusters pull him forward. He draws himself in until, at a mere thirty-five thousand kilometers per hour, he mounts on top of his quarry. There he waits, weathering the GAZ and its bumps, watching for the chaperone buoy to signal the all clear. The buoy flashes three times, and Chanziu unhooks his tether.

The rest is easy—a task accomplished innumerable times before—and Chanziu scrambles to the craft's cargo bay, forces it open, and climbs inside.

"I apologize," he says, his weapons set for stun, "but I require use of your vessel."

CHAPTER 14

Konran runs. Cassio is next to him, a hand on his elbow as they follow Ruzcier down a narrow hallway. The old Xolian disappears abruptly, slipping into what moments before had been solid wall. Zenara brings up the rear, pushing the two to enter.

"Go," she says with a shove. "In."

They go, entering a tunnel of neatly hewn stone lit by an amber, shadowless glow. The corridor curves ever downward as they run, chilling the air. Konran is vaguely aware of the thud of his feet against the stone floor, the rhythm of his breath, the coldness of sweat pooling above his brow.

Ruzcier stops in a large cavern, but all Konran can see are the images of his parents, smiling kindly back at him.

"He's shivering!" Zenara calls out, stepping next to and bracing Konran. "Are you OK?"

"I- I..." Konran replies, looking down at his hands. One is clenched tightly to his chest, grasping the holo-cube in a death grip. The other shakes visibly. He can't feel it shaking. "I don't know," he finally answers.

"Here, eat this," Cassio says, handing a small, flat morsel to Konran. Konran takes it in shaking fingers, bringing the corner to his mouth. The bite wasn't boost cake, but it brings warmth with it, and Konran nibbles again.

"Are we there?" the marine asks.

"No," Ruzcier replies. "We are in the caverns beneath my mountain. Zenara, do you remember the way to the room I told you to never enter?"

"The one with the warp yacht? Yes, I went there all the time as a child," she replies.

"Bless your insubordinate spirit," Ruzcier says. "Go there now. Take my yacht. Exit through the tunnels. They will bring you on the far side of the mountain. Make your way to the warp margin. The warp protocol for Kapteyn b is preprogrammed into the yacht.

Warp there, and find your cousin Xubarif—he will protect you. I will come if I am able. Whatever you do, keep Konran safe."

"Wait? Father, you want us to just warp out of here?" Zenara asks. "Why can't he just hide? There's tons of space down here."

"I just got word that the NACs discharged," Ruzcier replies. "Something else just tried to penetrate Arzibanian space. None of this is coincidence, daughter. You must go—I feel it is the only way to assure his safety. I will see to it that our guests are delayed."

"Why don't you just shoot them down?" Zenara says defiantly.

"Because then you will be targets. Trust me. Go. Take Konran to Kapteyn b. We will delay them."

"Yes, Father," Zenara says soberly. Her gaze follows Ruzcier as he sprints like a twenty-year-old from the room.

"Are you OK to run?" she asks Konran.

"Yeah," he says. "I think I was going into shock for a minute, but I feel better."

"You're still pale," she replies.

"Eat that while we run," Cassio says, handing Konran a small packet. "You will be fine." He gestures for Zenara to lead the way.

"This isn't boost cake?" Konran asks, dubious.

"No. Better for action. Let us run," Cassio urges.

Zenara nods, grabbing Konran's hand as he stuffs the better-than-boost-cake into his mouth. "Stay close," she says.

No light precedes their path this time, and the illumination of the corridor fades into shadow behind them. Zenara doesn't falter, and Konran is grateful for her hand. Their footsteps echo across the high cavern as they run, filling the darkness with hollow reverberations. The sound stretches in all directions, the protuberance of shadow the only hint of structure.

Shortly, the echoes descend from many meters above to less than a meter overhead, and Konran realizes they had entered a new corridor. He can't see anything now, but Cassio and Zenara seem unaffected by the darkness. They follow the corridor for a minute and then Zenara stops.

"Which one is it?" she says, more to herself than Konran or Cassio.

"You don't remember the way?" Cassio asks.

"No, I do. It's just been awhile since I came down here," Zenara replies. Konran feels her tug as she pulls him back the way they had come.

"What are you looking for?" Konran asks. "I can't see a thing in here."

"A side tunnel," Cassio responds. "We have passed many side tunnels down here, which makes her memory loss all the better."

"Here, this is it," she says, ignoring Cassio's sarcasm.

Her pull drags Konran into the side tunnel, perpendicular to their original direction. The tunnel curves downward again. The air becomes colder as they descend, but Konran doesn't shiver as before. Having escaped the numbing effects of shock, his muscles keep pace easily thanks to Cassio's boost cake training, warming him as he runs.

Zenara guides them through a maze of twisting, turning tunnels. They wind their way like this for several minutes, but to Konran it could have been an hour. Finally Zenara stops, a latch clicks, and a heavy-sounding door swings open. Another click, and light floods the hallway.

Konran blinks furiously as his eyes adjust to the sudden influx of light. It wasn't really that bright, but his irises had adjusted so well to the darkness that even the low level of luminosity makes his retinas rebel. His regenerative lenses respond quickly, and as sight returns, he sees rows of piled equipment occupying a large cave: machinery and tools, stacked atop each other, as if their future usage had been intentionally factored out of the arrangement. The equipment looks old, like it had been stashed there before the moon that became Maehn Arziban had been colonized—which made no sense, but neither did the room.

"Is the warp yacht hiding in this pile of garbage?" Cassio asks.

"No," Zenara says, making a low, long whistle with fingers pressed to her lips. A small platform drops from the ceiling, hovering a few centimeters above the ground. Zenara pulls Konran on with her. "It's hiding here." The platform raises suddenly, leaving Cassio behind.

The marine's curses echo as the platform floats higher. Cassio whistles, mimicking Zenara's, but the platform does not pause. Konran holds tight to Zenara's hand until they reach the top,

Cassio's shouts ascending with them. A hole in the wall opens behind her, high above the floor below, and she steps through, dragging Konran with her. The platform drops and Zenara pokes her head out.

"It's coming down for you," she says. "There wasn't room to lift all three of us."

"Don't ever do that again!" Cassio bellows from below. "Do you understand how critical it is that I remain with Konran? This is not a game. Or did you forget our purpose in fleeing?" His shouts continue as he rises.

"Cool it, big guy, it's fine, we're right here," Zenara calls down. But when Cassio reaches the top, he comes off the platform like a bull.

"It is my duty to stay with Konran," he yells. "Do not compromise that again!"

"I didn't compromise anything," she yells back. "We didn't all fit."

"Then you let me take him. Never do that again."

"What difference does it make? We're here now, aren't we?"

Konran realizes Zenara's accent has faded. It sounds more normal—although after his conversation with Ruzcier he wasn't sure what classified as normal anymore.

Had I really been thirty-five light-years from Earth before I could even walk, born to non-Earthling parents?

The thought was so foreign, but he had seen them in the holo-projection, had heard the story from Ruzcier's own mouth. Konran's mind spins. And he realizes Cassio and Zenara are still arguing.

"Ungrateful Solarian," Zenara is saying. "Maybe try, for a minute, to comprehend the honor my father bestowed on you by inviting you into his house. But no, you all just own the universe, right?"

"You think I ask for honor?" he snarls. "While you drift here on your isolated moon," he spits the word, "we fight and die to protect the solar system. Once you spacewalk through a war zone and fight Nolvarics hand to hand, personally preventing them from ravaging defenseless civilians, then we can talk about honor."

"Guys," Konran starts.

"You call that honor?" Zenara retorts. "What else could they pay you to do? Yet here you are, ungrateful for the most obvious fortune."

"Hey, guys," Konran tries again.

"Don't speak to me of fortune, girl, when your daddy has gold-plated servants waiting to tie your shoes for you."

"I only count one servant down here. And he should apologize now," she says, anger burning in her eyes.

"If you are any reflection of him," Cassio jabs, "what need have I of profanity?"

"How dedicated are you to fighting and dying, servant? Or do you fear what a Xolian *girl* is capable of?"

"Guys!" Konran yells, waving his arms.

"Are you threatening me?" Cassio hisses.

"Impressive, you figured it out."

"If not for the respect of my captain..." Cassio begins.

"Ugh, ihh, aghk," Konran gurgles, falling to the ground, groaning. "Help me, please!" He shivers, hugging himself and trying to look ill.

"Konran!" Cassio runs to his side. "Are you well?" Zenara is right beside him, a look of concern on her face.

"He's in shock," she says, squatting next to them, "shivering again."

Konran continues the ruse, hoping to prevent Cassio and Zenara from fighting further. He sits up as if the effort costs him dearly. "Can I get something to drink?" he asks weakly. "And somewhere to sit?"

They help him to his feet and Zenara leads him across the room. Unlike the room they just passed through, this one is clean, sterile, and metallic. A control panel occupies the near side of the room, and shiny lockers run along the far wall. In between it all a warp yacht perches, a great eagle frozen on the precipice of flight. Zenara gives Konran some water.

"Let us make haste," Cassio says, moving toward the warp yacht.

"I need to engage the system first," Zenara says, sitting at the control panel. Holo-feeds pop to life around her, depicting images of ten large transport ships and twelve smaller starfighters descending toward Ruzcier's compound.

"This is not 'firing up the system,'" Cassio complains. "Let us go now."

"First I think we should find out what's going on out there."

"My orders are to..." Cassio starts.

"Protect Konran," Zenara cuts him off. "Relax, I know, I was standing next to you." She leans into the command console, and the warp yacht begins to hum in the center of the room.

"Don't you want to know the threat status before we blast out of here? It will only take a minute anyway."

"The surest way to mitigate the threat is to get out of here now," Cassio says, voice growing stern again. "Konran and I will board. Open the doors."

Zenara ignores the marine, and more holo-feeds pop up around her. She cycles through different views, and Konran watches images of Ruzcier's compound flash past. One display stops on five USFN heavy landing craft, hovering authoritatively in the air directly above Ruzcier's lake. Another finds Ruzcier himself, speaking hurriedly to armored Xolian servants. A third finds Captain Granicks, standing in the pouring rain before Ruzcier's home, three of the landing craft having touched down no more than ten meters before him. The lead craft's front access ramp is extended, and a hologram descends the opening, flanked by a row of tough-looking humanoid assaultbots on either side. Konran had read about the prototype robot soldiers. Rumors suggested they were getting close to entering military service again for the first time since the Nolvaric Invasion.

Apparently that time was now.

"Wait, zoom in on that man," Cassio says, pointing to the hologram exiting the landing craft. Zenara zooms in, and his face fills the viewport. Cassio groans.

"Who is he?" she asks.

"Vadic Heesor," Cassio answers. "The United Space Federation minister of defense. This makes no sense at all. We should go now!"

"Can we hear what they're saying?" Konran asks.

"Yes," Zenara says, "here."

The sound of heavy rain comes into the room and then mutes as Zenara fiddles with the controls. She zooms in to show both men facing each other, and suddenly Captain Granicks's voice comes in. He is shouting.

CHAPTER 15

Darius Granicks stands in the cold rain, facing Vadic Heesor's flickering hologram. Five all-too-real assaultbots flank the minister. Three heavy landing craft stand ominously behind the minister's entourage, their four medium plasma cannons and one heavy autocannon each indicating this wasn't just a political consultation. Five more of the landing craft linger in the air above, protected by two squadrons of Dronehawks, the controversial, unmanned, yet-to-be-deployed version of the mighty Sparrowhawk starfighter.

At least Granicks had his two best pilots up there. Ace's and Valkyrie's Sparrowhawks maintain courteous escort positions on either side of the airborne party, hovering in place. At Granicks's recommendation, no Xolian forces had gone airborne yet. Instead he had Ruzcier's pilots move their Xarbas to secure locations to keep their numbers hidden in case this got hot. There were only six of them anyway—five, since Ruzcier's daughter Zenara had personally gone to see Konran to safety.

That Heesor wasn't there in person didn't surprise Granicks one bit—the man's self-importance was legendary within the ever-turning rumor mill of brass and politics, and the minister's fingers ran as deep as his budget ran broad. He was just the type of man Granicks expected to face down when he made the call to not take Konran to USFN headquarters. Granicks's plan had worked, and he had drawn out the enemy.

After hearing Ruzcier's story, Granicks wished he had sent Konran straight to Kapteyn b without this Arzibanian detour. But that was how combat always felt. You never knew everything upfront. You just used whatever you had at the moment to win, and improvised when circumstances forced you. And if one thing was certain in Granicks's mind, this was combat.

Heesor may have weaseled his way into Maehn Arziban and slammed our backs against the wall with superior firepower, but I still have Andacellos.

And no one can take Andacellos without his permission.

It wasn't the first time Granicks had placed himself between an invading party and his own forces. The feeling of vulnerability was more like an old friend than anything. He steps forward, hands out at his sides, rain dripping into his eyes and soaking his uniform.

"I don't understand, Minister," he shouts over the din of rain, "is there a problem I don't know about?"

"Since when did it become your prerogative to question direct orders, Captain?" Heesor's hologram calls back. "I already told you, I'm here for Andacellos on official business. Now do your duty, and bring him to me."

"I haven't received any orders, Minister," Granicks shouts back. "If you are suggesting my aide is in danger, I assure you, my crew is more than capable of protecting him. Why don't you tell me what's going on?"

* * * * *

Chanziu drops his weapon and holds his hands where they can be seen, and the Arzibanian patrolmen encircling him converge. One binds his arms and legs. Another passes a scanner around his body. Another collects his weapons. A fourth points her weapon at Chanziu's head.

"Get the idiot out of here," their commander orders gruffly. "What audacity. The circuits are going to love dealing with this one."

"You're lucky we don't throw you out here," the patrolman behind him hisses in his ear.

I could still make that work, Chanziu quickly analyzes the possibility, *although it would be a little more difficult.*

The patrolmen push him brusquely toward the airlock where, on the other side, their sky-interceptor awaits, attached to the vessel Chanziu hijacked and flew into Maehn Arziban's atmosphere. As they shove him through the airlock, Chanziu catches the eye of the crew member who called in the abduction. The man smirks at him.

"Saturnese filth," he growls. "Enjoy rotting in prison—if you're lucky."

Chanziu hangs his head in response, dropping his gaze as if despondent. Rough hands shove his head down, making him duck to get into the airlock. More rough hands grab him on the other side, forcing him through and throwing him into a restraining system. Locks click and independent systems bind him down under heavy manacles. Chanziu keeps his gaze downward, but his peripheral vision watches, waiting for the airlock to seal.

CLICK—HISS!

The airlock closes and Chanziu's shackles fall open. He stands calmly, weaponless. His hand flashes out, dropping the nearest guard. He steps forward smoothly. Two more hands flash out, and two more guards drop. A fourth guard grabs for his weapon. Chanziu's heel breaks his jaw, and Chanziu catches the weapon before its owner hits the ground.

"Don't move," he says to the pilot, "and I will not need to harm you." She remains frozen in place.

"Did you send a distress signal?"

She nods, eyes widening in fear as Chanziu steps forward.

"Do not fear," he says, resting a hand on her shoulder. "You will receive no harm, but this must be done." His hand moves, and her eyes close. He catches her carefully, removing her from the chair and laying her with her fellow officers. In moments they are bound.

Chanziu takes the pilot's seat and accesses the Arzibanian entrance databases. His eyes flit across the information, then his hands take the controls and the sky-interceptor rockets toward Maehn Arziban's mountain estates, sirens blaring.

* * * * *

"With due respect, sir," Captain Granicks shouts over the rain, "Aide Andacellos is a member of my staff, and as such is subject to my authority. Now if you don't have any more information, I believe we're done here."

"I don't know how else to say it, Captain, that information is classified!" Heesor's hologram bellows into the rain.

"I have all the clearance you need," Granicks yells back. "If there is something I should know regarding personnel under my command, I demand to know it."

"You would discuss federation secrets unsecured on an unfederated planet?" Heesor clamors. "I believe your security clearance will require review, Captain."

"I'm not the one jamming USFN military transmissions and invading personal property unannounced and uninvited," Granicks retorts. "We can discuss who needs reviewing for what later. If you have nothing further to say, I suggest you go file your report."

"Fine! You want to obstruct official USFN business and leak sensitive information? This will be on your head, Captain."

"Spill it, Minister!"

"We have information that an attack is impending. The Nolvarics have identified Andacellos as a potential asset and intend to capture him. We don't know how, but we expect an attack any hour now. My orders are to take and protect him. We can't have him falling into their hands."

"That's it?" Granicks yells through the rain. "The entire solar system has that plastered across their social media accounts. And if you're so worried, why aren't you warning the Arzibanian's of the attack? I'm sure they would like to know."

"I will have no more of this," Heesor yells, his fury growing as his hologram flickers in the rain. "Hand over Andacellos or consider yourself relieved of duty, Captain."

"Just like that? Where did you get that authority?" Granicks yells back. "Or shall we add this to your growing list of indiscretions for the afternoon?"

"Do not stand in my way, Captain," Heesor shouts. "Consider your career over. Take him into custody." At Heesor's command, three ranks of assaultbots step forward. They move toward Granicks, Heesor's image following behind them.

"Do you think this is actually going to stick?" Granicks yells back, unmoving. Rain splashes in his mouth as he speaks. "You realize you're being recorded, right? The only head this will fall on is your own, Minister. You've overstepped your authority. The only way out of this is to back off. And then we negotiate, on my terms."

"Why do you think I've been jamming you?" Heesor replies, walking closer to Granicks. "History only records that which gets reported, Captain. And only one of us will be doing the reporting after today. Shoot him."

A bolt of red plasma flashes, and Darius Granicks feels a burst of pain in his side. Cobblestone crashes hard against his face as he crumples to the ground. He struggles to breathe, the gasps gurgling hot in his throat. Everything looks red.

"Find Andacellos," Heesor orders, "and bring him to me. Preferably alive." With that, the hologram disappears.

* * * * *

Chanziu comes in low toward the compound, seven Arzibanian sky-interceptors close on his tail. His countdown timer hits two minutes, and he checks that the craft's autopilot function is set properly—it is.

At ninety seconds he leaves the pilot's seat and unsheathes his utility knife and a small syringe. Stepping to the prisoner hold he crouches at the feet of his former captors, cuts their bonds, and gives each an injection from the syringe. Their eyes pop open, and Chanziu helps them sit up. Fear flares in their eyes as they recognize him. A quick check shows they are all right—even the one with the broken jaw.

"You will regain function of your limbs in a few moments," Chanziu says to them. "I leave this craft in your hands and present to you your true enemies. Always remember, the Saturnese would be your allies, if you would have us."

With that he climbs into the airlock, overrides its access control, seals it from the cargo hold and pilot cabin, and waits for his timer to reach zero.

Thirty seconds: Chanziu snaps his stealth suit's embedded face shield closed.

Twenty seconds: he activates his internal breathing system.

Ten seconds: he double-checks his weapons.

Four, three, two, one.

Chanziu bursts the airlock and jumps from the sky-interceptor. The rush of air and rain are momentarily incapacitating, but nothing new to the Saturnese spy. His stealth suit stiffens at the change in environment, bracing his body and activating descent mode. Chanziu extends his arms like a bird and thin wings extend from his wrists to his feet. He glides forward like a bullet, inertial thrusters in his boots adding momentum. His suit automatically orients itself on the Xolian compound, and he zips quickly over its defensive walls.

Through the rain his suit visually confirms five state-of-the-art heavy USFN landing craft hovering above his target—so new as yet to be released for military use. His visual heads-up display lists their specifications:

Hull: 50 mm thick zyrcasium armor

Shielding: 300 terawatt gravito-electric

Armament:

4 x 15 mm medium-range plasma cannons, 2.5s refresh rate

1 x 90 mm long-range autocannon, 0.1s refresh rate, 650 rounds

Designated Cargo: 10 x RGF-4X0-B prototype assualtbots

Chanziu zips around a tall building, evading a weapons lock from the Arzibanian sky-interceptors behind him. Only recently had the United Space Federation approved assaultbots for reintroduction to the military. The bots were so new that the Saturnese hadn't even stolen complete development specs yet.

There was no time like the present to finish the job.

The visual message appears on his display: *500 METERS TO TARGET.* He scans the target area through the rain, searching for more enemy craft. He had only identified five heavy landing craft so far, but the Arzibanian entrance manifest had listed a total of eight.

They must have landed, Chanziu calculates. *That is where I begin.*

He deactivates his suit's autopilot function and angles upward. His inertial thrusters wouldn't be able to provide much altitude, but it would be enough.

There! He identifies three heavy landing craft nestled into a small canyon-shaped cove before an enormous Xolian palace. Flashes of blaster fire spark in the space, the battle having commenced without him.

Time to disappear, he thinks. Pulling arms and legs into his chest, he activates stealth mode, plummeting toward the ground.

* * * * *

Darius Granicks lies on Ruzcier's cobblestone courtyard, drenched in ever-pouring rain, struggling to breathe, let alone reach his sidearm. The crackle of blaster fire echoes through the courtyard, repeatedly superheating the air above his skin. People scream and explosions rumble and weapons whine. He tries to lift his head, but his stomach howls in agony and his body curls reflexively at the pain, tripling its intensity.

His mouth forms a scream, but his vocal folds only manage a gasp. The redness around him begins fading into black. He thinks of Konran, angry to be dying but satisfied he had done everything to protect the boy.

This is the end. He accepts the moment like every warrior when the moment comes. *I just hope I've done enough.*

He becomes conscious of someone, or something next to him. A new hum of blaster fire roars. Its sound becomes more distant, like a lullaby.

Then his body erupts in pain, wracking him from head to toe. His eyes jolt open and his lungs gasp for air, sucking in rainwater instead. He coughs violently, but the pain in his side doesn't reply. Someone is next to him firing a weapon. It's not the sound of a USFN or Xolian firearm. Assaultbot return fire silences as the weapon systematically picks them off. Granicks feels himself lifted from the ground, his limp form flopping over his unseen rescuer's shoulder.

"We must protect Andacellos," an unfamiliar voice says, its inflection almost Saturnese. Then his rescuer jumps, covering the ten meters to the barricades set down by Ruzcier's guards.

"Tell me where to find him," the voice says as Xolian guards rush to Granicks's side, "and I will save him."

* * * * *

"Captain down! Captain down!" Ace shouts into his comm, communicating with Valkyrie and Revenshal over laser link. "Weapons hot, Val! Take them out!"

"On it." Her voice is deadly.

Out of the corner of his cockpit, the smoking hulks of two Dronehawks fall from the sky. Then a third. He squeezes his own trigger and two more of Heesor's escort squadron join their comrades in free fall.

* * * * *

"Noooo!" Konran screams at the holo-display. "They shot him. I can't believe they shot him!"

"Come!" Cassio yells. "We must flee now!"

Every holo-display shows assaultbots streaming toward Ruzcier's home. Bots drop from the sky, landing on Ruzcier's roof. A firefight breaks out on the ground as Ruzcier's guards fight to defend the fallen captain.

Zenara gets up from the console. Visibly shaken, she scrambles to the warp yacht. Konran and Cassio follow close on her heels.

"Do you know how to fly her?" Cassio asks, standing by the elegant craft.

The warp yacht stands five meters high, twenty meters long. A toroidal bulge protrudes from its midline where the warp field generator wraps around its otherwise sleek girth. Unlike the warp drives USFN warships used to traverse the solar system, this generator was made to propel the craft over light-years.

"It's like any other craft while subluminal," Zenara says. "The warp protocol for Kapteyn b is already loaded. We just have to make it past the warp margin, say go, and it will do the rest."

"If we make it that far," Cassio yells. "We should not have delayed."

"You said that a hundred times already," Zenara yells back, struggling with the warp yacht's entrance. "Open," she grunts. Nothing happens.

"How do we get in?" Konran asks.

"That's what I'm working on."

"You don't know how to open the door?" Cassio's voice is on its last thread. "How incompetent are you, girl?"

"It's Ms. Exeunt to you, jarhead. And something isn't right. The door should have already opened."

"If it hasn't been opened in a while, the actuators could be rusted," Konran says. "Some older craft have that problem."

"Not this yacht," Zenara says. "Dad keeps it in prime working order."

"So open the door, then," Cassio says.

"Maybe it needs an external power source," Konran offers, mind racing. "Some old ships go into a hibernation-type mode. It may just need reawakening."

"Yes, that's it," Zenara says. "I forgot that—everything I fly is so much more modern. Wait here." She turns and runs back to the command console.

"You should have already DONE THAT!" Cassio bellows, face red. Zenara ignores him.

Then the lights go dark, and the warp yacht ceases humming. Zenara curses from across the room, her epithet echoing between the walls with one of Cassio's own.

"It's not working!" she calls out. "I can't get it back up!"

"They killed the power," Konran realizes. "We're stuck."

"They can't have done that," Zenara replies. "They'd have to be right on top of us to do that."

"Guys, do you hear that?" Konran asks before Cassio can reply. A muted crash sounds from the direction of the entrance, down below, in the junk room.

"They're down there," Konran says.

"How?" Zenara asks, voice rising. "How did they find us so fast?"

244

"Assaultbots do not experience human limitations," Cassio hisses. "Is there another way out?"

"Yes," Zenara says, nearly panicking. "I can get us out. I think we can get to another hangar." She runs back to Konran's side. "There are some guns in the lockers. Quick, let's go." She takes Konran's hand.

"Get ready to run," Cassio says, unslinging his plasma rifle. "And get ready to fight."

* * * * *

Vadic Heesor sits in on the bridge of the *Tartaglia*, watching his assaultbots collapse in the Xolian courtyard more than a million kilometers below.

This wasn't going right.

He had rushed it. Granicks got under his skin, and he rushed it. Ever since the NACs discharged, he had been rushing it. There was nothing else to do. As the master of orchestrating coincidences, Heesor knew when something wasn't. And that wasn't a coincidence. Whatever it was that had been obliterated while trying to penetrate Arzibanian space had unsettled him. And he had rushed it.

Heesor wipes sweat from his forehead, scanning the status readout for each assaultbot squad. Three of the five squads were already inside Ruzcier's complex—they were doing fine. But of the thirty bots that landed with his hologram, only half remained functional. That number drops from fifteen to ten, then four, then zero.

What?

He looks back at the status readout.

How?

Suddenly Darius Granicks's prone figure lifts into the air. It lands out of sight behind the Xolian barricades.

"What just happened?" he shouts, but the officers around him look as dumbfounded as he does.

And then the whine of Arzibanian sirens joins the percussive clamor of rain.

The Arzibanian forces should not be responding so quickly.

245

"Give me control of a Dronehawk," he orders. "I need to see what's going on down there."

A holo-feed appears in his display, transmitting point-of-view visual from one of his Dronehawks. Heesor slows the craft down, allowing him to take in the full situation.

At least a half dozen Arzibanian police craft circle Ruzcier Exeunt's complex, and they are quickly honing in on Vadic's exposed landing craft.

"Focus the Dronehawks against Granicks and the Xolians," he orders. "We need to take out those Sparrowhawks!"

Too late. He sees the attack coming before it hits.

A Sparrowhawk dives from the clouds, sending plasma bolts into one, then two, then all of his landing craft. Their hulls burgeon with billowing smoke. Heesor searches for the attacker, itching to release his own plasma blast in reply. Then his holo-feed goes black, his own Dronehawk blasted from the sky.

"You understand you made that craft an easy target?" a voice speaks from beside his command chair.

Vadic turns to the emerald eyes and a long, catlike face behind the words; a sharp black goatee and mustache demarcate thin lips. Emersav Firnuendal, Level 19 naval combat strategist, peers back at him. Although transmitted over a distance of fifty-seven light-years, the hologram perfectly depicts the condescending amusement shining between Emersav's slitted eyelids. How Vadic hated his life's work at times.

Emersav's hologram speaks again. "I would suggest refraining from tampering too much with the drones, Minister, as they are known to be quite *intelligent* of their own accord."

Vadic hides his anger beneath his next words.

"I'd like to see you do better."

"Is that an invitation?" Emersav asks, his tone eager, like a hyena hunched in the bushes, watching the antelope drink.

"Do you require me to repeat myself?" Vadic replies.

Emersav just peers back at him, his expression unchanging—or had his smile increased ever so slightly? The combat strategist stands, addressing rows of unseen officers from the command bridge of his stolen Saturnese Huoxing.

246

"Jump," he says, his smile widening into a sneer. "Attack groups one through six, jump, now."

* * * * *

Commander Jasyn Revenshal listens from the bridge of the *Gamma*, heart pounding, to the intermittent broadcasts from Ace's and Valkyrie's Sparrowhawks, the laser links falling in and out of contact. *Curse the communication jamming.*

"Captain ... hit ... bleeding."

"Taking fire..."

"Reinforcements..."

"Do we have any update from Orbital Twelve?" he shouts across the *Gamma*'s bridge—which was not large. The massive Arzibanian orbital defense station known as Orbital Twelve lurked silently out the *Gamma*'s forward viewport, refusing to acknowledge Revenshal's pleas to aide his captain.

"No, sir," his sensors officer replies. "All communications are jammed, and they refuse to acknowledge our laser link."

"Keep trying," he shouts back. "And how about those Bestiphan trajectiles we traded for?"

"Installed and loaded, sir," his weapons officer calls back. "It was a crude job, but they should work."

"Good," Revenshal replies. "Double-check them and make sure."

He studies his holographic space-time emulator, estimating the odds of circumventing Orbital Twelve, getting past the NACs, and reaching Maehn Arziban in one piece. He'd gotten past worse before—but he always told himself that when preparing to do something crazy.

Suddenly more than twenty new signatures appear in his space-time emulator: ships of all sizes, well behind the NACs, deep within Maehn Arziban's gravitationally affected zone. His emulator lists their designations as the *Gamma*'s targeting system automatically identifies the craft.

Nolvaric Rezakar

Nolvaric Rezakar

Nolvaric Rezakar

Nolvaric Rezakar
Nolvaric Evariz
Nolvaric Evariz
Nolvaric Evariz
Nolvaric Nicransin
Nolvaric Nicransin
Nolvaric Nicransin
Saturnese Huoxing
Saturnese Huoxing

Revenshal stops reading, his eyes nearly bulging out of his skull. "What is going on here?" he shouts, even louder than before. "Since when did the Saturnese join forces with the Nolvarics? And how did they get all these ships so close to Maehn Arziban?"

"No idea, sir!" the reply comes back, as if reading Revenshal's mind. "The Nolvarics somehow just jumped twenty-three ships within five millicks of the moon! There's no way that was warp technology. They should have been torn apart by Summanus more than a meglick out—not to mention the warp dampeners."

"What have we gotten ourselves into, Darius?" Revenshal says, looking at the staggering enemy force.

"Sir!" his communications officer calls out. "We just received Arzibanian authorization to enter the system!"

"Advance now!" Revenshal barks. "And everyone get ready to earn some medals."

CHAPTER 16

Chanziu runs silently down the marbled hallway, calming his nervous system as he follows a mentally uploaded map of Ruzcier's compound. Somehow the Nolvarics had jumped more than twenty ships into Summanus's gravity well—a feat impossible for present warp technology, but they had done it. But despite the impossibility, the Nolvarics had done it, and they were here. And now, positioned so closely to the city-moon, the enemy fleet was impervious to the Arzibanian's mighty orbital defense stations and no-admittance cannons. It was the glaring weakness of an otherwise impenetrable defense: Arzibanian law prohibited the weapons from firing toward their own populace. However, the Nolvaric presence wasn't what threatened to spike Chanziu's heart rate.

They brought the Huoxings, he thinks, recalling the plot he had eavesdropped upon in the USFN command center. *They're framing Saturno-China for the attack.*

Chanziu stops abruptly. No more than fifteen meters ahead, assaultbots bustle in an adjoining room. He estimates their numbers: there were no more than seven of them.

A perfect target.

Crouching, Chanziu makes a noise. A bot springs around the corner with a recoilless bazooka on its shoulder. Its adjustable camouflage matches the marbled décor as it scans the hallway. Heesor had certainly sent in the big guns.

Stupid.

Chanziu places a blaster bolt through its head and three more through its torso. The bot crashes to the ground and Chanziu bolts forward, taking position above its smoking remains, clinging to the ceiling.

Assaultbots pour into the hallway and Chanziu lets them pass, but not unaffected. Nanobots sprinkle them from above.

Time to see what they're made of.

* * * * *

Commander Revenshal bites his lip, squinting into his space-time emulator at the blips indicating the enemy ships.

"They still don't acknowledge our approach," he says. "Well, I'm not complaining. Keep alternating our jamming protocol and try to keep it that way."

So far none of the Nolvaric capital ships had successfully made the atmospheric plunge, though they had released a sizeable amount of fighters which had. Three of the Nolvaric Rezakars and two of the Nicransin cruisers had been destroyed by the NACs already, but plenty of enemy craft had found shielding close to the moon. Arzibanian law prevented the NACs from firing toward the moons they protected, so unless the Arzibanians held a vote in the next five minutes, those Nolvaric craft were all here to stay.

"Commander!" Revenshal's second-in-command, Lieutenant Umjab Cauli, shouts. "The *Tartaglia* is gaining on us. Convergence rate of one point three."

"One point *three*?" Revenshal repeats, incredulous. "Is he mad? That thing must be maxed out."

"That's how I see it, sir," Cauli replies.

The *Tartaglia* was the kind of ship every officer wanted to command: the first of its generation. It was huge, powerful, and apparently blazingly fast. Its jamming equipment was good enough to hinder the *Gamma* from communicating with the rest of the *Nova Scotia*, its stealth capabilities good enough to hide it from the cutter's active scanners. But Heesor had been sloppy, and the *Gamma* had traced its location as soon as it launched that accursed landing party.

I still wish I could have shot those carizan lovers down, Revenshal sulks. Had the all-seeing babysitter Orbital Twelve not been present, he would have blasted Heesor's landing party from orbit without blinking.

"Sitrep, Cauli," Revenshal orders. "Call it like you see it."

"Well, sir," Cauli says, turning from his position on the officer's deck. "The *Tartaglia* will be right on top of us when we hit Maehn Arziban. Assuming they're in league with the Nolvaric forces..."

"Yes, we assume that," Revenshal inserts.

250

"Right," Cauli resumes. "Assuming that, we're going to enter the fight both pinned and flanked. It will be dirty, and we may not last long—but I don't see any other way to dig the captain out. We have to try."

"Thanks, Cauli," Revenshal replies. The Cameroonian officer always read it straight, and he had more than enough courage to serve on Revenshal's bridge. Bouncing ideas off him often spurred Revenshal's greatest machinations.

"How about we do both?" he adds.

"Both, sir?"

"Yeah, why not dig them out and live for more than one minute."

"I say yes, sir."

"You ready for some crazy?"

"Aye, sir," the reply comes from more voices than just Lieutenant Cauli's.

"All right, people," Revenshal orders, "push velocity to maximum! I want 100 percent subluminal! They're not faster than us, I don't care how special they think they are. Navigation, take us around Summanus. We're going to use it to sling ourselves at the moon. That means all active shields drop as soon as we enter Summanian orbit. We're going to use the gravity generator instead to propel ourselves around the planet. And we'll need every centimeter per second of velocity we can get, because when we get there, we're blowing the carizans off the map with a thermo-gravitic shock to the face."

Cauli looks at Revenshal. "This is illegal, sir."

"On federated planets, yes."

"Pretty much everywhere, sir."

"I don't see another option, Cauli. Do you?"

"No, sir. I just needed you to know I'm with you, despite that."

Revenshal nods. He encouraged his officers' inquisitive and independent natures. He needed their best selves, and that often meant taking critical feedback during critical moments. More than once, Cauli and his sharp, detail-oriented mind had prevented Revenshal from taking illegal or controversial action like this. Cauli hated breaking the rules, and Revenshal let him speak his mind. But even more, Cauli hated injustice. Revenshal admired the man for his ability to carefully balance the two, and so made him second-in-command.

"Let's go be the lever, sir," the Cameroonian officer says.

"Let's go be the lever," Revenshal repeats. "Oh, and weapons, transfer firing control of the Bestiphan trajectile system to me."

* * * * *

Konran runs down the subterranean corridor, a small plasma blaster in each hand and a pair of vision-enhancement goggles over his eyes. Zenara runs ahead of him, a large scatterblaster from her father's supply lockers at the ready. Cassio brings up the rear. He throws another plasmo-shrapnel grenade down the tunnel. Behind Cassio, assaultbots lurk around corners, keeping pace but staying away from the grenades. A warm wind rustles Konran's hair as the grenade's shockwave washes over him. A volley of assaultbot plasma bursts up the corridor in reply, thundering within the confined space.

"They have orders to capture us alive," Cassio calls up, "or we'd already be in a firefight. They're herding us!"

"We're almost there," Zenara calls back.

"I know!" Cassio shouts. "That's where they capture us!"

"Can we hide somewhere?" Konran asks, grateful once again for his boost-cake-enhanced running ability.

"Look behind," Cassio replies. "Our thermal signature is a kilometer wide."

Konran ventures a glance, and, sure enough, his goggles reveal a tunnel scoured with heat marks where their feet and arms had brushed its walls.

"And they can image us through fifty centimeters of steel and hear our heartbeats through a meter of duracrete," Cassio says, ripping off a series of shots with his plasma rifle.

"That's it!" Zenara says. "Give me your grenades!"

A plasma blast explodes in the corridor nearby and Cassio rattles off another barrage in return.

They turn another corner, and Zenara stops abruptly. She grabs Konran as he almost runs into her, arresting his momentum by grabbing onto his shirt and redirecting him into the tunnel wall. He crashes into it with an "Oof!"

"Grenades! Now! All of them!" Zenara hisses, bracing Konran and keeping him on his feet.

Cassio hastily hands her his grenades, which she piles along the side of the tunnel. Then she drags Konran forward again.

"Come on!" she urges, but Konran doesn't need the motivation. He and Cassio sprint with the Xolian. They dive when she dives, taking cover behind a bend. But Zenara doesn't stay down. She rolls back to her feet, levels her scatterblaster, and fires.

A deafening roar shatters the space as both Cassio and Zenara smash Konran against the wall to shield him. Zenara's scatterblaster fires again and again, joined in cacophony by Cassio's plasma rifle. The air fills with smoke and dust, flashing with the diffuse glow of plasmic weapons' fire. The chaos lingers, crashing and exploding in violent, angry dissonance, and then the dust begins to settle. Konran risks a glance up, and then Zenara helps him all the way. He feels his plasma pistols in his hands, hot against his palms.

"Wooo!" Zenara shrieks, raising her scatterblaster in triumph. She lifts her sleeve to wipe sweat from her brow, and dust smudges across her forehead.

"Do not be too jubilant," Cassio says, caked with dust smears of his own. "They were not trying to kill us."

"Maybe I took that into consideration, Marine," Zenara replies, still jubilant. "Through here."

She leads them back down the dusty, rubble-strewn tunnel, over the corpses of assaultbots. "That's the one you got, Konran," she says, indicating a crumpled robot. "Nice shooting."

"I got that one?" Konran says.

"You did," Cassio confirms. "My line of fire was occupied, and you hit it before I could take a shot."

When did I take the shot? Konran wonders, looking at the pistols still radiating heat into his hands. The whole ordeal was such a blurred mess, he couldn't recall anything but noise, dust, and headache. The pads of his trigger fingers even feel fatigued, now resting lightly against the triggers.

Zenara crouches at the side of the tunnel. "Here we go," she says, shoving her scatterblaster through a hole in the wall. "Tight squeeze, but we'll make it."

She crawls in after her gun. Konran follows, twisting and undulating to press through the cramped space. His arm breaks into free space, and Zenara grabs it, tugging him through and back to his feet. He stands, but not all the way, stooping in a contorted cavern of rocks, cables, piping, and thick mustiness. His vision-enhancement goggles auto-adjust, sending out an infrared beam to illuminate the darkness.

"Stand back," Cassio calls through the hole. "I don't fit yet."

Zenara and Konran scramble back into the cavern, wedging their way between rocky outcroppings and drooping ledges before winding far enough that Zenara calls, "All clear!"

Cassio's plasma rifle jumps to life with a CRACK, CRACK, CRACK, CRACK. He grunts for a moment, before another CRACK, CRACK, CRACK rings out. Finally, he wiggles his way through and joins them.

"I trust this does not get any tighter than that?" he says.

"We don't have to go far," Zenara says, leading Konran forward again. "I know of some retired maintenance shafts in here. They're just on the other side. They'll bring us up inside the mountain— and then we find one of our internal hangar bays. We can take a ship and get out of here."

"I hope so," Cassio says, "or this will end badly."

They wiggle their way through the cavern, smacking heads and knocking elbows, knees, and ankles against the unforgiving rocks. True to Zenara's word, the passage opens up after only a few tight squeezes, not into a passageway, but into a cave-like bubble of rock.

"These mountains are full of caves and tunnels," she says, stepping beneath an outcropping and into the space. "I used to play down here until my father found out. There's our way out."

She points to the left, where a large shaft protrudes like a steel stalagmite from rock floor to ceiling. Behind the shaft, the cave ends in a harsh rock wall, although more than a few spots appeared like they might lead on. It was hard to say in the darkness.

They pick their way to the two-meter-wide shaft. An impressive calcified crust grows up from its base, strengthened, no doubt, by water seeping down its length over the years. Rusty lines peek out behind the growths, demarcating a nearly obscured access hatch at its base.

"We blast it?" Cassio asks, kicking at the calcification, which doesn't break.

"Definitely," Zenara replies, leveling her scatterblaster and firing. The boom echoes through the cave, and the door converts into wreckage and dusty debris.

"A little warning next time!" Cassio growls, coughing up and brushing away dust.

"No time to waste, let's go," she replies, ducking and stepping through the twisted metal hole.

Konran follows Zenara onto a grated platform, which covers most of the shaft. A ladder runs along the side opposite from the door, continuing unseen distances upward and downward. Zenara climbs without a word, and the sound of feet and hands on rungs becomes the drumbeat of ascension. The discordant clang of metal on metal bangs out as loose ladder supports bounce precariously at the trio's motion.

They climb past three more platforms, a distance that Konran judges to be around thirty meters. Finally, at the fourth platform, the shaft ends with just enough standing room for the three of them. The lines of an access hatch are visible on the ceiling. Zenara holds her arm up to it, and a beam of scanning energy emanates from her wrist, analyzing the structure.

"Kirzot," she utters an unknown-to-Konran curse. "The shaft's been completely sealed off, with two meters of duracrete above us. I can blast through, but it's going to take at least ten shots, and this shaft is in worse condition than I anticipated."

"At least the assaultbots can't hear our hearts beating while we wait," Konran says, garnering a rueful laugh from the Xolian but not the marine.

"Let me see your gun," Cassio says to Zenara. "I have an idea." She hesitates, but he insists, and she hands over the weapon. Within a few seconds he has its cover partially disassembled.

"What are you doing?" she asks.

"Bypassing the firing regulator," Cassio says, his fingers fiddling with something inside the gun, "so we can bleed the capacitor in one shot. Take cover on the level below, and I'll get this set up."

"Give me your gun, and I'll open the door on that level, in case you demolish this shaft," Zenara says.

Cassio stares at Zenara for a long moment before relinquishing his plasma rifle. "I want that back as soon as you're done," he says.

"As soon as you blow up my gun, it's yours," Zenara replies, taking his plasma rifle and descending.

She and Konran descend the ten meters back to the last platform.

"There's not a door on this level," Zenara shouts up as Konran steps beside her.

"This better work, then," Cassio shouts back.

"Should we go down another?" Konran asks, already sure he knew the answer.

"No, we'll need to get out as fast as we can. We just have to hope it works," Zenara says.

"Set!" Cassio shouts down. "Brace yourselves!"

An orange light emanates from above, accompanied by a roar like a freight train passing meters overhead, and, as Cassio lands on their platform, the ceiling explodes. Without a word, the marine yanks the ladder hard once, and then scrambles back up when it holds.

Konran tries not to breathe as he follows Zenara up the ladder, but the acrid smoke from the blast stings his nostrils anyway. And then a completely unexpected sensation hits him: wetness, landing hard on his face. Confused, he grabs Zenara's hand as she pulls him from the shaft and into the Arzibanian afternoon thunderstorm.

* * * * *

Commander Yoana Exeunt was improvising. It wasn't her ideal mode of operation, preferring rather to execute solid orders from a trusted source. But years serving under Granicks and alongside

256

Revenshal would teach anyone to appreciate the art of improvisation.

She had already fulfilled her original directive, providing the captain a positive ID on Vadic Heesor's invading party before the minister landed. It galled her that she hadn't been at Granicks's side when Heesor shot him. She curses again at the thought. But orders were orders, and she always trusted the captain's judgment completely.

Yoana pauses, taking one deep breath and cuing her mind to focus attention on her purpose at hand. She feels her mental clarity build, and then Salazar interrupts her, the enthusiastic scientist grinning broadly from the chair next to hers in the control tower.

"I've decoded their transmissions, ma'am! And I've broken their jamming protocol! It was harder than I thought—I've been working on it in my spare time, just, you know, to see how well USFN communications protocols can hold up—but once I pegged the encryption layers running on top of what turned out to be nothing more than standard USFN transmission codes, backing out their jamming protocols underneath was easier than stoking civil unrest on the nets—which, er, I've never actually attempted—officially, at least."

"Can you contact our forces?" Yoana asks, willing patience with the man.

Salazar nods. "I'm trying. It will take me a minute to set them all up on the same bypass channels."

"Do it. And do not interrupt me for that minute."

Yoana breathes again, and thoughts drain from her mental canvas, replaced by pure focus on the present moment. But the emotion remains. She breathes again and lets the stage of her mind simply be. If the emotion was going to stay, she was going to use it.

The captain's overall plan revolved around protecting Konran, which, from Granicks's rash urgency and willingness to be shot, was of clear criticality. Now, as second-in-command, that initiative rested directly upon Yoana's shoulders.

Yoana opens her eyes, tuning to the various holo-feeds broadcasting uplinks from across Ruzcier's estate. Assaultbots scour the compound. Her uncle's guards and servants scramble to set up defenses. Some of them flee—not all Xolians were created equal.

She opens her ears, directing her data console to tune into the enemy transmissions Salazar had decoded. They are speaking about Konran.

"Show me that location," she says, but not to Salazar. Mentally uploaded into her brain, the map of her uncle's compound zooms in, indicating a location on the side of his mountain.

"Ah," she says as everything integrates into one seamless whole.

Konran, her cousin Zenara, and Konran's bodyguard Cassio were in the tunnels beneath the compound. Her uncle's warp-yacht bay had been overrun by assaultbots, who were herding the trio toward the mountain. There, the assaultbots intended to cut them off. Yoana follows Konran's path on her mental schematic, calculating his logical destinations. Heesor's forces do the same on the holo-feed monitors as assaultbots reroute to Ruzcier's mountain.

"We are connected!" Salazar shouts, listening to some transmission only he can hear.

"You have Revenshal?" Yoana asks.

"Yes, ma'am!" Salazar replies. "I've got the Xolian pilots, too. They already scrambled their Xarbas—five of them; those things are slick. They've joined the fighting, and I've linked them to Ace and Valk."

"Salazar," Yoana cuts the scientist off, "give Revenshal these coordinates," she says, indicating the region where Konran was heading.

"Yes, ma'am!" he agrees enthusiastically and relays the information. Though vertically challenged, the South American man was not short on energy. Suddenly a startled look crosses his face, and he turns to Yoana.

"All right, go for it," Salazar mutters into the comm. "Ma'am," he addresses her, "Revenshal is going to throw a thermo-gravitic shock."

"Good," she replies, appreciating yet again her colleague's insatiable bravado. "It will buy us time to unite with Konran. Come, we must make haste."

258

Yoana turns from her seat and runs out the door, exiting the control tower with Salazar close on her heels. Tactical improvisation, she learned by observing Granicks, simply meant finding the angles that maximized your chances of success while minimizing those of your enemies—and always trusting your gut.

It had taken her years to assimilate that lesson. She was the knife, not the tactician, and as any precision instrument, Yoana worked best when directed by the master surgeon. She only lived today because Granicks saved her all those years ago. The captain had rescued her task force during the hottest moments of the Battle of Terra Fina, brilliantly reversing tactical blunders that should have been her doom. And then the man took her under his command and wiped the Shavinaeri pirates out of the system within the day (which, for the planet Terra Fina, was only eighteen Earth hours long).

Granicks understood her true potential, and the captain hadn't stopped pulling strings until she became the first—and only—Xolian officer within the United Space Federation Navy. Today, for perhaps the first time ever, he truly needed her back.

Yoana steps into a hover-vehicle—selecting one with strong vertical capabilities.

She knew the enemy's location, she knew the enemy's target, and she knew the target's destination. Now all that remained was assuring the target succeeded and the enemy failed. It was simple, once you knew how to frame the puzzle.

Salazar scrambles into the seat beside her, and Commander Yoana Exeunt guns the accelerator. It was time to introduce Heesor's forces to the inner Xolian—and that was something she utterly excelled at.

* * * * *

"I thought we were supposed to be under the mountain! Where is the hangar?" Cassio yells at Zenara.

Konran looks around, surveying his surroundings through the driving rain. They are on a plateau of sorts, a small platform cut into the side of Ruzcier's mountain. He can see the towers of the nearest Arzibanian city center in the near distance, its spires

259

sparkling with a rainbowlike glow as Solis cuts beneath the dark clouds.

The stark, eerie beauty of the vista is lost on him. His eyes fix instead on the starfighters filling the sky, pouring through the clouds like burning asteroids toward Ruzcier's mountain. Ruzcier's defense cannons fire angrily from his thick perimeter wall at Heesor's invaders. Below, smoke billows from the Xolian's estate. Konran's ears attune to the sound of naval-grade plasma fire, and a Dronehawk falls from the sky, flailing like a giant flaming quail.

"Where is the hangar you promised, Zenara?" the marine demands again. "We need to get off this platform now!"

"Over here!" Zenara shouts, gathering her wits and running toward the mountain wall. "There is an entrance."

"Halt, humans!" an authoritative, humanoid voice commands. Konran obeys, but not out of desire to comply. Hairs prickle on his neck as the rumble of military-grade antigravity repulsors shakes the plateau. He turns to see two of Heesor's landing craft hovering at the plateau edge, cannons glaring at him like multipronged snouts of two ancient dragons. The landing craft don't touch down or advance, and wind and rain whip at Konran's face as he wonders what they are waiting for.

Then, as Cassio pulls Konran behind him, five more craft emerge from the clouds above, descending purposefully toward the plateau. Three of them have Saturnese markings, the others are Nolvaric.

Something else catches Konran's eye, and he ducks instinctively as a large object hurtles over the plateau edge. It stops without hitting the ground—a long, tubular shape with a conical tip protruding from one end. It hovers a little more than a meter above the plateau in the space between Konran and Heesor's minions. Then a wiry man appears alongside it, his black jumpsuit sleek as if untouched by rain. His gloved hands clutch the object, which he raises easily to his shoulder. Fire belches and the hull of the nearest landing craft crumples in a violent inferno.

Comprehension dawns on Konran as Cassio tackles him backward, shielding him from the blast with his body.

Oh, I think that was a bazooka.

CHAPTER 17

"Run, Konran, run!" Chanziu yells.

He drops the bazooka and reengages stealth mode, becoming invisible. He fires his inertial thrusters, jumping laterally to change his angle of attack before propelling himself forward, onto the remaining USFN landing craft. There he drops stealth—heightening the effect of his attack by suddenly reappearing atop the enemy—and fires point-blank with his sidearm, blasting away at sensory equipment, viewports, and anything exposed.

The ship's access hatch hisses open and Chanziu goes invisible again, jumping high and firing as he falls, picking off two emerging assaultbots. He jumps again before hitting the ground, straining his inertial thrusters, and narrowly avoids vaporizing beneath the landing craft's plasmic return fire.

Got you now.

Chanziu's hijacked army of assaultbots leaps from the mountainside and onto the landing craft. Only four of the bots had succumbed to his nanobot-inflicted hacking infestation, but it was enough. They clamber quickly up the landing craft's armored sides, jump down its open hatch, and, using a few moves Chanziu personally programmed into them, take control of the craft.

* * * * *

Still alive and wanting to stay that way, Ace dives his Sparrowhawk hard, hurtling toward Maehn Arziban at suicidal speed. Sweat drips off an eyebrow and into an eye. Behind him, he can sense Valkyrie pulling the same maneuver. Behind her, the squad of five Xolian starfighters follows suit. Led by Majorkai Yazzi, their formation of egg-like, shape-shifting Xarbas dive with the Sparrowhawks toward Maehn Arziban.

"Please confirm no Arzibanian forces or civilians are present near the target," a communications officer from the *Gamma* crackles into Ace's comm.

"Wiped out!" Ace shouts, staring at the rapidly approaching ground. "Gone; destroyed!"

"You are clear?" the officer asks.

"Affirmat-rrggh!" Ace manages, leveling off and skimming less than a meter above the ground. Even with the Sparrowhawk's impressive inertial compensation system, the maneuver taxes his body. He fights dimming vision as his instincts take control of the craft, dodging obstacles in his path like a mosquito braving the autobahn.

"T minus five seconds to thermo-gravitic shock," the officer relays.

Five ticks of eternity later the *Gamma* slams into the Arzibanian troposphere. The entire sky explodes above Ace, converting instantaneously from roiling thunderheads into a scathing, fiery fury as the *Gamma*'s incredible momentum converts into thermo-gravitic shock energy.

Ace's visor automatically dims against the harsh light, and he pulls back on his stick, angling his Sparrowhawk upward and into the fray. Beside him, Valkyrie has already done the same.

* * * * *

"Arzibanian first responders have all been destroyed, sir!"

Captain Revenshal slams his fist onto his console as the familiar acrid mixture of grief and anger forms its knot within his heart.

"The Xolian fighters?" he asks.

"Fine, sir, they've formed with our squad."

Revenshal lets out a half breath of air, holding to the other half out of spite. After orbiting Summanus to gravitationally slingshot themselves at Maehn Arziban, the *Gamma* had already made eight truncated elliptical orbits of the moon. And the Nolvaric and Saturnese ships lurking nearby were starting to pay special notice to his little cutter and its meteoric circuits around the moon—the kind involving plasma bursts, rail gun rounds, and advanced anti-ship missiles.

Revenshal had anticipated only needing one pass at Maehn Arziban before executing his plan, but the circumstances of atmospheric battle had forced him to delay the maneuver. Not wanting to destroy friendly Arzibanian forces, the *Gamma* had continued to orbit Maehn Arziban, altering its trajectory with each pass to avoid the enemy guns. His crew had adjusted to the opportunity expertly, and the *Gamma* had gained velocity with each successive orbit and also positively identified every enemy craft on Granicks's side of the planet.

The Arzibanian police forces surrounding Granicks's location had succumbed quickly as Nolvaric starfighters descended upon the moon. That Ace and Valkyrie had managed to evade the now more than 120 starfighters swarming the skies did not surprise Revenshal at all—he knew their prowess. But he had seen enough combat to know that luck and skill could only delay the inevitable so long when the inevitable became this ravenous.

"Fighters reporting all clear!" his officer shouts.

"Do it!" Revenshal orders through gritted teeth, checking his inertial restraints and life-support systems for the fiftieth time. "And keep to the upper troposphere so the shockwave primarily remains atmospheric. I want to minimize surface casualties."

"Yes, sir!"

Revenshal stares into the *Gamma*'s forward view display, watching its real-time point-of-view broadcast rather than his space-time emulator. The Arzibanian sunset fades to darkness and then back to sunrise as the *Gamma* orbits the moon again, and the overlaid countdown timer ticks toward zero.

At T minus two seconds the *Gamma* dips on its trajectory, plummeting through Arzibanian atmosphere until just kissing the outer reaches of its troposphere. Revenshal can see the top of the thunderstorm hovering over the spot where Heesor shot Granicks. The tall, tumultuous clouds speckle with the flitting dots of a hundred buzzing starfighters.

The *Gamma* covers the distance in a blink, converging on the thunderhead like a meteoric piece of Armageddon itself. The countdown timer hits zero, and the *Gamma*'s gravitational shields reconfigure, releasing their grasp on the moon below. Angling forward, the shields invert their polarity to resist instead of assist the *Gamma*'s motion. And the cutter's momentum transfers into every molecule—and every ship—in the Arzibanian sky before it.

And everything explodes.

In humble deference to the law of conservation of momentum, and in complete insubordination to the laws of intersolar warfare, the *Gamma*'s thermo-gravitic shockwave rips through the thunderhead like a warp yacht through warm cheese.

Revenshal's inertial compensation system braces his body. Life-support systems interface with his veins and organs, protecting him from the sudden forces. The *Gamma*'s internal gravity compensates for what the restraints can't, and he hears the shriek of metal as the *Gamma* convulses within a hurricane of fire and wind and death. He tastes blood, feeling the salty wetness creep onto his tongue and up his nose. And then the firestorm stops, and his officers go to work.

"Firing systems coming online!"

"Reassessing enemy position!"

"Hostile craft 74 percent eliminated!"

"Remaining targets acquired!"

"Fire," Revenshal orders, the taste of iron wet on his throat.

* * * * *

Konran disappears into the mountain, and Chanziu jumps, climbing the mountainside. He would have preferred to follow and protect Konran, but his work out here was not done. In the sky above him, Nolvaric and Saturnese landing craft fire upon the plateau, blasting away at the spot he had just vacated. Chanziu sends a command to his assaultbots, and the USFN landing craft they had appropriated turns its turret, firing back into the sky.

Chanziu activates his inertial thrusters and jumps again, soaring upward toward the next plateau. There were many of these landing plateaus cut into the mountain, and, using the mentally uploaded map Ruzcier's servants gave him after rescuing Darius Granicks, Chanziu charts the quickest course to Konran.

His assaultbots ascend with him, but not near him. Keeping the stolen landing craft close enough to provide cover but far enough to not give away his position, Chanziu orders his assaultbots to head for a different landing plateau. The enemy takes the bait, focusing their attempts away from his actual position.

I could get used to working with these bots, he reasons, climbing ever higher.

As he ascends, he instinctively surveys the battle swarming about him. His eyes and ears track the action automatically, feeding the chaotic patterns into his mind to be distilled into meaning. He identifies two USFN Sparrowhawks in the melee, fighting for their lives against impossible odds. Chanziu silently bids them farewell, removing them from his mental list of potential allies.

Then, as Chanziu lands softly upon a new plateau, he discerns something odd: a deviation in the pattern that immediately registers within his brain as significant. The two friendly craft are diving straight down, set on a collision course with the moon itself.

Fatal mistake, his mind notes: losing so much altitude, so highly outnumbered in an atmospheric furball was a fighter pilot's final mistake.

These are no amateurs, he analyzes, listening to the ascending whine of the diving craft. *This is a tactical maneuver. That must mean...*

Chanziu's body reacts before his mind concludes its analysis, sprinting across the plateau in two inertial-thruster-assisted leaps. He takes what cover he can, crouching against the mountainside, sensing by instinct he was right.

And then the world explodes in a colossal flash of gale-force wind. Chanziu strains, grasping to the rock with fingers, elbows, knees, and toes.

Suddenly the wind stops and the thunderstorm clears. Silver skies and an orange sunset glow across the not-so-distant horizon. The only sound in the air is a rhythmic thump. Chanziu looks upward. A ship hovers there, thousands of meters above. Puffs of light blink around its girth as it fires at the Nolvaric starfighters still inhabiting the sky. Distant explosions reach his ears as kills crash to the earth.

That must be the Nova Scotia's Gamma *cutter,* Chanziu identifies. *And it just released a thermo-gravitic shock front—a desperate and devastating move within the capacity of its commander, Jasyn Revenshal.*

Nearby, Chanziu's hijacked assaultbots continue the fight in their hijacked landing craft. All three Saturnese landing craft had survived the thermo-gravitic shock, as had their two Nolvaric counterparts.

And then one landing craft explodes, followed by three more as coil gun rounds from the *Gamma* find their mark. The thunderous BOOM, BOOM, BOOM, BOOM of the hypersonic projectiles echoes across the mountain seconds after obliterating the ships. Chanziu's own landing craft takes a rail gun round to the skull, crumpling backward into a smoking crater within the mountainside, destroying his hijacked assaultbots with it.

So much for that asset.

Two Saturnese landing craft escape the bombardment, maneuvering quickly about the mountain to avoid the *Gamma*'s fire. Chanziu tracks them until they fall out of view behind a ridge.

Jumping back to action, he finds the platform's mountain entrance, hacks its control panel, and steps inside.

The race to Andacellos was on.

* * * * *

Alandie peers intently from the top floor of Vycrz Tower, a glass of Maehn Arziban's finest wine in one hand, Kyalia's hand in the other. Patrons of the skyscraper's famed penthouse restaurant surround them. All eyes stare across the city-filled moon valley, beyond the twin rainbows floating beneath the roiling thunderhead, to the mountain twenty kilometers to the north.

Nolvaric starfighters dive through the stormy sky, their glowing contrails adding a surreal effect as they pop in and out of view. Plasma blasts flash like lightning to and from the churning clouds as surface guns exchange fire with the invaders. Alandie's fist clenches tight to Kyalia's. All he can think of is that day, not yet a distant memory, when Konran launched himself into the darkness of asteroidal space to save the *Viona Grande*.

266

To save Alandie.

"We have to do something," he mutters, feet frozen in place. "We have to help him." Kyalia quivers on his elbow in response— no doubt thinking of the same fateful moment.

"But what can we do?" she breathes, almost too quiet to hear.

Then, suddenly, the sky around the mountain explodes in brilliant, unfurling fire.

Alandie and everyone screams, and the room dives for cover. The skyscraper shakes with a roar, shuddering as if hit by a hurricane. Windows shatter and people scream again. And everything goes silent.

Alandie brushes glass off Kyalia, cutting his hands with the little shards and getting blood onto her fancy clothes. But she appears unhurt, and he helps her to her knees. The two of them risk a glance through the newly opened window, Alandie trying to be brave, Kyalia shaking under his arm.

The sky is clear, thunderstorm gone. Something occupies the sky above the mountain, drawing Alandie's eye.

Was that the Gamma?

Bursts of weapons' fire spray from its distant form. The blasts streak across the sky in all directions, terminating in tiny starfighter-shaped explosions.

Then Alandie's mouth drops. Above the *Gamma*, faint at first but growing in size with every second, a ship as large as one hundred *Gamma*s appears through the haze of Arzibanian atmosphere. Its gradual descent is graceful rather than fiery, more ominous than anything Alandie has seen today.

The ship exchanges weapons' fire with the *Gamma*, which swoops from its firing perch to evade the descending monstrosity.

"What about the warp yacht?" Alandie's mouth speaks. "There was a warp yacht docked atop the tower, right?"

"What can we do with that?" Kyalia asks.

"I don't know," Alandie replies. "Get Konran out of here? Somehow? You know they're after him. We have to do something."

Kyalia looks at him, struggling not to tremble but only shaking harder. Her vibrant yellow eyes glow up at him. Her pulsating hair cycles in phase with her tears.

"It..." she tries to speak. "It belongs to Zimak Jin," she says, pointing weakly across the restaurant at a tan-skinned, terrified man in his early twenties. "He's the one I wanted to meet."

Next to Alandie, Philipe, Kyalia's languorous co-star, stirs from his motionless state on the floor. The man had lingered at Kyalia's side since arriving at Maehn Arziban, murmuring nonsensical complaints every time Alandie spoke. That was, until the Nolvaric attack began, at which point the celebrity assumed a trancelike, wide-eyed state on the floor, arms hugging his knees.

"I will bring him to you," Philipe says simply, standing and walking through the petrified crowd.

* * * * *

Yoana Exeunt leans against inertia as she careens around a corner, weaving the hover-vehicle through tight corridors never intended for vehicular passage. She and Salazar were under the mountain now, gunning for the hangar bay she predicted Konran and his party would attempt to access.

"It's just one level up from here," Salazar says, bobbing in his seat as she threads the vehicle through another series of turns.

"Do we have anything more from the *Gamma*?" she asks, slamming her foot on the gravitational repulsor pedal and causing the hover-vehicle to rise, jumping over an assortment of crates and containers in her path.

Revenshal's ploy, insane as it was, had worked. The thermo-gravitic shock had decimated the initial Nolvaric-Saturnese forces that had entered the atmosphere, buying precious time. But time had passed since they last corresponded, and Yoana worried about the *Gamma*'s fate.

"No, not yet," Salazar says before blurting, "Wait, yes! Incoming message! It's from Revenshal!"

"Yoana!" Revenshal's voice comes through. "Saturnese forces breached the mountain before I hit them. Are you in position to respond?"

"Yes, Commander," she replies, crashing through a set of doors and into a fresh corridor. "Send me what you have."

"Sending coordinates now," Revenshal replies, breathless. "The *Tartaglia* just entered the atmosphere, so we won't be able to support you. We estimate fifteen to twenty commandos inserted into the mountain before we destroyed their ships."

"They will not have Konran," Yoana replies, guiding the hover-vehicle into a twisting, upward-rising tunnel.

* * * * *

The mountain shakes, and Zenara stops.

"What was that?" she asks, looking around.

"Something above," Cassio says, pushing her forward. "Do not stop. Keep running."

Konran runs, taking his usual place behind Zenara and in front of Cassio. The tunnels inside the mountain wind erratically, expanding and contracting without any real transitions between spaces. Large rooms full of crates, boxes, and storage shrink into twisting corridors before widening into broad caverns with ceilings so high they were invisible. The tunnel walls are smooth, fused solid by whatever processes had formed them.

"My father bought this place from the original miners," Zenara explains as they run. "That's why the layout is so disorganized. I remember a hangar down this way. We'll be able to find something with some juice behind it."

"Like a smuggling vessel?" Cassio asks from behind Konran.

"You just don't know when to shut it, do you?" Zenara barks.

"I would take a smuggling vessel," Cassio says. "Ideal for our situation."

"You should be grateful my father doesn't bend to every rule," Zenara spits out. "Or else where would you run from all these attackers you brought to his doorstep?"

"We would have no need to run," Cassio says, "if you had not failed to engage the warp yacht as instructed."

"Shut it, grunt," Zenara retorts. At the next fork, she leads them down the tunnel on the right, stops, retraces her steps, then takes the tunnel on the left.

"Do you even know where you are going?" Cassio demands.

"Guys!" Konran urges. "Stop it! It's my fault! They're after me. I can't change anything of this. Let's just get out of here. I trust Zenara to get us out."

They run on in silence, three rhythmic sets of footfalls and breaths. Shortly they arrive at a large, high-ceilinged confluence of tunnels. Openings spread in every direction.

"Here we are!" Zenara says, sprinting across to one particularly gaping tunnel. But as they enter it, she suddenly stops.

"Kirzot!" she spits out the word. "It's locked. Stand guard while I grant us access." She begins to work at a control panel.

Cassio turns and takes position at the mouth of the tunnel. Suddenly he crouches, plasma rifle raised, head swiveling. Konran un-holsters his plasma pistols.

"It's not responding," Zenara grumbles. "I'm going to hack it."

"Quiet," Cassio says, his voice tense. He drops to a prone position with his body tucked behind the tunnel wall, plasma rifle against his shoulder, barrel protruding into the opening.

"What is it?" Zenara hisses.

Cassio doesn't reply, but the marine's posture conveys the danger, and the Xolian woman pulls Cassio's sidearm from his belt.

A small, metallic object bounces off the tunnel beside them, clinking on the rough, rocky floor.

"Flash-bang grenade!" Cassio yells, and a blinding light bursts into the tunnel with a deafening pop.

Konran's regenerative lenses work to reestablish his vision as his ears throb within his skull. He trips into Zenara, and both end up on the tunnel floor. Zenara untangles them, shoving him back against the unmoving durasteel door.

"Stay down," she hisses. Cassio's plasma rifle cracks off shots behind her, and Zenara turns, firing Cassio's sidearm down the tunnel, over the crouching marine's head.

"Saturnese commandos," Cassio grunts. "A lot of them."

Konran only has one of his guns now—the other lost in the commotion. He slinks there, back against the door, lone gun raised, struggling to see anything. Plasma fire crackles back and forth through the tunnel, exploding against the walls and pelting him with rock and smoke.

Suddenly a door rises behind Konran, and someone pulls him to his feet. Cassio and Zenara are still in front of him, but before he can struggle against the newcomer's grip, a voice speaks into his ear.

"Come, run!"

It was the voice of the man who appeared with the bazooka on the plateau.

The man fires above Cassio's head to get the marine's attention. Cassio looks back, as does Zenara, startled, and then the man whisks Konran down the tunnel.

* * * * *

Revenshal's teeth grind and his brow scowls. The viewport, which has converted to provide a 360-degree view around the *Gamma*, depicts Vadic Heesor's massive super-frigate *Tartaglia* behind them. It churns toward them, an angry whale intent on digesting that one last elusive krill. Various holo-displays list additional information, nearly all of which Revenshal hates—especially the one with Nolvaric and Saturnese capital ships diving into the atmosphere after the *Tartaglia*.

This is turning the bad kind of ugly fast.

"Sir!" Officer Cauli calls out. "The *Alpha* and *Beta* have achieved firing range and are prepared to engage!"

"Let them at it!" Revenshal barks.

"Lieutenant Vilkoj is requesting clarification on the scope of engagement, sir," Cauli says.

"Tell him to pretend he's me," Revenshal replies, scanning another holo-display for information.

The *Tartaglia* had made its atmospheric entry strategically, cutting off the *Gamma*'s best escape vectors. Now the *Gamma* sprinted, but like the fullback preventing the speedy striker from reaching the goal by taking the right angle, the *Tartaglia* bears down on the smaller ship. Revenshal calculates the time until the *Tartaglia*'s tractor beam strength would outmuscle the *Gamma*'s thrust capacity.

Moments at most.

"Sir!" Cauli calls out more urgently. "Heesor is demanding an audience."

"Tell him I'm on the toilet," Revenshal replies, "and cease all communications with that carizan lover."

"Yes, sir!"

"Hold it, Cauli," Revenshal says, his mouth working faster than his brain. "Engines, drop power 15 percent!"

"Sir?"

"Do it!" Revenshal yells, and the *Gamma* slows. Revenshal feels the grip of the *Tartaglia*'s powerful tractor beams snare the *Gamma*.

"All right, engines, go full power! Try to escape like your lives depend on it!"

Thrust back to full power, the *Gamma* struggles against the *Tartaglia*'s noose like a bull snared around the neck. Focused gravitational wells, or "tractor beams," as they were colloquially known, were a recent technological advent. And they were performing exactly as advertised: once a larger ship locked onto a smaller ship, that smaller ship wasn't going anywhere. The side with the sumo always won the tug of war.

Unless, of course, you punch them in the face, Revenshal thinks.

The *Gamma* slowly reverses course, reeling toward the *Tartaglia* like a barracuda on the line.

"All right, Cauli, patch the slimesack in."

"Yes, sir."

Part of the *Gamma*'s view screen converts to show a baroque office adorned with precious metals, woods, and artifacts from around the inhabited universe. At the center, a man in his late fifties, portly, but not overly so, with black, curled hair and dark penetrating eyes, stares at Revenshal like a rubicund raven peering at its next taste of roadkill.

"Commander," Minister Heesor begins, "how kind of you to return my hail. What do you think of my new ship?"

Revenshal looks down, making his face go red and his body shake slightly. "Er, sir..." he hesitates, then looks up, pretending to remove the strain he was trying to force onto his expression. "It's impressive, sir."

"Indeed," Heesor tisks. "I am afraid you forced me to act with a heavy hand, seeing how *busy* you have been this afternoon."

"Yes, sir," Revenshal replies, his face contorting into a mask of contrition. "I wish it born on record, sir, that I have been about my sworn duty today—to defend my captain."

"I know your reputation, Commander, and your record," Heesor croons with polished diction. "Which is why I am prepared to be lenient for your crimes, if you are willing to accept my terms."

"You are, sir? Thank you, sir. I am, sir," Revenshal replies, invoking relief into the rambling and trying to insert a tinge of panic. "My crew is most grateful for your mood—considering ... er..." he pauses, as if searching for the right word, "events."

"*Events*, indeed, Commander," Heesor says. "I trust you are aware of the implications of your actions?"

"I am, sir," Revenshal replies crisply.

"And you are willing to accept my terms?"

"I am, sir, whatever they are, sir," Revenshal squishes as much polish as he can into the words.

"Then why are you still running?" Heesor asks. "You know I could have killed you already."

"I do, sir," Revenshal lies as honestly as possible. "I was just waiting for your word."

"My word?"

"That my crew will be treated fairly." Around the bridge Revenshal's officers stare at him like he has gone insane—of a flavor they aren't already used to.

"You have it," Heesor replies, his tone so oily Revenshal feels the urge to run and bathe.

"Engines!" Revenshal barks authoritatively. "Cut all power immediately, save to maintain altitude above the moon. Weapons, deactivate all systems. Shields, drop protective energy fields."

Around him, the *Gamma*'s crew looks pale. To their credit, however, the *Gamma* stops struggling to escape, and status indicators depicting the health of the weapon and shielding systems go dim. The *Gamma* shakes as the *Tartaglia*'s tractor system grips the cutter intimately.

"An excellent choice," Heesor preens. "You may well find yourself atop a new command in not so long a time, under my supervision, of course."

"Of course, sir," Revenshal replies, evoking as many lines of defeat into his expression as possible. Although downcast, his eyes yet watch, waiting for the moment when the *Gamma* would enter the *Tartaglia*'s gravitational shield well.

There!

"I just have one question for you, Minister," Revenshal says, keeping his tone neutral as he keys commands into his console.

"And what is that?" Heesor replies, peering at Revenshal like the school principal who had just finished his finest lecture.

"What is your opinion of the Bestiphans? I find them to be fascinating people."

"What...?" Heesor says, his expression souring between that of a scorpion and that of a bat.

"In fact, there were Bestiphans here just yesterday—not on record, of course; you know how they like to keep a low profile, especially anywhere near USFN territory. But if you can find them, they're always interested in a little *trade*."

"All systems—!" Heesor begins to shout, but doesn't finish.

Out the *Gamma*'s viewport, five vapor trails streak toward the *Tartaglia*. The monstrous super-frigate's guns track and fire at the Bestiphan trajectiles, but the alien works of weaponry dodge as artfully as their boastful vendors had promised.

Revenshal had chosen well—again.

Electric explosions erupt across the *Tartaglia* as the trajectiles find their mark, skittering across and scouring its hull like ten million frenetic spiders. More explosions burst in the wake of the wave, puffing about the *Tartaglia* like so many bursting balloons (of hydrogen). And the tractor beam releases its hold on the *Gamma*.

"OK, everyone, back to work," Revenshal orders as the crew roars in celebration. "We have hunting to do."

* * * * *

Cassio runs at a dead sprint, gaining ground on Konran with every step. He recognized the man who had taken Konran—it was the same man who blasted Heesor's landing craft on the platform outside the mountain. His were not the actions of an enemy—he could have easily shot Cassio and Zenara instead of alerting them to run—and Cassio elects to trust him.

That didn't mean he had to like his methods.

"I," he begins, through heavy breaths, "I had our position secure," he says to the man.

"They are more than you can fight," the man replies simply, still running.

"Who are you?"

"Your friend."

"How did you find us?"

"Does it matter?"

"Why are you here?"

"The same reason you are."

"How did you—?"

"Would you rather I shot you through your head or let the traitors slaughter you?" The mystery man cuts Cassio off before he can finish his question.

"I told you that you don't know when to shut it," Zenara says behind Cassio.

The mystery man leads them in silence, picking his way through the tunnels without hesitation, ever maintaining his grip on Konran's arm.

"There it is!" Zenara suddenly shouts as the tunnel widens out again into a cavern. "The hangar!"

Inside, Cassio sees a handful of ships amidst an assortment of boxes, crates, and storage containers of various sizes. Suddenly, something feels off, and he grabs Zenara as she runs past him toward the nearest ship.

"Stop," he hisses, as the Xolian whirls on him. He is ready for her move and blocks her arm and restrains her further. In front of him the mystery man pulls Konran down behind a crate.

And then something whizzes over their heads, and the tunnel behind them explodes.

The hover-vehicle shakes as Yoana Exeunt accelerates through the tunnel. That blast had been close.

Too close.

She swerves through the final turns on her mental map, and the hover-vehicle bursts into a large, open hangar. Instantly, her mind attunes to the firefight within. She identifies Cassio's plasma rifle by its sound and hones in on its location. Konran would be with him, as would Zenara. And they were pinned down and nearly surrounded.

Yoana stops the vehicle, jumps out, and drags Salazar behind a crate with her. A rocket slams into the hover-vehicle, detonating its engine.

"Stay low and keep cover," she whispers to Salazar. And then she darts forward, straight for the nearest pocket of enemies.

"Valk, can you hit the *Tartaglia* on Flight Deck 2?" Ace yells as he turns his Sparrowhawk toward Flight Deck 1. Below him, the massive *Tartaglia* writhes under an electrical storm—courtesy of Revenshal's latest playing card. But Ace's training told him what was coming next, and he needed to prevent as much of it as possible.

"On target," Valkyrie's voice crackles into his ear. "Here they come."

Ace pulls the trigger as Dronehawks deploy en masse in response to Revenshal's surprise attack. Ace's four guns fire, one from each wingtip and two from the nose, tearing apart the first wave of unmanned starfighters with vicious bursts. His targeting system auto-tracks the Dronehawks as they continue to pour out, and his guns send half of them careening to the ground below.

Ace inverts his Sparrowhawk's weapons and propulsion systems. His seat flips with the reorientation, facing him toward the Sparrowhawk's large aft gravito-nuclear thruster. He feels the change within his craft as its propulsion system reconfigures, converting his speed-producing thruster into a plasmic megacannon.

With ease borne of fifteen thousand hours of high-intensity training, Ace maneuvers the Sparrowhawk swiftly with what had moments ago been his wingtip and nose guns. He fires, releasing a super-punch from his now forward cannon. Like Godzilla's atomic belch itself, the blast vaporizes the *Tartaglia*'s flight deck.

Just as quickly, he reverts his Sparrowhawk and sends it streaking upward, into the sky, trailed by at least fifteen surviving Dronehawks. Ace's wingtip guns spray repressive fire behind him, buying some breathing room as he races toward the vacuum of space. On the other side of the paralyzed *Tartaglia*, Valkyrie's Sparrowhawk matches his vector.

As Ace rises through the atmosphere, so does the overwhelming sensation that he had crossed a line from which there was no return. The sensation doubles as a status report displays secondary explosions ripping through the midsection of the *Tartaglia* far below.

Heesor crossed the line first, Ace reminds himself. *Now it's war.*

"Majorkai, we've got them on the hook. Are you set?" he speaks into his comm, addressing the Xolian starfighter commander.

"In position," the Xolian pilot crackles into Ace's ear.

"Let's do this," Ace orders.

Ace pulls his stick hard right, careening toward Valkyrie's position. She does the same, passing within meters of his Sparrowhawk as they swap places. The maneuver pulls the two Dronehawk tails in toward each other as autonomous craft angle after their respective targets.

See ya, suckers, Ace thinks as the five Xolian starfighter pilots zip in from all angles. Their Xarbas unleash on the Dronehawks, slicing into their formation with cascades of sapphire plasmic energy. Dozens fall, and Ace and Valkyrie dive in. Together, they rip the remaining Dronehawks apart from all sides.

And then Ace's gut sinks: swarms of Askeras and Miratans empty from the bellies of two Rezakars within the atmosphere. Midsize, manta-ray-shaped Nolvaric Evariz destroyers descend with them.

"Valk, you see that?"

"Yep."

"First one to fifty kills owes the other dinner," Ace says.

"Bet," Valkyrie crackles back.

* * * * *

Lieutenant Vilkoj, acting commander of the *Nova Scotia* in the absence of Captain Granicks and Commanders Exeunt and Revenshal, was lower on ammunition than he thought he should be.

At least he was following orders.

"*Alpha* and *Beta*, partition," he commands. "*Beta* to commence flanking maneuver from Arzibanian southwestern hemisphere. *Alpha* to set dead pursuit course of Saturno-Nolvaric task force. Continue present firing rate, but hold tesseracts. Launch missile frigates and flight wings once within the exosphere."

"Yes, sir," the cries ring out across the bridge.

Vilkoj considers his orders, weighing them against the instruction he had received from the *Gamma*.

Pretend you're me, is all Commander Revenshal had replied when Vilkoj asked about the *Nova Scotia*'s scope of engagement.

Too conservative, he concludes.

"On second thought," he says, "set tesseracts for maximal shield penetration, and target the two nearest enemy ships. We take them out two at a time."

* * * * *

Darius Granicks moans as the medical bot's appendages work his insides, mending blood vessels and organs where the plasma bolt had burned through his belly. Beside him, two Xolian nurses push his hover-gurney at a run through Ruzcier's compound.

"Closer," he manages to say, instructing the holo-feed to position closer to his face, which it does. He squints at it, which depicts a waterfall of enemy ships cascading into Maehn Arziban from the sky above.

278

"We can't escape this," Granicks wheezes to his nurses. They round a corner and he grunts with the inertia, closing his eyes.

"We're not escaping, sir," one of the nurses replies.

"Where then?"

"To the bunker."

"What of Konran?" Granicks asks, his eyes still closed.

"Attacked," the nurse says.

"Did he escape?" Granicks's question sounds less like words and more like a breath from his tired lips.

"We don't know."

"We have to..." Granicks tries, but unconsciousness takes him once again, leaving the thought to drift as an untenable ghost within his mental ether:

We have to save Konran.

* * * * *

Konran's heart thuds like blaster fire within his chest. He ducks down behind the barricade of maintenance carts and spaceship parts that Cassio had hastily thrown down. Konran tries to breathe, clutching his gun. His eyes dart left and right, trying to find a target, but in that moment, surrounded by destruction and chaos, his muscles remain frozen in place. The others, each trained warriors, fight ferociously beside him, and he tries to help, but all he can do is cringe. The hangar had not been their salvation; it had been a trap.

"Keep moving," the mystery man hisses, pulling Konran's arm and sending him scrambling behind a mechanics' bay. Something detonates against Cassio's barricade, scattering spaceship parts as the marine and mystery man dive in beside Konran. Zenara ducks the other way, behind the smoking fuselage of a light transport craft. Cassio fires a quick barrage with his plasma rifle, and a someone cries out in pain. Then the mystery man pulls Konran again, tossing him out of the way as the mechanics' bay explodes.

Cassio gets off another set of shots before ducking back down.

"We must—" the marine begins through heavy breaths.

A thunderous explosion cuts him off, reverberating from the other side of the hangar. Gunfire bursts across the room in response, but not toward Konran's position. Cries and screams and crashes resound through the space for a terrifying moment. The flurry of unseen devastation ceases, and the hangar goes silent—save for the voice of one woman: sharp, punctuated, and deadly.

"How many follow you, and how soon?" the voice demands from across the hangar.

Commander Exeunt!

"That's Exeunt," Konran says, struggling to stand.

"Konran?" another voice calls tentatively. "You OK?"

Salazar!

The mystery man wastes no time, dragging Konran, who stumbles into the hangar, in the direction of Exeunt's and Salazar's voices. They stop and Konran catches his balance. Before them, Commander Exeunt stands, silhouetted in the darkness. She dangles a Saturnese commando by his neck from the end of her long, slender, outstretched arm. Similar uniforms lie scattered in the shadows about the commander, unmoving.

"How many? How soon?" Exeunt demands again.

"Four hundred Nolvarics," the man grunts, his weak grimace an almost-smile, "coming before you can escape." He kicks a leg out, but the commander is faster, slamming him into the ground with a twist of her elbow and shoulder. He doesn't get up.

Commander Exeunt surveys the hangar, lithe form poised for combat, daring more foes to appear with the ferocity of a mother jaguar. Her gaze finds Konran before settling on the mystery man. "You are Saturnese." The way she breathes the words gives Konran chills.

"Yes," he replies. "I am here to protect Konran—these others are traitors."

"He is on our side, Commander," Cassio says, still catching his breath from the battle. "He helped us escape twice already."

"It's true," Zenara confirms. "How did you do this?" she asks the commander, surveying the destruction around her cousin. "I've studied under Achana Vak masters ... but this ... you're incredible."

"You must hurry, my cousin," Commander Exeunt replies. "The starcraft within this hangar are useless—sabotaged. But there is another hangar nearby. See Konran to safety. Go, now."

"I know which hangar you speak of," the mystery man states. "We go." He pulls Konran with him, but Konran pulls back, stumbling against the man's strength.

"Commander, you're coming with us, right?" he asks.

In response, a dozen crashes ring from somewhere high above, echoing as if reverberating through many tunnels. A dozen inhuman, cybernetic shrieks waft into the hangar bay: the battle cry of Nolvaric Clan Selkaska. Not known for subtlety, Clan Selkaska was renowned for merciless savagery. The cyborgs had breached the mountain.

"Yoana..." Zenara breathes.

"Go," Commander Exeunt replies, the word more of an order than any Granicks had ever given. And the mystery man whisks Konran away.

Konran's feet work more to catch his fall than propel him forward. The group sprints out of the hangar. Salazar joins them, but the commander does not. The short man breathes hard but keeps pace as they reenter the winding subterranean tunnel system.

These tunnels are wider than before: clearly cut from the mountain for cargo transportation. The mystery man navigates them easily, never wavering at a turn, never slackening his pace. Behind them, the din of battle slowly swells—muted, desperate, and hollow, it echoes through the tunnels.

Their path dead-ends at a gate, but the mystery man does not hesitate.

"We are here," he speaks. Still clutching Konran, his free hand manipulates a control panel, and the gate slides upward.

No surprise attack greets them this time, and in moments the mystery man has the lights on. Konran blinks as he adjusts to the brightness, and then his heart sinks.

There are no starcraft in the room.

CHAPTER 18

Crates, boxes, and containers litter the room: some open, some closed, some stacked into piles more than five meters high. Straight rows of neatly arranged storage racks stand some distance behind, stretching on into the cavernous space. It smells fresher than other areas under the mountain, as if the room had been recently reconfigured.

"What?" Cassio yells. "This is not a hangar! Zenara?"

"I..." she says. "This isn't right."

"This place is marked a hangar on the map," the mystery man replies, still holding on to Konran's wrist. Dragging Konran to a control panel inside the room, he works it with his free hand, and the hangar door closes behind them. Then he blasts the control panel with his gun and shoots the drive mechanism.

"So where is this 'hangar'?" Cassio asks, looking at the multitude of crates and containers with frustration. "We have to get out now!"

"This is the last hangar on the map," the mystery man replies, his voice calm. "Unless the Xolian knows of another location, all other flying craft are behind us," he adds.

He walks into the room, bringing Konran with him between the crates. The room was huge—completely full of stuff in various stages of shipment or storage.

"I..." Zenara says, "I don't know." She climbs up one of the smaller crate-stacks for a better vantage. "There's nothing else in here," she confirms. "What do we do?"

"What do we do?" Cassio yells. "You tell us, Xolian!"

"I don't live on Maehn Arziban most of the time," she replies, searching around. "I..." she trails off.

"Is there a storage room like this on the map?" Salazar asks. "Maybe things got swapped. Maybe that's a hangar now?"

"There are no rooms large enough on this level," the mystery man replies. "The commandos destroyed the only hangar."

"Maybe we can find another escape route?" Konran offers, his mind racing to find a solution. "Or go help Commander Exeunt?"

"She is fighting to give us time to escape, but there's nowhere to go!" Cassio replies, his anger getting the best of him. "This is your fault." He points at Zenara, who looks stricken, standing against the stack she had climbed on.

"We must see Konran to safety," the mystery man replies. "Bickering will not change anything. We will flee into the mountain and make our options as we go."

"How is that a plan?" Cassio shouts. "Who are you, anyway, little man?"

"My name is Chanziu Guan," the mystery man replies, "and I will save Konran with or without your compliance."

"Hey, everyone," Salazar says with deep concern on his face. "The *Gamma* just said Nolvaric capital ships are dropping more troops. It's a hornet's nest up there."

Without another word, Chanziu whisks Konran into the room. Passing row after row of containers, they wind awkwardly through the randomly collocated arrangement.

"You can let go," Konran says. "I'll follow you."

"No risks; I protect you," Chanziu says as they pass a particularly tall open crate. A bronze statue stands inside: a woman poised regally before an alien planet, her arms outstretched in greeting.

Konran can hear the others around them. He glances at Salazar running along a parallel path from the corner of his eye, and then runs straight into a crate as the mystery man changes direction. Chanziu pulls him hard, suddenly staring directly into Konran's eyes.

"Do not stop again. Your life is of critical importance. You must escape. Do you understand?" The man's glare is not angry, but the sense of clarity behind his dark eyes is more frightening than anything Konran has experienced yet.

"Yeah," Konran breathes, shouldering his way past the crate. "OK, let's run."

They run again, even faster than before. They reach the rows of storage racks and dart between two. Artifacts of all kinds line their shelves, gleaming gold and silver, glittering with jeweled greens,

283

blues, and reds. Konran doesn't have time to take them all in, and after a short sprint they enter another maze of crates.

The room seems to go on forever, but finally the cavernous ceiling begins to taper downward, forming into a wall. Chanziu changes direction with it, leading Konran along its length before stopping suddenly at a sealed large cargo door, wide enough for a freighter to pass through.

If this place isn't a hangar now, it was certainly built to be one.

In seconds Chanziu opens the door. Close behind, Cassio, Zenara, and Salazar exit the jumbled rows of containers, all jogging over to Konran's side. And then the cries begin—Nolvaric battle cries, echoing from the far side of the cavernous room, no more than 150 meters away.

"They're here," Konran whispers, strength draining from his legs. "They got in here. That means Exeunt..." he trails off.

"She gave us time to escape, had there been starcraft," Chanziu says. "Quickly now."

The door leads into another long, wide cargo tunnel. Large storage bays line its sides, filled with more of Ruzcier's interstellar acquisitions. Zenara and Salazar sprint close behind Konran, but Cassio is back by the cargo door, attempting to blockade it. Chanziu doesn't stop for the marine, and Konran's breath becomes ragged as he presses even deeper into the mountain, wrist locked in the man's iron grip.

Konran's vision-enhancement lenses activate as the tunnel's ambient lighting dims. Even with the lenses on, the storage bays lining the tunnel are shadowy. His lungs scream for air and his side aches against the exertion of running so far, but he doesn't stop. When he can think, the only thought is of Commander Exeunt.

Nolvaric cries rise behind them, the unintelligible shrieks of so many bedtime monsters. Konran's neck hairs rise with every scream, and Chanziu's pace increases further, the incessant, interlinked run becoming more of the main event than a means to an end. Konran's ability to run diminishes as his will to escape grows stronger, and somehow he continues stride after stride on the hard, hewn subterranean stone.

Suddenly, something catches Konran's eye from one of the cargo bays—a word, gleaming in the darkness. He stops, and the mystery man almost drags him off his feet. His knee hits hard as he struggles to resist the forward momentum.

"We have to go back!" he says, gasping for air as he stumbles forward. "I saw something. In there."

Chanziu doesn't hesitate, allowing Konran to lead for the first time. He scrambles to the side of the tunnel, searching for the word.

"Where is it, where is it?" Konran asks, panicking.

Then, at the side of the storage bay, he sees it: one word, painted white, illuminated just enough in the murk of the tunnel.

Kazrick.

"That's my dad's name," he says, pulling Chanziu into the bay. Salazar and Zenara follow, and Salazar lights a flare. The bay is empty.

A blast crashes through the confines of the tunnel, and a series of return blasts reply, reminiscent of the subterranean fight with the assaultbots not more than thirty minutes ago. Two words burst through the cacophony, Cassio's shouting, "Take cover!"

Chanziu pulls Konran down, releasing his arm.

"Stay here, stay down," he says. Picking up Salazar's flare and hurling it from the bay, he takes up a defensive position at its edge. Zenara takes position next to him, firing down the tunnel.

Salazar crouches next to Konran.

"You said you saw your dad's name?" he whispers.

"Yeah, it was on this bay."

"You think Ruzcier has some of his stuff?" Salazar asks.

"I don't know. I thought maybe, but there's nothing here."

Salazar gets up, ducking back down quickly as blaster fire crashes against the bay like an elephant in a china store.

"Come on," he urges. "Look for a door or something."

Konran gets up, searching frantically with his hands across the back of the bay—nothing but smooth rock. He struggles not to panic, but each blast roars louder than the last. Gurgled shrieks join the clangor, echoing as Nolvarics howl—either from being hit or just from being Nolvaric. Plasmic ozone and charred rock pollute the air, along with the thick chemical stench of burning polymer.

Then Konran's fingers sink into a crack. He searches hastily up and down its length, holding his breath.

"Sal, I think I found it," he says. "This feels like a door."

Salazar joins him, they strain together, but the door won't budge.

"We need the new guy," Salazar grunts, pulling one last time.

Konran ducks, crawling across the bay with head low. If anyone could open the door, it was Chanziu. Konran searches, but the man is across the tunnel, fifteen meters away, firing from the opposite bay.

The rock wall of Konran's bay explodes right next to Zenara, sending her jolting backward amidst a thunderous roar. Specks of rock smack Konran, stinging his face and arms. Coughing, struggling to get up, he reaches for Zenara. Trickles of blood ooze from her chest, arms, and forehead, but she is still breathing. Konran moves to her side, cradling her head as he drags her to the back of the bay by her shoulders. Another explosion hits the bay, and Konran hugs her tight as more rock particles sting his body.

Suddenly, Chanziu reappears in the bay. He picks up Zenara's sidearm (which used to be Cassio's) and shoves it into Salazar's hands.

"Fight," he urges, and Salazar takes the weapon without hesitation.

In Konran's arms, Zenara coughs.

"Zenara, Zenara," he whispers urgently. "Are you OK? Can you hear me?"

"Too many," she moans, coughing again and wincing. "Too many Nolvarics."

"Zenara, listen," Konran says. "There's a door here. I think some of my dad's old stuff is in there. Can you help me open it?"

Suddenly clear, but not without pain, Zenara's eyes pop open. She gasps as she rises to her feet. Konran holds her close.

"How do we open it?" he presses.

"Open it," she repeats. "My father locked it ... you need the code."

Another explosion rocks the bay, and Salazar falls backward. The scientist crawls back to his post, head bleeding.

"What's the code?" Konran pleads. "Come on, you have to know it."

"I don't know," she says, stooping against him. "Could be anything."

Konran wracks his brain. "What about HR9038? There's a planet there. My parents were there. Does that ring a bell?"

Zenara breathes against him, shaking. "Intaurus. Moons of Intaurus," she says.

With a hefty rumble and the grate of metal on metal, a pair of doors slide open.

Konran drags Zenara inside, but he can't see anything. He sets her down, bracing her against a crate or whatever it was in the darkness.

"Sal!" he hisses back into the bay. "Sal! We got it open!"

Salazar continues firing down the tunnel, but he pauses long enough to toss a flare back toward the door. Konran reaches out and grabs it, igniting it with a flick of his finger.

* * * * *

Chanziu sees the flare ignite and jumps across the corridor, ready to dismantle whatever threat had made its way to Konran. He propels himself into the bay with inertial thrusters, searching for the enemy.

The rear wall of the bay is opened, but no enemy appears. Konran simply stands inside, illuminated by the red glow of the emergency flare in his hand.

And there, before him in cold glory, is a Sparrowhawk.

* * * * *

Cassio's plasma rifle was running low on power. It didn't help that Nolvarics kept streaming into the tunnel.

It also didn't help that he was the only one trying to hold the position. At least it felt that way.

That Cassio had chosen his position well did help—at least it had for the first three minutes until the Nolvarics blew up that spot. He had Chinsing—*or Chanziu, whatever his name is*—to thank for covering his scrambled sprint into the adjacent bay. But what the mystery man brought in accuracy he lacked in firepower.

Although the mystery man's pinpoint precision had prevented the Nolvarics from blowing Cassio up again, it wasn't doing much more than that. And then there was Salazar, who had Cassio's sidearm now. To the scientist's credit, Salazar had picked the gun up once Zenara went down, but the man couldn't hit the broadside of a battleship. Bless him for trying, but Cassio was in almost as much danger from him as the Nolvarics.

And so, it was Cassio, the marine, the only one with any real firepower, who held off the Nolvarics, dropping them with his plasma rifle as they poked their nasty little heads around the curve of the tunnel wall. Every now and then a Nolvaric would manage to get a rocket off or a group would scramble for cover in an adjacent bay, and Cassio would have to strafe them down. But he had the pattern figured out now, and the Nolvarics' wild charges weren't gaining any more ground.

Yet.

If only he had more firepower. It was a matter of time until he ran out of juice, got overrun by Nolvarics, and then everyone got eaten by cyborgs—or whatever they did when they got you.

Suddenly Chanziu and Salazar's support fire cuts off. As little help as they added, they still added something, and Cassio curses. Whatever they were doing better be good—better be getting Konran to safety. Cassio knew he wouldn't mind dying here if Konran made it out. Every bodyguard accepted the risks well before ever facing them.

He amplifies his firing rate to make up for the lack of support, draining his plasma rifle even further. Nolvarics charge, and Cassio struggles to make up the difference himself.

If they reach another bay, I am toast, he thinks, motivating himself to prevent them from setting up multiple angles of attack.

The Nolvarics make it, dodging Cassio's plasma and diving into another bay.

Ferrospit.

Cassio trades shots with his enemy, alternating shots with Nolvarics on both sides of the tunnel. They charge again, and their forces spill into another bay.

"I'm going down there," a voice speaks suddenly into Cassio's ear, freaking him out before he realizes it's just Chanziu in his invisibility suit. "Konran found a Sparrowhawk. I confirmed it's operational. We need to hold. Here's your gun."

Chanziu drops Cassio's sidearm beside him.

"Watch for me in the second bay," the invisible man says. "And we'll catch them in a crossfire."

* * * * *

Zenara sits next to the Sparrowhawk trying not to groan. Nearby, Konran dons his flight suit. It fits him perfectly, as do the boots, gloves, and helmet—like they were made for him.

I have to do something, Zenara urges herself.

Konran taps the flight suit's chest twice, and it responds as if made yesterday, sealing around the gloves and boots and integrating with the headgear.

Behind Konran, Salazar fiddles with the Sparrowhawk, hooking and unhooking hoses and cables as he brings the bird back to life from dusty hibernation.

Cassio and Chanziu can't hold out forever. I have to do something.

She tries to sit up, and pain explodes in her chest and head, but she does it.

After confirming that the Sparrowhawk was operational, and before sealing the doors and leaving to fight with Cassio, Chanziu had turned the lights on. If he hadn't done that, Zenara might not have seen it.

Across the room: What is that? she wonders.

She forces herself to stand, sending the pain to suffer by itself in the back of her mind. She trudges across the room, stooping beneath the wing of the Sparrowhawk. A rack of equipment stands on the other side.

I can't believe it.

She reaches out, flicking a power switch with her finger, and the object of her attention hums to life before her.

A bio-augmentation exoskeleton. Just like in Father's stories.

She turns around, backing into the exoskeleton. As soon as she sits into it, the suit embraces her, hugging around her arms and legs and torso and head. A holographic display runs through a series of start-up diagnostics, and she stands. It doesn't hurt anymore—the suit was masking her pain. Searching through the equipment rack, she finds a chain gun and checks its power.

Eighteen percent. I can use that.

Now too tall to stoop beneath the Sparrowhawk with the smooth, metallic exoskeleton armor encompassing her form, Zenara walks around the sleek bird of prey. The suit's joints respond to hers, and her arms and legs feel light despite the added bulk. Salazar is checking the starfighter's weapon bay; Konran is setting up a ladder to the cockpit. Both stop to gape at her.

"For Yoana," she says, hitting the switch to open the door Chanziu had closed moments earlier. It rumbles open, she charges, and the door closes behind her.

Around the corner Cassio is pinned down. Nolvarics had advanced nearly all the way up the tunnel. The marine fires with his sidearm rather than his plasma rifle, but it isn't enough. Nolvarics descend upon him.

And Zenara pounces.

* * * * *

Cassio watches the Nolvarics charge. He drops one, then two of them, but there are more than six in the pack. The lead Nolvaric reaches him, and Cassio flies backward, kicked in the chest.

Wider and taller than a normal human, the Nolvaric's bristling muscles ripple beneath the same Saturnese uniform worn by the commandos Exeunt had defeated back in the hangar. It hulks dark and ominous in the dusty bay entrance. Bionic implants bulge from its skin, protruding from its face, neck, and chest in a random pattern of metallic, cybernetic tattoos. Its eyes are yellow, nearly glowing as they stare at Cassio with a deranged hunger. Two spear-like guns emerge from its shoulders, rising upward before angling down, directly at Cassio. It steps toward him, licking its lips as three more Nolvarics enter the bay, shrieking in triumph at having cornered their prey.

Back in the tunnel, the battle rages as hot as ever, with the invisible mystery man holding his own against the hordes. But these three had bypassed Chanziu, and now Cassio was out of options. He struggles to stand.

The Nolvaric smiles at him, displaying rows of longer-than-human teeth. And then something smashes it. The other Nolvarics react, but whatever it is lashes out. They fall in a whirl of motion as something huge and robotic smashes their faces into the ground. And then Zenara steps out of the dust, armored in an exoskeleton suit, violence upon her face.

"Take this," she says, tossing Cassio a Nolvaric gun.

*****

"Up!" Salazar urges, and Konran scrambles up the ladder.

The cockpit opens automatically, responding to the proximity of Konran's flight suit. He sets himself into the pilot seat, and the firm cushioning presses familiarly into his back and legs. His right hand finds the control stick while his left flips the ignition switches, ten thousand hours of simulated practice making the movements automatic. Salazar scrambles up behind Konran, dragging the life-support connection system behind him.

"Don't forget this," he grunts as he plugs Konran into the Sparrowhawk.

Konran helps as much as he can, twisting and bending so Salazar can get to the appropriate connection ports. As he bends forward, Konran feels the holo-cube, which he tucked into his flight suit pocket. He retrieves it with a gloved hand and reaches below his seat for the small personals compartment he knew would be there. He pulls it open and, to his surprise, finds a holograph already inside. A smiling man and a beautiful woman stand against a stunning red, unearthly backdrop: his parents.

"Sal," Konran says, holding up the holograph.

291

"*Santa muchacha,* this is definitely your dad's Hawk," Salazar utters, exchanging a meaningful glance with Konran. "It's a sign. You were meant to have this Hawk."

Konran nods, tucking the hologragh quickly back under his seat. "I'm ready to do this."

"Go," the scientist replies, climbing down before yelling, "Wait! Wait! Wait!" and climbing back up. "Communication codes!"

Salazar leans into the cockpit. "Where is it? This thing is so old. Ah-ha! OK, you should be patched in. Oh, and eat this." Salazar tosses in a packet of better-than-boost cake before climbing down and dislodging the ladder.

The cockpit closes around Konran. He stashes the holograph and holo-cube into the personals compartment, settling into the pilot seat as a holographic heads-up display paints status indicators and, most importantly, targeting indicators across his field of vision. The Sparrowhawk's reactor displays optimal status, its complement of twelve missiles signals full.

All right, show me the ropes, Dad, Konran thinks, pride tingling with excitement in his chest. Not only was this his dad's Sparrowhawk, but it was vintage.

I just hope this old bird still has what it takes.

His feet lock into the multi-axis rudder pedals. His right hand grasps the control stick and his left rests upon the throttle as the Sparrowhawk vibrates like a racehorse beneath him. He makes eye contact with Salazar and points forward repeatedly. *Let's get this thing going!*

Salazar pumps his fist and runs to open the door. Its stone walls rumble open, and Salazar scrambles out of the way.

"Auto-tune visibility," Konran says, and the dust in the tunnel fades as the Sparrowhawk's sensors cut through. "Weapons hot, antigrav on," he adds, and the Sparrowhawk disengages from the ground, hovering in place.

"Would you like to activate your shields, sir?" a voice speaks into Konran's ear.

"Er, yes," he replies, surprised at the question. Fourth-generation Sparrowhawks hadn't sported shield systems beyond the rudimentary photon deflection shield every craft had back then.

"Active engagement detected," the voice replies. "Anti-Nolvaric tracking and targeting engaged." *Another unexpected feature— time to put it to use.*

Konran guides the craft around, maneuvering slowly through the bay and into the tunnel, which is more than wide enough for his Sparrowhawk. As he turns, Zenara dives into a storage bay next to him.

The tunnel crawls with Nolvarics, and targeting indicators sprout up on Konran's heads-up display, readily marking each target—at least sixty of them. Konran presses the trigger.

For Commander Exeunt.

Orange plasma bursts from his guns: two streams from his nose and one from each wingtip. Pulses of plasma track back and forth, washing the tunnel of Nolvarics as the guns jump from target to target. Konran pushes the throttle, picking up speed and winding through the tunnel, heading for the hangar.

Cassio, standing with assistance from Zenara, raises his fist as Konran glides past. Chanziu appears farther down the tunnel amidst a pile of motionless Nolvarics, likewise cheering. His fists pump upward in a double salute of victory.

Konran cruises past, feeling the Sparrowhawk take to the tunnel like a feather on an air current. The thing rides smoother than a dream, as if tuned to his every preference. More Nolvarics stream up the winding passage, and Konran's guns track back and forth, blasting each with swift judgment.

He reaches the end of the tunnel in less than a minute and blows the cargo door to fragments with a flick of his finger. Cruising into the massive storage room—the room he had hoped so shortly before was a hangar, the room Exeunt had paid dearly to buy them time to reach—Konran clears it of Nolvarics with one swoop of the Sparrowhawk.

Another flick of his finger later and the hangar bay door explodes backward in a crash of melting metal. Konran zips through, trigger depressed, plasma cannons blazing. The tunnels on the other side are too small for his Sparrowhawk, and the Nolvarics in the area flee into them or fall to his guns.

Although the tunnels are narrow, the space outside the false hangar is wide, expanding upward toward some unseen avenue of departure from the mountain. With a tick of his feet in the rudder straps, Konran rises slowly upward, the Sparrowhawk more an extension of his mind than his fingers, arms, and feet. Then, with a nudge of a lever next to his throttle, and a simultaneous depression of a button on his control stick, he inverts the Hawk.

His pilot seat flips effortlessly, facing him toward his rear thruster. His body courses with energy at the maneuver, having longed to experience it in reality for nearly twenty years. His wingtip and nose guns now converted into thrusters, Konran maneuvers the inverted craft easily, angling its new nose downward. With a flick of his eyes he aims his rear-thruster-now-megacannon, directing it to point toward the tunnels below. He fires, and the energy within him releases, pouring as plasma through the Sparrowhawk's massive cannon, demolishing each access point into the area.

Nobody was going to attack his remaining friends using this passageway.

Demolition complete, Konran soars upward, still thrusting with his wingtip and nose guns, maintaining his Sparrowhawk in its inverted state. He reaches a large access hatchway and vaporizes it along with the shielded counterpart behind it with another flick of his finger.

And then, reverting his Sparrowhawk to its normal configuration, Konran blasts into the darkening Arzibanian atmosphere, his father's son.

* * * * *

Chanziu hadn't smiled in more days than he could remember. It just wasn't very useful to him. Now he smiles as wide as he had in memory, still cheering as the sound of Konran's warfare fades from the tunnel.

Chanziu had succeeded, and now, after so many hours, so many millions of miles of effort, and so much fighting, Konran had a Sparrowhawk. If there was any way to keep the young man safe—the certified Level 20 spatial combat tactical genius—it was within the confines of a starfighter.

Exhausted, Chanziu looks back up the tunnel. Cassio, the marine, is there, tired and broken, but alive. Salazar, the scientist, stands beside him, along with Zenara, the Xolian, in her wonderful bio-augmentation suit.

They had won.

They had done it.

Then it dawns on him.

Konran is safe.

Konran is gone.

Now what?

CHAPTER 19

"Sixteen more Askeras, coming in low, southwest beyond the city, making for the mountain," Ace says, scanning both the skies and his status displays simultaneously.

High above Ruzcier's mountain, Ace had just finished tangoing with six Saturnese Shandian starfighters, three of which he had converted into flaming debris (two with well-placed plasma bolts through their aft fuselages, the other with a bolt through two of its triple, equilaterally spaced wings). The others had fallen back to regroup, for now.

Across the western horizon, Maehn Arziban's sky flickers with glittery bursts of sparks—the *Nova Scotia*'s engagement with the Nolvaric and Saturnese capital ships barely discernible at such a distance. Ace's comrades were up there, fighting with every drop in their veins to keep the Nolvarics from devouring their captain and the aide he had sworn them all to protect. So far, the *Nova Scotia*'s efforts had stalled the enemy force from converging en masse on Ruzcier's mountain—and thank Mars that Lieutenant Vilkoj had ordered the *Alpha* and *Beta* to go tesseracts hot this close to the moon.

Even so, Ace was pressing hard to keep up with the constant influx of enemies; they all were. The two Rezakar corpses burning on the outskirts of the city spoke volumes enough, as did the one Revenshal had converted into a crater beside Ruzcier's mountain. Now the *Gamma* was hundreds of kilometers above the atmosphere, engaging three more Rezakars that had made it past the *Nova Scotia*'s ramshackle blockade.

And then there was the *Tartaglia*, Minister Heesor's goliath mega-cruiser having limped east with a handful of remaining Dronehawks, fleeing past Ruzcier's mountain and beyond the horizon after Revenshal jabbed his finger up its nose with that spectacular Bestiphan-proffered surprise attack. Indigestion in

Ace's gut told him that wasn't the last they would see of the *Tartaglia* today.

Valk and I should have destroyed more than just the Tartaglia's *flight deck*, Ace broods, scanning his sensor readouts and berating himself for not blasting it fully from the sky.

"Make that nineteen Askeras, Valk," he says, updating his previous estimate. "Nolvarics and their prime numbers. You want flank?"

"A minute. Almost got these Miratans," Valkyrie replies, as smooth as ever. "Seven remaining ... make that five."

"Rev, can you drag your guns across these Askeras?" Ace asks. "They're closing on the mountain."

"Negative. Still have two Rezakars and their fighters to deal with. Could use the backup myself."

At least it wasn't three Rezakars anymore.

"Yazzi," Ace says, directing himself to the commander of Ruzcier's Xolian starfighter force, "you've got incoming. Nineteen Askeras inbound."

Nothing.

"Yazzi? Yazzi?"

"Majorkai Yazzi fell, as did Siakan," an unfamiliar, Xolian-accented voice buzzes into Ace's ear. Her voice is pained, even through the comm.

"All right, get your Xarbas up here now," Ace orders the Xolian. "You aren't any use shot to pieces down there."

After the *Tartaglia* had been hit and the skies momentarily cleared, the Xolian pilots had refused to follow Ace and Valkyrie into the upper atmosphere, insisting to remain in their egg-shaped, shape-shifting Xarba starfighters near Ruzcier's mountain. As fresh waves of enemies began swarming the position, Ace's plan had been to harry, draw off, disrupt, and systematically destroy the enemy forces, but the Xolians had elected to punch them directly in the face.

"They did take out the first wave of Shandians themselves," Valkyrie crackles in, "and those Evariz destroyers, and the initial Askera escort."

But there's a lot of fighting left to do, and I would rather have them all alive to do it, Ace thinks, grateful he had only been forced to deal with six of the Saturnese fighters on his own.

"True, but at 40 percent casualties," he replies into the comm. "Xolian, what's your name? I want you up here now!"

"I am Tiswa," the Xolian pilot replies in her punctuated accent. "We come."

"Good. Valk, you OK with the five Miratans for now?"

"Three."

"Roger. I'm going to take a pass at the mountain—try to draw off some of the Askeras. Tiswa: take a flanking vector and pick them off as they come at me."

"Yes, Ace," Tiswa replies.

As Ace dives, he sees a series of explosions burst out far below.

Too far away from Tiswa and her squad to be the work of Xolians.

Plenty of enemies still buzzed the mountain, leaving ample targets for any friendly force to engage.

Could Ruzcier's perimeter guns be attacking them?

Ace checks, but the perimeter guns are occupied, belching plasma skyward as fast as they can cycle. Three more Nolvaric capital ships draw precariously low in the atmosphere, absorbing the punishment for now.

The tiny explosions below continue, popping in quick succession around Ruzcier's mountain like fireflies glowing and fading on a summer night.

"Ace! Valkyrie!" a familiar, unexpected, breathless voice cuts into Ace's comm. "You there?"

"Konran?" Ace asks, puzzled. A new entry appears within his Sparrowhawk's IFF registry—another Sparrowhawk, marked as friendly, transmitting the call sign Snakedust.

Ace watches the explosions progress into the formation of Askeras he had been tracking. Snakedust makes into their midst like a starving bat for a mosquito cloud.

"Yeah! It's me!" Konran replies. "I found a Sparrowhawk!"

* * * * *

My dad was a starfighter.

Konran spins, using the rudder controls strapped to his feet rather than his control stick to effect the maneuver. In response, his Sparrowhawk gyrates along a jagged, helical trajectory, its fuselage vent ports spouting successive, controlling bursts to change its direction. In front of him, a Nolvaric Askera plays a three-thousand-kilometer-per-hour game of chicken with his Sparrowhawk—his dad's Sparrowhawk.

My dad was one of the very best, according to Ruzcier.

The Askera fires, but Konran's erratic motion does its job: blue plasma crackles past him like a packaged burst of lightning, slashing directly into the cockpit of the Askera trailing him. Whatever modifications his dad had made to this Sparrowhawk, its maneuverability was off the charts.

It's in my blood. It's always been there.

Konran stops the spiral, kicking the rudder pedals and sending the Sparrowhawk jutting downward, upside down toward the ground, away from the Askera's follow-up burst.

All those years wishing and hoping. All those hours training in any simulator I could get my hands on—the only place I've ever felt truly myself.

A flick of the finger, and Konran's left wingtip cannon sends plasma through the Askera's ventral, spike-shaped wing. Its crab legs detach from its body with the detonation, scattering and smacking into a third Askera coming in on Konran's right flank.

I'm finally in a starfighter—my dad's starfighter.

Konran pulls back on his control stick as he pulls the trigger, dodging around the third Askera and converting it, too, into a fireball. Still on the trail of his actual target, Konran fires again, and three distant Askeras die under a barrage of orange plasma.

I am a starfighter.

Two more Askeras explode, their attempts to escape by diving sharply in opposite directions invalidated by Konran's guns.

This is so much easier than Y25LM90.

"Konran!" Ace's voice nearly screams into his comm. "You've got twelve Shandians coming down on you, high and five o'clock! Get out of there!"

Konran sets his jaw, angling his Sparrowhawk directly toward "high and five o'clock."

Shandians are Saturnese. If not for them, Exeunt would have escaped with me.

He picks up the enemies on his scanner. They had circled around to attack Ruzcier's mountain from the east and were making the plunge into the atmosphere. Konran sends a burst of plasma into the center of their formation, the long-range shot less of an attack than an indication of things to come. Anticipating their response to his initial burst, Konran's trigger finger sends a second plasma blast toward unoccupied space. One distant Shandian explodes as its evasive action fills the very spot. Its equilateral triple wings flutter down like butterfly wings without the butterfly, illuminated by the red rays of Solis at sunset.

The formation breaks up, and Konran fires another burst, targeting a group of four Shandian starfighters. He follows up with a second round of plasma as before, but they dodge. Anticipating that reaction, Konran's third burst of plasma strikes true, and six triangular panels flutter down as two more Shandians fall to his guns.

"I count nine," Konran says, rocketing forward and closing ground on the Shandians.

"Dude, we're almost there. Hold tight and we'll tear them up from behind," Ace crackles in.

"Not unless I get them first."

Konran begins evasive action, following a looping, S-shaped path as he gains altitude, never following the same pattern twice—except when he does, of course.

The Shandian formation separates farther, dispersing to engulf the lone attacker. Konran sets his guns to track and fire on the foremost Shandian, which was circling to engage him from an angle above and to his left. The pilot dodges Konran's attack expertly; however, two pilots attacking from Konran's right don't, and two more Shandians explode under quick bursts of plasma.

"Seven," Konran breathes.

Missile locks detected, the message displays within his cockpit, blinking in warning.

Konran wonders how much punishment his Sparrowhawk's shields can take as his guns track, and miss, another Shandian. He maneuvers quickly, bounced out of harm's way by his fuselage vent ports as white plasmic bolts pepper the air around him. He fires again, and his target erupts into an evening fireworks display.

"Six."

CFS activated, a new message appears, its meaning unknown to Konran.

"Describe CFS," he speaks to his ship's computer, muting his connection to Ace and Valkyrie, and dodging another burst of white Shandian plasma.

"The Coronal Flare System is a short-range, antimissile, antiaircraft engagement system which is coupled to and discharges from the shield system. It is also capable of disruption and penetration of enemy shields," the computer replies in a pleasant voice. "Effective radius: seventy-five meters."

Sparks, Dad, Konran thinks as the computer finishes the description. *How did you pack all this new tech into one Sparrowhawk? I can make use of that.*

The Shandians had closed within classical dogfighting range now. The lack of missile-launch warning tones, however, tells Konran their orders were not to kill him.

So you still want to capture me.

"Describe CFS shield-penetration capability," Konran orders his craft, angling into position behind a Shandian. He flicks his finger.

"Five," he breathes as the Shandian converts into glimmering particles of fire.

"The Coronal Flare System produces intense, short-range flares that are capable of disrupting light to medium shields and allowing close-range engagement of enemy defenses," his ship's computer replies with its pleasant voice.

"Konran, break due east on my mark." Konran is surprised to hear Valkyrie's voice in his ear.

"Mark!"

Konran breaks east, away from the lowering sun, away from the Arzibanian city gleaming beneath its rays, away from the two Shandians presently under his guns.

"Zero," Valkyrie crackles back. Konran studies his displays, noticing only two Sparrowhawks and three Xolian Xarba starfighters closing on his position. The immediate vicinity is clear.

"Nice shooting. Now follow us," Valkyrie says.

"Sure, you listen to her," Ace grumbles. "What were you thinking, man? That was crazy!"

"Avenging Commander Exeunt," is all Konran manages, his throat constricting with pain around the words.

He searches his sensor displays, seeking another target. More Nolvaric starfighters were inbound—less than a minute out, at the moment. High above Maehn Arziban in the vacuum of space, the *Gamma* struggles against five Rezakars. Beyond the city, the *Alpha* and *Beta* engage the bulk of the enemy forces. None of them could be doing well. Below, Cassio, Zenara, Chanziu, Granicks, and everyone else still need to escape.

Setting his jaw, Konran weighs his options. The only thing he knew for sure was that fleeing wasn't on the list.

* * * * *

Ace's fingers tighten, anger constricting them about his control stick. *They got Exeunt—they're all going to pay for that.*

"Commander Exeunt fell?" Valkyrie's voice is delicate, like the gasp of breath that follows the unexpected gust of freezing wind. To Ace, having flown hundreds of hours with Valkyrie, her brusque warrior persona may as well have cracked in half.

"We were ambushed by Saturnese commandos," Konran explains. "Exeunt stopped them and then fought off a hundred Nolvarics. If not for the Saturnese, she would have escaped with us."

"She fell fulfilling Granicks's orders," Ace says, watching Snakedust glide effortlessly in front of him. The sight of the vintage Sparrowhawk gives Ace a chill—that, or was it the thought of losing Exeunt? Throughout Ace's time with Granicks, the captain's right-hand commander had seemed nearly untouchable in battle. The thought of losing her was unthinkable.

Shoving his grief into the back of his mind, Ace forces himself to stay focused on the battle at hand. "OK, everyone, having Konran up here changes everything. Our number-one priority is seeing him to safety. Granicks wanted him to warp out of here, so that's what we're going to do: we make for the warp margin and hijack ourselves a yacht or a cruiser. Valk, you take point. Konran, you tail Valkyrie. Tiswa, form your Xarbas on me."

"Good plan," Konran says as Snakedust breaks upward, toward space, but not the space Ace intended.

"I'll catch up once I have Revenshal. Save me a seat."

Ace doesn't hesitate, veering his Sparrowhawk on vector with Konran's. Valkyrie isn't a moment behind him, nor the Xolian Xarbas. The six craft assume a double-wedged chevron formation as their six contrails sublimate upward—three USFN Sparrowhawks trailed closely by three Xolian Xarbas, an interspatial alliance unknown to more than a century of politics, led by a kid with no more than ten minutes in a starfighter.

He probably has as many kills as I do today.

Ace glances at his sensor display again, checking Revenshal's status; there were now five Rezakars engaging the *Gamma*.

Of course, there were five now.

* * * * *

"Kid, get out of here," Revenshal's stern voice speaks into Konran's ear.

"Commander, listen," Konran replies. "They're not playing shoot-to-kill with me. Take off at a sprint away from their fleet, but keep your guns ready."

"You're not going to listen, are you?"

"He ain't listening to nobody!" Ace interjects.

"Do it, Commander," Konran urges. Through his viewport he can just begin to make out the five Rezakars, glimmering like little stars shining through the thinning Arzibanian sky. Although they were close enough to the planet that the mighty NACs didn't want to fire at them, they were still a thousand kilometers away, beyond the reaches of the atmosphere. The *Gamma*'s shape was still too small to make out at this distance.

Konran continues his instruction to the commander. "Draw them away from the incoming fighters. We're gonna hit the middle of their formation, but we'll need the breathing room."

"You sound just like Granicks," Revenshal mutters. On Konran's sensor display, the *Gamma*'s blip begins separating from the Rezakars.

"I'm heading for the centermost Rezakar alone," Konran says. "Ace and Valkyrie, see if you can take out any fighters trailing the *Gamma*. Give them all the space you can."

"Yeah right," Ace balks. "We ain't going nowhere."

"We will cover the *Gamma*," Tiswa replies in her thick Xolian accent.

"Roger that," Konran acknowledges.

The trio of Sparrowhawks blasts through the atmosphere with the trio of Xarbas, ticking off kilometers faster than heartbeats.

"Konran, think, man," Ace says. "We need an actual plan here."

"I told you the plan," Konran says. "I can take them."

"That's what I'm saying—that ain't no plan."

"I'm in," Valkyrie replies.

"This was my dad's Sparrowhawk," Konran says, wishing Ace and Valkyrie would get off his six. "He made some modifications that you don't have."

"Your dad modified it?" Ace nearly chokes on the words. "What kind of crazy did Maehn Arziban beat into your head?"

"Trust me, Ace," Konran replies. "I've got this."

"They Rezakars have locks on our position," Valkyrie reports.

"Rev, give them some tesseracts," Konran orders. "Scramble their targeting."

"Ace is right, kid. Get out of here while you can," Revenshal replies. "I can hold them."

"I'll just do it without the tesseract screen," Konran threatens, continuing his trajectory toward the Rezakars.

In response, the space separating Konran from the Rezakars distorts, blasted into space-time soup by the *Gamma*'s tesseract barrage. The sky around Konran fades to black—it hadn't been more than a few hours since he'd taken the landing craft the other direction, into the Arzibanian atmosphere for the first time.

"You're out of your mind, you know that?" Ace asks, agitated.

304

"Time for some surfing," Konran answers, entering the space-time distortion field laid down by the *Gamma*.

CHAPTER 20

Being a multidimensional, multipurpose weapon, the USFN tesseract was capable of producing a variety of effects. It was the tesseract's ability to interact with the energy field of space-time, however, that facilitated creation of the gravitational waves Konran now surfed—an effect that very easily appeared to create roiling, undulating gravitational fields out of nothing (although the mass excitation of virtual particles within the space-time vacuum and the subsequent "flavoring" of these particles with graviton-like properties was certainly not nothing).

While the tesseract's capacity for gravitational disturbance did not equal that of the Nolvaric cattails, it still packed a considerable punch, and gravitational forces tug erratically as Konran enters the grav cloud. Rezakar plasma blasts bounce and split around him, refracted unnaturally through the ever-changing gravitational topology. Close to a massive body such as Summanus, the tesseracts' gravitational effect would wash out quickly. Although Maehn Arziban orbited some three hundred millicks away from the planet, the effect was still present.

Luckily the Sparrowhawk was fast. Cruising through the soup, Konran feels a surge of excitement, cresting gravitational waves upon his Sparrowhawk's considerable capacity for forward thrust.

Careful maneuvering keeps the gravitational gradient in his favor—a trick mastered by the original starfighters—and Rezakar plasma bolts refract away from his position rather than into it. But even if the plasma bolts had managed to strike or penetrate his Sparrowhawk's considerable shields, Konran was certain they wouldn't have killed him: if one thing was clear from Konran's interaction with the Nolvarics below Ruzcier's mountain, they wanted to capture him alive. He was sure the plasma bolts were at a fraction of their maximum power, intended to knock him out rather than destroy him. The result, of course, would be nearly as terrible either way, and Konran wasn't taking any chances.

He continues to surf the gravitational gradient, letting his Sparrowhawk dictate his course as much as his hands and feet. Instead of the straight path of the sprinter, his becomes that of the dancer: arcing and twisting, flipping and spinning, ever progressing toward his target. Five Rezakars loom on the other side of the grav cloud, but Konran only cares about the middle one.

The chaotic gravitational ripples play havoc with his sensors; anything more than a few ripples away displays as a fuzzy probability cloud rather than a definitive location. The *Gamma*, appearing as a sensor blip the size of Los Angeles, flees toward Maehn Arziban's south pole. The Rezakars' blips blur together, spreading out the length of Oahu within Konran's sensor display. Broad probability swaths indicate the location of Tiswa and her cadre of Xolian Xarbas as they continue to attack the Nolvaric starfighters trailing the *Gamma*. Ace's and Valkyrie's sensor blips are clear, however, as their Sparrowhawks follow Konran's closely through the soup.

They should have stayed behind, Konran thinks.

He dives through a gravitational wave like a wader on the beaches of California. Ace and Valkyrie don't bat an eye at the maneuver, and their blips remain glued to his tail. Konran knew they wouldn't leave him—he would do the same thing if put in their shoes, but his Sparrowhawk had abilities theirs didn't. Keeping them alive complicated what otherwise had been a simple, one-man charge. If he couldn't ditch them soon, it would be too late.

The grav field weakens slightly as he progresses through the soup, Summanus's influence evident. As a result, his path gradually becomes straighter and less acrobatic. The five Rezakars in front of him come into focus on his scopes, as does their target, the *Gamma*. Crisp little sensor blips mark the Xarbas as they engage the Askeras and the Miratans still out there.

No time for hesitation, he reminds himself, counting on the surprises tucked within his Sparrowhawk to provide the advantage he needed. *No misdirection or sleight of hand—just straight to the target.*

"Konran, let's think this through," Ace's voice crackles in, distorted through the rippling gravitational waves.

"Nothing to talk about. I already told you," Konran replies. "Stay back. I can handle this."

Valkyrie's laugh in response is a brief, sarcastic chortle.

Ace simply mutters, "I should shoot you down now to keep you from killing yourself."

"I'm serious, Ace," Konran demands, diving through rather than skimming across another set of gravitational waves, hoping to gain some distance and lose them.

"I could do it right now," Ace replies, his Sparrowhawk as close as ever to Konran's.

"Let me go, Ace!" Konran barks. "And no, you couldn't. Not with my dad's modifications to this Hawk."

"Granicks got himself shot for you, man," Ace argues, angry. "Exeunt sacrificed herself. To let you escape. And what are you doing? You're wasting their lives!"

"That's why I have to save Revenshal's!" Konran shouts in response, losing focus and bouncing spastically across a series of gravitational ripples. His inertial compensators and life-support systems sustain him through the series of abrupt, abusive forces.

"Dude, watch the ripples," Ace says, his tone shifting from frustration to concern. "We get it, man. We're here, whatever crazy you've got planned."

"I can do crazy," Valkyrie crackles in, allowing her craft to bounce along behind Konran, following his same, awkward path while somehow managing to appear graceful in the process.

"Guys," Konran says, collecting himself and regaining his rhythm with the ever-changing gradient, "if you're sticking with me, you have to stay within a seventy meter radius of my Sparrowhawk. Keep as close as you can and follow my changes. Don't vary from that radius or the Rezakars will get you. We'll alternate our leader every ten seconds, so Ace, you're up next, then Valkyrie, then me again. Our target is the midmost Rezakar."

"Tharsis free," Ace says, quoting part of the Tharsis Wildlynx slogan.

"Wildlynx strong," Valkyrie continues.

"Forever one," Konran finishes, a tingle rising on his spine as he sets his jaw.

"Let's do this," Ace adds.

Ace and Valkyrie fall into position behind Konran. Ten seconds later, Ace's Sparrowhawk takes the lead, passing within thirty meters of Konran's portside wingtip cannon. Ace continues Konran's trajectory, bearing on the midmost Rezakar, which was now discernible on sensors as a probabilistic entity distinct from its four companions. Surfing the gravitational gradient so close behind Ace's Sparrowhawk, Konran suddenly feels like he's back on a field trip to the Redwoods with his boys' home, tailgating hover-vehicles on the I-5.

"The Nolvarics don't want me dead yet," Konran says as Valkyrie's Sparrowhawk assumes the vanguard position. "But that will probably change when we get closer."

Konran follows Valkyrie's lead into a large gravitational wave, cringing as she makes the approach at a different angle than he preferred. The rough transition into the wave never occurs, and the change in gravitational gradient is barely noticeable.

I need her to teach me that, he makes a mental note.

"They will try, and they will fail," Ace declares, his tone assuming its natural, friendly manner. "So what's your master plan, chief?"

The trio exit Valkyrie's grav wave, and Konran resumes the lead position, preparing to plunge them into the next one.

"We're going to detonate the Rezakar's cattail supply," he answers. He tries to imitate Valkyrie's smooth transition between waves, vibrating as his Sparrowhawk doesn't quite hit the angle right.

"So you can punch us through their shields?" Ace asks. "'Cause we need at least two more Sparrowhawks to have enough bite to break through ourselves."

"My Sparrowhawk can do it," Konran answers, letting Ace take the lead again.

"Your dad's additions?" Ace says as the three Sparrowhawks loop through the remaining gravitational ripples like a spacefaring Chinese dragon.

"Yeah, he added stuff I've never seen before."

"I'm game," Valkyrie says, pulling into the lead ahead of Ace, out of turn.

"Man, you had to do that," Ace crackles in, pulling in front of Konran.

Konran laughs as the gradient lessens—soon they would reach its edge. "All right, guys, we take things evasive now," he orders. "Maintain close to me; keep them guessing; keep mixing it up like that."

The gravitational ripples bring them out between the foremost two Rezakars. Nolvaric plasma fire picks up immediately once the gravitational gradients allow for straight-line plasma beams. The foremost Rezakars are separated by more than a hundred kilometers, but the gap between them feels more like Beggar's Canyon to Konran as the space fills with destructive plasmic energy. Konran weaves evasively, and Ace and Valkyrie match his pace—up and down, side to side, twisting, diving, and climbing like three Brazilian free-tailed bats on the prowl.

A mere five hundred kilometers in front of them lurks the target, the midmost Rezakar reflecting Solis's light like a distant, arrowhead-shaped asteroid. Two more Rezakars glint some three hundred kilometers beyond that, their hulls glimmering like two new stars betwixt the mass of dazzling constellations plastering Konran's cockpit.

"Askeras incoming!" Valkyrie calls out. "We go weapons hot?"

"Stay on me, but fire away," Konran replies, tracking, firing, and blasting an Askera of his own. Their three Sparrowhawks rocket forward, dodging plasma blasts and destroying whatever Nolvarics come their way.

"It's nice to know my friends are crazier than I am," Revenshal's voice crackles in Konran's ear, communication with the *Gamma* reestablished now that the gravitational soup had fallen behind.

"You said it, man," Ace chirps as his guns blast three Askeras into space dust.

Konran senses pressure mounting above him, like the feeling of being watched, but more like that of being shot at. He surges upward (or the equivalent of the direction in open, gravity-less space), triggering his cannons as he does so. Blue Nolvaric plasma pops across his shields, crackling with so much silent energy that

Konran's view is temporarily obscured. Trusting on sensors alone, he fires, picking off the first of thirteen Askeras bearing down on him. His guns strike another, and then, as orange Sparrowhawk plasma flashes past him in a fury, the remaining eleven Askera blips wink out, demolished by Ace and Valkyrie's guns.

"I like your dad," Ace says.

"Nice shooting," Konran replies.

"On me!" Valkyrie calls out, and Konran dives, keeping her Sparrowhawk within his prescribed twenty-five-meter radius. Green plasma balls appear before him, growing ever larger as they surge to fill his viewport. Konran surges back at them, Valkyrie's vector allowing him to place his Sparrowhawk between the plasma balls and his friends. Surges of red coronal energy lick outward from his shields, leaping from invisible surfaces seventy-five meters away from his Sparrowhawk. Their fiery arms detonate against and quench the green onrushing threat.

Now oriented to the oncoming Miratans, Konran's guns belch plasma, targeting the herd of Nolvaric starcraft. Konran knocks out a few of the sharklike targets, and then, in a repeat of their former display of fury, Ace and Valkyrie demolish the rest.

"Scratch that," Ace crackles back in, "I love your dad."

The central Rezakar grows in size, looming in Konran's viewport as the distance to the target shrinks to one hundred kilometers. Cohorts of Askeras and Miratans swirl through the space, still firing at but now maintaining respectful distances from the deadly trio. Konran's shields continue to hold, and he, Ace, and Valkyrie press within eighty kilometers of the Rezakar. Nolvaric starfighters explode like bubble wrap in a five-year-old child's fingers.

"All right, guys, it's gonna get nasty," Konran says, anticipating the Nolvarics' willingness to preserve his life was about to expire. "Tuck it in close, I want you within twenty-five meters."

"Let's do this," Ace says.

"Missile locks," Valkyrie reports. "They're launching fishbones."

"We've got this," Konran replies. "Stay on target. Trust me."

"Ain't that what I'm doing?" Ace grunts.

"Not as well as I am," Valkyrie taunts, and Konran notices Valkyrie's Sparrowhawk draw closer to him than Ace's, then Ace's

311

draws even closer, then Valkyrie's, then Ace's. Shortly the two are less than five meters away.

"Here we go," Konran says. His status display shows a distance to target of fifty kilometers. Missile-lock alarms blare in his ears. And then the first wave of fishbones strikes.

Colossal, silent explosions crash all around him as the splintery, fragmented fishbones impact his shields. His Coronal Flare System activates, lashing out like it had with the Miratan plasma balls, and brilliant, fiery bursts of energy consume the fishbones with ten thousand explosions. As before, the coronal bursts emanate from an invisible field beyond Ace's and Valkyrie's craft, enshrouding them within the protective cocoon provided by Konran's shield system.

"Man, your dad is the man," Ace murmurs under the silent barrage.

"All right, guys, prepare for shield penetration—I'm not exactly sure how this works, but the system described the capability to me," Konran says.

"So far so good," Valkyrie crackles back.

"No time like the present," Ace adds, and the trio enters the Rezakar's shield-projection range.

Konran's CFS erupts like a plasma globe. Fingers of coronal energy extend and flicker in all directions, licking against the Rezakar's shields with a thousand hungry fingers. And then their Sparrowhawks break through.

The Rezakar awaits them, as large as the fully assembled *Nova Scotia*. Its sharp angles gleam Solis's rays in wicked angles. Another fishbone barrage hits, and the CFS licks up the fragmented splinters with ten thousand more silent coronal explosions.

Time to finish this.

"You guys have missiles left?" Konran asks.

"Full," Ace replies.

"Ditto," Valkyrie confirms.

"Empty everything into the ventral cattail bays," Konran says, switching to his missile system. "Valkyrie, you're going to fly us out. Ace and I will slave our Sparrowhawks to yours."

"Copy that."

Three Sparrowhawks arc around the Rezakar, separated by meters as they head for the ventral cattail bays. There, like the underbelly of the giant beast, the Rezakar's armor was most vulnerable.

More Askeras and Miratans swarm them. Blue plasma flickers against Konran's shields and his CFS licks up a continual barrage of ominous green plasma balls. Konran's appendages urge him to go evasive, scream he should get out of the onslaught, but he presses onward, trusting in whatever it was his dad had given him.

Konran swoops under the Rezakar, Ace and Valkyrie on his heels. His targeting system registers solid target acquisition, and his fingers work his weapons controls, signaling for full release of all missiles.

Although far less impressive than a Longbow missile frigate, Konran's full array of twelve small but potent missiles streaks forward, followed closely by Ace's and Valkyrie's: thirty-six missiles trailed by thirty-six plumes. And without further protestation, the Rezakar's underbelly ruptures in a ballooning inferno.

Konran flips the switch to slave his Sparrowhawk to his wingman, but his finger finds nothing but air. He looks down at the spot—his first time glancing at his controls since taking off from below the mountain.

His Sparrowhawk has no slave switch.

Konran grasps his controls, jamming his aft thruster to full power. Diving away from the Rezakar, he presses back into his seat as the full force of a million gravito-nuclear explosions accelerate him to full speed. His only chance of survival now is to get ahead of the impending gravitational wave and ride its fringe outward until the ripples inevitably engulf him. He had hoped to leverage Valkyrie's gravitational surfing skills, which were clearly superior to his own. But Ace and Valkyrie are gone, having already made their break.

Behind Konran and precisely on schedule, the Rezakar's supply of cattails detonates beneath the Sparrowhawks' missiles. Compressed beneath the compounded force of scores of the galaxy's most potent gravitational bombs, space-time converts into a grenade.

"They did what?" Captain Granicks groans, the surge of adrenaline accompanied by a surge of pain.

"They attacked a formation of Nolvaric cruisers above the atmosphere," Ruzcier's servant responds from Granicks's bedside.

"Our Xarba pilots report Konran led the attack," Ruzcier adds. "He must have found one of Kazrick's old Sparrowhawks. I have so many of Kazrick's former possessions."

"They won?" Granicks asks.

"Whatever they did, an enormous gravitational cascade obliterated the area," the servant explains. We have yet to reacquire their signal."

"They went for the cattail bays," Granicks surmises with another groan. "They would have ridden the gravitational wave out. Keep trying. And what news of the *Alpha* and *Beta*?"

"Not good," the servant responds, turning from Granicks's bedside. "Arzibanian forces joined them, but they appear to be barely holding."

Granicks nods, a grim line across his lips. "Have you contacted Salazar?" he adds, teeth gritting with the effort of continued speech.

"We just raised him on a comm channel," Ruzcier says, helping Granicks rest back onto his pillow. "He, my daughter, and the marine are alive. They have acquired a fourth companion who claims to be a Saturnese spy."

"I am aware of the fourth individual," Granicks replies. "I need to speak with him. And I need a ship."

* * * * *

Alandie stands helplessly as Philipe, Kyalia's co-holo-star, argues with Zimak Jin. Alandie glances back and forth between them and the shattered window. Either way he looked, battle raged.

In the distance, the mountain guns still fired at the invading Nolvarics, aiding the fleet of Arzibanian warships which had taken off en masse in response to the attack. At least four of the Arzibanian vessels had succumbed as they climbed to engage the

Nolvarics, falling in infernos back to the ground. Two of their smoldering craters were visible across the sprawling urban horizon, joined by several smoldering Nolvarics.

It was a bad day, and Zimak Jin had no intention of risking his own neck to experience the badness firsthand.

Alandie didn't know whether he was grateful for or furious at Philipe, who had escalated the confrontation with Zimak to the point of fisticuffs three times over the course of the previous half hour. Kyalia had hoped the famous entrepreneur, trillionaire, philanthropist, and sponsor of several blockbuster holo-pictures would understand their plight and, through his renowned generosity and soft spot for the cinema, lend them a hand. Zimak's warp yacht, however, still sulked atop the skyscraper's landing pad, ever the enervated eagle.

Had this been a normal day at the restaurant, Philipe and his companions (probably including Alandie and Kyalia) would have been thrown from the premises long ago. As it was, Zimak's bodyguard sat moaning, nursing a broken jaw beside Philipe's stagehand, Turnsil Vecani, who lay next to him unconscious (or, just as likely, feigning). Security and staff huddled with the rest of the patrons, chattering and whimpering in nervous pockets around the penthouse restaurant. Nobody was sticking their neck out.

Except Philipe, of course, who was more useful when he didn't.

Zimak yells at the holo-star through bloodied lips about a lawsuit for his damaged tooth.

Philipe spatters something back at him about being a false patron of the arts.

If Philipe's motivation had been driven by a desire to fulfill Kyalia's need, it now persisted for something more primal. Alandie glances at Kyalia, who, sitting beside him with tear-streaked cheeks, had stopped trying to prevent Philipe from arguing with her former idol. Her glowing hair throbs faintly, almost not at all, itself resigned. He reaches out and takes her hand.

"Do something," she says in a whisper, looking at him.

Alandie sits down. "But what?"

"There are lots of starcraft down in the parking bay. Nobody's going anywhere. You're a pilot."

"Are you saying ...?" Alandie asks.

Kyalia nods, looking around. Nobody was listening.

"But how?" he presses.

"A bribe? I've got money."

"I'll do it," a voice speaks behind them. They both whirl around. The voice's owner is tall, thin, and bald, and sitting very close to them.

"Who are you?" Alandie asks the man.

"Ryk Stinson, at your service, mate. I was about to make you an offer, and then you made it yourself. So, I'll do it."

"What do you want?" Alandie says.

"Nothing, mate," the man replies. "But I've got access codes to that warp yacht upstairs, and if you care to make a little trade..." He looks at Kyalia inquisitively.

"How do we know we can trust you?" Kyalia whispers (they had all been whispering).

"Easy, lass." Ryk tips his head toward Zimak Jin. "I'm his pilot. And he pays bilkrot."

"Deal," Kyalia says. "Take us there."

Ryk smiles. "Meet you on the roof in three minutes."

* * * * *

"Yes, sir, I understand, sir," Chanziu Guan replies, overtly cognizant of the fact that he had just addressed a USFN officer with a phrase of salute—twice. The strangest part wasn't that he had willingly allowed himself to receive orders from an officer of a rival, oft-antagonistic military force; the strangest thing was that it felt right. The race for Konran Andacellos was not over, and Chanziu knew if anyone desired to win that race more than he did, it was the man on the other side of the comm right now.

"Excellent," Captain Granicks replies. "Go to these coordinates across the compound. You'll find a transport vessel there." The captain pauses, and Chanziu can hear him breathing, laboring to continue. "And make it fast," he finally adds. "We don't want any Nolvaric attention."

"We will, sir. It won't be a problem."

"Excellent, I'm counting on you."

"I know."

* * * * *

Ace searches his sensors, seeking any sign of Snakedust's whereabouts.

Valk had done a stellar job navigating the Rezakar's gravitational detonation, catching the wave as perfectly as Ace had ever seen any pilot do so. But now the ripples had taken them, and Konran was nowhere to be found.

Ace knew better than to bother Valk while she was leading them through the soup. Not that it would do any good for both of them to look. Sensors were as useful as a parachute in this mess.

Frustrated, Ace turns his attention back to Valk's work, keeping an eye on the fishbone fragments circulating the grav waves like schools of piranha. Not to mention all the Rezakar debris.

* * * * *

Lieutenant Vilkoj stumbles, falling to his knees as the *Alpha* rocks beneath Nolvaric guns. Nearby, the *Beta* weathers a barrage of its own. Six millicks away, Rezakars thrash to pieces in the violence of their own cattails, destroyed by the audacity of Konran Andacellos.

Somehow the boy found a Sparrowhawk. And wiped out five Rezakars.

Now the Nolvaric fleet pushes for Konran, eager to claim their prize once and for all. Only the *Alpha* and *Beta* still stood in their way. One of the arrow-tipped, chevron-shaped Rezakars breaks away from the body of fighting, circumventing Vilkoj's guns.

"Tibo," Vilkoj calls out. "Head off that lead Rezakar! We can't let them break for Andacellos!"

"Tibo's down!" Pearl's voice calls back, the albino fighter pilot next in the Wildlynx chain of command. "But we're on it!"

On Vilkoj's space-time emulator seven blue blips race through the fray, heading for the cruiser.

If anyone can slow it down, the Wildlynx can.

A fresh Nolvaric deluge slams into the *Alpha*, nearly tossing Vilkoj off his feet again. He braces himself with his one arm. It

317

wouldn't take many more hits like that. Before him, a massive, Nolvaric Nicransin charges his position. Bulky, alligator-like, and armed to the teeth, the heavy warship was the sledgehammer of the Nolvaric fleet.

The *Alpha* was already throwing everything it had into the Nicransin's face. Tesseracts depleted, rail guns and plasma cannons release broadside after broadside into the Nolvaric monstrosity.

Nearby, the *Beta* does the same, presently releasing its store of ammunition into three Rezakars.

And then there were the thirteen other ships.

Below the *Alpha*, on the moon side of the battle, the final two Arzibanian Lancer-class attack frigates succumb to Nolvaric firepower. The *Nova Scotia* was alone.

The *Alpha* shakes.

It wasn't going to be long now.

What would Revenshal do? What would Exeunt do? What would Granicks do?

Vilkoj opens his mind, considering every out-of-the-box possibility. Something had to happen, and it had to happen now. But no ideas come.

So what would Vilkoj do?

How did you fight a gang when you only had one hand? Dirty. And with a whole lot of legs.

"*Alpha* and *Beta*, cease engagement with all Nolvaric craft," Vilkoj orders. "We're surrounded, outgunned, and outnumbered. We can't beat them. We won't be escaping this—and we all knew that was a possibility coming into it. But we can still finish our mission, to protect Andacellos—just like Captain Granicks did."

Vilkoj pauses, letting his words sink in. Defiant eyes stare back at him, unflinching. Nobody on the bridge was fooling themselves about the outcome of this battle—but nobody had quit fighting, either. He senses therein an electricity, an energy above any he had previously experienced in his entire life. It could have been what Leonidas felt, more than seventeen hundred years ago at Thermopylae, knowing he could not defeat the massive Persian army facing his meager forces, but refusing to stop trying.

"Target all Arzibanian warp dampeners within range," Vilkoj orders. "And prepare for warp-drive engagement. Let's take the Nolvarics with us."

* * * * *

Konran crashes through a series of gravitational waves, completely missing the angle, shuddering as his craft tosses end over end, out of control.

An alarm sounds, adding to the three already blaring. Konran struggles to maintain consciousness, his life-support system fighting with him as he throttles up the Sparrowhawk. He attempts to control its angle into the next grav wave, but three more hit him first, slapping him completely off course. He struggles to regain control.

This new alarm meant something important. What was it? The alarm grows in volume as the words, *Fishbones detected, impact inevitable,* flash across his cockpit.

Konran angles his Sparrowhawk into the gravitational gradient, trying to let it whisk him away. He feels its tug, and he guns the throttle, seeking the grav wave.

And the fishbones hit. Energy flashes like fireworks as his Coronal Flare System collides with the shards, completely blocking out Konran's view and wreaking total havoc with his sensors. Blind and disoriented, he closes his eyes, letting his mind and muscles dictate his next path.

He feels another wave. Its impact hits like a dump truck to the chest. His mind absorbs the information, seeing the gravitational fields, feeling them ebb and flow from every direction as another dump truck hits, this one to the top of his head. He can hear his systems straining, his head and body throbbing, can feel the vibrations as the Coronal Flare System fights the fishbones.

And then his hands react, jamming his throttle to full power and torqueing his flight stick; his feet slam the rudders, jostling them like a drummer on a freestyle riff. The Sparrowhawk reacts instantly, and finally he feels it catch a gradient, the sudden boost of acceleration like a breath of fresh air to his lungs.

The Sparrowhawk screams, exerting itself with the roar of a dying wraith to rip its way through the fishbone cloud. Konran keeps the throttle open. Opening his eyes, he angles with the undulating grav cloud. He anticipates its movements by following a trail of fishbone splinters, traversing it like the lost wanderer following bread crumbs along the forest floor.

His system flashes angrily, throwing messages like *Coronal System Failure*, *Reactor Temperature Critical*, and *Shield Capacity 24%* in panicky red letters on his heads-up display.

Sensing a bifurcation in the fishbone pattern, Konran rolls his Sparrowhawk, jutting into and catching a new gravitational gradient before it crashes into his position. He lingers with it less than a moment, the rhythm of his rudder pedals finding him a weakened gravitational subcurrent through which he rolls instantly. Inverting and then diving perpendicular to his former trajectory, he maintains alignment with this softer gradient until his Sparrowhawk bursts free of the fishbone splinters.

He immediately encounters another wave. It crests from every direction below and in front of him, like an enormous jaw moving to swallow him. Gravitational undulations behind him pull the fishbone splinters back his way. In moments all will be devoured in the gigantic maw, to be tossed and tumbled in whatever digestive gravitation chaos ensued. His chance for escape closing, he dives into the mouth, climbing against the direction of increasing gravitational strength.

His heads-up display screams at him, flashing with a dozen warnings. His Sparrowhawk slows, struggling against the space-time equivalent of a hundred zombies dragging it backward into the pit.

The two gradients converge, and fishbone splinters suck in with them. Konran maintains his course, no other options except to escape. The fishbones surge toward him, sucked down by intense gravitational peristalsis. But something in the complex wave interactions about him changes, and Konran shoots for the window. Accelerating like a slingshot, his Sparrowhawk bursts free from that gradient.

But not the next one. Or the three hundred after that.

He tosses and tumbles, crashing through the gravitational equivalent of the South Dakota Badlands at full speed, unconscious.

* * * * *

Konran's eyes snap open, and he gasps for breath.

Where am I?

He catches a glint of light shining above him, and turns his eyes in that direction, craning his neck toward the source. Maehn Arziban hangs overhead, turning slowly away as his Sparrowhawk spins around. The moon is large enough in size that Konran knows he hadn't drifted far.

Why is it so blurry? he wonders, worrying about what had happened to him.

He looks at his sensor displays, finding nothing but darkness in its place. Then he realizes how clammy he feels. He exhales, and a wisp of vapor puffs from his mouth. A layer of frost crusts his shell-shaped viewport, and Konran shivers as intense coldness penetrates his consciousness.

The grav cloud. I escaped it. At least I'm not dead, he thinks. *Not yet.*

Something was obviously wrong with his Sparrowhawk. Whatever the escape from the grav cloud had done, it had knocked out his power systems. He unstraps his harness and stands as much as possible in the confined space, using his forearm to wipe the frost from his viewport. He has to wait a moment before the craft's rotation brings light to bear on its sleek, black surface. From what he can see, the Sparrowhawk was still structurally integral.

I'll just have to assume the hull is fine, he concludes. *If it's not, nothing else I do is going to matter much.*

He sits back down and straps back in, shivering and collecting his thoughts.

The CFS was failing before I got out, he reasons, recalling the lines drilled into him during his starfighting coursework: *A starfighter is the closest thing to a nonorganic living being you'll ever meet. It thinks, it breathes, and it wants to live. If injured in battle, it will respond like your own human system, shutting down nonessential functions in favor of preserving its life, which is you.*

The chill of vacuous space permeates his chest, and Konran shivers again.

The Hawk must have diverted all energy to the CFS to keep me alive in the grav cloud, he reasons. *When the CFS failed, it took everything else with it.*

So am I a dead man or not?

Konran conjures what he remembers of cold-starting a Sparrowhawk. It wasn't a skill you used very much during simulated battles, where all of his experience lay, but it was one of the first things they taught you in spaceflight school. Even if you were only majoring in the subject and not *actually* training to use one.

Stupid acceptance policies.

Konran closes his eyes, fighting against the frustration that always accompanied the memory. The cards had always been stacked against him. From the very beginning, the world—the entire solar system, for that matter—had closed its doors to his aspirations, funneling him, in all their wisdom and despite his every effort to the contrary, into the "honorable" position of astrofreighter captain. Every time he tried to raise his head, to stand above, to get noticed, to break through, to change his fortunes, to grasp his dreams, to find some opportunity to somehow move his life in some direction *he* cared about, every time he was met with the same warm, bureaucratic logic: *Let go of the ladder and your safety net goes with you; we already said no.*

Anger swirls inside him, building to its familiar, insoluble storm of emotion. He feels the unfairness of it all, the weight of the rejection of his deepest desires, the whack of the mallet every time he tried to peer above the corporate throngs. He feels the discouragement that, no matter his effort, he would never receive his due, the despair that it would never amount to enough. He feels the cold of the Sparrowhawk's flight stick against his palm, his hand having drifted to the familiar position. The shock of the icy temperature shoots up his arm.

What am I doing? he thinks, his mind jerking back into the present. *I'm in my dad's sparking Sparrowhawk right now.*

I am a starfighter, by blood right.

Konran sets to work, his emotions dispelling with the energy of action. He pulls back a small panel near his throttle, exposing a set of switches. Wired to their own independent battery source, these were useful for jump-starting things when things went cold. He jogs the one for life-support, jabbing it once, and then, after no response, three more times. A sudden jolt of energy courses into his body as the system kicks to life, infusing him with much-needed nutrients. A gentle warmth emanates from his flight suit and into his skin as the system counteracts his dropping body temperature.

Konran jogs another switch, and his heads-up display kicks back to life with a series of diagnostic messages. He works through each systematically, jump-starting sensors, communications, navigation, and finally his engines. The familiar hum of life around him is like the patter of rain on his bedtime window.

Now revitalized, his Sparrowhawk does the rest. It boots back to full power, initializes weapons and targeting systems, and populates Konran's cockpit with a full array of information. The lone protestant is the shielding system, which, along with its integrated Coronal Flare System, only musters 6 percent capacity.

I'll take it.

Konran evaluates the wealth of information laid before his eyes, angling his Sparrowhawk to face Maehn Arziban. His sensors mark signatures of the *Gamma*, Ace's and Valkyrie's Sparrowhawks, and the Xolian Xarbas. They had congregated some fifteen hundred kilometers from his position, toward Maehn Arziban's south pole. No Nolvaric sensor blips existed in the vicinity. And the Rezakars had been completely destroyed.

Good, we all survived.

He probes the system for information regarding the greater battle, eager to know how the *Alpha* and *Beta* were doing. He engages the Sparrowhawk's optical zoom features, maneuvering his craft to scan the space around the moon. Now that the *Gamma* had been saved, his next step involved rescuing the rest of Granicks's force. The lack of the Coronal Flare System would complicate the process, especially with so many enemies in the region, but Konran isn't fazed.

Then, as his mind registers meaning from the sensors' information presented by his system, Konran's eyes behold the truth of the battle before him:

The Alpha *and* Beta: *They're completely surrounded. How am I going to do this?*

Then, across Maehn Arziban, the heart of the starship battle lights off like a supernova.

* * * * *

"Retreat!" Emersav Firnuendal, commander of the mixed Nolvaric-Saturnese attack force, screams as the USFN warships destroy the last of the warp dampeners. "All ships retreat!"

His pirated Huoxing falls back with alacrity. But too many of the Nolvarics don't. Too stupid to see what was happening, and too slow to follow orders, the bulk of the force continues to fight, oblivious to the impending threat.

And tattered yet still standing, the *Nova Scotia*'s guns knock out the last warp dampener.

Bedamn Heesor and his idiotic plans. If I had been permitted to bring in the Krona, this never would have happened.

* * * * *

Vilkoj looks into the eyes of his officers. An hour ago these people may have belonged to Granicks, but now they were his.

That's what happened when you chose this end together.

Beside him, Lieutenant Giulia da Catra's hologram stares back with pure resolve, projected from the *Beta*'s command deck.

"We have confirmation, sir," da Catra reports. "Andacellos's Sparrowhawk just powered back up—he survived the grav soup."

Vilkoj nods, and every eye in the room nods back.

Vilkoj didn't understand everything. But he knew enough. He had seen the boy in action, had witnessed the breadth of his capability. Granicks had gotten himself shot to keep Andacellos safe. The minister of defense had betrayed the entire United Space

Federation in an attempt to take the boy. The stench of deep evil wreaked below the action today, and the Nolvarics had deployed breathtaking new technology for the endeavor, bringing in firepower worthy of subduing a planet. All bent on capturing Andacellos.

Well, they couldn't have him.

Vilkoj had always cherished his freedom. It had been that love which propelled him to pursue his military career in the first place. To him the choice had never been complicated: freedom simply mattered. And when an enemy this bent on taking it away wanted something as badly as this enemy did, you stopped them. Whatever the cost. Because allowing them to reach their end was unacceptable.

Freedom was worth it.

"For freedom!" he yells, punching his fist into the air.

"For freedom!" they all yell back, steadfast before their leader like the three hundred before Thermopylae.

The Hot Gates may fall, but not without cost.

Per Vilkoj's orders, the *Alpha* and *Beta* had destroyed every Arzibanian warp dampener within range of their guns. Now there was only one thing left to do.

"Warp," he commands.

Trapped within the gravity well of Summanus, the *Alpha* and *Beta* warp.

And Vilkoj closes his eyes, breathing in one last, beautiful breath.

For freedom, he thinks, at peace with his role in the conflict. *Now it's up to you, Andacellos.*

* * * * *

Summanus had occupied its current location in the solar system for nearly 4.5 billion years. Out here so far from the sun, the planet had orbited in freedom for millennia, liberated from the meddling influence of the solar system's larger bullies. Frozen in frigid blackness, Summanus had accepted its fate long ago. Such was the price to be the undisputed master of this domain.

So, when two tiny bubbles of distorted space-time emanated from the *Nova Scotia's* two sub-ships, Summanus barely noticed. The bubbles strained against Summanus's enormous gravity well with mighty energy, growing in size and strength factorially over femtoseconds. But Summanus was not to be disturbed, and, just as quickly as the warp bubbles began they burst asunder, and Summanus's gravity well flowed back to its customary space-time smoothness.

* * * * *

In a violent nanosecond, a full two-thirds of the *Nova Scotia* is gone, completely obliterated in a blinding, colossal fury along with the bulk of the Nolvaric forces surrounding them. Konran panics, disbelieving.

But they were gone.

No.

They warped.

Why did they warp?

They knew they couldn't engage warp engines inside the planet's gravity well and survive.

Everyone knew that.

It was the reason every planet, every moon, every celestial body big enough had warp dampeners.

"Kid! Get moving now. We'll hold them off," Commander Revenshal's urgent voice crackles into Konran's ear.

On the far side of Maehn Arziban, two Saturnese Huoxings, two Nicransins, and three Rezakars sprint around the moon, unabated en route to their primary target: Konran. Then, out of nowhere, ten more Nolvaric warships suddenly appear behind them, followed instantaneously by five others.

The Nolvarics just jumped more forces into the system.

CHAPTER 21

Konran watches the Nolvarics come at him.

The Alpha *and* Beta.

That chef, Franco.

Those nurses.

The Wildlynx ... how many?

Granicks.

The Relrick.

Natauli.

The VIPs.

His parents.

He stares at the distant, onrushing attackers, but all he sees is the ever-growing list of casualties.

"Kid, get moving! Now!" Revenshal yells into his ear. "Get out of there!"

Soon to include Revenshal and the Gamma, *Ace and Valkyrie, Cassio, Zenara, Chanziu, Ruzcier...*

"Konran." Valkyrie's voice is earnest. "Get up."

His hands tighten about the flight stick and throttle. He isn't dead yet.

But some Nolvarics are about to be.

He jams his throttle and the Sparrowhawk kicks toward the enemies.

"Konran!" a new voice breaks into his comm—a familiar voice he hadn't expected to hear again. "Andacellos, do you read me?" Captain Granicks asks.

"Captain! I read you! You're alive!"

"Listen fast!" Granicks orders. "Do not engage the enemy. Do everything in your power to stay alive for the next twenty minutes. Whatever it takes. I've got some help coming."

"Copy that," Konran replies, breaking off his attack vector immediately, "as long as you give Revenshal, Ace, and Valkyrie the same order."

"We're coming with you, kid," Revenshal crackles in. "Lead the way."

Konran breaks hard toward Maehn Arziban. Granicks's voice had felt like a lightning bolt to his brain. When fleeing had meant abandoning his friends to destruction, the thought had been out of the question. Now, it encompasses the entirety of Konran's being.

"I'll come to you," Konran says. "I don't trust the NACs after that. I'm heading for the city. Let's give them a chase."

Since there is nowhere else to go.

"Copy that," Revenshal replies. "We'll cover your approach."

"About time you listen to someone," Ace rebukes.

"How many tesseracts do you have left?" Konran asks.

"Six," Revenshal says. "But I've got plenty of plasma cannons left."

Streaks of light burst from the *Gamma*, shooting across Maehn Arziban from the *Gamma's* position near the Arzibanian southern hemisphere toward the Nolvarics occupying the northwest. The flashes culminate as tiny bursts of energy against Nolvaric and Saturnese shields. Blue Nolvaric plasma peppers the *Gamma's* shields in response. From Konran's vantage point, the entire vista fills his view.

And then the missile locks sound.

"They've got missile locks on me!" Konran says, feeling exposed out here with no cover.

"What about your shield system?" Ace asks.

"The grav cloud took it down," Konran replies. "We're going to have to do this the old-fashioned way."

"Crap," Ace says.

"Do you have stealth skin?" Valkyrie asks.

Konran hadn't thought of that. "Engage stealth skin," he speaks, and a thin, oozy substance secretes from his Sparrowhawk's fuselage.

"Yeah! I've got it!"

"OK, kid," Revenshal says. "Mix it up. Here comes your ink cloud. Get to us and we'll hide you in the city."

Three tesseracts launch from the *Gamma*, visible only on Konran's sensor display. They pop between him and the Nolvarics, giving Konran a distorted space-time smokescreen to hide behind.

Fishbone blips careen for him nonetheless, but the *Gamma*'s plasma cannons pick them off.

Two thousand kilometers to go.

"Rev," Konran asks, using the respite to scheme, "do you have the locations of Maehn Arziban surface defense batteries?"

"Are you kidding me?" the commander replies. "We mapped this rock eight times before breakfast."

"OK, good. Send the locations to us. We're going to lure the Nolvarics into them; I want to use them to our advantage."

"Done and done. I like it, kid."

One thousand kilometers to reentry, Konran's display reads. Déjà vu sets in as he counts down.

Four hundred kilometers, three hundred, two hundred.

Ace and Valkyrie form up with him.

One hundred kilometers. Here we go!

Now upside down with respect to Maehn Arziban, Konran enters an orbit of the moon. He retracts his stealth skin before descending, and the glowing burn of atmospheric reentry washes pink around him. Ace and Valkyrie flank his Sparrowhawk to the left and right. Even the Xolian Xarbas form up, creating an elongated hexagon formation with the USFN craft. Finally, the *Gamma* follows, taking a different descent vector, which places it between Konran and the Nolvarics.

Of course Revenshal did that, Konran worries. *I have to find a way to use everyone's overprotectiveness to our advantage.*

Konran's cockpit overlays with data from Revenshal, indicating the location of Arzibanian defense batteries across the moon. Those closest to Ruzcier's mountain have all been destroyed—but they were on the other side of the moon right now. He searches for the right target, watching the Nolvarics come down into the atmosphere as he dips into a city center for cover.

Skyscrapers, spires, and towers sprout around him, more than double the number growing near Ruzcier's mountain. The Nolvarics were mostly coming in northwest of him, and, using Revenshal's data, Konran identifies an industrial complex nearby. It appears heavily defended. If he could get a cruiser or two to follow him, they would be easy prey for the Arzibanian guns lurking inside.

Several Nolvaric starfighters take a more direct approach, converging straight down on Konran's position. The *Gamma* thins their ranks, converting them into atmospheric fireballs with orange bursts from its plasma cannons. Easy enough targets, the starfighters were of no interest to Konran.

Beyond them, however, two Rezakars and a more massive Nicransin burn through the atmosphere, their bulks glowing hot across the sky. Konran tracks them as he skips between buildings, calculating how to attract the trio. A pair of Askeras dives down toward him, and he dodges around a skyscraper, angling upward and around it. He cuts the spiral short and, turning sharply back on his course, brings the Nolvarics beneath his crosshairs. He fires twice, and their debris rains down amidst the urban canyon walls.

A sharklike Miratan juts in front of him, coming up from below a skyway. A green plasma ball zips toward Konran, who barrel rolls: jutting upward and away from the attack, he spins his craft upside down, righting it as he angles back toward the city. His maneuver takes him up and over the Nolvaric, which had expected the move to be a full reverse loop. Konran's wingtip guns track it, rotate behind him, and blast two holes through its hull. The Miratan falls unceremoniously, crashing in flames on the city floor two hundred meters below.

Konran whips through a series of skyways, intent on the incoming Nolvaric cruisers filling the not-so-distant sky. He ignores a quintet of Askeras collecting on his tail, allowing Tiswa's trio of Xarbas to knock them out for him. For some reason, despite his attempt to bait the Nolvarics' bigger ships, they weren't heading into the mix as Konran expected. Instead, the Rezakars and Nicransins take a trajectory beyond the city center.

He inverts his Sparrowhawk's weapon system. Three more Askeras angle between the large, multi-helical beams of a towering, twisting skyscraper. His Sparrowhawk somersaults with the inversion, bringing its megacannon to bear and vaporizing the three in their tracks. He reverts the system and rockets down a perpendicular urban avenue.

Through it all he synthesizes meaning from his Sparrowhawk's array of sensor data. Then, his heart skipping a beat as his fingers blast another Miratan from the cityscape, he comprehends the

Nolvarics' true target: *They're targeting the Arzibanian guns at the industrial complex.*

"Guys!" Konran yells. "Abort plan! They're going for the ground guns!"

In the distance, blue Nolvaric plasma rains down in a fury like a modern, intensely more deadly visitation of the Leonids meteor shower of 1833. Arzibanian plasma flashes from the ground, peppering the Nolvaric cruisers, but as quickly as the firestorm starts, it is over, the ground guns destroyed.

Konran expands his map to show more of the Arzibanian hemisphere, and his fears compound. Around the moon, as far as his Sparrowhawk can indicate, clusters of Nolvaric cruisers engage each and every one of the Arzibanian defense batteries.

They knew our plan, he realizes.

"Konran!" Ace screams.

Konran jerks his controls, immediately going evasive. He had been distracted, analyzing the distant Nolvarics and failing to focus on the battle at hand.

His cockpit flashes green, and he loses all sense of direction. His Sparrowhawk flails, tossing backward into a skyscraper and busting through a massive window. It tumbles ferociously into the building, crashing with awful vengeance through a fifty-story office complex.

Konran's mind comprehends the end as it comes. His last thought is of the simulator he played so many times as a child: green Nolvaric plasma ending his attempt to win the day. It was poetic, in a brutal sort of way.

If there ever was a way to end, this was it.

He closes his eyes.

And then he opens them. His lungs gasp. His body hangs upside down, wedged with his Sparrowhawk somewhere deep inside the building. His vision comes back into focus and one flashing red message catches his eyes.

Shield capacity: 2.02%.

Thanks, Dad.

He checks his system diagnostics. His left wing had been smashed, its wingtip cannon demolished. His aerodynamics were shot. His firepower was at two-thirds. His maneuverability—he

331

could only guess—had to be at 40 percent. Fuzzy crackles of communication buzz: allies struggling to avoid the same fate. Their dispatches come broken and halting into Konran's ears.

Adrenaline surges as his life-support system (both physiological and Sparrowhawk driven) kicks in with force. He fires all maneuvering thrusters simultaneously and debris blasts away, dislodging his Sparrowhawk. He activates his gravity repulsor system, and the craft rises from the ground, hovering there with him upside down.

His father's holo-photo flutters in the cockpit, sticking to the face shield of his helmet. He grabs it with a gloved hand, noticing for the first time the look on his father's smiling face: so confident, so capable, so eager. And his mother: so determined, so intelligent, so genuine. The strain of their struggle was apparent, but their faces were happy. Salty moisture burns as tears pool in Konran's eyes and drip down his forehead. He looks up (which was down) and finds his holo-cube nestled into the bulbous arc of his cockpit. He grabs it, stuffs it into his flight suit, and wedges the holo-photo next to his sensor display.

"Nolvarics detected," his Sparrowhawk speaks. "Activating suppression system."

Konran's remaining guns burst to life. Blasting in rapid succession through the darkness, plasma explodes in fiery punches against everything and anything in their path. He jostles the throttle, and the Sparrowhawk surges through the devastated office complex, retracing its path of ingress and breaking into the urban skyscape.

High above, a Nolvaric Nicransin cruiser blocks out the sky, the enormous, alligator-like ship dropping landing craft toward his position. Konran's guns tear into the descending convoy, and they veer and tumble clumsily.

Konran doesn't wait for the Nicransin's response, zigging away from his hole in the skyscraper. He dodges this way and that, across streets, below skyways, between skyscrapers, and through immaculately crafted gaps in the magnificent architecture. His Sparrowhawk handles like a bird with a rock tied to one leg—but it can still fly.

This is still nothing compared to Y25LM90.

"Ace, Valkyrie, Revenshal," Konran speaks into his comm, unsure if anyone can hear him as he blasts a pair of Saturnese Shandians against the side of a skyscraper—he didn't know there were any of those left in this battle. "This is Konran. I'm alive. What's your status?"

Garbled static returns, inflected like something Ace would have said.

Konran's sensors indicate a mixed group of Askeras and Miratans on his tail. Rather than dodging, he whirls on end. The movement is awkward, but he is ready for it—planning on it—and his right wingtip cannon blasts two Askeras while his nose cannon takes out a Miratan.

He doesn't flee, remaining between the skyscrapers as he flips his Sparrowhawk end over end, maintaining altitude with timely bursts of maneuvering thrusters. He fires again, and plasma finds an Askera coming from above the skyscrapers. He fires again, and his guns knock the ventral wing off another Askera, sending it flailing into a skyway. He gyrates farther, his Sparrowhawk wheeling like a gymnast on her final approach, and he fires again. His cannons blast one Miratan each, and the sharklike starfighters detonate forcibly, ejecting shards of debris in every direction. He inverts his weapons system and a blast from his megacannon crumples two Askeras like ants beneath the hammer. He reverts and jams his thruster, rocketing after the lone Miratan remaining from the pack. His Sparrowhawk wobbles after it like a clipped, radioactive duck.

The Miratan takes a corner sharply, clipping the side of a skyscraper in an attempt to elude him. More enemies converge from above, and, sensing their pressure, Konran inverts and sends a mega blast of plasma straight through the side of the skyscraper. The blast echoes with a BOOM through the urban canyons as he bolts through in pursuit of his prey. The Miratan is down the avenue, but not far, thrashing like a skewered fish. Exposed holes in its hull spark with red smoke.

Konran's fingers cover his triggers as his crosshairs sight on the craft. And then his gut lurches within him, a warning he knew to trust more by instinct than by academics. He remembers Hot Sauce and her battle against the Miratan.

Grav bombs. These Miratans have grav bombs.

Konran pulls up, performing a quick flip and angling back through his hole in the skyscraper. Behind him another swarm of Askeras bank hard, trying to keep pace. He yanks the controls upward, toward the hulking Nicransin above. Then the city shrieks behind him, the gravity bomb deafening even inside his cockpit. Like a tsunami meeting a black hole, the skyscrapers buckle, twist, collapse, and then burst asunder, shattered by hellacious gravitational distortions. At least ten fall to the blast.

Konran banks his Sparrowhawk, surging into the sky but away from the Nicransin's deadly bulk. His stomach rebels at the destruction, churning once, then twice, before sending vomit up his throat. He lets it out, smelling its acrid stench before his flight suits sucks it away. A cleansing taste of lemon meets his tongue as his support system mitigates the effect. And in moments his nausea is no more.

"Hahahaha," a new voice echoes into his comm system, sending chills into Konran's neck hairs. "You truly are remarkable. But you will not escape me."

Konran's fingers pull the triggers, shooting a cast of six crablike Askeras from the sky at three kilometers. His right wingtip gun tracks backward, firing and knocking another pair of Nolvarics from his tail. His mind whirls at the words. Had he really just heard that voice?

Konran's cockpit alerts him to a tractor beam focusing in his direction. Tractor beams were too new for an old Sparrowhawk like his to need a detection system—or even Ace's or Valkyrie's Sparrowhawks, for that matter—but even as the warning displays, the gravitational energy tugs against his craft like the tentacles of an octopus finagling its prey.

Engage Countermeasures. The holographic button appears within his cockpit—yet another prescient innovation added by Konran's parents.

Without worrying how they had done it, Konran engages the countermeasure. His Sparrowhawk reacts automatically, inverting itself and pointing its megacannon at the tractor beam source. The system fires repeatedly, releasing brief belches of massive orange plasma. Glorious explosions impact the Nicransin's hull far above.

The tractor beam dies, the warning in Konran's cockpit desists, and he rockets off, putting as much space between him and the enormous ship as possible.

"I applaud you," the voice crackles in again, unamused. "You are slippery, but let me be clear about this little game: you *will* be mine."

"Who are you?" Konran demands, diving as a fresh swarm of Miratans shower his position with green plasma balls. He blasts two from the sky before angling away from them, keeping his distance from their grav bombs.

"I am your match, and your new master," the voice speaks.

"What are you talking about?" Konran's peripheral vision catches a glimpse of battle taking place some thirty kilometers to his northeast. He angles toward it, magnifying the area on his screen. His friends had to be that way. More Askeras bear down on his position.

"Let me introduce you to Emersav Firnuendal," another voice speaks into Konran's comm. "Emersav is a Level 19 naval combat strategist, and he will be your new superior officer." This voice Konran recognizes, and his blood boils at the sound of Vadic Heesor, United Space Federation minister of defense.

"You shot Granicks!" he yells, turning his Sparrowhawk into the swarm of Askeras. Blue plasma peppers the Arzibanian air, but none touches him. Konran allows his craft's mangled aerodynamics to jolt him around randomly, mingling the effect with his own evasive maneuvers. Unrelenting on the triggers, he rushes the attackers like a cowboy on a broken horse. Eight of them fall before he pulls a quick flip and sends his Sparrowhawk streaking back toward his friends.

"Remind me to keep you angry when I require your services," Heesor mocks him. "Why don't you settle down? Emersav and I have so much to discuss with you."

Konran seethes, struggling to compose himself. What was going on here? His fingers depress the triggers as he processes the information, releasing long-range shots that score at least another kill.

"You were listening the whole time!" he finally accuses. "You heard our transmissions; that's how you knew to attack the gun batteries instead of us. You're a traitor and a liar! You villain! You fiend! You scum!" Konran spits the words, blasting two more Miratans at distance for emphasis.

He was getting close to his friends: those two Miratans had been harrying the *Gamma* before the cutter disappeared behind a cloud.

"Now, now," Heesor tisks. "You have quite the temper. What do you think, Emersav? I believe he will work out nicely."

"He will," Emersav's liquid voice leaks back into Konran's ear. "Under my command, he will prove pivotal to our cause."

They don't care about any of this, Konran realizes. *They've got me trapped, and they know it. This is a game to them.*

He checks his long-range sensors again. Nolvarics surrounded him, and not just the starfighters. Capital ships were closing from every angle, some ships high, some low. Their starfighters dart within the space. Amidst the Nolvaric numbers, Konran notes three non-Nolvarics: lurking at the periphery of the battle, two Huoxing battleships flank one ultra-massive USFN frigate. Konran's system designates the third as the *Tartaglia*.

"Shall we finish this?" Emersav's words drip against Konran's will into his auditory canal. His wingtip and nose cannons take out a pair of Askeras flitting within the *Gamma*'s cloud bank in reply.

"Yes, Commander, we've seen enough. Take him," Heesor orders.

"Revenshal? Ace? Valkyrie? Tiswa? Do you read me?" Konran pleads into his comm, but only static replies.

However he's doing it, Heesor jammed our communications and hacked my comm, Konran thinks.

"Well, aren't you the hopeful type?" Heesor mocks him again. "Haven't you figured out we're jamming your transmissions?"

"Shut up," Konran replies, concentrating on the thermal mass signatures of a large group of Askeras hidden in the cloud bank. The Askeras' images superimpose holographically on his viewport, augmented with heading and velocity for each craft. His fingers twitch, and orange plasma sizzles into the cloud. Four of the holographic signatures wink out.

He maneuvers parallel to the cloud, not entering its vapor as the Askeras within turn to track his position. He extrapolates their original trajectory, using the information to set a waypoint within his navigation system.

The Gamma *will be that way.*

Konran banks as if fleeing their attack. High above him and nearly overhead, two Rezakars converge. More capital craft follow, ever tightening the noose.

"My, my," Heesor taunts, "you will be a fun one to break."

"Shut. Up!" Konran grunts.

The Askeras emerge from the cloud and Konran cuts his engine power, letting his Sparrowhawk free fall. He spins without control for a moment, timing his enemies' reactions. About half of the fifteen Askeras overshoot his position while the others make clean dives toward him. He reactivates his engines, stabilizing himself with a deft burst of maneuvering thrusters. Angling below the Askeras, Konran sprints beneath the cloud, entering from the bottom.

Once inside, he reengages his stealth skin. Despite the damage to his Hawk, the marvelous oozy material seeps quickly around its current form, molding to the mangled geometry. He kills his speed, letting his heat signature melt away, and he waits.

Askeras converge from both sides, and Konran lets them surround him. He tunes his plasma cannons to fire diffuse, unfocused plasma rather than cohesive bursts. Then he pounces like an angry badger.

His remaining cannons flash to life, spinning within their rotating turrets and spewing plasmic energy everywhere. Crablike craft fracture, splinter, or explode, devastated by his point-blank attack. Konran juts this way and that in their midst, bouncing like an uncontrollable pinball as he evades counterattack. He feels them shift within the cloud, anticipating their jabs like a veteran boxer bobbing and weaving in the ring. His Sparrowhawk jumps high, an Askera goes low; his Sparrowhawk tumbles, and Konran lets it, adding a burst of thrust as an Askera takes aim from below; his Sparrowhawk climbs, jostling erratically into the curving path of a cornering Askera. At each step his guns find their mark, and the fifteen Askeras soon dwindle to four. He tunes his plasma cannons to fire cohesive bursts of focused plasma once more and drops their number to zero with four final well-placed shots. And then, not waiting for the next wave to hit, he rockets through the cloud, following his waypoint toward the *Gamma*.

"They can't see you," Heesor harasses him. "To their sensors, every starfighter in the sky now registers as your own—your friends are quite good, but achieving visual confirmation of every kill is taking its toll. It will only be a matter of time now."

"You can't have them," Konran says, cloud vapors whipping past his cockpit.

"Oh, but I can," Heesor insists, "just as I held your father's life in my hands all those years ago, and just as I now hold yours—they are mine."

Konran's blood freezes at the words. He bursts out of the cloud, finally obtaining visual on the *Gamma*. The cutter is in a desperate fight, pinned down by two Rezakars, some twenty kilometers away—a distance a Sparrowhawk can cover in moments at top speed.

The *Gamma* dives as Konran watches, trying to use its superior speed to escape the larger ships. Despite their bulk, however, the Rezakars move nimbly, keeping pace with the cutter.

They're upgraded, he realizes. The Rezakars he fought earlier had not demonstrated such adroitness; neither had the ones back in the Kuiper Belt. Heesor had saved the best for last. Konran's mind absorbs the information without thinking, his cognitive processes dedicated to another, more pressing thought.

My father.

A shiver of Miratans attacks him, coming from the direction of the Rezakars and blocking his approach to the *Gamma*. Konran destroys two before diverting around the deadly craft. Green plasma balls fill the air, seeking his Sparrowhawk. Konran lets himself bounce awkwardly, wielding the damaged aerodynamics for whatever value they had left.

"Yes." Heesor's voice is thick with mirth as he crackles back into Konran's comm. "I knew your father. Kazrick Anavos. Our forces finally killed him and his pesky wife on July 15, 2195, if you had to know—they had been quite the thorns in our side for some time, but never more than that. It was actually Emersav who connected the dots first on this point. Until today, we had suspected they concealed a child; never had any evidence. They were a clever pair. Not clever enough, but clever."

My father. My mother. He looks down at the holograph tucked next to his sensor display.

"The connection to the Xolians, the flying style, the elegant creativity of the attack patterns, the intuitive battle awareness, and especially the unorthodox, advanced starfighter technology—it is nearly a perfect match," Emersav summarizes as if reading a text book (to Dracula). "As is the primary weakness."

I was five years old.

"Would you like to know what that weakness is?" Heesor exults.

Konran doesn't reply. He knows instinctively what the answer will be. He allows his Sparrowhawk to continue its current course despite the knowledge, skirting the Miratans and closing the gap on the *Gamma.* The Rezakars loom across the urban landscape like gleaming, chevron-shaped silver daggers, poised to plunge through the heart of Maehn Arziban. Their substantial forms cast dark shadows on the earth below, darkening kilometers from sunlight. Their guns pound the *Gamma.*

"He must defend those he loves," Emersav concludes, "and therefore may be manipulated at will upon this fulcrum."

"Aaaagghh!" Konran yells in frustration, pulling up on his flight stick so his Sparrowhawk gains altitude. He blazes upward at top speed, ticking off kilometers until exiting the thermosphere.

"You've already lost, my boy," Heesor speaks consolingly. "Your defensive system has been compromised."

Two Nicransin cruisers materialize above him, converting from ghostlike outlines into crisp silhouettes. Their alligator-like forms appear to slither as they rush toward Konran's gnat of a starfighter.

"You have no options. Give up now, and we'll let your friends live," Heesor tempts.

"Konran!" Granicks's voice crackles in, severely scattered by static. "Hold out for a few more minutes! We've got help incoming!"

"My, your captain is persistent—I applaud him for even managing to break through our jamming at all," Heesor leans into the smarmy kudos. "Do you think we don't already know of the reinforcements coming from Maehn Kahlikstan at this very moment to your 'rescue'?" He lengthens the final word, emphasizing its futility.

Konran's Sparrowhawk reaches the apex of its climb, and he turns, reacquiring the point of action far below.

"Let me be clear: neither the Kahlikstani forces nor the entirety of the Arzibanian Collective pose a threat to us," Heesor boasts. "You have no idea what you're facing, Konran. Give up now, and your remaining friends need not be destroyed."

Konran finds his mark below. Maneuvering on thrusters, he aligns himself with the target. And his Sparrowhawk feels an external tug—the Nicransin tractor beams had reached him.

"Hahaha! We have him!" Heesor preens. "Emersav, kill them all!"

"YOU! CANNOT! HAVE! THEM!" Konran screams.

He doesn't wait for the Nicransins to pull him in, he doesn't wait for Heesor's reply, he doesn't even fire back to break their grasp. Rather, sighting his Sparrowhawk—his dad's Sparrowhawk—on the Rezakar pair far below, Konran slams his thruster, tearing free of the beam as it coalesces around him. Then, shoving fundamental atmospheric reentry protocol to the curbside, he dives straight down.

"Reengage CFS," he orders his computer as the air around his hull rapidly superheats.

"The CFS has been irreparably damaged," the computer says in its pleasant way, displaying the familiar set of warning messages.

"Fix it—whatever you have left, use it," Konran demands.

"Attempting to bypass CFS damage may destabilize the ship," the ship replies. "System failure is likely."

"Risk acknowledged. Do it, anyway!" Konran utters as the drag on his left wing mounts. The hull there is glowing white, with a vapor trail gushing behind it.

"Acknowledged," the computer replies. "Reengaging."

Kilometers hurtle, but Konran holds. The Rezakars grow from specks to baseballs to hover-vehicles to sinister battle cruisers before him, but even this fades from view as superheated atmosphere grows to block out his visual filtration system. Navigating by sensors alone, he nears the limit of the Rezakar's

340

shield projection zone. And, his hands and feet full perceiving the task laid before them, Konran closes his eyes.

His Sparrowhawk punches through the nearest Rezakar's shields with bloody knuckles leaking fiery contrails all the way back to outer space. The atmosphere entrained around his craft explodes upon impact, sending a shockwave that only he outpaces. Sparks flash as CFS energy crackles maniacally around him, licking outward in frenzied, diabolical madness. The weight of accelerative force presses against Konran, and blood drains from his face and torso despite his life-support system's best efforts. But Konran holds to the controls, arcing his Sparrowhawk within the Rezakar's shield projection zone by blind intuition alone.

And then he inverts the weapons system and goes to work.

CHAPTER 22

Memories flood him as the Sparrowhawk's megacannon unleashes upon the Rezakar.

There was the time, at age five, when he first encountered a starfighting simulator. He had watched an older boy lose repeatedly to a Rezakar, torn to pieces by its fishbone swarms.

He always made the same mistake, trying to take out the plasma cannons first.

Konran arcs beneath the Rezakar, feigning the boy's mistake by angling for the ventral plasma cannon deck. The fishbone tubes open, and he reacts, skidding his Sparrowhawk sideways at audacious velocity. He blasts the ports shut, whipping around as his fiery arc takes him close to the Arzibanian cityscape below him. A satisfying set of internal shudders shake the Rezazar as he continues his loop around the giant beast.

He remembers the first time he saved enough money to plug himself into a veracitonic simulator. It was the only such device with a true-to-life biophysical rendering system within a half day's walk from the glorified orphanage he grew up in. He had been seven, and only had enough money to play one round, which he lost quickly before making the disheartened return on foot.

I didn't trust the Sparrowhawk's life-support system enough at first, he recalls, allowing himself to whip around the Rezakar with velocity barely attenuated from the atmospheric dive. He takes out the Rezakar's dorsal fishbone tubes as he passes over the top side of the craft, not giving the Nolvarics inside time to react to the implications of his attack. Until moments ago, they hadn't even considered him a threat. Now their ventral and dorsal fishbone tubes shuddered in ruination.

Memories of hundreds of hover-bus rides meld together, journeys Konran made over the ensuing years from money scraped together in order to enjoy more than one round at the veracitonic simulator.

Konran zips back toward the Rezakar's ventral side like a comet. The plasma cannons would be charged by now. He remembers the hours he had spent practicing to defeat such weapons, the extra chores he doled as favors to the boys who covered for his extended, late-night absences. It had taken effort to get a handle on the plasma ball launchers.

And plasma ball launchers were always best to hit when hot.

Konran arrests his speed at the edge of the Rezakar, slowing suddenly before passing from its dorsal to ventral side. A set of maneuvering thrusters on his left wing give out under extreme forces, rocking him off course with claps of smoke and sparks. But Konran adjusts easily, and the plasma balls flash past him prematurely, expecting his former velocity. He realigns himself and unleashes his own burst of thunder into a launcher which had yet to fire. Under the same chain reaction as the cannon Konran hit with the gun-craft on Y25LM90, the entire launch deck explodes with destabilized energy.

The hover-bus rides had proffered more than just turns on the simulator, and Konran recalls the autobiographies, histories, and documentaries he watched so many times on library-loaned retinal-projection lenses. After his twentieth checkout, a kind librarian had given him a pair to keep. Now, here in his father's Sparrowhawk, his mind courses with memory of those accounts, settling upon Commander Vurumira Patalun's masterful attacks during the Battle of Celsis.

Once she knocked the plasma launchers out, the rest of the guns couldn't track her at such close range.

The Rezakar's ventral side now cleared of plasma launchers, Konran gets down to the dirty work. His Sparrowhawk darts about, releasing plasmic energy into every nuance of the surface: shield projectors, sensor hubs, weapon hard points, and straight into the raw, glistening hull itself. Everything has to go. Battle damage mounts as Konran systematically peels the Rezakar down for the decisive blow. And then two more Sparrowhawks swoop in to join him.

"You ... attention ... incoming ... now..." Ace's semi-coherent voice hums into Konran's comm through a non-jammable hard laser link between their Sparrowhawks. The Wildlynx leaders add

343

their own blasts to the Rezakar's hull before sprinting off across the moon. Konran understands.

There are more Nolvarics incoming.

He disengages, following Ace and Valkyrie away from the Rezakar. The Nolvaric cruiser hangs pathetically in the air behind him, ravaged, burning, and listing gracelessly. Smoke gushes from more than thirty holes in its once silvery hull. Ten kilometers away distant, the Rezakar's sister rushes to its aide—and then they both explode in a massive fireballs.

"And now I'm out of tesseracts," Revenshal's voice hums in on its own laser link.

Konran looks back at the destruction, peering through his Sparrowhawk with helmet-enhanced vision as if the body of the craft were not there. Not seeing the *Gamma*, Konran searches his sensors. At last he finds it: crashed on the ground, smoking heavily itself, having been pounded from the air.

"They had me done, kid," Revenshal says with a weary voice, "only a few shots from dead. Your crazy kamikaze dive saved my neck. I see what Granicks sees in you."

"You think that matters?" Heesor's snarling voice bites into Konran' ear. "There is no escape. Your friends will still die."

"People," Granicks's voice crackles with halting static. "Heesor … tap … links. Urgent…"

Konran soars forward, his Sparrowhawk thrashing clumsily behind Ace's and Valkyrie's, away from the dead Rezakars.

"Yes, I have you trapped," Heesor growls. "What did you expect? Toys? I control the military."

Fresh waves of enemies surge toward them: Rezakars, Nicransins, Evarizs, Askeras, Miratans, Huoxings, Shandians, and the *Tartaglia*, all converging on Konran's location.

"May I, Minister?" Emersav's oil interrupts Heesor's vitriol.

Ace and Valkyrie are breaking for outer space, attempting to outrun the Nolvaric pursuit. Konran sticks on their tail, limping at best speed after his friends.

"Certainly," Heesor replies without emotion. "Finish this."

Konran's long-range sensors show an armada approaching from the direction of Maehn Arziban's cousin, Maehn Kahlikstan.

There they are!

"Shivari 2 and 3," Emersav states arrogantly, "concentrate fire on the Xolian mountain estate. Remove it from the map. Shivari 1, 4, and 5, dispatch the Kahlikstani threat. Tankari 7, relieve us of the *Nova Scotia*'s *Gamma* cutter. All remaining forces: obtain Andacellos. And just to be certain, Krona Task Force Epsilon, full jump now."

Konran watches sensors helplessly as Nolvaric ships move to execute orders.

They're all upgraded—all superior to their normal specs, he observes.

Another kamikaze atmospheric dive wouldn't work against one more enemy ship, let alone so many. Konran scours his brain, working to find something—anything—to escape this trap. Heesor wasn't at all threatened by the incoming forces from Maehn Kahlikstan, but there were no other reinforcements, no other options. Konran makes his choice, and his fingers tighten around his flight stick—the real fight was only just beginning.

I hope Maehn Kahlikstan is up to the fight, he thinks, angling toward the Kahlikstani armada.

Then Konran's long-range scanner erupts with new signatures. A dozen ships appear in front of him, outside Maehn Arziban's atmosphere but inside its NAC-support radius—right in the path of the Kahlikstani forces.

The Nolvarics jumped in even more ships. Konran's eyes go wide at the sight.

The fresh Nolvarics engage immediately, and two Kahlikstani ships wink off Konran's sensor display. Then four. Then seven. Then ten. Some turn to flee, but few escape the withering attack.

It happened so fast.

Konran can feel the noose tightening around him.

We're out of options.

Ace and Valkyrie arc with the curvature of Maehn Arziban, angling away from the Nolvarics toward free space. Konran tries to cue his laser link system to communicate with them, but it fails to transmit. Far below him, a fishbone swarm slams into the grounded *Gamma*.

"NOOOO!" he yells, fighting against the urge to turn back. A plethora of enemy starfighters prowl back there. His trigger finger itches, and the desire for vengeance wins out. He turns his Sparrowhawk, his first target already acquired.

"Konran ... hold ... backup..." Granicks crackles in, barely discernible amidst the static.

Konran stops his attack run, diverting his Sparrowhawk upward, back toward space. Anger boils as he scans the burning, empty crater below. The *Gamma*, and everything within a kilometer of it, had been destroyed, leaving nothing but an enormous, rubble-filled crater. Tears fall freely along his cheeks, and he gasps in anguish, but he follows Granicks's order.

"You started this war," Heesor speaks into his ear again. "Whether you like it or not. You could have stopped this. Now you bear responsibility for your friends' destruction."

"No, I didn't!" Konran yells back. "I saved people that day—from you and your scum! I'll do it again today! And if I can't, I'll take you out trying!"

"Such harsh words from such an insignificant player," Heesor censures. "I gave you your chance. I gave Revenshal a chance. I gave your captain a chance. I have been more than merciful today. Do you know who just jumped into the system? Until now you've been fighting mercenaries, placeholders, brainless oafs. If you couldn't defeat them, you wouldn't be worth my time. But now you face true warriors, and your friends will be killed. And you will be mine."

Konran breathes hard, struggling to compose himself. His hand shakes on the flight stick. His fingers itch for action. His entire body desires to descend back into the fray, wishing to fight for his friends.

But the odds were impossible, and there was nothing left to do.

Nothing left except to follow orders.

He holds fast to his course, tailing Ace and Valkyrie around Maehn Arziban and into space, their vector the only direction that didn't have some Nolvaric lurking at its end. Konran watches the enemy focalize toward him. Any remaining Kahlikstani forces have turned back to protect their own moon.

"Kon ... back ... ming," Granicks's staticky voice repeats. Konran's sensors pick up three Nolvaric ships posted on the other side of the planet, ringing Ruzcier's compound. Soon they, too, would accomplish their objective.

Why me? Konran wonders at last. *I didn't ask for any of this.*

"There is no backup incoming," Heesor crows, invading Konran's thoughts yet again. "You will be within tractor beam range within 1.2 minutes. You are damaged, limping like a wounded animal, and outgunned three hundred to one. You have no chance."

An Askera fighter wing was drawing ahead of them. Judging from the angle of approach, these Nolvarics were from the newest forces—the "true warriors."

Konran watches them, yearning to blast their smug carcasses out of his sight. But Ace and Valkyrie curve away, fleeing the impending attack.

Konran considers them. He considers Granicks's staticky words. He considers the Askeras' approach.

We can't circle this moon more than once without being caught. And they'll get us well before that.

But Ace and Valkyrie don't vacillate. They had the same information as Konran. They all knew the inevitable. He elects to follow them, trusting in his friends and distancing himself as much as possible from the enemies. Above the glowing bubble of atmosphere enshrouding Maehn Arziban, Nolvaric capital ships loom larger and larger, shimmering against Summanus's blackness.

Static crackles into Konran's comm, Granicks's words completely inaudible.

"It seems your captain has some last words," Heesor sneers.

"Granicks?" Konran asks weakly, addressing the static and not Heesor.

More static.

"Captain?" Konran tries again.

Heesor laughs in response, a dark, hateful sound. "Do you think he could persist long with his transmissions? My forces unraveled his encryption—a hack job, mind you. We destroyed his hastily constructed transmission points. We will fully destroy him in short order, just as we have done with his entire force. He never proved more than a nuisance—never more than a scratch to my dragon.

We had his communication protocols sliced from the beginning—we heard everything, knew everything, saw everything. He was a fool to stand in our way. We came for you, Andacellos, and would have let the rest go. I showed Granicks mercy. I showed him restraint, but he dared to stand in my way. His actions, and yours, Andacellos, have only stirred the pot, only furthered our plans. You could never stop me, could never stand before the might of the Krona, which I wield at will against you. You will be mine today, or you will die. Nothing you or he can do can change that."

"I have just one question for you, then, Minister," Darius Granicks voice suddenly comes loud and clear into Konran's comm.

"What is this?" Heesor demands. "How is he doing this?"

"If you defeated me so fully, why did I let you hear my plans?"

* * * * *

Chanziu Guan makes his way through the tunnel system below the nondescript Arzibanian home. It had been fifteen minutes since he had penetrated the façade, subverted the guards, eluded the top-layer detection systems, and entered the heart of the secret facility. He knew time was running out, and the guards down here were wise to his presence. There had been no way to avoid it. Some jobs were simply like that, and Chanziu presses forward without regret, toward the target.

Captain Granicks had persuaded him to bring Zenara with him—an unprecedented step for the solitary spy, but Chanziu had relented, agreeing to the captain's plan more out of necessity to be moving than for its tactical nuances. Cassio, the marine, awaited outside, hovering around the corner in their escape vehicle. Both the marine and the Xolian were battered from the battle, but modern medicine had worked its magic, and they were still in fighting form. And when time was of the essence, you made do with what you had.

And time was of the essence.

Chanziu nods across the dim tunnel, making eye contact with the Xolian woman. Zenara steps into the tunnel, disguised in the clothes of one of the guards they had "humanely encountered."

The clothing fits horribly—the man had been both shorter and wider than Zenara—but that didn't matter. All they needed was a moment.

"Did you see him? Did you see him?" Zenara shouts frantically at a pair of Arzibanian guards, running down the tunnel toward them. "He was here."

She stops, breathing hard, playing the part well. "He got Qumar and Zensk already. I thought he got you as well. This guy knows what he's doing."

"Who are you?" one of the guards barks warily, raising his weapon toward Zenara. The ID badge Chanziu hastily implanted in her arm had allowed the Xolian to access the tunnel without getting paralyzed by the bioelectric arresting system, but there had been no time to configure an actual disguise.

"The ID reads Qumar," the other guard shouts. "She's the imposter. Shoot her!"

Chanziu drops from the ceiling above the guards, having used Zenara's distraction to crawl down its length, invisible. The guards fall instantly before Chanziu, unconscious but otherwise unharmed.

"Take these," Chanziu says, tossing their weapons to Zenara, "and bar the tunnel. No one can enter until I leave."

She nods, taking the weapons and running back down the tunnel. Chanziu cuts an ID badge from one of the guards. Then, stepping into the room they had been guarding, Chanziu speaks four words, holding a device to his throat.

"*Azatut'yun yerknk'um yndmisht.*" The voice is not his own, belonging rather to the director of Arzibanian planetary defense, Kiril Nevrinian.

Another door opens, and Chanziu steps into the control room.

"*Cherangi!*" Zenara shouts the Xolian word for "company," her voice echoing behind him. The harsh reports of blaster fire follow as Chanziu sets himself to work.

In truth, the facility had been both well designed and well hidden. Had Chanziu intended to penetrate such a facility for his own purposes, he would have needed at least a day on the planet to pin down its location, and another day to plot the deed. As it

349

was, Ruzcier Exeunt had already found the secret facility—the Xolian "businessman" of the more astute variety.

What little else Chanziu already knew about the facility had been enough, and he had pieced the full picture together while en route to the target.

He had defeated the system of mazes beneath the otherwise nondescript home in less than a minute, using the last of his supply of nanobots in the process. The nanobots had combed the maze for him, providing an optimal path through its twists and turns and reconnaissance on the deeper security systems. Chanziu was glad he had used the bots sparingly when searching for Andacellos back in Ruzcier's compound.

Now he hacks. His hands fly across multiple input terminals as his mind processes data from as many holo-displays. He pulls himself deeper and deeper through the intricate labyrinth that was the Arzibanian mutual defense network. He falls into a trance as he does so.

Trusting fully in Zenara's protection, Chanziu enters the mental state ingrained in him by Saturnese intelligence instructors as best suited for high-speed data processing. His eyes don't move, his eyelids don't blink, data just sinks straight into his subconscious. His hands flash faster, and Chanziu plunges ever further toward his target. Security protocol melts. System warnings crumble. Obstacles divide asunder. It was crude, and the path would invariably be detected. In fact, at most Chanziu would have less than a minute after reaching his cyber destination.

His hands slow and his mind re-attunes its normal rhythms and his eyes regain their focus. Chanziu was in, and he wastes no time. He assumes full control. He designates targets, and an eternity of seconds later, the system confirms all targets locked.

The window would close in a matter of moments.

"Captain, I'm in. Targets locked. We have thirty seconds at most."

If he didn't hear back, Chanziu was going to make the hard decision himself—although it wasn't going to be hard. If there was a way to save Konran, Chanziu could never have conjured a better one than this.

Adding to his lengthy list of impossible accomplishments for the day, Chanziu Guan had just hacked Maehn Arziban's network of NACs.

* * * * *

"Do it," Captain Granicks speaks simply.

Ace's and Valkyrie's Sparrowhawks divert immediately from their current course toward open space, instead turning head-on to meet the incoming swarm of enemy starfighters. Konran follows suit, not knowing what had caused their change in tactics.

And then, in a demonstration of power unknown to the galaxy before that day, sixty geyser-like columns of refulgent energy simultaneously annihilate every single Nolvaric Rezakar, Evariz, and Nicransin in the region, as well as the two Saturnese Huoxings and Heesor's *Tartaglia*. From Konran's vantage above the atmosphere, he witnesses at least forty of the explosions as if forty suns had suddenly grown and died at the same instant.

The afterimage glows in Konran's eyes, fading slowly despite the dedicated work of Ruzcier's regenerative lenses.

"Great shot, Valk," Ace's voice crackles into Konran's ear as communications suddenly restore. "You got the lead Askera."

"I had him in my eye for the past three minutes," Valkyrie crackles back.

The pilots' voices jog Konran into action, and he spurs his Sparrowhawk after his friends. The NACs had taken out the enemy capital ships, but not the starfighters. Konran's radioactive duck of a Sparrowhawk hurtles itself at the remaining enemy craft, guns blazing. Before any serious counterattack can be mounted, Konran, Ace, and Valkyrie wipe their twenty-three Askera pursuers from existence, the astonished hunters falling languidly to the celerity of the prey.

Without ado or time for an adieu, and at the behest of Captain Granicks, the trio of Sparrowhawks heads toward the solar warp margin.

They pass Arzibanian defenses along the way, and Konran makes out NACs as well as the heavily armed orbital defense stations hanging in the blackness, their ghostlike apparitions reflecting tenuous, fifty-seven-hour-old light rays from the sun back to his eyes. None so much as acknowledge the trio's presence.

Before they reach the warp margin, Ace and Valkyrie stop their Sparrowhawks. Konran follows suit, unsure what was going on.

"We've reached the coordinates, Captain," Ace speaks. "Tell us what you want us to do from here."

"Take a ride," Granicks replies, and suddenly a large warp cruiser appears in front of them, manifesting out of pure spatial darkness into physical form not more than two hundred meters from their position. Its hull is bulbous yet sleek, the craft long and lithe before them—with thrice the length and twice the girth of the *Nova Scotia*.

"Holy sparking feculence," Ace blurts in concert with the apparition. "Wait, are these Bestiphans?"

"They're Revenshal's contacts," Granicks explains. "He negotiated this with them on the contingency that we won. Salazar's patched them into our comm channel."

"Come, friends," a soothing monotone voice speaks into Konran's comm. A hangar bay opens on the side of the ship, its welcoming light pouring into the vacuum of empty space. Three docking beacons emerge, guiding the way in.

"Here goes nothing," Ace says, turning toward the ship.

"Thank you, friends," Valkyrie adds, "we are most grateful for your hospitality."

"Yes, thank you," Konran says, passing the docking buoys and waiting his turn to enter behind Ace and Valkyrie.

"You are welcome," the voice answers. "Your feats will surely go spoken within our halls for generations. It is with gratification we greet you so forth."

Konran guides his Sparrowhawk through the seamless hangar bay opening. His craft touches down on a shiny, unobstructed platform within. No other craft are visible, save their three.

He searches for a moment for the switch to raise his cockpit, finally giving up and speaking the words, "Open cockpit."

It raises, and he removes his helmet. Stashing it between his legs, he collects his parent's hologragh and holo-cube. He stands, unhooking his life-support system, and looks out at his

Sparrowhawk. She looks beautiful: torn, bent, broken and smoking with as much glory as any starfighter ever had.

A step extends from the platform beneath him, hovering placidly. He steps out, unsteady at first, but the platform moves politely, granting him balance.

He touches down and instantly finds himself in Ace's and Valkyrie's arms. The three of them stand there together for a long moment, laced in mutual embrace.

"We did it, man, we did it, man," Ace repeats. The pilot's tears and smile flow freely as his short, black dreadlocks plaster his forehead.

"Anytime you want," Valkyrie says through her own set of tears.

"Want what?" Konran asks, relishing if not fully comprehending the moment.

"Kribasa," Valkyrie replies. "Anytime you want, I'll make you some."

Ace gags audibly, loosening his grip and ending the hug.

"Ah, man," he groans, "you had to go and ruin the moment."

CHAPTER 23

"We have multiple reports of a massive battle taking place over Maehn Arziban this morning," a newswoman recounts. "Initial eyewitness accounts describe an intense encounter between USFN, Saturnese, Arzibanian, Xolian, and Nolvaric forces, which culminated in a mass discharge of Arzibanian no-admittance cannons at 2:17 a.m. Earth Standard Time. As you can see behind me, the densely populated planetoid received severe damage as a result of the action, with casualties estimated in the thousands to tens of thousands."

Gaared Jariksson, leader of the Tiyaka Reservists, sits in the small, austere room within the space station he currently called home. Orbiting the super-earth Raschon-2, which in turn orbited Barnard's Star, the space station had been given to him by the Raschonian government in gratitude for his actions delivering the system from recent Nolvaric attacks. It wasn't much, but the Tiyaka Reservists had found a new home.

Gaared sits there, considering news reports as one after another stream into his battle room. Their holographic projections fill the space, mixing in frantic hysteria as every news agency strives to convey something special about the Battle of Maehn Arziban.

"Nolvaric technology has advanced beyond anything we anticipated," a military analyst states. "Their ability to jump multiple warships within the gravity well of massive bodies like Summanus is unprecedented and unexpected. We as a solar system have collectively fallen behind our enemy while deluding ourselves that we were winning."

Gaared's chief pilots chatter aggressively between themselves, even shouting as they work to distill news opinion from actual fact. Two pilots argue whether a segment of holo-footage was synthesized or not, their hands mimicking the holographic replay of a single Sparrowhawk destroying swarms of Nolvarics within the junglelike forest of Arzibanian skyscrapers.

"Konran Andacellos has been confirmed as a participant in today's fighting," another news anchor reports. "Top sources within the United Space Federation, speaking on the condition of anonymity, suggested Andacellos may have been involved in a detailed plot to subvert USFN defenses in order to facilitate a second Nolvaric invasion of the inner planets."

Some broadcasts proclaim Konran's innocence, others declare him a hero of the grandest proportions. Others yet doubt his participation in the battle at all, questioning whether it made sense for him to be involved both at Y25LM90 and Maehn Arziban within such a short period of time. The more cynical doubt Konran's existence altogether, asserting that it wouldn't be the first time the government had fabricated an identity in order to mold public opinion according to their own desires.

Gaared's pilots argue and analyze, growing in animated debate, but he just sits, aware of his pilots, aware of the conflicting, oft-sensationalized reports, aware of his own mental efforts to synthesize significance out of everything.

"We're here on the deck of the *Estrellas Vigilantes*, which just arrived on the scene at Maehn Arziban," an excited reporter proclaims, his perfect hair blowing in Maehn Arziban's artificial wind. "This is a remarkable moment for the respective governments—representing the first time since Maehn Arziban declared independence that a USFN military force of this magnitude has received official invitation into the reclusive colony."

It had been twenty years since Gaared left behind his career as a colonel in the Fighter Defense branch of the United Space Federation Navy.

"This just in," an excited woman states. "No more than ten hours since the conclusion of the Battle of Maehn Arziban, we have confirmed reports of Nolvaric strikes on both Venus and Mars. From what we can gather, the Nolvarics jumped in using the same technology witnessed at Maehn Arziban, launched brief assaults on USFN defense facilities, and jumped out before significant counterattacks could be mounted."

It had been twenty years since Gaared took a group of forty like-minded pilots out of the solar system, away from the molasses of bureaucracy, far from the futility of red tape and the inanity of politics, to a place where they could actually do something useful.

"The Saturnese are to blame!" an angry politician proclaims from another news outlet. "Their secretive, militaristic nature has long been suspect, and their disruptive efforts into the trans-solar network have long been established. What more proof do we need than two of their own Huoxing warships jumping into the Arzibanian system with the Nolvarics? This is clear collusion. It is clear cause for war. Yet we waste our time driveling like fools while our enemies mount further attacks against us."

Life may be cold and dark outside Solar System One, but to Gaared, at least life out here meant he was living—meant he was making a difference.

"This just in: Captain Darius Granicks, commanding officer of the USFN Riot-class cruiser *Nova Scotia*, which was involved in heavy fighting at Maehn Arziban, has released a message. We are pleased to bring you this breaking news first, from CNSTC."

"This is Captain Darius Granicks of the *Nova Scotia*," a bedridden man speaks through a fuzzy hologram. Gaared recognizes the eyes of a warrior therein. Suddenly, and for the first time since news of the attack broke, every news outlet is broadcasting the same footage.

"My forces participated yesterday in military engagement against what appeared to be a combined Nolvaric-Saturnese force," Darius Granicks continues. "This was not as it appeared, however. USFN Minister of Defense Vadic Heesor orchestrated the attack with the sole aim of capturing Konran Andacellos. Minister Heesor was in league with an advanced military force known as the Krona, which has been preparing for decades to strike at and overthrow the inner planets. I know this due to the efforts of a heroic Saturnese intelligence agent who participated in the fighting on our behalf and proved instrumental in preserving both Konran's life and his freedom. I have provided battle footage as well as recordings and transcripts involving Minister Heesor, which more than clearly demonstrate the truth of the matter."

Subsequent footage shows Heesor ordering Granicks's execution and depicts assaultbots ravaging an Arzibanian mountain estate. One poignant piece provides point-of-view holo-video from one of Granicks's pilots, known as Valkyrie, who had managed to both record and survive the battle.

Silence falls over Gaared's Tiyaka pilots as they watch Valkyrie fight USFN Dronehawks after her captain had been shot by assaultbots. Then she charges with two other Sparrowhawks and destroys a fleet of Rezakars with a well-placed missile salvo, continuing on to battle overwhelming Nolvaric forces on the Arzibanian moon below.

Stillness reigns as Valkyrie flees two Rezakars, she and her wingman trapped near the moon's surface. Then a lone Sparrowhawk plunges through the Arzibanian atmosphere, contrails bleeding fire and smoke, straight for the nearest Rezakar. It falls out of view before flashing back in, whipping around the Rezakar and blasting it with holes. Valkyrie and her wingman race to assist their comrade. Communications are jammed, but they get there in time, and the pilot escapes with them before more Nolvaric fighters bear down on the position.

Granicks's message continues with Heesor's mocking voice, his arguments with Konran, his willingness to destroy USFN personnel, Granicks's final challenge, and the minister's ultimate demise beneath the NACs.

News blurbs explode in response to the broadcast, dissecting every nuance, decrying the captain for warping out of the system instead of remaining to give the statement in person, applauding his admirable bravery in exposing the scheme, screaming in outrage at his subversion and unlawful utilization of the Arzibanian NACs, finding fault and veracity within the same words, decomposing the syllables and frames until any meaning all but dissolves.

Gaared's pilots clamor in response, growing in both intensity and volume, pointing, standing, shouting, gesturing, arguing. Gaared, however, just sits—aware that his lower lip had become pinched slightly between his teeth, aware that his pulse had risen within his chest, aware that his gaze had grown distant, outward, into the depths of the Milky Way galaxy.

Aware that his time in the new space station was over, Gaared simply sits, allowing his pilots to reach the conclusion on their own.

357

EPILOGUE

"Hey, man, you've been in there forever." Ace's voice is muffled behind the sleek, sliding, steel panel that was the door to Konran's room.

Konran arises, picking up his holo-cube from its place on the crisp, white hover-desk and crossing his simple yet sumptuous quarters within the Bestiphan warp cruiser. The door slides open, revealing Ace. The pilot inclines his head at the holo-cube.

"You memorized it yet?"

"I think I had it memorized three days ago," Konran acknowledges. "But I keep watching it. It's all I have of them, you know?"

"Yeah, man, it's cool," Ace replies. "You gotta take your time. I try to tell them, but, you know..."

Konran raises an eyebrow. "I missed dinner again, didn't I?" He still hadn't adjusted to the Bestiphan thirty-hour day, or their customary—that would be mandatory—group gatherings at mealtimes.

"You could say that," Ace says. "I was about to tell them to send meals to your room, but Val stopped me—said I would offend them."

"She's probably right," Konran replies. "Again."

Ace rolls his eyes. "Watching her you'd think it was easy."

"So, how bad was it?" Konran asks.

"Not too bad, man. The captain is figuring us out, but he was for certain disappointed. It's like you spend three days on a Bestiphan warp cruiser and you're expected to know their every custom."

"I should set an alarm for the meals," Konran says, "but I couldn't figure out their interfaces and kind of just quit. I get so wrapped up with the holo-cube. After everything went down the way it did, I just need some time, you know?"

"Man, you are preaching to the circus," Ace replies.

Konran laughs. "I think you mean the choir."

"What, you're singing to the circus?"

Konran laughs more. "Yeah, singing to the circus is about right." He often couldn't tell if Ace's verbal gaffs were satirical or otherwise.

"Anyway, Val's enrolled us in tutoring. She figures we need the help before we ruin all this hospitality for ourselves."

"Yep," Konran replies, "right again."

Now Ace laughs. "Man, did you ever think..." he trails off with a sigh and his eyes go distant, searching for the words. "I sure didn't," he finally concludes. There was no need to finish the thought; there was simply too much.

"No," Konran says, sitting back and sighing toward the ceiling. "I can barely wrap my head around any of it. I kind of stopped trying. It just is what it is, you know?"

"Yeah, man," Ace replies. "I mean, we're on our way to Bestipha, after tearing Maehn Arziban apart, violating something like thirty-seven intersolar laws, and nearly starting an all-out war. It's not every day you have a price on your head from your own government, let alone three."

Bestipha, a rocky super-earth, orbited the star Gliese 667C in the constellation Scorpio. Due to the existence of liquid water on its surface and an abundance of rocky neighbor planets in the system, Bestipha had been identified as an early candidate for colonization. The twenty-three-light-year distance from Earth had proved daunting for early planetary travelers, however, and Bestipha wasn't colonized until exasperated inhabitants of the Orion Belt left their colonies, intent on distancing themselves from the ravages of the Orion Wars.

After five years of effort, including the loss of an entire warp cruiser on the initial attempt, the colonists, known collectively as the Bestiphan Refugees, reached and established the Bestiphan Republic. In the ensuing years, the republic had expanded to include two nearby sister stars, Gliese 667A and 667B, making it the first system to be colonized entirely of non-Earth native humans. Aside from Bestiphan forays for trade and gambling, the system had since become completely self-sustaining.

"We're lucky the Bestiphans got us," Konran says. "I think they take pleasure in the fact that we're essentially outlaws now. That, and our embodiment of the warrior quintessence."

"They sure love how we embody that 'warrior quintessence.'"

"Ace! Are you bringing him or not?" Val's voice shouts from around the corner. They turn to see Val standing there, hands on hips, laser beams crisping them from her eyes.

"Val, hey, yeah!" Ace replies hastily. "We just got to chatting again. It's been such an ordeal, you know."

"Your ordeal is just about to get started," she says. "Come on, Granicks wants to talk with us."

"Granicks?" Konran repeats.

"Cap made contact?" Ace adds eagerly.

"Yeah, Salazar worked something up and patched him in. You would know this if you paid any attention during dinner."

"Val. My brain. I tried," Ace complains. "I can't focus on so many pleasantries for so long."

"Your tutoring sessions start tonight," she scolds, walking briskly in front of them.

Ace glances at Konran, fear in his eyes. Again, the glance is so real that Konran has a hard time deciphering whether Ace is sincere. He assumes satire, making his own terrified face by raising his eyebrows.

They follow Val through the corridor without further exchange. Valkyrie, whose actual name was Valerie Melendez, did not have patience for overt stupidity. Once you crossed that line in her mind, you had to earn your way back.

Not that anything else is new, Konran surmises.

They reach the meal hall and Konran turns to enter, but Val waves him on with a "huh uh."

They continue walking down the wide-arched, immaculate spacecraft corridor—a luxury of luxuries in the generally confined quarters known to space travel. Val finally stops, leading them into a small, office-like room full of communications equipment. Its entrance is crafted with the customary Bestiphan arch, with thick, gunmetal trim reaching a point at the apex. The walls inside the room, though not ornate by comparison to the dining hall, exude a practical classiness that Konran's old apartment in the Apogees never reached.

The Bestiphan captain, Shir Vunu, awaits them, a tall man, with characteristic long Bestiphan cheekbones and narrow shoulders. Three Bestiphan technicians operate communications equipment next to their captain. Konran can only tell them apart from the captain because of their different uniforms.

Konran salutes him, nodding deeply and touching the knuckle of his index finger to his forehead—like taking a drink without the cup and aiming for the top of his face. Shir Vunu returns the salute, performing the gesture against his chest rather than his forehead.

"Captain," Konran apologizes, "I'm sorry I missed dinner again. I am not ungrateful for your hospitality. Valerie has arranged for tutoring sessions to help me improve my behavior."

"It is no matter, Mr. Konran," Captain Vunu replies. "I was hasty in my original judgments, and all is forgiven. Your lack of understanding is to be expected, which I did not consider at first. As you know, assertive judgment is a highly prized Bestiphan skill, of which I particularly pride myself, for without it I could not have risen to the station I now call my own. I am also aware of the tutoring sessions Ms. Valerie has arranged for yourself and Mr. Ace, and I myself have orchestrated for our linguist to educate you. In addition, your participation in our meal arrangements will likewise be most anticipated and appreciated, of course, as you are able."

"Yes, sir, thank you," Konran replies. He gives Ace a nudge with his elbow, and the pilot's eyes come back into focus.

"Without further delay," Captain Vunu says, "we have established contact with your captain. Crewmen, please initiate communication."

The technicians work their consoles for a moment, and then a holographic projection of Captain Granicks appears. His left arm is in a sling, but he otherwise appears to be well.

"People," he addresses them, "we won't have much time. I'm glad to see you alive and well." He pauses, smiling sadly. "We triumphed over inestimable odds at terrible cost. Your continued

361

survival assures the sacrifice of so many of our comrades was not in vain."

"That traitor, Heesor," Ace spits, suddenly angry. "I should have finished his stupid *Tartaglia* off instead of letting it limp away."

"The galaxy spins as it does, Ace," Granicks replies. "It may not have made a difference if you did. I'm just glad we're alive, and that we're the ones who get to face this evil down. I'm not aware of any other team I would entrust with this job."

"Yes, sir. Right, sir," Ace says. "You can count on that."

"Thank you, Commander," Granicks replies. "So to be frank," he continues, "our enemy is immense. We know nearly nothing about them; however, thanks to the Saturnese spy who assisted you, Konran, we have a strong foundation to build from. For security reasons, I will keep the rest of this briefing to the essentials. Commander Revenshal and most of his crew are with me, as are many of Ruzcier's servants and ground defense personnel. Sadly, Ruzcier's Xarba pilots each perished while attempting to defend his estate from the Nolvaric bombardment."

"Revenshal? How?" Konran asks. "I saw him get hit. How did he make it?"

"Revenshal and his crew abandoned ship after their final tesseract salvo," Granicks explains. "He anticipated the Nolvaric counterattack and forced everyone to sprint away from the area. Let's just say his crew was grateful he demands they keep themselves in top physical condition."

"Ah," Konran replies, relieved at the welcome words. "That's awesome."

At least some of them survived.

"In fact, Konran," Granicks continues, "Revenshal, Ruzcier, and their staff escaped with me because of your PIT."

"Alandie?" Konran says. "He's with you?"

"He and Ms. Rennasent stole themselves a rather fine warp yacht and came looking for you. They found us instead. If not for them, we may not have made it out, since Ruzcier's only other warp yacht—the one you were intended to take—was thoroughly destroyed by Heesor's assaultbots."

"Kyalia came, too?" Konran asks, recalling Cassio laughing at him (and the smell of her hair again).

"The pair did an admirable job," Granicks commends. "With Alandie as our pilot, my group warped to the Kapteyn b system. We will arrive shortly and hope to unite with Ruzcier's nephew, Xubarif. Ruzcier anticipates this will be the case. This leaves us about twenty-nine light-years from Bestipha, which makes coordinating our reunion paramount. We can discuss this further once I reach Kapteyn b and establish more secure communication."

Granicks pauses, allowing a moment for them to consider his words before continuing.

"The trio of Cassio, Chanziu, and Zenara also hijacked a warp yacht after hacking the Arzibanian NACs. They warped on your tail toward the Bestiphan system; however, since optimal warp route parameters to Bestipha are not maintained within standard USFN or Saturnese databases, we estimate they may trail your arrival by a week to a month's time. If we can establish communication with their vessel, the Bestiphans have graciously agreed to provide warp parameters to speed them on their way. But nothing is certain at this point."

Granicks's hologram looks at Konran, Ace, and Valerie in turn, his expression deepening.

"Now, a word of caution. As you are aware, after Maehn Arziban things really heated up in the solar system. USFN and Saturnese forces narrowly avoided confrontation three times in the ensuing day, and Nolvaric forces have been making guerrilla-style jump attacks into the inner solar system ever since. Fortunately, Salazar figured out some nuances of how they manage to jump their ships so close to planets. Evidently, the Nolvarics rely on disguised beacon ships at each target location, which allow them to create a sort of interspatial intertwining between points. This grants them what we suspect to be instantaneous transportation capability between these points, which could be light-years apart. The technology is at least a half century ahead of the established bleeding edge, but at least we have a handle on how they're pulling it off. If not for Lieutenant Vilkoj's sacrifice, which forced the Nolvarics to jump more ships into the Arzibanian system, we never would have figured this out. Once we reach Kapteyn b, Salazar will provide the Bestiphans with details on how to detect and engage any of these jump beacons. The good news is the enemy must physically deposit the beacon in a location before they can jump in any craft. Bestipha should be safe for now, but stay sharp—with this foe, anything is possible."

Konran exchanges glances with the other pilots. This was heavy stuff.

"Due to the security of this transmission," Granicks says, "your orders are limited to the following: You are to develop and maintain relations with your Bestiphan hosts. Do everything in your power to understand your enemy, and protect yourselves from them at all costs. We will speak on this in more detail when we establish more secure communication. Excellent work, you three. I hope to speak with you shortly."

Granicks's hologram fades abruptly.

"Man, no time for questions," Ace complains.

"We got enough," Val says. "Thank you, Captain, for preparing this communication," she addresses Shir Vunu.

"It is my pleasure, Ms. Valerie," Vunu replies. "I assure you we will work to establish a more secure means of communication at the shortest interval possible. As envoy of the Bestiphan people in this regard, I reiterate our respect for your courage and warrior quintessence. We are committed to serve and protect you."

"Thank you, Captain," Valerie says, performing the Bestiphan salute with her knuckle to her head. Konran and Ace repeat the gesture. "With your leave, we would like some time to process this information," she adds.

"Certainly, Ms. Valerie. You and your fellow crewmen are welcome to roam the ship as you please."

Captain Vunu departs, the door to the communications room closes, and Konran, Ace, and Valerie are left in the corridor alone. Konran feels Valerie at his side, the pilot suddenly close.

"Konran, how are you?" she asks, the alternate, compassionate side of her personality exuding itself now that the meeting had subsided. Konran was still getting used to the mixture of fire and feather within the pilot: Valerie could switch between them without so much as a catch in her stride.

"I'm good, Val," he says. "It's just been so much to process. Less than a week ago, I was an orphan piloting an astrofreighter—now I'm fleeing the solar system and suddenly have parents to get to know. It's just a holo-cube, but it's all I have of them. From what Heesor said, they were still alive when I was five years old, fighting the same fight we just fought. And Heesor—I know we got him, but the way he spoke of them ... like it was so satisfying..."

Konran trails off, leaning into Valerie as she offers her arm. He realizes she got him rambling, but the feeling isn't one of embarrassment. It was good to talk to your friends.

"Why don't you show us again?" Valerie says, moving the trio toward Konran's room. "You've spent a lot of time alone, and we could use your company, too."

Konran looks at her, turning as they walk. "I didn't think of it that way," he says.

"After Maehn Arziban, we're all we have left now," she replies, her face steeling against a mask of emotion. "Besides," she manages with a soft croak, "Granicks ordered us to learn as much as we can."

The trio passes through the arched, comfortably lit, gently peaked Bestiphan corridor in silence. Konran enters his room first, waving over the sofa, which glides out from its storage location in the wall. The furniture plumps as it arrives, becoming comfortable and plush from flat and angular. Konran waves over his hover-desk next, and they sit, Ace to his left, Valerie to his right. It's tight with all three of them together, but it doesn't feel awkward—more like *family*, he realizes.

The holo-cube hums as he deposits it on the hover-desk. The ambient lighting within the room dims, and the cube emits a stream of light, which solidifies into a man and woman in the air.

Kazrick stands to Linaya's left, his arm around her slender waist. Konran always noticed the look in their eyes first, the tenderness and courage by which he had come to identify them in his still-forming memories and dreams.

"Konran," Linaya begins, and Kaz smiles. "My precious little boy. If you are watching this message, then terrible things have happened. Our plan has failed, and you have lived your life without us, alone in a world foreign and alien." She pauses, closing her eyes as Kaz squeezes her shoulders.

"You are now our last hope for success," she goes on, voice steadying. "You are our greatest hope, our deepest joy, and now, though we are gone, we must ask you to finish the work we have started. Everything depends on this," her voice drops to a whisper, becoming urgent, "for there is more at stake than anyone can possibly imagine, and once you receive this message, it will already be so late. Your gift is the only thing that can stave off the impending disaster."

"You see, my son," his mother continues, "you are more than a boy born to parents through natural means. You embody certain characteristics, chosen carefully, which are designed to combat and bring an end to the threat which faces us all."

"What your mother is trying to say," Kazrick chimes in, "is that she is a sparking genius. And that you are the most fantastic baby in the entire galaxy."

Linaya laughs, nestling a little more beneath Kazrick's arm. "Your father always knows what I need," she says, smiling. "It's just so hard to consider that this may actually be the only way our son knows us," she says.

His mother's emotion always took Konran's breath away, like staring into the eyes of love itself. Valerie gives his arm a light squeeze.

Linaya takes a breath, composing herself. "There is an organization within this galaxy, hidden and evil, known only to the few as the Krona. They have been stealing gifted children, adolescents, and even adults for the past decade at least. They cover up the abductions as accidents or murders, often implicating parties guilty for other crimes as the culprit. They are never seen and never get caught. I myself was abducted by them in a feigned warp accident and taken to a secret facility on the planet Raiota, where I was ultimately saved by your father."

She tightens her side hug on Kazrick before continuing.

"Since then we have dedicated our lives to fighting this enemy. We have dug into their secrets over years and months, and though our efforts have nearly cost our lives, we have scratched the surface deeply enough to comprehend what it is we fight. We

366

understand their methods. We know from where they draw their means. We have pieced together this puzzle from a thousand bits of what otherwise would be unrelated information. And we have contained all we know within this holo-cube, for you, our son, when you are ready, if it so be you are left without us."

Valerie gives Konran another squeeze, and he notices tears spilling down her cheeks. She doesn't wipe them, and Konran doesn't look, but he understands something finally: he had been so focused on his own emotional scars since leaving Maehn Arziban that he had failed to recognize those of his friends. They, too, had lost entire chunks of everything they held dear. They, too, had seen friends fall, helpless to assist in any way. The dawning sense of responsibility ignites like a candle inside his heart, not hot, but illuminating as he reaches out with his arms to either side, pulling the pilots a little bit closer. They weren't just his new friends; he was theirs, too.

"Linaya," Kazrick says, "it's OK. It's all right. You know this is right. Everything will work out. You know it will." He emphasizes the last words by holding fast to her hands and staring into his wife's eyes with conviction. Konran sees therein a man capable of unearthing his mother from the awful, hidden depths of the Raiotan prison.

Linaya peers straight into Konran's eyes. "To be straightforward, my son, we genetically prepared you for the task which lays before you. Due to the extremity of our present circumstance, our means for achieving your genetic alteration have been dissimilar from any others known to the galaxy. It had to be so, or our enemy would have found you and taken you. But we encoded your talents to be hidden and undetectable to your enemies until the time is right. How we did this is beyond the purpose of this message, but suffice it to say that your traits will express themselves fully when the time is right. You will know when the time has come. You are the only being in the galaxy upon which this technology has been utilized—a hero with capacity to rise and face the terrible evil of your day."

"Now, don't think that you're not still human or even our son," Kazrick interjects. "It's not like your genius mother completely altered you in every way—it's more like she took what was already in there and tweaked it to give you what you will need."

Linaya smiles again. "Kaz, I didn't mean that," she says, giving him a hip bump and making his holographic image bounce partially out of view. "But your father is right," she addresses Konran. "You naturally inherited his ability for tactical starfighting warfare, as well as many other traits from each of us. What I have done is like he said: tweak your genomics such that your traits and abilities are accentuated to the necessary levels."

"Spoken like a scientist," Kazrick banters, and Linaya laughs again.

"You'll find a complete description of your genomics within the data package included with this message," Linaya explains, "as well as methods you can employ to efficiently train and hone your skills. You have almost certainly found one of the most simple yet effective means, which involves starfighter simulator training."

"That was my idea," Kazrick adds.

"Yes, it was," Linaya confirms with another smile, "as were many of our best ideas. I could never have made it this far without your father, Konran. You should be proud of him."

Kazrick shakes his head. "Not true, son. Everything good you inherited came from this beautiful woman. I'm just lucky to be standing on the same rock as her eminence."

Linaya laughs again, punching Kazrick three times with the playful words, "Liar, liar, liar." Then she pauses, gathering her thoughts, her face clouding with emotion.

"My little Konran," she says, choking up, "how I wish I could hold you for longer. How I wish I could be your mother and be at your side as you learn about the galaxy. I would give you everything, if I could. But there is so much evil out there, and you are not safe; no one is safe. Oh, Kaz, will I ever see him again?"

"I believe you will," Kazrick says, taking Linaya by the shoulders as solemn conviction returns to his face. Then he steps out of the holo-projection. Moments later he returns with a sleeping baby in his arms.

"He looks just like you," Valerie says, as Kazrick and Linaya hold baby Konran, gazing at him together without speaking.

"Well, he sure as sparks doesn't look like me," Ace quips, and the three of them laugh.

The transmission plays on for another five minutes, Linaya and Kazrick holding Konran in their arms, holding each other, their foreheads touching. No one speaks until Linaya turns back to the camera.

"I love you, Konran."

"I love you, son," Kazrick repeats, "my little warrior."

The holo-cube goes still, and Konran's parents disappear from view.

"I love you, too," he whispers, and Valerie squeezes his hand.

Silence persists among the trio for another moment. Then Ace stands up, stretches, picks up the holo-cube, and tosses it to Konran.

"So, you figured out how to access the rest yet?" he asks.

Konran shakes his head. "No idea. Maybe when Salazar gets here, we can figure it out."

"That's too long," Valerie says, taking the holo-cube and looking at it with a scrutinizing eye. "He's twenty-nine light-years away with Granicks—we may not see them for months."

She looks at Konran. "What do you say we crack it?"

Konran nods, the same sense of certainty filling his chest as when his fingers pressed the Sparrowhawk's trigger.

"Let's do this," he says.

FREE STUFF!

Like what you read?

Visit www.danielseegmiller.com/free to receive to free short
stories!

ABOUT THE AUTHOR

Daniel Seegmiller grew up loving Star Wars, the great outdoors, and all things sports. He started out as an English major before switching to his other love, science. He has an MS in mechanical engineering and has worked on everything from biomechanics, to machine learning, to defense technology.

Daniel loves dreaming up awesome adventures...like, literally, he wakes up in the middle of the night with the best ideas. Most of the stories he writes are for his kids. Starfighter Rising is his debut novel.

He lives in Albuquerque, New Mexico with his wife and three squirrelly children.

To find out about future releases and free stuff you can visit www.danielseegmiller.com.

Contact him at: dan@danielseegmiller.com.

If you enjoyed Starfighter Rising, please take a few minutes to leave a reivew. This is a great way to show your support, give back to the community, and help other readers find books they might enjoy.